The Last Song

Also by Nicholas Sparks

The Notebook
Message in a Bottle
A Walk to Remember
The Rescue
A Bend in the Road
Nights in Rodanthe
The Guardian
The Wedding
Three Weeks with My Brother
(with Micah Sparks)
True Believer
At First Sight
Dear John
The Choice
The Lucky One

NICHOLAS SPARKS

The Last Song

GRAND CENTRAL
PUBLISHING

NEW YORK   BOSTON

Grand Central Publishing
Hachette Book Group
237 Park Avenue
New York, NY 10017

Visit our website at www.HachetteBookGroup.com.

Printed in the United States of America

First Edition: September 2009
10 9 8 7 6 5 4 3 2 1

Grand Central Publishing is a division of Hachette Book Group, Inc.
The Grand Central Publishing name and logo is a trademark of Hachette Book Group, Inc.

Library of Congress Cataloging-in-Publication Data

Sparks, Nicholas.
    The last song / Nicholas Sparks.—1st ed.
        p.   cm.
    ISBN 978-0-446-54756-7
    1. Teenage girls—Fiction. I. Title.

PS3569.P363L37   2009
813'.54—dc22
                            2009024801

For Theresa Park and Greg Irikura
My friends

Acknowledgments

· · · · ✦ · · · ·

As always, I have to start by thanking Cathy, my wife and my dream. It's been an amazing twenty years and when I wake in the morning, my first thought is how lucky I am for having spent these years with you.

My children—Miles, Ryan, Landon, Lexie, and Savannah—are sources of endless joy in my life. I love you all.

Jamie Raab, my editor at Grand Central Publishers, always deserves my thanks, not only for her brilliant editing, but for the kindness she always shows me. Thank you.

Denise DiNovi, the producer of *Message in a Bottle*, *A Walk to Remember*, *Nights in Rodanthe*, and *The Lucky One* is not only a genius, but one of the friendliest people I know. Thanks for everything.

David Young, the CEO of Hachette Book Group, has earned my respect and gratitude in the years we've been working together. Thanks, David.

Jennifer Romanello and Edna Farley, my publicists, are not only good friends, but wonderful people. Thanks for all.

Harvey-Jane Kowal and Sona Vogel, as usual, deserve my thanks, if only because I'm always late with my manuscripts, thus making their jobs a whole lot harder.

Howie Sanders and Keya Khayatian, my agents at UTA, are fantastic. Thanks for everything, guys!

Scott Schwimer, my attorney, is quite simply the best at what he does. Thanks, Scott!

Thanks also go to Marty Bowen (the producer of *Dear John*), as well as Lynn Harris and Mark Johnson.

Amanda Cardinale, Abby Koons, Emily Sweet, and Sharon Krassney also deserve my thanks. I appreciate all that you do.

The Cyrus family deserves my thanks not only for welcoming me into their home, but for all they've done with the film. And a special thanks goes to Miley, who chose Ronnie's name. As soon as I heard it, I knew it was perfect!

And finally, thanks to Jason Reed, Jennifer Gipgot, and Adam Shankman for their work on the film version of *The Last Song*.

The Last Song

Prologue

· · · · 𝄌 · · · ·

Ronnie

Staring out the bedroom window, Ronnie wondered whether Pastor Harris was already at the church. She assumed that he was, and as she watched the waves breaking over the beach, she questioned whether he was still able to notice the play of light as it streamed through the stained-glass window above him. Perhaps not—the window had been installed more than a month ago, after all, and he was probably too preoccupied to notice anymore. Still, she hoped that someone new in town had stumbled into the church this morning and experienced the same sense of wonder she'd had when she'd first seen the light flood the church on that cold day in November. And she hoped the visitor had taken some time to consider where the window had come from and to admire its beauty.

She'd been awake for an hour, but she wasn't ready to face the day. The holidays felt different this year. Yesterday, she'd taken her younger brother, Jonah, for a walk down the beach. Here and there were Christmas trees on the decks of the houses they passed. At this time of year, they had the beach pretty much to themselves, but Jonah showed no interest in either the waves or the seagulls that had fascinated him only a few months earlier. Instead, he'd wanted to go to the workshop, and she'd taken him there, although he'd stayed only a few minutes before leaving without saying a single word.

On the bedstand beside her lay a stack of framed photographs from the alcove of the small beach house, along with other items she'd collected that morning. In the silence, she studied them until she was interrupted by a knock on the door. Her mom poked her head in.

"Do you want breakfast? I found some cereal in the cupboard."

"I'm not hungry, Mom."

"You need to eat, sweetie."

Ronnie continued to stare at the pile of photos, seeing nothing at all. "I was wrong, Mom. And I don't know what to do now."

"You mean about your dad?"

"About everything."

"Do you want to talk about it?"

When Ronnie didn't answer, her mom crossed the room and sat beside her.

"Sometimes it helps if you talk. You've been so quiet these last couple of days."

For an instant, Ronnie felt a crush of memories overwhelm her: the fire and subsequent rebuilding of the church, the stained-glass window, the song she'd finally finished. She thought about Blaze and Scott and Marcus. She thought about Will. She was eighteen years old and remembering the summer she'd been betrayed, the summer she'd been arrested, the summer she'd fallen in love. It hadn't been so long ago, yet sometimes she felt that she'd been an altogether different person back then.

Ronnie sighed. "What about Jonah?"

"He's not here. Brian took him to the shoe store. He's like a puppy. His feet are growing faster than the rest of him."

Ronnie smiled, but her smile faded as quickly as it had come. In the silence that followed, she felt her mom gather her long hair and twist it into a loose ponytail on her back. Her mom had been doing that ever since Ronnie was a little girl. Strangely, she still found it comforting. Not that she'd ever admit it, of course.

"I'll tell you what," her mom went on. She went to the closet and put the suitcase on the bed. "Why don't you talk while you pack?"

"I wouldn't even know where to start."

"How about at the beginning? Jonah mentioned something about turtles?"

Ronnie crossed her arms, knowing the story hadn't started there. "Not really," she said. "Even though I wasn't there when it happened, I think the summer really began with the fire."

"What fire?"

Ronnie reached for the stack of photographs on the bedstand and gently removed a tattered newspaper article sandwiched between two framed photos. She handed the yellowing newsprint to her mother.

"This fire," she said. "The one at the church."

Illegal Fireworks Suspected in Church Blaze
Pastor Injured

Wrightsville Beach, NC—A fire destroyed historic First Baptist Church on New Year's Eve, and investigators suspect illegal fireworks.

Firefighters were summoned by an anonymous caller to the beachfront church just after midnight and found flames and smoke pouring from the back of the structure, said Tim Ryan, chief of the Wrightsville Beach Fire Department. The remains of a bottle rocket, an airborne firework, were found at the source of the blaze.

Pastor Charlie Harris was inside the church when the fire started and suffered second-degree burns to his arms and hands. He was transported to New Hanover Regional Medical Center and is currently in the intensive care unit.

It was the second church fire in as many months in New Hanover County. In November, Good Hope Covenant Church in Wilmington was completely destroyed. "Investigators are still treating it as suspicious, and as a case of potential arson at this point," Ryan noted.

Witnesses report that less than twenty minutes before the fire, bottle rockets were seen being launched on the beach behind the church, likely in celebration of the New Year. "Bottle rockets are illegal in North Carolina, and are especially dangerous considering the recent drought conditions," cautioned Ryan. "This fire shows the reason why. A man is in the hospital and the church is a total loss."

When her mom finished reading, she looked up, meeting Ronnie's eyes. Ronnie hesitated; then, with a sigh, she began to tell a story that still felt utterly senseless to her, even with the benefit of hindsight.

1

······ ♪ ······

Ronnie

Six months earlier

Ronnie slouched in the front seat of the car, wondering why on earth her mom and dad hated her so much.

It was the only thing that could explain why she was here visiting her dad, in this godforsaken southern armpit of a place, instead of spending time with her friends back home in Manhattan.

No, scratch that. She wasn't just *visiting* her dad. *Visiting* implied a weekend or two, maybe even a week. She supposed she could live with a *visit*. But to stay until late August? Pretty much the entire summer? That was banishment, and for most of the nine hours it had taken them to drive down, she'd felt like a prisoner being transferred to a rural penitentiary. She couldn't believe her mom was actually going to make her go through with this.

Ronnie was so enveloped in misery, it took a second for her to recognize Mozart's Sonata no. 16 in C Major. It was one of the pieces she had performed at Carnegie Hall four years ago, and she knew her mom had put it on while Ronnie was sleeping. Too bad. Ronnie reached over to turn it off.

"Why'd you do that?" her mom said, frowning. "I like hearing you play."

"I don't."

"How about if I turn the volume down?"

"Just stop, Mom. Okay? I'm not in the mood."

Ronnie stared out the window, knowing full well that her mom's lips had just formed a tight seam. Her mom did that a lot these days. It was as if her lips were magnetized.

"I think I saw a pelican when we crossed the bridge to Wrightsville Beach," her mom commented with forced lightness.

"Gee, that's swell. Maybe you should call the Crocodile Hunter."

"He died," Jonah said, his voice floating up from the backseat, the sounds mingling with those from his Game Boy. Her ten-year-old pain-in-the-butt brother was addicted to the thing. "Don't you remember?" he went on. "It was really sad."

"Of course I remember."

"You didn't sound like you remembered."

"Well, I did."

"Then you shouldn't have said what you just said."

She didn't bother to respond a third time. Her brother always needed the last word. It drove her *crazy*.

"Were you able to get any sleep at all?" her mom asked.

"Until you hit that pothole. Thanks for that, by the way. My head practically went through the glass."

Her mom's gaze remained fixed on the road. "I'm glad to see your nap put you in a better mood."

Ronnie snapped her gum. Her mom hated that, which was the main reason she'd done it pretty much nonstop as they'd driven down I-95. The interstate, in her humble opinion, was just about the most boring stretch of roadway ever conceived. Unless someone was particularly fond of greasy fast food, disgusting rest-stop bathrooms, and zillions of pine trees, it could lull a person to sleep with its hypnotically ugly monotony.

She'd said those exact words to her mother in Delaware, Maryland, *and* Virginia, but Mom had ignored the comments every time. Aside from trying to make nice on the trip since it was the last time they'd see each other for a while, Mom wasn't one for conversation in the car. She wasn't all that comfortable driving, which wasn't surprising since they either rode the subways or took cabs when they needed to get somewhere. In the apartment, though . . . *that* was a different story. Mom had no qualms about getting into things there, and the building super had come by twice in the last couple of months to ask them to keep it down. Mom probably believed that the louder she yelled about Ronnie's grades, or Ronnie's friends, or the fact that Ronnie continually ignored her curfew, or the *Incident*—especially the *Incident*—the more likely it would be that Ronnie would care.

Okay, she wasn't the worst mom. She really wasn't. And when she was feeling generous, Ronnie might even admit that she was pretty good as far as moms went. It was just that her mom was stuck in some weird time warp in which kids never grew up, and Ronnie wished for the hundredth time that she'd been born in May instead of August. That was when she'd turn eighteen, and her mom wouldn't be able to force her to do anything. Legally, she'd be old enough to make her own decisions, and let's just say that coming down here wasn't on her to-do list.

But right now, Ronnie had *no choice* in the matter. Because she was still *seventeen*. Because of a *trick of the calendar*. Because Mom conceived *three months earlier than she should have*. What was that about? No matter how fiercely Ronnie had begged or complained or screamed or whined about the summer plans, it hadn't made the tiniest bit of difference. Ronnie and Jonah were spending the summer with their dad, and that was final. *No if, ands, or buts about it*, was the way her mom had phrased it. Ronnie had learned to *despise* that expression.

Just off the bridge, summer traffic had slowed the line of cars to a crawl. Off to the side, between the houses, Ronnie caught glimpses of the ocean. Yippee. Like she was supposed to care.

"Why again are you making us do this?" Ronnie groaned.

"We've already been through this," her mom answered. "You need to spend time with your dad. He misses you."

"But why all summer? Couldn't it just be for a couple of weeks?"

"You need more than a couple of weeks together. You haven't seen him in three years."

"That's not my fault. He's the one who left."

"Yes, but you haven't taken his calls. And every time he came to New York to see you and Jonah, you ignored him and hung out with your friends."

Ronnie snapped her gum again. From the corner of her eye, she saw her mother wince.

"I don't want to see or talk to him," Ronnie said.

"Just try to make the best of it, okay? Your father is a good man and he loves you."

"Is that why he walked out on us?"

Instead of answering, her mom glanced up into the rearview mirror.

"You've been looking forward to this, haven't you, Jonah?"

"Are you kidding? This is going to be great!"

"I'm glad you have a good attitude. Maybe you could teach your sister."

He snorted. "Yeah, right."

"I just don't see why I can't spend the summer with my friends," Ronnie whined, cutting back in. She wasn't done yet. Though she knew the odds were slim to none, she still harbored the fantasy that she could convince her mom to turn the car around.

"Don't you mean you'd rather spend all night at the clubs? I'm not naive, Ronnie. I know what goes on in those kinds of places."

"I don't do anything wrong, Mom."

"What about your grades? And your curfew? And—"

"Can we talk about something else?" Ronnie cut in. "Like why it's so imperative that I spend time with my dad?"

Her mother ignored her. Then again, Ronnie knew she had

every reason to. She'd already answered the question a million times, even if Ronnie didn't want to accept it.

Traffic eventually started to move again, and the car moved forward for half a block before coming to another halt. Her mother rolled down the window and tried to peer around the cars in front of her.

"I wonder what's going on," she muttered. "It's really packed down here."

"It's the beach," Jonah volunteered. "It's always crowded at the beach."

"It's three o'clock on a Sunday. It shouldn't be this crowded."

Ronnie tucked her legs up, hating her life. Hating everything about this.

"Hey, Mom?" Jonah asked. "Does Dad know Ronnie was arrested?"

"Yeah. He knows," she answered.

"What's he going to do?"

This time, Ronnie answered. "He won't do anything. All he ever cared about was the piano."

Ronnie *hated* the piano and swore she'd never play again, a decision even some of her oldest friends thought was strange, since it had been a major part of her life for as long as she'd known them. Her dad, once a teacher at Juilliard, had been her teacher as well, and for a long time, she'd been consumed by the desire not only to play, but to compose original music with her father.

She was good, too. Very good, actually, and because of her father's connection to Juilliard, the administration and teachers there were well aware of her ability. Word slowly began to spread in the obscure "classical music is all-important" grapevine that constituted her father's life. A couple of articles in classical music magazines followed, and a moderately long piece in *The New York Times* that focused on the father-daughter connection came next, all of which eventually led to a coveted appearance in the Young Performers series at Carnegie Hall four years ago. That, she supposed, was the highlight of her career. And it was a highlight; she wasn't naive about what she'd accomplished. She knew how rare an opportunity like that was, but lately she'd found herself wondering whether the sacrifices had been worth it. No one besides her parents probably even remembered the performance, after all. Or even cared. Ronnie had learned that unless you had a popular video on YouTube or could perform shows in front of thousands, musical ability meant nothing.

Sometimes she wished her father had started her on the electric guitar. Or at the very least, singing lessons. What was she supposed to do with an ability to play the piano? Teach music at the local school? Or play in some hotel lobby while people were checking in? Or chase the hard life her father had? Look where the piano had gotten him. He'd ended up quitting Juilliard so he could hit the road as a concert pianist and found himself playing in rinky-dink venues to audiences that barely filled the first couple of rows. He traveled forty weeks a year, long enough to put a strain on the marriage. Next thing she knew, Mom was yelling all the time and Dad was retreating into his shell like he usually did, until one day he simply didn't return from an extended southern tour. As far as she knew, he wasn't working at all these days. He wasn't even giving private lessons.

How did that work out for you, Dad?

She shook her head. She *really* didn't want to be here. God knows she wanted nothing to do with any of this.

"Hey, Mom!" Jonah called out. He leaned forward. "What's over there? Is that a Ferris wheel?"

Her mom craned her neck, trying to see around the minivan in the lane beside her. "I think it is, honey," she answered. "There must be a carnival in town."

"Can we go? After we all have dinner together?"

"You'll have to ask your dad."

"Yeah, and maybe afterward, we'll all sit around the campfire and roast marshmallows," Ronnie interjected. "Like we're one big, happy family."

This time, both of them ignored her.

"Do you think they have other rides?" Jonah asked.

"I'm sure they do. And if your dad doesn't want to ride them, I'm sure your sister will go with you."

"Awesome!"

Ronnie sagged in her seat. It figured her mom would suggest something like that. The whole thing was too depressing to believe.

2

......♪......

Steve

Steve Miller played the piano with keyed-up intensity, anticipating his children's arrival at any minute.

The piano was located in a small alcove off the small living room of the beachside bungalow he now called home. Behind him were items that represented his personal history. It wasn't much. Aside from the piano, Kim had been able to pack his belongings into a single box, and it had taken less than half an hour to put everything in place. There was a snapshot of him with his father and mother when he was young, another photo of him playing the piano as a teen. They were mounted between both of the degrees he'd received, one from Chapel Hill and the other from Boston University, and below it was a certificate of appreciation from Juilliard after he'd taught for fifteen years. Near the window were three framed schedules outlining his tour dates. Most important, though, were half a dozen photographs of Jonah and Ronnie, some tacked to the walls or framed and sitting atop the piano, and whenever he looked at them, he was reminded of the fact that despite his best intentions, nothing had turned out the way he'd expected.

The late afternoon sun was slanting through the windows, making the interior of the house stuffy, and Steve could feel beads

of sweat beginning to form. Thankfully, the pain in his stomach
had lessened since the morning, but he'd been nervous for days,
and he knew it would come back. He'd always had a weak stomach; in his twenties, he'd had an ulcer and was hospitalized for
diverticulitis; in his thirties, he'd had his appendix removed after
it had burst while Kim was pregnant with Jonah. He ate Rolaids
like candy, he'd been on Nexium for years, and though he knew
he could probably eat better and exercise more, he doubted that
either would have helped. Stomach problems ran in his family.

His father's death six years ago had changed him, and since the
funeral, he'd felt as though he'd been on a countdown of sorts. In
a way, he supposed he had. Five years ago, he'd quit his position
at Juilliard, and a year after that, he'd decided to try his luck as a
concert pianist. Three years ago, he and Kim decided to divorce;
less than twelve months later, the tour dates began drying up,
until they finally ended completely. Last year, he'd moved back
here, to the town where he'd grown up, a place he never thought
he'd see again. Now he was about to spend the summer with his
children, and though he tried to imagine what the fall would
bring once Ronnie and Jonah were back in New York, he knew
only that leaves would yellow before turning to red and that in
the mornings his breaths would come out in little puffs. He'd long
since given up trying to predict the future.

This didn't bother him. He knew predictions were pointless,
and besides, he could barely understand the past. These days, all
he could say for sure was that he was ordinary in a world that
loved the extraordinary, and the realization left him with a vague
feeling of disappointment at the life he'd led. But what could he
do? Unlike Kim, who'd been outgoing and gregarious, he'd always
been more reticent and blended into crowds. Though he had certain talents as a musician and composer, he lacked the charisma
or showmanship or whatever it was that made a performer stand
out. At times, even he admitted that he'd been more an observer
of the world than a participant in it, and in moments of painful

honesty, he sometimes believed he was a failure in all that was important. He was forty-eight years old. His marriage had ended, his daughter avoided him, and his son was growing up without him. Thinking back, he knew he had no one to blame but himself, and more than anything, this was what he wanted to know: Was it still possible for someone like him to experience the presence of God?

Ten years ago, he could never have imagined wondering about such a thing. Two years, even. But middle age, he sometimes thought, had made him as reflective as a mirror. Though he'd once believed that the answer lay somehow in the music he created, he suspected now that he'd been mistaken. The more he thought about it, the more he'd come to realize that for him, music had always been a movement away from reality rather than a means of living in it more deeply. He might have experienced passion and catharsis in the works of Tchaikovsky or felt a sense of accomplishment when he'd written sonatas of his own, but he now knew that burying himself in music had less to do with God than a selfish desire to escape.

He now believed that the real answer lay somewhere in the nexus of love he felt for his children, in the ache he experienced when he woke in the quiet house and realized they weren't here. But even then, he knew there was something more.

And somehow, he hoped his children would help him find it.

A few minutes later, Steve noticed the sun reflecting off the windshield of a dusty station wagon outside. He and Kim had purchased it years ago for weekend outings to Costco and family getaways. He wondered in passing if she'd remembered to change the oil before she'd driven down, or even since he'd left. Probably not, he decided. Kim had never been good at things like that, which was why he'd always taken care of them.

But that part of his life was over now.

Steve rose from his seat, and by the time he stepped onto the porch, Jonah was already out of the car and rushing toward him. His hair hadn't been combed, his glasses were crooked, and his arms and legs were as skinny as pencils. Steve felt his throat tighten, reminded again of how much he'd missed in the past three years.

"Dad!"

"Jonah!" Steve shouted back as he crossed the rocky sand that constituted his yard. When Jonah jumped into his arms, it was all he could do to remain upright.

"You've gotten so big," he said.

"And you've gotten smaller!" Jonah said. "You're skinny now."

Steve hugged his son tight before putting him down. "I'm glad you're here."

"I am, too. Mom and Ronnie fought the whole time."

"That's no fun."

"It's okay. I ignored it. Except when I egged them on."

"Ah," Steve responded.

Jonah pushed his glasses up the bridge of his nose. "Why didn't Mom let us fly?"

"Did you ask her?"

"No."

"Maybe you should."

"It's not important. I was just wondering."

Steve smiled. He'd forgotten how talkative his son could be.

"Hey, is this your house?"

"That's it."

"This place is awesome!"

Steve wondered if Jonah was serious. The house was anything but awesome. The bungalow was easily the oldest property on Wrightsville Beach and sandwiched between two massive homes that had gone up within the last ten years, making it seem even more diminutive. The paint was peeling, the roof was missing numerous shingles, and the porch was rotting; it wouldn't surprise him if the next decent storm blew it over, which would no doubt please the neighbors. Since he'd moved in, neither family had ever spoken to him.

"You think so?" he said.

"Hello? It's right on the beach. What else could you want?" He motioned toward the ocean. "Can I go check it out?"

"Sure. But be careful. And stay behind the house. Don't wander off."

"Deal."

Steve watched him jog off before turning to see Kim approaching. Ronnie had stepped out of the car as well but was still lingering near it.

"Hi, Kim," he said.

"Steve." She leaned in to give him a brief hug. "You doing okay?" she asked. "You look thin."

"I'm okay."

Behind her, Steve noticed Ronnie slowly making her way toward them. He was struck by how much she'd changed since the last photo Kim had e-mailed. Gone was the all-American girl he remembered, and in her place was a young woman with a purple streak in her long brown hair, black fingernail polish, and dark clothing. Despite the obvious signs of teenage rebellion, he thought again how much she resembled her mother. Good thing, too. She was, he thought, as lovely as ever.

He cleared his throat. "Hi, sweetie. It's good to see you."

When Ronnie didn't answer, Kim scowled at her. "Don't be rude. Your father's talking to you. Say something."

Ronnie crossed her arms. "All right. How about this? I'm not going to play the piano for you."

"Ronnie!" Steve could hear Kim's exasperation.

"What?" She tossed her head. "I thought I'd get that out of the way early."

Before Kim could respond, Steve shook his head. The last thing he wanted was an argument. "It's okay, Kim."

"Yeah, Mom. It's *okay*," Ronnie said, pouncing. "I need to stretch my legs. I'm going for a walk."

As she stomped away, Steve watched Kim struggle with the impulse to call her back. In the end, though, she said nothing.

"Long drive?" he asked, trying to lighten the mood.

"You can't even imagine it."

He smiled, thinking that for just an instant, it was easy to imagine they were still married, both of them on the same team, both of them still in love.

Except, of course, that they weren't.

After unloading the bags, Steve went to the kitchen, where he tapped ice cubes from the old-fashioned tray and dropped them into the mismatched glasses that had come with the place.

Behind him, he heard Kim enter the kitchen. He reached for a pitcher of sweet tea, poured two glasses, and handed one to her. Outside, Jonah was alternately chasing, and being chased by, the waves as seagulls fluttered overhead.

"It looks like Jonah's having fun," he said.

Kim took a step toward the window. "He's been excited about coming for weeks." She hesitated. "He's missed you."

"I've missed him."

"I know," she said. She took a drink of her tea before glancing around the kitchen. "So this is the place, huh? It's got . . . character."

"By character, I assume you've noticed the leaky roof and lack of air-conditioning."

Kim flashed a brief smile, caught.

"I know it's not much. But it's quiet and I can watch the sun come up."

"And the church is letting you stay here for free?"

Steve nodded. "It belonged to Carson Johnson. He was a local artist, and when he passed away, he left the house to the church. Pastor Harris is letting me stay until they're ready to sell."

"So what's it like living back home? I mean, your parents used to live, what? Three blocks from here?"

Seven, actually. Close. "It's all right." He shrugged.

"It's so crowded now. The place has really changed since the last time I was here."

"Everything changes," he said. He leaned against the counter, crossing one leg over the other. "So when's the big day?" he asked, changing the subject. "For you and Brian?"

"Steve . . . about that."

"It's okay," he said, raising a hand. "I'm glad you found someone."

Kim stared at him, clearly wondering whether to accept his words at face value or plunge into sensitive territory.

"In January," she finally said. "And I want you to know that with the kids . . . Brian doesn't pretend to be someone he isn't. You'd like him."

"I'm sure I would," he said, taking a sip of his tea. He set the glass back down. "How do the kids feel about him?"

"Jonah seems to like him, but Jonah likes everyone."

"And Ronnie?"

"She gets along with him about as well as she gets along with you."

He laughed before noting her worried expression. "How's she really doing?"

"I don't know." She sighed. "And I don't think she does, either. She's in this dark, moody phase. She ignores her curfew, and half the time I can't get more than a 'Whatever' when I try to talk to her. I try to write it off as typical teenage stuff, because I remember what it was like . . . but . . ." She shook her head. "You saw the way she was dressed, right? And her hair and that god-awful mascara?"

"Mmm."

"And?"

"It could be worse."

Kim opened her mouth to say something, but when nothing came out, Steve knew he was right. Whatever stage she was going through, whatever Kim's fears, Ronnie was still Ronnie.

"I guess," she conceded, before shaking her head. "No, I know you're right. It's just been so difficult with her lately. There are times she's still as sweet as ever. Like with Jonah. Even though they fight like cats and dogs, she still brings him to the park every weekend. And when he was having trouble in math, she tutored him every night. Which is strange, because she's barely passing any of her classes. And I haven't told you this, but I made her take the SATs in February. She missed every single question. Do you know how smart you have to be to miss every single question?"

When Steve laughed, Kim frowned. "It's not funny."

"It's kind of funny."

"You haven't had to deal with her these last three years."

He paused, chastened. "You're right. I'm sorry." He reached for his glass again. "What did the judge say about her shoplifting?"

"Just what I told you on the phone," she said with a resigned expression. "If she doesn't get into any more trouble, it'll be expunged from her record. If she does it again, though . . ." She trailed off.

"You're worried about this," he started.

Kim turned away. "It's not the first time, which is the problem," she confessed. "She admitted to stealing the bracelet last year, but this time, she *said* she was buying a bunch of stuff at the drugstore and couldn't hold it all, so she tucked the lipstick in her pocket. She paid for everything else, and when you see the video, it seems to be an honest mistake, but . . ."

"But you're not sure."

When Kim didn't answer, Steve shook his head. "She's not on her way to being profiled on *America's Most Wanted*. She made a mistake. And she's always had a good heart."

"That doesn't mean she's telling the truth now."

"And it doesn't mean she lied, either."

"So you believe her?" Her expression was a mixture of hope and skepticism.

He sifted through his feelings about the incident, as he had a dozen times since Kim had first told him. "Yeah," he said. "I believe her."

"Why?"

"Because she's a good kid."

"How do you know?" she demanded. For the first time, she sounded angry. "The last time you spent any time with her, she was finishing middle school." She turned away from him then, crossing her arms as she gazed out the window. Her voice was bitter when she went on. "You could have come back, you know. You could have taught in New York again. You didn't have to travel around the country, you didn't have to move here . . . you could have stayed part of their lives."

Her words stung him, and he knew she was right. But it hadn't been that simple, for reasons they both understood, though neither would acknowledge them.

The charged silence passed when Steve eventually cleared his throat. "I was just trying to say that Ronnie knows right from wrong. As much as she asserts her independence, I still believe she's the same person she always was. In the ways that really matter, she hasn't changed."

Before Kim could figure out how or if she should respond to his comment, Jonah burst through the front door, his cheeks flushed.

"Dad! I found a really cool workshop! C'mon! I want to show you!"

Kim raised an eyebrow.

"It's out back," Steve said. "Do you want to see it?"

"It's awesome, Mom!"

Kim turned from Steve to Jonah and back again. "No, that's okay," she said. "That sounds like more of a father and son thing. And besides, I should really be going."

"Already?" Jonah asked.

Steve knew how hard this was going to be for Kim, and he answered for her. "Your mom has a long drive back. And besides, I wanted to take you to the carnival tonight. Could we do that instead?"

Steve watched Jonah's shoulders sink a fraction.

"I guess that's okay," he said.

After Jonah said good-bye to his mom—with Ronnie still nowhere in sight and, according to Kim, unlikely to return soon—Steve and Jonah strolled over to the workshop, a leaning, tin-roofed outbuilding that had come with the property.

For the last three months, Steve had spent most afternoons here, surrounded by assorted junk and small sheets of stained glass that Jonah was now exploring. In the center of the workshop was a large worktable with the beginnings of a stained-glass window, but Jonah seemed far more interested in the weird taxidermy pieces perched on the shelves, the previous owner's specialty. It was hard not to be mesmerized by the half-squirrel/half-bass creature or the opossum's head grafted onto the body of a chicken.

"What is this stuff?" Jonah asked.

"It's supposed to be art."

"I thought art was like paintings and stuff."

"It is. But sometimes art is other things, too."

Jonah wrinkled his nose, staring at the half-rabbit/half-snake. "It doesn't look like art."

When Steve smiled, Jonah motioned to the stained-glass window on the worktable. "Was this his, too?" he asked.

"Actually, that's mine. I'm making it for the church down the street. It burned last year, and the original window was destroyed in the fire."

"I didn't know you could make windows."

"Believe it or not, the artist who used to live here taught me how."

"The guy who did the animals?"

"The same one."

"And you knew him?"

Steve joined his son at the table. "When I was a kid, I'd sneak over here when I was supposed to be in Bible study. He made the stained-glass windows for most of the churches around here. See the picture on the wall?" Steve pointed to a small photograph of the Risen Christ tacked to one of the shelves, easy to miss in the chaos. "Hopefully, it'll look just like that when it's finished."

"Awesome," Jonah said, and Steve smiled. It was obviously Jonah's new favorite word, and he wondered how many times he'd hear it this summer.

"Do you want to help?"

"Can I?"

"I was counting on it." Steve gave him a gentle nudge. "I need a good assistant."

"Is it hard?"

"I was your age when I started, so I'm sure you'll be able to handle it."

Jonah gingerly picked up a piece of the glass and examined it, holding it up to the light, his expression serious. "I'm pretty sure I can handle it, too."

Steve smiled. "Are you still going to church?" he asked.

"Yeah. But it's not the same one we went to. It's the one where Brian likes to go. And Ronnie doesn't always come with us. She locks herself in her room and refuses to come out, but as soon as we leave, she goes over to Starbucks to hang out with her friends. It makes Mom furious."

"That happens when kids become teenagers. They test their parents."

Jonah put the glass back on the table. "I won't," he said. "I'm always going to be good. But I don't like the new church very much. It's boring. So I might not go to that one."

"Fair enough." He paused. "I hear you're not playing soccer this fall."

"I'm not very good at it."

"So what? It's fun, right?"

"Not when other kids make fun of you."

"They make fun of you?"

"It's okay. It doesn't bother me."

"Ah," Steve said.

Jonah shuffled his feet, something obviously on his mind. "Ronnie didn't read any of the letters you sent her, Dad. And she won't play the piano anymore, either."

"I know," Steve answered.

"Mom says it's because she has PMS."

Steve almost choked but composed himself quickly. "Do you even know what that means?"

Jonah pushed his glasses up. "I'm not a little kid anymore. It means pissed-at-men syndrome."

Steve laughed, ruffling Jonah's hair. "How about we go find your sister? I think I saw her heading toward the festival."

"Can we ride the Ferris wheel?"

"Whatever you want."

"Awesome."

3

....✦....

Ronnie

The fair was crowded. Or rather, Ronnie corrected herself, the *Wrightsville Beach Seafood Festival* was crowded. As she paid for a soda from one of the concession stands, she could see cars parked bumper to bumper along both roads leading to the pier and even noted a few enterprising teenagers renting out their driveways near the action.

So far, though, the action was boring. She supposed she'd been hoping that the Ferris wheel was a permanent fixture and that the pier offered shops and stores like the boardwalk in Atlantic City. In other words, she hoped it would be the kind of place she could see herself hanging out in the summer. No such luck. The festival was temporarily located in the parking lot at the head of the pier, and it mostly resembled a small county fair. The rickety rides were part of a traveling carnival, and the parking lot was lined with overpriced game booths and greasy food concessions. The whole place was kind of . . . gross.

Not that anyone else seemed to share her opinion. The place was *packed*. Old and young, families, groups of middle-schoolers ogling one another. No matter which way she went, she always seemed to be fighting against the tide of bodies. Sweaty bodies. Big, sweaty bodies, two of whom were squashing her between them as the crowd came to an inexplicable stop. No doubt they'd had both the fried hot dog and fried Snickers bar she'd seen at the concession stand. She wrinkled her nose. So gross.

Spying an opening, she slipped away from the rides and carnival game booths and headed toward the pier. Fortunately, the crowd continued to thin as she moved down the pier, past booths offering homemade crafts for sale. Nothing she could ever imagine herself buying—who on earth would want a gnome constructed entirely from seashells? But obviously someone was buying the stuff or the booths wouldn't exist.

Distracted, she bumped into a table manned by an elderly woman seated on a folding chair. Wearing a shirt emblazoned with the logo SPCA, she had white hair and an open, cheerful face—the type of grandmother who probably spent all day baking cookies before Christmas Eve, Ronnie guessed. On the table in front of her were pamphlets and a donation jar, along with a large cardboard box. Inside the box were four gray puppies, one of which hopped up on its hind legs to peer over the side at her.

"Hi, little guy," she said.

The elderly woman smiled. "Do you want to hold him? He's the fun one. I call him Seinfeld."

The puppy gave a high-pitched whine.

"No, that's okay." He was cute, though. Really cute, even if she didn't think the name suited him. And she did sort of want to hold him, but she knew she wouldn't want to put him down if she did. She was a sucker for animals in general, especially abandoned ones. Like these little guys. "They're going to be okay, right? You're not going to have them put to sleep, are you?"

"They'll be fine," the woman answered. "That's why we set up the table. So people would adopt them. Last year, we found homes for over thirty animals, and these four have already been claimed. I'm just waiting for the new owners to pick them up on their way out. But there are more at the shelter if you're interested."

"I'm only visiting," Ronnie answered, just as a roar erupted from the beach. She craned her neck, trying to see. "What's going on? A concert?"

The woman shook her head. "Beach volleyball. They've been playing for hours—some kind of tournament. You should go watch. I've heard the cheering all day, so the games must be pretty exciting."

Ronnie thought about it, figuring, Why not? It couldn't be any worse than what was happening up here. She threw a couple of dollars into the donation jar before heading toward the steps.

The sun was descending, giving the ocean a sheen like liquid gold. On the beach, a few remaining families were congregated on towels near the water, along with a couple of sand castles about to be swept away in the rising tide. Terns darted in and out, hunting for crabs.

It didn't take long to reach the source of the action. As she inched her way to the edge of the court, she noticed that the other girls in the audience seemed fixated on the two players on the right. No surprise there. The two guys—her age? older?—were the kind that her friend Kayla routinely described as "eye candy." Though neither of them was exactly Ronnie's type, it was impossible not to admire their lanky, muscular physiques and the fluid way they moved through the sand.

Especially the taller one, with dark brown hair and the macramé bracelet on his wrist. Kayla would have definitely zeroed in on him—she always went for the tall ones—in the same way the bikini-clad blonde across the court was obviously zeroing in on him. Ronnie had noticed the blonde and her friend right away. They were both thin and pretty, with blindingly white teeth, and obviously used to being the center of attention and having boys drool all over them. They held themselves apart from the crowd and cheered daintily, probably so they wouldn't mess up their hair. They might as well have been billboards proclaiming it was okay to admire them from a distance, but don't get too close. Ronnie didn't know them, but she already didn't like them.

She turned her attention back to the game just as the cute guys scored another point. And then another. And still another. She didn't know what the score was, but they were obviously the better team. And yet, as she watched, she silently began to root for the other guys. It had less to do with the fact that she always rooted for the underdog—which she did—and more to do with the fact that the winning pair reminded her of the spoiled private school types she sometimes ran into at clubs, the Upper East Side boys from Dalton and Buckley who thought they were better than everyone else simply because their dads were investment bankers. She'd seen enough of the so-called privileged crowd to recognize a member when she saw one, and she'd bet her life that those two were definitely part of the popular crowd around here. Her suspicions were confirmed after the next point when the brown-haired guy's partner winked at the blonde's tanned, Barbie-doll friend as he got ready to serve. In this town, the pretty people clearly all knew one another.

Why wasn't she surprised by that?

The game suddenly seemed less interesting, and she turned to leave just as another serve sailed over the net. She vaguely heard someone shouting as the opposing team returned the serve, but before she had taken more than a couple of steps, she felt the spectators around her beginning to jostle one another, knocking her off balance for just an instant.

An instant too long.

She turned just in time to see one of the players rushing toward her at full speed, his head craning to catch sight of the wayward ball. She didn't have time to react before he slammed into her. She felt him grab her shoulders in a simultaneous attempt to stop his momentum and prevent her from falling. She felt her arm jerk on impact and watched almost in fascination as the lid flew off the Styrofoam cup, soda arcing through the air before drenching her face and shirt.

And then, just like that, it was over. Up close, she saw the brown-haired player staring at her, his eyes wide with shock.

"Are you okay?" he panted.

She could feel the soda dripping down her face and soaking through her shirt. Vaguely, she heard someone in the crowd begin to laugh. And why shouldn't someone laugh? It had been such a *fantastic* day already.

"I'm fine," she snapped.

"Are you sure?" the guy gasped. For what it was worth, he seemed genuinely contrite. "I ran into you kind of hard."

"Just . . . let me go," she said through clenched teeth.

He hadn't seemed to realize he was still gripping her shoulders, and his hands instantly released their pressure. He took a quick step back and automatically reached for his bracelet. He rotated it almost absently. "I'm really sorry about that. I was going for the ball and—"

"I know what you were doing," she said. "I survived, okay?"

With that, she turned away, wanting nothing more than to get as far away from here as possible. Behind her, she heard someone call out, "C'mon, Will! Let's get back to the game!" But as she pushed her way through the crowd, she was conscious somehow of his continuing gaze until she vanished from sight.

Her shirt wasn't ruined, but that didn't make her feel much better. She liked this shirt, a memento from the Fall Out Boy concert that she'd sneaked out to with Rick last year. Her mom had almost blown a gasket about that one, and it wasn't simply because Rick had a tattoo of a spiderweb on his neck and more piercings in his ears than Kayla did; it was because she'd lied about where they were going, and she hadn't made it home until the following afternoon, since they'd ended up crashing at Rick's brother's place in Philadelphia. Her mom forbade Ronnie from seeing or even speaking to Rick ever again, a rule that Ronnie broke the very next day.

It wasn't that she loved Rick; frankly, she didn't even like him that much. But she was angry at her mom, and it felt right at the time. But when she got to Rick's place, he was already stoned and drunk again, just as he'd been at the concert, and she realized that if she continued to see him, he'd continue to pressure her to try whatever it was he was taking, just as he'd done the night before. She spent only a few minutes at his place before heading to Union Square for the rest of the afternoon, knowing it was over between them.

She wasn't naive about drugs. Some of her friends smoked pot, a few did cocaine or ecstasy, and one even had a nasty meth habit. Everyone but her drank on the weekends. Every club and party she went to offered easy access to all of it. Still, it seemed that whenever her friends smoked or drank or popped the pills they swore made the evening worthwhile, they'd spend the rest of the night slurring their words or staggering or vomiting or losing control completely and doing something *really stupid.* Something usually involving a guy.

Ronnie didn't want to go there. Not after what happened to Kayla last winter. Someone—Kayla never knew who—slipped some GHB into her drink, and though she had only a vague recollection of what happened next, she was pretty sure she remembered being in a room with three guys she'd met for the first time that night. When she woke the following morning, her clothes were strewn around the room. Kayla never said anything more— she preferred to pretend it had never happened at all and regretted having told Ronnie even that much—but it wasn't hard to connect the dots.

When she reached the pier, Ronnie set down her half-empty drink cup and dabbed furiously at her shirt with her wet napkin. It seemed to be working, but the napkin was disintegrating into tiny white flakes that resembled dandruff.

Great.

She wished the guy had rammed into someone else. She was only there for what, ten minutes? What were the odds that she'd turn away at the same instant the ball came flying her way? And that she'd be holding a soda in a crowd at a volleyball game she didn't even want to watch, in a place she didn't want to be? In a million years, the same thing could probably never happen again. With odds like that, she should have bought a lottery ticket.

And then there was the guy who did it. Brown-haired, brown-eyed cute guy. Up close, she realized he was way better looking than *cute*, especially when he got that expression of . . . concern. He might have been part of the popular crowd, but in the nanosecond their eyes had met, she'd had the strangest sense that he was as real as they came.

Ronnie shook her head to clear her mind of such crazy thoughts. Clearly the sun was affecting her brain. Satisfied that she'd done the best she could with the napkin, she picked up the cup of soda. She planned to throw the rest away, but as she spun around, she felt the cup get jammed between her and someone else. This time, nothing happened in slow motion; the soda instantly covered the front of her shirt.

She froze, staring down at her shirt in disbelief. *You've got to be kidding.*

Standing before her was a girl her age holding a Slurpee, seemingly as surprised as she was. She was dressed in black, and her stringy dark hair hung in unruly curls framing her face. Like Kayla, she had at least half a dozen piercings in each ear, highlighted with a couple of miniature skulls that dangled from her earlobes, and her dark eye shadow and eyeliner gave her an almost feral appearance. As the remains of her soda soaked through Ronnie's shirt, Goth-looking chick motioned with her Slurpee toward the spreading stain.

"Sucks being you," she said.

"Ya think?"

"At least the other side matches now."

"Oh, I get it. You're trying to be funny."

"'Witty' is more like it."

"Then you might have said something like 'Maybe you should stick with sippy-cups.'"

Goth-chick laughed, a surprisingly girlish sound. "You're not from around here, are you?"

"No, I'm from New York. I'm here visiting my dad."

"For the weekend?"

"No. For the summer."

"It does suck being you."

This time, it was Ronnie's turn to laugh. "I'm Ronnie. It's short for Veronica."

"Call me Blaze."

"Blaze?"

"My real name's Galadriel. It's from *Lord of the Rings*. My mom's weird like that."

"At least she didn't name you Gollum."

"Or Ronnie." With a tilt of her head, she motioned over her shoulder. "If you want something dry, there are some Nemo shirts in the booth over there."

"Nemo?"

"Yeah, Nemo. From the movie? Orange-and-white fish, gimpy flipper? Gets stuck in a fish tank and his dad goes to find him?"

"I don't want a Nemo shirt, okay?"

"Nemo's cool."

"Maybe if you're six," Ronnie retorted.

"Suit yourself."

Before Ronnie could respond, she spied three guys pushing their way through a parting mob. They stood out from the beach crowd with their torn shorts and tattoos, bare chests showing beneath heavy leather jackets. One had a pierced eyebrow and was carrying an old-fashioned boom box; another had a bleached Mohawk and arms completely covered with tattoos. The third, like

Blaze, had long black hair offset by milky white skin. Ronnie turned instinctively to Blaze, only to realize that Blaze was gone. In her place stood Jonah.

"What did you spill on your shirt?" he asked. "You're all wet and sticky."

Ronnie searched for Blaze, wondering where she'd gone. And why. "Just go away, okay?"

"I can't. Dad's looking for you. I think he wants you to come home."

"Where is he?"

"He stopped to go to the bathroom, but he should be here any minute."

"Tell him you didn't see me."

Jonah thought about it. "Five bucks."

"What?"

"Gimme five bucks and I'll forget you were here."

"Are you serious?"

"You don't have much time," he said. "Now it's ten bucks."

Over Jonah's head, she spotted her dad searching the crowd around him. Instinctively she ducked, knowing there was no way she could sneak past him. She glared at her brother, the black-mailer, who'd obviously realized it as well. He was cute and she loved him and she respected his blackmailing abilities, but still, he was her little brother. In a perfect world, he would be on her side. But was he? Of course not.

"I hate you, you know," she said.

"Yeah, I hate you, too. But it's still gonna cost you ten bucks."

"How about five?"

"You missed your chance. But your secret will be safe with me."

Her dad still hadn't seen them, but he was getting closer.

"Fine," she hissed, digging through her pockets. She passed over a crumpled bill and Jonah pocketed the money. Glancing over her shoulder, she saw her father moving in her direction, his head still going from side to side, and she ducked around the booth. Surprising her, Blaze was leaning against the side of the booth, smoking a cigarette.

She smirked. "Problems with your dad?"

"How do I get out of here?"

"That's up to you." Blaze shrugged. "But he knows what shirt you're wearing."

An hour later, Ronnie was sitting beside Blaze on one of the benches near the end of the pier, still bored, but not quite as bored as she'd been before. Blaze turned out to be a good listener, with a quirky sense of humor—and best of all, she seemed to love New York as much as Ronnie did, even though she'd never been there. She asked questions about the basics: Times Square and the Empire State Building and the Statue of Liberty—tourist traps that Ronnie tried to avoid at all costs. But Ronnie humored her before describing the real New York: the clubs in Chelsea, the music scene in Brooklyn, and the street vendors in Chinatown, where it was possible to buy bootlegged recordings or fake Prada purses or pretty much anything else for pennies on the dollar.

Talking about those places made her absolutely *long* to be back home instead of here. Anywhere but here.

"I wouldn't have wanted to come here either," Blaze agreed. "Trust me. It's boring."

"How long have you lived here?"

"Just my whole life. But at least I'm dressed okay."

Ronnie had bought the stupid Nemo shirt, knowing she looked ridiculous. The only size the booth had in stock was an extralarge, and the thing practically reached her knees. Its only redeeming feature was that once she donned it, she'd been able to slip unseen past her father. Blaze had been right about that.

"Someone told me Nemo was cool."

"She was lying."

"What are we still doing out here? My dad's probably gone by now."

Blaze turned. "Why? Do you want to go back to the carnival? Maybe go to the haunted house?"

"No. But there's got to be something else going on."

"Not yet. Later there will be. But for now, let's just wait."

"For what?"

Blaze didn't answer. Instead, she stood and turned around, facing the blackened water. Her hair moved in the breeze, and she seemed to stare at the moon. "I saw you earlier, you know."

"When?"

"When you were at the volleyball game." She motioned down the pier. "I was standing over there."

"And?"

"You seemed out of place."

"So do you."

"Which is why I was standing on the pier." She hopped up onto the railing and took a seat, facing Ronnie. "I know you don't want to be here, but what did your dad do to make you so mad?"

Ronnie wiped her palms on her pants. "It's a long story."

"Does he live with his girlfriend?"

"I don't think he has a girlfriend. Why?"

"Consider yourself lucky."

"What are you talking about?"

"My dad lives with his girlfriend. This is his third one since the divorce, by the way, and she's the worst by far. She's only a few years older than I am and she dresses like a stripper. For all I know, she was a stripper. It makes me sick every time I have to go there. It's like she doesn't know how to act around me. One minute she tries to give me advice like she's my mom, and the next minute she's trying to be my best friend. I hate her."

"And you live with your mom?"

"Yeah. But now she has a boyfriend, and he's at the house all the time. And he's a loser, too. He wears this ridiculous toupee because he went bald when he was like twenty or something, and he's always telling me that I want to think about giving college a try. Like I care what he thinks. It's just all screwed up, you know?"

Before Ronnie could answer, Blaze jumped back down. "C'mon. I think they're getting ready to start. You've got to see this."

Ronnie followed Blaze back up the pier, toward a crowd surrounding what seemed to be a street show. Startled, she realized that the performers were the three thuggish guys she'd spotted earlier. Two of them were break-dancing to music blaring from the boom box, while the one with long black hair stood in the center juggling what seemed to be flaming golf balls. Every now and then he would stop juggling and simply hold the ball, rotating it between his fingers or rolling it across the back of his hand or up one arm and down the other. Twice, he closed his fist over the fireball, nearly extinguishing it, only to move his hand, allowing the flames to escape out the tiny opening near his thumb.

"Do you know him?" Ronnie said.

Blaze nodded. "That's Marcus."

"Is he wearing some sort of protective coating on his hands?"

"No."

"Doesn't it hurt?"

"Not if you hold the fireball right. It's awesome, though, isn't it?"

Ronnie had to agree. Marcus extinguished two of the balls and then relit them again by touching them to the third. On the ground lay an upturned magician's hat, and Ronnie watched as people began tossing money into it.

"Where does he get the fireballs?"

"He makes them. I can show you how. It's not hard. All you need is a cotton T-shirt, needle and thread, and some lighter fluid."

As the music continued to blare, Marcus tossed the three fireballs to the guy with the Mohawk and lit two more. They juggled them back and forth between each other like circus clowns using bowling pins, faster and faster, until one throw went awry.

Except that it didn't. The guy with the pierced eyebrow caught it soccer-ball style and began bouncing it from foot to foot as though it were nothing more than a Hacky Sack. After extinguishing three of the fireballs, the other two followed suit, the entire troupe kicking the two fireballs back and forth between them. The crowd started to clap, and money rained into the hat as the music built to a crescendo. Then all at once, the remaining fireballs were caught and extinguished simultaneously as the song thundered to a close.

Ronnie had to admit she'd never seen anything like it. Marcus walked over to Blaze and folded her into a long, lingering kiss that seemed wildly inappropriate in public. He opened his eyes slowly, staring right at Ronnie before he pushed Blaze away.

"Who's that?" he asked, motioning in Ronnie's direction.

"That's Ronnie," Blaze said. "She's from New York. I just met her."

Mohawk and Pierced Eyebrow joined Marcus and Blaze in their scrutiny, making Ronnie feel distinctly uncomfortable.

"New York, huh?" Marcus asked, pulling a lighter from his pocket and igniting one of the fireballs. He held the flaming orb motionless between his thumb and forefinger, making Ronnie wonder again how he could do that without getting burned.

"Do you like fire?" he called out.

Without waiting for an answer, he threw the fireball in her direction. Ronnie jumped out of the way, too startled to respond. The ball landed behind her just as a police officer rushed forward, stamping out the flame.

"You three," he called out, pointing. "Out. Now. I've told you before that you can't do your little show on the pier, and next time, I swear I'm gonna bring you in."

Marcus held up his hands and took a step backward. "We were just leaving."

The boys grabbed their coats and began moving up the pier, toward the carnival rides. Blaze followed, leaving Ronnie alone. Ronnie felt the officer's gaze on her, but she ignored him. Instead, she hesitated only briefly before going after them.

4

·····✦·····

Marcus

He'd known she would follow them. They always did. Especially the new girls in town. That was the thing with girls: The worse he treated them, the more they wanted him. They were stupid like that. Predictable, but stupid.

He leaned against the planter that fronted the hotel, Blaze wrapping her arms around him. Ronnie was sitting across from them on one of the benches; off to the side, Teddy and Lance were slurring their words as they tried to get the attention of the girls who walked past them. They were already tanked—hell, they were a little tanked even before the show—and as usual, all but the ugliest of girls ignored them. Half the time, even he ignored them.

Blaze, meanwhile, was nibbling on his neck, but he ignored that, too. He was sick of the way she always hung on him whenever they were out in public. Sick of her in general. If she weren't so good in bed, if she didn't know the things that really turned him on, he would have dumped her a month ago for one of the three or four or five other girls he regularly slept with. But right now he wasn't interested in them, either. Instead, he stared at Ronnie, liking the purple streak in her hair and her tight little body, the glittery effect of her eye shadow. It was sort of an upscale, trampy style, despite the stupid shirt she was wearing. He liked that. He liked that a lot.

He pushed against Blaze's hips, wishing she weren't here. "Go get me some fries," he said. "I'm kind of hungry."

Blaze pulled back. "I only have a couple of dollars left."

He could hear the whine in her voice. "So? That should cover it. And make sure you don't eat any of them, either."

He meant it. Blaze was getting a little soft in the belly, a little puffy in the face. No surprise considering that lately she'd been drinking almost as much as Teddy and Lance.

Blaze made a show of pouting, but Marcus gave her a little shove and she headed to one of the food booths. The line was at least six or seven deep, and as she reached the end of it, Marcus sauntered toward Ronnie and took a seat beside her. Close, but not too close. Blaze was the jealous type, and he didn't want her running Ronnie off before he had a chance to get to know her.

"What did you think?" he asked.

"About what?"

"The show. Have you ever seen anything like it in New York?"

"No," she admitted, "I haven't."

"Where are you staying?"

"Just down the beach a little way." He could tell by her answer that she was uncomfortable, probably because Blaze wasn't there.

"Blaze said you ditched your dad."

In response, she simply shrugged.

"What? You don't want to talk about it?"

"There's nothing to say."

He leaned back. "Maybe you just don't trust me."

"What are you talking about?"

"You'll talk to Blaze, but not me."

"I don't even know you."

"You don't know Blaze, either. You just met her."

Ronnie didn't seem to appreciate his snappy comebacks. "I just didn't want to talk to him, okay? And I don't want to have to spend my summer here, either."

He pushed the hair out of his eyes. "So leave."

"Yeah, right. Where am I supposed to go?"

"Let's go to Florida."

She blinked. "What?"

"I know a guy who's got a place down there just outside of Tampa. If you want, I'll bring you. We can stay there as long as you want. My car's over there."

She stared at him as if in shock. "I can't go to Florida with you. I . . . I just met you. And what about Blaze?"

"What about her?"

"You're with her."

"So?" He kept his face neutral.

"This is too weird." She shook her head and stood. "I think I'll go see how Blaze is doing."

Marcus reached into his pocket for a fireball. "You know I was kidding, right?"

Actually, he hadn't been kidding. He'd said it for the same reason he'd thrown the fireball at her. To see how far he could push her.

"Yeah, okay. Fine. I'm still going over there to talk to her."

Marcus watched her stalk off. As much as he admired that dynamite little body, he wasn't sure what to make of her. She dressed the part, but unlike Blaze, she didn't smoke or show any interest in partying, and he got the sense that there was more to her than she was letting on. He wondered if she came from money. Made sense, right? Apartment in New York, house at the beach? Family had to have money to afford things like that. But . . . then again, there wasn't a chance she'd fit in with people around here who had money, at least the ones he knew. So which one was it? And why did it matter?

Because he didn't like people with money, didn't like the way they flaunted it, and didn't like the way they thought they were better than other people because of it. Once, before he'd dropped out, he'd heard a rich kid at school talking about the new boat he got for his birthday. It wasn't a piece-of-crap skiff; this was a twenty-one-foot Boston Whaler with GPS and sonar, and the kid kept bragging about how he was going to use it all summer and dock it at the slips at the country club.

Three days later, Marcus set the boat on fire and watched it burn from behind the magnolia tree on the sixteenth green.

He'd told no one what he'd done, of course. Tell one person, and you might as well have confessed to the cops. Teddy and Lance were cases in point: Put them in a holding cell and they'd crumple as soon as the door clanged shut. Which was why he insisted they do all the dirty work these days. Best way to keep them from talking was to make sure they were even more guilty than he was. Nowadays, they were the ones who stole the booze, the ones who beat the bald guy unconscious at the airport before taking his wallet, the ones who painted the swastikas on the synagogue. He didn't necessarily trust them, didn't even particularly like them, but they always went along with his plans. They served a purpose.

Behind him, Teddy and Lance continued to act like the idiots they were, and with Ronnie gone, Marcus was antsy. He didn't intend to sit here all night, doing nothing. After Blaze got back, after he ate his fries, he figured they'd go wandering. See what came up. Never knew what might happen in a place like this, on a night like this, in a crowd like this. One thing was certain: After a show, he always needed something . . . *more*. Whatever that meant.

Glancing over to the food booth, he saw Blaze paying for the fries, Ronnie right behind her. He stared at Ronnie, again willing her to turn his way, and eventually, she did. Nothing much, just a quick peek, but that was enough to make him wonder again what she'd be like in bed.

Probably wild, he thought. Most of them were, with the right kind of encouragement.

5

Will

No matter what he was doing, Will could always feel the weight of the secret pressing down on him. On the surface, everything seemed normal: In the last six months, he'd gone to his classes, played basketball, attended the prom, and graduated from high school, college-bound. It hadn't been all perfect, of course. Six weeks ago, he'd broken up with Ashley, but it had nothing to do with what had happened that night, the night he could never forget. Most of the time, he was able to keep the memory locked away, but every now and then, at odd times, it all came back to him with visceral force. The images never changed or faded, the images never blurred around the edges. As though viewing it through someone else's eyes, he would see himself running up the beach and grabbing Scott as he stared at the raging fire.

What the hell did you do? he remembered screaming.

It's not my fault! Scott had screamed back.

It was only then, however, that Will realized they weren't alone. In the distance, he noticed Marcus, Blaze, Teddy, and Lance, watching them, and he knew at once they'd seen everything that happened.

They knew . . .

As soon as Will grabbed for his cell phone, Scott stopped him.

Don't call the police! I told you it was an accident! His expression was pleading. *Come on, man! You owe me!*

News coverage had been extensive the first couple of days, and Will had watched the segments and read the articles in the paper, his stomach in knots. It was one thing to cover for an accidental fire. Maybe he could have done that. But someone had been injured that night, and he felt a sickening surge of guilt whenever he drove by the site. It didn't matter that the church was being rebuilt or that the pastor had long since been released from the hospital; what mattered was that he knew what had happened and hadn't done anything about it.

You owe me . . .

Those were the words that haunted him most.

Not simply because he and Scott had been best friends since kindergarten, but for another, more important reason. And sometimes, in the middle of the night, he would lie awake, hating the truth of those words and wishing for a way to make things right.

Oddly enough, it was the incident at the volleyball game earlier in the day that triggered the memories this time. Or rather, it had been the girl he'd collided with. She hadn't been interested in his apologies, and unlike most girls around here, she hadn't tried to mask her anger. She didn't simmer and she didn't squeal; she was self-possessed in a way that struck him instantly as different.

After she'd stormed off, they'd finished out the set, and he had to admit he'd missed a couple of shots he ordinarily wouldn't have. Scott had glared at him and—maybe because of the play of light—he'd looked exactly as he had on the night of the fire when Will had pulled out his cell phone to call the police. And that was all it took to set those memories loose again.

He'd been able to hold it together until they'd won the game, but after it ended, he'd needed some time alone. So he'd wandered over to the fairgrounds and stopped at one of those over-priced, impossible-to-win game booths. He was getting ready to shoot an overinflated basketball at the slightly too high rim when he heard a voice behind him.

"There you are," Ashley said. "Were you avoiding us?"

Yes, he thought. *Actually, I was.*

"No," he answered. "I haven't taken a shot since the season ended, and I wanted to see how rusty I am."

Ashley smiled. Her white tube top, sandals, and dangly earrings showed off her blue eyes and blond hair to maximum effect. She'd changed into the outfit since the final volleyball game of the tournament. Typical; she was the only girl he'd ever known who carried complete outfit changes as a regular rule, even when she went to the beach. At the prom last May, she'd changed three times: one outfit for dinner, another for the dance, and a third for the party afterward. She'd actually brought along a suitcase, and after pinning on her corsage and posing for photographs, he'd had to lug it to the car. Her mother hadn't found it unusual that she packed as though she were heading off on vacation instead of a dance. But maybe that was part of the problem. Ashley had once taken him to glimpse inside her mom's closet; the woman must have had a couple of hundred different pairs of shoes and a thousand different outfits. Her closet could have housed a Buick.

"Don't let me stop you. I'd hate for you to be out a dollar."

Will turned away, and after zeroing in on the rim, he sent the ball arcing toward the basket. It bounced off the rim and backboard before dropping in. That was one. Two more and he'd actually win a prize.

As the ball rolled back, the carnival worker sneaked a glance at Ashley. Ashley, meanwhile, hadn't seemed to have even noticed the worker's presence.

When the ball rolled down the net and back to Will, he picked it up again and glanced at the carnival worker. "Has anyone won today?"

"Of course. Lots of winners every day." He continued to stare at Ashley as he answered. No surprise there. Everyone always noticed Ashley. She was like a flashing neon sign for anyone with an ounce of testosterone.

Ashley took another step forward, pirouetted, and leaned against the booth. She smiled at Will again. Ashley had never been one for subtlety. After being crowned homecoming queen, she'd worn the tiara all night.

"You played well today," she said. "And your serve has gotten a lot better."

"Thanks," Will answered.

"I think you're almost as good as Scott."

"No way," he said. Scott had been playing volleyball since he was six; Will had taken up the game only after his freshman year. "I'm quick and I can jump, but I don't have the complete game Scott does."

"I'm just telling you what I saw."

Focusing on the rim, Will exhaled, trying to relax before shooting the ball. It was the same thing his coach had always told him to do at the free-throw line, not that it ever seemed to improve his percentage. This time, though, the ball swished through the net. Two for two.

"What are you going to do with the stuffed animal if you win?" she asked.

"I don't know. Do you want it?"

"Only if you want me to have it."

He knew she wanted him to offer it to her as opposed to asking him for it. After two years together, there were few things he didn't know about her. Will grabbed the ball, exhaled again, and took his final shot. This one, however, was a touch too hard, and the ball bounced off the back rim.

"That was close," the worker said. "You should try again."

"I know when I'm beat."

"Tell you what. I'll take a dollar off. Two dollars for three shots."

"That's all right."

"Two dollars and I'll let both of you take three shots." He grabbed the ball, offering it to Ashley. "I'd love to see you give it a try."

Ashley stared at the ball, making it obvious she'd never even contemplated such an idea. Which she probably hadn't.

"I don't think so," Will said. "But thanks for the offer." He turned toward Ashley. "Do you know if Scott is still around?"

"He's at the table with Cassie. Or at least that's where they were when I went to find you. I think he likes her."

Will headed in that direction, Ashley right beside him.

"So we were talking," Ashley said, sounding almost casual, "and Scott and Cassie thought it might be fun to head over to my place. My parents are in Raleigh for some event with the governor, so we'd have the place to ourselves."

Will had known this was coming. "I don't think so," he said.

"Why not? It's not like anything exciting is happening around here."

"I just don't think it's a good idea."

"Is it because we broke up? It's not like I want us to get back together."

Which was why you came to the tournament, he thought. And got dressed up tonight. And came to find me. And suggested going to your place, since your parents aren't home.

But he didn't say those things. He wasn't in the mood to argue, nor did he want to make things any harder than they already were. She wasn't a bad person; she just wasn't for him.

"I've got to be at work early tomorrow morning, and I spent all day playing volleyball in the sun," he offered instead. "I just want to go to sleep."

She grabbed his arm, bringing him to a stop. "Why don't you take my calls anymore?"

He said nothing. There was really nothing he could say.

"I want to know what I did wrong," she demanded.

"You didn't do anything wrong."

"Then what is it?"

When he didn't answer, she gave him a beseeching smile. "Just come over and we'll talk about it, okay?"

He knew she deserved an answer. The only problem was that it was an answer she wouldn't want to hear.

"Like I said, I'm just tired."

"You're *tired*," Scott bellowed. "You told her you were *tired* and you wanted to go to *sleep?*"

"Something like that."

"Are you insane?"

Scott stared at him across the table. Cassie and Ashley had long since headed up the pier to talk, no doubt dissecting everything Will had said to Ashley, adding unnecessary drama to a situation that probably should have remained private. With Ashley, though, there was always drama. He had the sudden sense that the summer was going to be a long one.

"I *am* tired," Will said. "Aren't you?"

"Maybe you didn't hear what she was suggesting. Me and Cassie, you and Ashley? Her parents' place at the beach?"

"She mentioned it."

"And we're still here because . . . ?"

"I already told you."

Scott shook his head. "No . . . see, that's where you lose me. You use the '*I'm tired*' excuse on your parents when they want you to wash the car, or when they tell you to get up so you can make it to church. Not when it comes to an opportunity like this."

Will said nothing. Though Scott was only a year younger—he'd be a senior at Laney High School in the fall—he often acted as if he were Will's older and wiser brother.

Except that night at the church . . .

"See that guy over there at the basketball booth? Now him, I get. He stands there all day trying to get people to play the game so he can earn a little money and buy himself some beer and cigarettes at the end of his shift. Simple. Uncomplicated. Not my kind of life, but one I can understand. But you, I don't get. I mean . . . did you *see* Ashley tonight? She's gorgeous. She looks like that chick in *Maxim*."

"And?"

"My point is, she's hot."

"I know. We were together for a couple of years, remember?"

"And I'm not saying you have to get back together with her. All I'm suggesting is that the four of us head over to her place, have some fun, and see what happens."

Scott leaned back in his seat. "And by the way? I still don't understand why you broke up with her in the first place. It's obvious she's still into you, and you two always seemed perfect together."

Will shook his head. "We weren't perfect together."

"You've said that before, but what does that mean? Is she, like . . . psycho or something when you two are alone? What happened? Did you find her standing over you with a butcher knife, or did she howl at the moon when you went to the beach?"

"No, nothing like that. It just didn't work out, that's all."

"It just didn't work out," Scott repeated. "Can you even hear yourself?"

When Will showed no signs of relenting, Scott leaned across the table. "C'mon, man. Do this for me, then. Live a little. It's summer vacation. Take one for the team."

"Now you sound desperate."

"I am desperate. Unless you agree to go with Ashley tonight, Cassie won't go with me. And we're talking about a girl who's ready to 'Romance the Stone.' She wants to 'Free Willy.'"

"I'm sorry. But I can't help you."

"Fine. Ruin my life. Who cares, right?"

"You'll survive." He paused. "You hungry?"

"A little," Scott grumbled.

"C'mon. Let's get some cheeseburgers."

Will got up from the table, but Scott continued to pout. "You

need to practice digging," he said, referring to the earlier volleyball games. "You were sending the ball in every direction. It was
all I could do to keep us in the games."

"Ashley told me I was as good as you are."

Scott snorted and pushed up from the table. "She doesn't know
what she's talking about."

After standing in line for their food, Will and Scott moved to the
condiment stand, where Scott drenched his burger in ketchup. It
squeezed out the sides as Scott put the bun back on.

"That's disgusting," Will commented.

"So get this. There was this guy named Ray Kroc and he
started this company called McDonald's. Ever heard of it? Anyway, on his original hamburger—in many ways the original
American hamburger, mind you—he insisted that ketchup be
added. Which should tell you how important it is to the overall
taste."

"Keep talking. You're just so fascinating. I'm going to get something to drink."

"Get me a bottled water, will you?"

As Will walked off, something white flashed by him, heading
in Scott's direction; Scott saw it, too, and instinctively lunged
out of the way, dropping his cheeseburger in the process.

"What the hell do you think you're doing?" Scott demanded,
spinning around. On the ground lay a wadded-up box of French
fries. Behind him, Teddy and Lance had their hands stuffed in
their pockets. Marcus was standing between them, trying and
failing to appear innocent.

"I don't know what you're talking about," Marcus answered.

"This!" Scott snarled, kicking the box back at them.

It was the tone, Will would later think, that made everyone
around them tense. Will felt the hair on his neck prickle at the
palpable, almost physical dislocation of air and space, a tremor
that promised violence.

Violence that Marcus obviously wanted . . .

As if he were baiting him.

Will saw a father scoop up his son and move away, while Ashley and Cassie, back from the pier, froze on the outskirts. Off to the side, Will recognized Galadriel—she called herself Blaze these days—circling closer.

Scott glared at them, his jaw clenching. "You know, I'm getting sick and tired of your crap."

"Whatcha gonna do?" Marcus smirked. "Shoot a bottle rocket at me?"

That was all it took. As Scott took a sudden step forward, Will pushed his way frantically through the crowd, trying to reach his friend in time.

Marcus didn't move. Not good. Will knew he and his friends were capable of anything . . . and worst of all, they knew what Scott had done . . .

But Scott, in a fury, didn't seem to care. As Will surged forward, Teddy and Lance fanned out, drawing Scott into their midst. He tried to close the gap, but Scott was moving too quickly, and suddenly everything seemed to happen at once. Marcus took a half step backward as Teddy kicked over a stool, forcing Scott to jump out of the way. He slammed into a table, toppling it. Scott caught his balance and balled his hands into fists. Lance closed in from the side. As Will forced his way forward, gaining momentum, he vaguely heard the wailing sounds of a toddler. Breaking free of the crowd, he veered toward Lance when all at once a girl stepped forward into the fray.

"Just stop!" the girl shouted, thrusting her arms out. "Knock it off! All of you!"

Her voice was surprisingly loud and authoritative, enough to make Will stop in his tracks. Everyone else froze, and in the sudden silence, the cries of the toddler sounded shrill. The girl pivoted, glaring at each of the brawlers in turn, and as soon as Will saw the purple streak in her hair, he realized exactly where he'd seen her before. Only now she was wearing an oversize T-shirt with a fish on the front.

"The fight's over! There is no fight! Can't you see this kid is hurt?"

Challenging them to contradict her, she pushed her way between Scott and Marcus and stooped to the crying toddler, who had been knocked over in the commotion. He was three or four, and his shirt was pumpkin orange. When the girl spoke to him, her voice was soft, her smile reassuring.

"Are you okay, sweetie? Where's your mom? Let's go find her, okay?"

The toddler seemed to focus momentarily on her shirt.

"This is Nemo," she said. "He got lost, too. Do you like Nemo?"

Off to the side, a panic-stricken woman holding a baby pushed through the crowd, oblivious to the tension in the air. "Jason? Where are you? Have you seen a little boy? Blond hair, orange shirt?"

Relief crossed her features as soon as she spotted him. She adjusted the baby on her hip as she rushed to his side.

"You can't run off like that, Jason!" she cried. "You scared me. Are you okay?"

"Nemo," he said, pointing at the girl.

The mother turned, noticing the girl for the first time. "Thank you—he just wandered off when I was changing the baby's diaper and—"

"It's okay," the girl said, shaking her head. "He's fine."

Will watched the mother lead her kids away, then he turned back to the girl, noticing the kind way she smiled as the young boy toddled off. Once they'd moved far enough away, however, the girl suddenly seemed to realize that everyone in the crowd was staring at her. She crossed her arms, self-conscious when the crowd began to part for a rapidly approaching police officer.

Marcus quickly murmured something to Scott before melting back into the crowd. Teddy and Lance did the same. Blaze turned to follow them as well, and surprising Will, the girl with the purple streak reached out to grab her arm.

"Wait! Where are you going?" she called out.

Blaze shook her arm free, walking backward. "Bower's Point."

"Where's that?"

"Just head down the beach. You'll find it." Blaze turned and rushed after Marcus.

The girl seemed unsure what to do. By then the tension, so thick only moments before, was dissipating as quickly as it had arisen. Scott righted the table and headed toward Will just as the girl was approached by a man he assumed was her father.

"There you are!" he called out with a mixture of relief and exasperation. "We've been looking for you. You ready to go?"

The girl, who'd been watching Blaze, was obviously unhappy to see him.

"No," she said simply. With that, she strode into the crowd, heading for the beach. A young boy walked up to the father.

"I guess she's not hungry," the boy offered.

The man put his hand on the boy's shoulder, watching as she descended the steps to the beach without a backward glance. "I guess not," he said.

"Can you believe that?" Scott raged, pulling Will away from the scene he'd been observing so closely. Scott was still hyped up, the adrenaline surging. "I was about to pound that freak."

"Uh . . . yeah," he responded. He shook his head. "I'm not sure Teddy and Lance would have let you."

"They wouldn't have done anything. Those guys are all show."

Will wasn't so sure about that, but he didn't say anything.

Scott took a breath. "Hold up. Here comes the cop."

The officer approached them slowly, obviously trying to gauge the situation.

"What's going on here?" he demanded.

"Nothing, Officer," Scott answered, sounding demure.

"I heard there was a fight."

"No, sir."

The officer waited for more, his expression skeptical. Neither Scott nor Will said anything. By then, the condiment area was filling with people going about their business. The officer surveyed the scene, making sure he wasn't missing anything, then suddenly his face lit up with recognition at the sight of someone standing behind Will.

"Is that you, Steve?" he called out.

Will watched him stride off toward the girl's father.

Ashley and Cassie sidled up to them. Cassie's face was flushed. "Are you okay?" she fluttered.

"I'm fine," Scott answered.

"That guy's crazy. What happened? I didn't see how it started."

"He threw something at me, and I wasn't going to put up with it. I'm sick and tired of the way that guy acts. He thinks everyone's afraid of him and that he can do whatever he wants, but the next time he tries it, it's not going to be pretty . . ."

Will tuned him out. Scott was always a big talker; he did the same thing during their volleyball matches, and Will had learned long ago to ignore it.

He turned away, catching sight of the officer chatting with the girl's dad, wondering why the girl had been so intent on getting away from her father. And why she was hanging out with Marcus. She wasn't like them, and he somehow doubted she knew what she was getting into with them. As Scott went on, assuring Cassie that he could easily have handled the three of them, Will found himself straining to overhear the police officer's conversation with the girl's father.

"Oh, hey, Pete," the father said. "What's going on?"

"Same old stuff," the officer responded. "Doing my best to keep things under control out here. How's the window coming?"

"Slowly."

"That's what you said the last time I asked."

"Yeah, but now I've got a secret weapon. This is my son, Jonah. He's going to be my assistant this summer."

"Yeah? Good for you, little man . . . Wasn't your daughter supposed to come down here, too, Steve?"

"She's here," the father said.

"Yeah, but she left again," the boy added. "She's pretty mad at Dad."

"Sorry to hear that."

Will watched the father point toward the beach. "Do you have any idea where they might be going?"

The officer squinted as he scanned the waterline. "Could be anywhere. But a couple of those kids are bad news. Especially Marcus. Trust me, you don't want her keeping company with him."

Scott was still boasting to a rapt Cassie and Ashley. Blocking him out, Will suddenly felt the urge to call out to the police officer. He knew it wasn't his place to say anything. He didn't know the girl, didn't know why she'd stormed off in the first place. Maybe she had a good reason. But as he saw the concern crease her dad's face, he recalled her patience and kindness when she'd rescued the toddler, and the words were out before he could stop them.

"She went to Bower's Point," he announced.

Scott stopped talking in midsentence, and Ashley turned to him with a frown. The other three studied him uncertainly.

"Your daughter, right?" When the father nodded slightly, he went on. "She's going to Bower's Point."

The officer continued to stare at him, then turned back to the father. "When I finish up here, I'll go talk to her and see if I can convince her to go home, okay?"

"You don't have to do that, Pete."

The officer continued to study the group in the distance. "I think in this instance, it's better if I go."

Inexplicably, Will felt a strange wave of relief. It must have shown, because when he turned back toward his friends, each of them was staring at him.

"What the hell was that all about?" Scott demanded.

Will didn't answer. He couldn't, because he didn't really understand it himself.

6

· · · · ♪ · · · ·

Ronnie

Under normal circumstances, Ronnie probably would have appreciated an evening like this. In New York, the lights from the city made it impossible to see many stars, but here, it was just the opposite. Even with the layer of marine haze, she could clearly make out the Milky Way, and directly to the south, Venus glowed brightly. The waves crashed and rolled rhythmically along the beach, and on the horizon, she could see the faint lights of half a dozen shrimp boats.

But the circumstances weren't normal. As she stood on the porch, she glared at the officer, livid beyond belief.

No, change that. She wasn't just livid. She was *seething*. What had happened was so . . . overprotective, so *over the top*, she could still barely process it. Her first thought was simply to hitchhike to the bus station and buy herself a ticket back to New York. She wouldn't tell her dad or her mom; she'd call Kayla. Once she was there, she would figure out what to do next. No matter what she decided, it couldn't be any worse than this.

But that wasn't possible. Not with Officer Pete here. He stood behind her now, making sure she went inside.

She still couldn't believe it. How could her dad—her own flesh-and-blood father—do something like this? She was almost an adult, she hadn't been doing anything wrong, and it wasn't even midnight. What was the problem? Why did he have to turn this into something far bigger than it was? Oh sure, at first Officer Pete had made it sound like it had been an ordinary, run-of-the-mill order to vacate their spot on Bower's Point—something that hadn't surprised the others—but then he'd turned to her. Zeroed in on her specifically.

"I'm taking you home," he'd said, making it sound as if she were eight years old.

"No thanks," she'd responded.

"Then I'll have to arrest you on vagrancy charges, and have your dad bring you home."

It dawned on her then that her dad had asked the police to bring her home, and there was an instant when she was frozen in mortification.

Sure, she'd had problems with her mom, and yeah, she'd blown off her curfew now and then. But never, ever, not even once, had her mother sent the police after her.

On the porch, the officer intruded on her thoughts. "Go on in," he prompted, making it fairly clear that if she didn't open the door, he would.

From inside, she could hear the soft sounds of the piano, and she recognized the sonata by Edvard Grieg in E minor. She took a deep breath before opening the door, then slammed it shut behind her.

Her father stopped playing and looked up as she glared at him.

"You sent the cops after me?"

Her dad said nothing, but his silence was enough.

"Why would you do something like that?" she demanded. "How could you do something like that?"

He said nothing.

"What is it? You didn't want me to have fun? You didn't trust me? You didn't get the fact that I don't want to be here?"

Her father folded his hands in his lap. "I know you don't want to be here . . ."

She took a step forward, still glaring. "So you decide you want to ruin my life, too?"

"Who's Marcus?"

"Who cares!" she shouted. "That's not the point! You're not going to monitor every single person I ever talk to, so don't even try!"

"I'm not trying—"

"I hate being here! Don't you get that? And I hate you, too!"

She stared at him, her face daring him to contradict her. Hoping he'd try, so she'd be able to say it again.

But her dad said nothing, as usual. She hated that kind of weakness. In a fury, she crossed the room toward the alcove, grabbed the picture of her playing the piano—the one with her dad beside her on the bench—and hurled it across the room. Though he flinched at the sound of breaking glass, he remained quiet.

"What? Nothing to say?"

He cleared his throat. "Your bedroom's the first door on the right."

She didn't even want to dignify his comment with a response, so she stormed down the hall, determined to have nothing more to do with him.

"Good night, sweetheart," he called out. "I love you."

There was a moment, just a moment, when she cringed at what she'd said to him; but her regret vanished as quickly as it had come. It was as if he hadn't even realized she'd been angry: She heard him begin to play the piano again, picking up exactly where he'd left off.

In the bedroom—not hard to find, considering there were only three doors off the hallway, one to the bathroom and the other to her dad's room—Ronnie flipped on the light. With a frustrated sigh, she peeled off the ridiculous Nemo T-shirt she'd almost forgotten she was wearing.

It had been the worst day of her life.

Oh, she knew she was being melodramatic about the whole thing. She wasn't stupid. Still, it hadn't been a great one. About the only good thing to come out of the whole day was meeting Blaze, which gave her hope that she'd have at least one person to spend time with this summer.

Assuming, of course, that Blaze still wanted to spend time with her. After Dad's little stunt, even that was in doubt. Blaze and the rest of them were probably still talking about it. Probably laughing about it. It was the kind of thing Kayla would bring up for years.

The whole thing made her sick to her stomach. She tossed the Nemo shirt into the corner—if she never saw it again, it would be too soon—and began slipping off her concert shirt.

"Before I get too grossed out, you should know I'm in here."

Ronnie jumped at the sound, whirling around to see Jonah staring at her.

"Get out!" she screamed. "What are you doing in here? This is my room!"

"No, it's our room," Jonah said. He pointed. "See? Two beds."

"I'm not going to share a room with you!"

He tilted his head to the side. "You're going to sleep in Dad's room?"

She opened her mouth to respond, considered moving to the living room before quickly realizing she wasn't going out there again, then closed her mouth without a word. She stomped toward her suitcase, unzipped the top, and flung open the lid. *Anna Karenina* lay on top, and she tossed it aside, searching for her pajamas.

"I rode the Ferris wheel," Jonah said. "It was pretty cool to be so high. That's how Dad found you."

"Great."

"It was awesome. Did you ride it?"

"No."

"You should have. I could see all the way to New York."

"I doubt it."

"I could. I can see pretty far. With my glasses, I mean. Dad said I have eagle eyes."

"Yeah, right."

Jonah said nothing. Instead, he reached for the teddy bear he'd brought with him from home. It was the one he clutched whenever he was nervous, and Ronnie winced, regretting her words. Sometimes the way he talked made it easy to think of him as an adult, but as he pulled the bear to his chest, she knew she shouldn't have been so harsh. Though he was precocious, though he was verbal to the point of annoyance at times, he was small for his age, more the size of a six- or seven-year-old than a ten-year-old. It had never been easy for him. He'd been born three months prematurely, and he suffered from asthma, poor vision, and a lack of fine-motor coordination. She knew kids his age could be cruel.

"I didn't mean that. With your glasses, you definitely have eagle eyes."

"Yeah, they're pretty good now," he mumbled, but when he turned away and faced the wall, she winced again. He was a sweet kid. A pain in the butt sometimes, but she knew he didn't have a mean bone in him.

She went over to his bed and sat beside him. "Hey," she said. "I'm sorry. I didn't mean it. I'm just having a bad night."

"I know," he said.

"Did you go on any of the other rides?"

"Dad took me on most of them. He almost got sick, but I didn't. And I wasn't scared at all in the haunted house. I could tell the ghosts were fake."

She patted him on the hip. "You've always been pretty brave."

"Yeah," he said. "Like that time when the lights went out in the apartment? You were scared that night. I wasn't scared, though."

"I remember."

He seemed satisfied with her answer. But then he grew quiet, and when he spoke again, his voice was barely above a whisper. "Do you miss Mom?"

Ronnie reached for the covers. "Yeah."

"I kind of miss her, too. And I didn't like being here alone."

"Dad was in the other room," she said.

"I know. But I'm glad you came home anyway."

"Me, too."

He smiled before looking worried again. "Do you think Mom is doing okay?"

"She's fine," she assured him. She pulled up the covers. "But I know she misses you, too."

In the morning, with sunlight peeking through the curtains, it took Ronnie a few seconds to realize where she was. Blinking at the clock, she thought, *You've got to be kidding me.*

Eight o'clock? In the morning? In the *summer*?

She plopped back down, only to find herself staring at the ceiling, already knowing that sleep was out of the question. Not with the sun shooting daggers through the windows. Not with her father already hammering on the piano in the living room. As she suddenly remembered what had happened last night, the anger she felt at what her father had done resurfaced.

Welcome to another day in paradise.

Outside the window, she heard the distant roar of engines. She rose from the bed and pulled aside the curtain, only to jump back, startled at the sight of a raccoon sitting atop a torn bag of garbage. While the strewn garbage was gross, the raccoon was cute, and she tapped the glass, trying to get its attention.

It was only then that she noticed the bars on the window.

Bars. On. The. Window.

Trapped.

Gritting her teeth, she whirled around and marched into the

living room. Jonah was watching cartoons and eating a bowl of cereal; her dad glanced up but continued to play.

She put her hands on her hips, waiting for him to stop. He didn't. She noticed that the picture she'd thrown was back in place atop the piano, albeit without the glass.

"You can't keep me locked up all summer," she said. "It's not going to happen."

Her dad glanced up, though he continued to play. "What are you talking about?"

"You put bars on the window! Like I'm supposed to be your prisoner?"

Jonah continued to watch the cartoon. "I told you she'd be mad," he commented.

Steve shook his head, his hands continuing to move across the keyboard. "I didn't put them up. They came with the house."

"I don't believe you."

"They did," Jonah said. "To protect the art."

"I'm not talking to you, Jonah!" She turned back to her dad. "Let's get one thing straight. You're not going to spend this summer treating me like I'm still a little girl! I'm eighteen years old!"

"You won't be eighteen until August twentieth," Jonah said behind her.

"Would you please stay out of this!" She whirled around to face him. "This is between me and Dad."

Jonah frowned. "But you're not eighteen yet."

"That's not the point!"

"I thought you forgot."

"I didn't forget! I'm not stupid."

"But you said—"

"Would you just shut up for a second?" she said, unable to hide her exasperation. She swiveled her gaze back to her dad, who'd continued to play, never missing a note. "What you did last night was . . ." She stopped, unable to put all that was going on, all that had happened, into words. "I'm old enough to make my own decisions. Don't you get that? You gave up the right to tell me what to do when you walked out the door. And would you *please* listen to me!"

Abruptly, her dad stopped playing.

"I don't like this little game you're playing."

He seemed confused. "What game?"

"This! Playing the piano every minute I'm here! I don't care how much you want me to play! I'm never going to play the piano again! Especially not for you!"

"Okay."

She waited for more, but there was nothing.

"That's it?" she asked. "That's all you're going to say?"

Her dad seemed to debate how to answer. "Do you want breakfast? I made some bacon."

"Bacon?" she demanded. "You made *bacon*?"

"Uh-oh," Jonah said.

Her dad glanced at Jonah.

"She's a vegetarian, Dad," he explained.

"Really?" he asked.

Jonah answered for her. "For three years. But she's weird sometimes, so it makes sense."

Ronnie stared at them in amazement, wondering how the conversation had been hijacked. This wasn't about bacon, this was about what happened last night. "Let's get one thing straight," she said. "If you ever send the police to bring me home again, I won't just refuse to play the piano. I won't just go home. I'll never, ever speak to you again. And if you don't believe me, try me. I've already gone three years without talking to you, and it was the easiest thing I've ever done."

With that, she stomped back to her room. Twenty minutes later, after showering and changing, she was out the door.

* * *

Her first thought as she trudged through the sand was that she should have worn shorts.

It was already hot, the air thick with humidity. Up and down the beach, people were already lying on towels or playing in the surf. Near the pier, she spotted half a dozen surfers floating on their boards, waiting for the perfect wave.

Above them, at the head of the pier, the festival was no more. The rides had been disassembled and the booths had already been hauled away, leaving behind only scattered garbage and food remnants. Moving on, she wandered through the town's small business district. None of the stores were open yet, but most were the kind she'd never set foot in anyway—touristy beach shops, a couple of clothing stores that seemed to specialize in skirts and blouses that her mom might wear, and a Burger King and Mc-Donald's, two places she refused to enter on principle. Add in the hotel and half a dozen upscale restaurants and bars, and that was pretty much it. In the end, the only interesting locales were a surf shop, a music store, and an old-fashioned diner where she could imagine hanging out with friends . . . if she ever made any.

She headed back to the beach and skipped down the dune, noting that the crowds had multiplied. It was a gorgeous, breezy day; the sky overhead was a deep, cloudless blue. If Kayla had been here, she'd even consider spending the day in the sun, but Kayla wasn't here and she wasn't about to put on her suit and go sit by herself. But what else was there to do?

Maybe she should try to get a job. It would give her an excuse to be out of the house most of the day. She hadn't seen any "Help Wanted" signs in the windows downtown, but someone had to be hiring, right?

"Did you make it home okay? Or did the cop end up making a pass at you?"

Looking behind her, Ronnie saw Blaze squinting up at her from the dune. Lost in thought, she hadn't even noticed her.

"No, he didn't make a pass at me."

"Oh, so you made a pass at him?"

Ronnie crossed her arms. "Are you done?"

Blaze shrugged, her expression mischievous, and Ronnie smiled.

"So what happened after I left? Anything exciting?"

"No. The guys took off and I don't know where they went. I ended up just crashing at Bower's Point."

"You didn't go home?"

"No." She got to her feet, brushing the sand from her jeans. "Do you have any money?"

"Why?"

Blaze stood straight. "I haven't eaten since yesterday morning. I'm kind of hungry."

7

Will

Will stood in the well beneath the Ford Explorer in his uniform, watching the oil drain while simultaneously doing his best to ignore Scott, something easier said than done. Scott had been haranguing him about the previous evening on and off since they'd arrived at work that morning.

"See, you were thinking about this all wrong," Scott continued, trying yet another tack. He retrieved three cans of oil and set them on the shelf beside him. "There's a difference between *hooking up* and *getting back together*."

"Aren't we done with this yet?"

"We would be if you had any sense. But from where I stand, it's obvious you were confused. Ashley doesn't want to get back together with you."

"I wasn't confused," Will said. He wiped his hands on a towel. "That's *exactly* what she was asking."

"That's not what Cassie told me."

Will set aside the towel and reached for his water bottle. His dad's shop specialized in brake repairs, oil changes, tune-ups, and front-end alignments, and his dad always wanted the place to look as though the floor had been waxed and the place just opened for business. Unfortunately, air-conditioning hadn't been quite as important to him, and in the summer, the temperature was some-where between the Mojave and the Sahara. He took a long drink, finishing the bottle before trying to get through to Scott again. Scott was far and away the most stubborn person he'd ever known. The guy could seriously drive him nuts.

"You don't know Ashley the way I do." He sighed. "And besides, it's over and done. I don't know why you keep talking about it."

"You mean aside from the fact that Harry didn't meet Sally last night? Because I'm your friend and I care about you. I want you to enjoy this summer. I want to enjoy this summer. I want to enjoy Cassie."

"So go out with her, then."

"If only it was that easy. See, last night I suggested the same thing. But Ashley was so upset that Cassie didn't want to leave her."

"I'm really sorry it didn't work out."

Scott was dubious. "Yeah, I can tell."

By that point, the oil had drained. Will grabbed the cans and headed up the steps while Scott stayed below to replace the plug and dump the used oil into the recycling barrel. As Will opened the can and set the funnel, he glanced at Scott below.

"Hey, by the way, did you see the girl who stopped the fight?" he asked. "The one who helped the little boy find his mom?"

It took a moment for the words to register. "You mean the vampire chick in the cartoon shirt?"

"She's not a vampire."

"Yeah, I saw her. On the short side, ugly purple streak in her hair, black fingernail polish? You poured your soda over her, re-member? She thought you smelled."

"What?"

"I'm just saying," he said, reaching for the pan. "You didn't notice her expression after you slammed into her, but I did. She couldn't get away from you fast enough. Hence, you probably smelled."

"She had to buy a new shirt."

"So?"

Will added the second can. "I don't know. She just surprised me. And I haven't seen her around here before."

"I repeat: So?"

The thing was, Will wasn't exactly sure why he was thinking about the girl. Particularly considering how little he knew about her. Yeah, she was pretty—he'd noticed that right off, despite the purple hair and dark mascara—but the beach was full of pretty girls. Nor was it the way she'd stopped the fight in its tracks. Instead, he kept coming back to the way she'd treated the little boy who'd fallen. He'd glimpsed a surprising tenderness beneath her rebellious exterior, and it had piqued his curiosity.

She wasn't like Ashley at all. And it wasn't that Ashley was a bad person, because she wasn't. But there was something superficial about Ashley, even if Scott didn't want to believe it. In Ashley's world, everyone and everything was put into neat little boxes: popular or not, expensive or cheap, rich or poor, beautiful or ugly. And he'd eventually grown tired of her shallow value judgments and her inability to accept or appreciate anything in between.

But the girl with the purple streak in her hair . . .

He knew instinctively that she wasn't that way. He couldn't be absolutely sure, of course, but he'd bet on it. She didn't put others into neat little boxes because she didn't put herself in one, and that struck him as refreshing and different, especially when compared with the girls he'd known at Laney. Especially Ashley.

Though things were busy at the garage, his thoughts kept drifting back to her more often than he expected.

Not all the time. But enough to make him realize that for whatever reason, he definitely wanted to get to know her a little better, and he found himself wondering whether he would see her again.

8

....♪....

Ronnie

Blaze led the way to the diner Ronnie had seen on her walk through the business district, and Ronnie had to admit that it did have some charm, particularly if you were fond of the 1950s. There was an old-fashioned counter flanked with stools, the floor was black and white tiles, and cracked red vinyl booths lined the walls. Behind the counter, the menu was written on a chalkboard, and as far as Ronnie could tell, the only change to it in the last thirty years had been the prices.

Blaze ordered a cheeseburger, a chocolate shake, and French fries; Ronnie couldn't decide and ended up ordering only a Diet Coke. She was hungry, but she wasn't exactly sure what kind of oil they used in their deep fryer, and neither, it seemed, was anyone else at the diner. Being a vegetarian wasn't always easy, and there were times when she wanted to give up the whole thing.

Like when her stomach was growling. Like right now.

But she wouldn't eat here. She couldn't eat here, not because she was a *vegetarian-on-principle* kind of person, but because she was *vegetarian-because-she-didn't-want-to-feel-sick* kind of person. She didn't care what other people ate; it was just that whenever she thought about where meat actually came from, she'd imagine a cow standing in a meadow or Babe the pig, and she'd feel herself getting nauseated.

Blaze seemed happy, though. After she placed her order, she leaned back in the booth. "What do you think about the place?" she asked.

"It's neat. It's kind of different."

"I've been coming here since I was a kid. My dad used to bring me every Sunday after church for a chocolate shake. They're the best. They get their ice cream from some tiny place in Georgia, but it's amazing. You should get one."

"I'm not hungry."

"You're lying," Blaze said. "I heard your stomach growling, but whatever. It's your loss. But thanks for this."

"No big deal."

Blaze smiled. "So what happened last night? Are you like . . . famous or something?"

"Why would you ask that?"

"Because of the cop and the way he singled you out. There had to be a reason."

Ronnie made a face. "I think my dad told him to go find me. He even knew where I lived."

"Sucks being you."

When Ronnie laughed, Blaze reached for the saltshaker. After tipping it over, she began sprinkling salt onto the table while using a finger to mold it into a pile.

"What did you think of Marcus?" she asked.

"I didn't really talk to him. Why?"

Blaze seemed to choose her words carefully. "Marcus never liked me," she said. "Growing up, I mean. I can't say that I liked him very much, either. He was always kind of . . . mean, you know? But then, I don't know, a couple of years ago, things changed. And when I really needed someone, he was there for me."

Ronnie watched the salt pile grow. "And?"

"I just wanted you to know."

"Fine," she said. "Whatever."

"You too."

"What are you talking about?"

Blaze scraped some of the black polish from her fingernails. "I used to compete in gymnastics, and for maybe four or five years, it was the biggest thing in my life. I ended up quitting because of my coach. He was a real hard-ass, always telling you what you did wrong, never complimenting you on what you did right. Anyway, I was doing a new dismount off the beam one day, and he marched forward screaming at me about the proper way to plant and how I have to freeze and everything I'd heard him scream about a million times before. I was tired of hearing it, you know? So I said, 'Whatever,' and he grabbed my arm so hard that he left bruises. Anyway, he says to me, 'Do you know what you're saying when you say, "Whatever"? It's just a code word for the f-word, followed by "you." And at your age, you never, ever say that to anyone.'" Blaze leaned back. "So now, when someone says it to me, I just say, 'You too.'"

Right then, the waitress arrived with their food, and she placed it in front of them with an efficient flourish. When she was gone, Ronnie reached for her soda.

"Thanks for the heartwarming story."

"Whatever."

Ronnie laughed again, liking her sense of humor.

Blaze leaned across the table. "So what's worst thing you've ever done?"

"What?"

"I'm serious. I always ask people that question. I find it interesting."

"All right," Ronnie countered. "What's the worst thing you've ever done?"

"That's easy. When I was little, I had this neighbor—Mrs.

Banderson. She wasn't the nicest lady, but she wasn't a witch, either. I mean, it's not like she locked her doors on Halloween or anything. But she was really into her garden, you know? And her lawn. I mean, if we ever walked across it on our way to the school bus, she'd come storming out, screaming that we were ruining the grass. Anyway, one spring, she planted all these flowers in her garden. Hundreds of them. It was gorgeous. Well, there was this kid across the street named Billy, and he didn't like Mrs. Banderson much, either, because one time he'd hit a baseball and it went into her backyard, and she wouldn't give it back. So one day, we were poking around his garden shed, and we came across this big sprayer filled with Roundup. The weed killer? Well, he and I snuck out after dark one night and sprayed all those new flowers, don't ask me why. I guess at the time we thought it would be kind of funny. No big deal. Just buy some new ones, right? You couldn't tell right away, of course. It takes a few days before it starts working. And Mrs. Banderson was out there every day, watering and pulling weeds before she noticed that all her new flowers had started to wilt. At first, Billy and I laughed about it, but then I started to notice she'd be out there before school trying to figure out what was wrong, and she'd still be out there when I came back from school. And by the end of the week, all of them were dead."

"That's terrible!" Ronnie cried, giggling despite herself.

"I know. And I still feel bad about it. It's one of those things that I wish I could undo."

"Did you ever tell her? Or offer to replace the flowers?"

"My parents would have killed me. But I never, ever walked across her lawn again."

"Wow."

"Like I said, it's the worst thing I've ever done. Now it's your turn."

Ronnie thought about it. "I didn't talk to my dad for three years."

"I already know that. And it's not that bad. Like I said, I try not to talk to my dad, either. And my mom has no idea where I am most of the time."

Ronnie glanced away. Above the jukebox was a picture of Bill Haley & His Comets.

"I used to shoplift," she said, subdued. "A lot. Nothing big. Just more for the thrill of doing it."

"Used to?"

"Not anymore. I got caught. Actually, I got caught twice, but the second time it was an accident. It went to court, but the charges were continued for a year. Basically, it means that if I don't get in trouble again, the charges will be dismissed."

Blaze lowered her burger. "That's it? That's the worst thing you've ever done?"

"I never killed someone's flowers, if that's what you mean. Or vandalized anything."

"You've never stuck your brother's head in the toilet? Or crashed the car? Or shaved the cat or something?"

Ronnie gave a small smile. "No."

"You're probably the most boring teenager in the world."

Ronnie giggled again before taking a sip of her soda. "Can I ask you a question?"

"Go ahead."

"Why didn't you go home last night?"

Blaze took a pinch of the salt she'd piled up and sprinkled it over her fries. "I didn't want to."

"What about your mom? Doesn't she get mad?"

"Probably," Blaze said.

Off to the side, the door to the diner swung open and Ronnie turned to see Marcus, Teddy, and Lance heading toward their booth. Marcus wore a T-shirt emblazoned with a skull, and a chain was attached to the belt loop of his jeans.

Blaze scooted over, but strangely, Teddy took a seat beside her while Marcus squeezed in next to Ronnie. As Lance pulled up a chair from an adjoining table and flipped it around before sitting, Marcus reached for Blaze's plate. Both Teddy and Lance automatically grabbed for the fries.

"Hey, that's for Blaze," Ronnie cried, trying to stop them. "Get your own."

Marcus turned from one to the other. "Yeah?"

"It's okay," Blaze said, pushing the plate toward him. "Really. I won't be able to eat it all anyway."

Marcus reached for the ketchup, acting as though he'd proved his point. "So what are you two talking about? From the window, it looked intense."

"Nothing," Blaze said.

"Let me guess. She's telling you about her mom's sexy boyfriend and their late night trapeze acts, right?"

Blaze wiggled in her seat. "Don't be gross."

Marcus gave Ronnie a frank stare. "Did she tell you about the night one of her mom's boyfriends came sneaking into her room? She was like, 'You've got fifteen minutes to get the hell out of here.'"

"Shut up, okay? That's not funny. And we weren't talking about him."

"Whatever," he said, smirking.

Blaze reached for her shake as Marcus began eating the burger. Teddy and Lance grabbed more fries, and over the next few minutes, the three of them devoured most of what was on the plate. To Ronnie's dismay, Blaze said nothing, and Ronnie wondered about that.

Or actually, she didn't wonder. It seemed obvious that Blaze didn't want Marcus to get mad at her, so she let him do whatever he wanted. She'd seen it before: Kayla, for all her tough posturing, was the same way when it came to guys. And generally, they treated her like dirt.

But she wouldn't say that here. She knew it would only make things worse.

Blaze sipped her milkshake and put it back on the table. "So what do you guys want to do after this?"

"We're out," Teddy grunted. "Our old man needs me and Lance to work today."

"They're brothers," Blaze explained.

Ronnie studied them, not seeing the resemblance. "You are?"

Marcus finished the burger and pushed the plate to the center of the table. "I know. It's hard to believe parents could have two such ugly kids, huh? Anyway, their family owns a piece-of-crap motel just over the bridge. The pipes are like a hundred years old, and Teddy's job is to plunge the toilets when they get clogged."

Ronnie wrinkled her nose, trying to imagine it. "Really?"

Marcus nodded. "Gross, huh? But don't worry about Teddy. He's great at it. A real prodigy. He actually enjoys it. And Lance here—his job is to clean the sheets after the noontime crowd rolls through."

"Ew," Ronnie said.

"I know. It's totally disgusting," Blaze added. "And you should see some of the people that go for the hourly rates. You could catch a disease just walking into the room."

Ronnie wasn't sure how to respond to that, so instead she turned to Marcus. "So what do you do?" she asked.

"Whatever I want," he answered.

"Which means?" Ronnie challenged.

"Why do you care?"

"I don't," she said, keeping her voice cool. "I was just asking."

Teddy grabbed the last of the fries from Blaze's plate. "It means he hangs out at the motel with us. In his room."

"You have a room at the motel?"

"I live there," he said.

The obvious question was why, and she waited for more, but Marcus stayed quiet. She suspected he wanted her to attempt to tease the information out of him. Maybe she was reading too much into it, but she had the sudden sense that he wanted her to be interested in him. Wanted her to like him. Even though Blaze was right there.

Her suspicions were confirmed when he reached for a cigarette. After he lit it, he blew the smoke toward Blaze, then turned to Ronnie.

"What are you doing tonight?" he asked.

Ronnie shifted in her seat, suddenly uncomfortable. It seemed like everyone, Blaze included, was waiting for her answer.

"Why?"

"We're having a little get-together at Bower's Point. Not just us. A bunch of people. I want you to come. Without the cops this time."

Blaze studied the tabletop, toying with the pile of salt. When Ronnie didn't answer, Marcus rose from the table and headed for the door without turning back.

9

·· ·· ·♪·· ·· ·

Steve

"Hey, Dad," Jonah called out. He was standing behind the piano in the alcove as Steve brought the plates of spaghetti to the table. "Is that a picture of you with Grandma and Grandpa?"

"Yeah, that's my mom and dad."

"I don't remember that picture. From the apartment, I mean."

"For a long time, it was in my office at school."

"Oh," Jonah said. He leaned closer to the photo, studying it. "You kind of look like Grandpa."

Steve wasn't sure what to think about that. "Maybe a little."

"Do you miss him?"

"He was my dad. What do you think?"

"I'd miss you."

As Jonah came to the table, Steve reflected that it had been a satisfying, if uneventful, day. They'd spent the morning in the shop, where Steve had taught Jonah to cut glass; they'd eaten sandwiches on the porch and collected seashells in the late afternoon. And Steve had promised that as soon as it was dark, he would take Jonah for a walk down the beach with flashlights to watch the hundreds of spider crabs darting in and out of their sand burrows.

Jonah pulled out his chair and plopped down. He took a drink of milk, leaving a white mustache. "Do you think Ronnie's coming home soon?"

"I hope so."

Jonah wiped his lip with the back of his hand. "Sometimes she stays out pretty late."

"I know."

"Is the police officer going to bring her back home again?"

Steve glanced out the window; dusk was coming, and the water was turning opaque. He wondered where she was and what she was doing.

"No," he said. "Not tonight."

After their walk along the beach, Jonah took a shower before crawling into bed. Steve pulled up the covers and kissed him on the cheek.

"Thanks for the great day," Steve whispered.

"You're welcome."

"Good night, Jonah. I love you."

"Me, too, Dad."

Steve rose and started for the door.

"Hey, Dad?"

Steve turned. "Yes?"

"Did your dad ever take you out to look for spider crabs?"

"No," Steve said.

"Why not? That was awesome."

"He wasn't that kind of father."

"What kind was he?"

Steve considered the question. "He was complicated," he finally said.

At the piano, Steve recalled the afternoon six years earlier when he took his father's hand for the first time in his life. He had told his father that he knew he'd done the best he could in raising him, that he didn't blame his father for anything, and that most of all, he loved him.

His father turned toward him. His eyes were focused, and despite the high doses of morphine that he'd been taking, his mind was clear. He stared at Steve for a long time before pulling his hand away.

"You sound like a woman when you talk like that," he said.

They were in a semiprivate room on the fourth floor of the hospital. His father had been there for three days. IV tubes snaked out of his arms, and he hadn't eaten solid food in more than a month. His cheeks were sunken, and his skin was translucent. Up close, Steve thought his father's breath smelled of decay, another sign the cancer was announcing its victory.

Steve turned toward the window. Outside, he could see nothing but blue skies, a bright, unyielding bubble surrounding the room. No birds, no clouds, no visible trees. Behind him, he could hear the steady beep of the heart monitor. It sounded strong and steady, with regular rhythm, making it seem that his father would live another twenty years. But it wasn't his heart that was killing him.

"How is he?" Kim asked later that night when they were talking on the phone.

"Not good," he said. "I don't know how much longer he has, but . . ."

He trailed off. He could imagine Kim on the other end, standing near the stove, stirring pasta or dicing tomatoes, the phone cocked between her ear and shoulder. She'd never been able to sit still when talking on the phone.

"Did anyone else come by?"

"No," he answered. What he didn't tell her was that according to the nurses, no one else had visited at all.

"Were you able to talk to him?" she asked.

"Yes, but not for long. He was drifting in and out most of the day."

"Did you say what I told you to say?"

"Yes," he said.

"What did he say?" she asked. "Did he say he loved you, too?"

Steve knew the answer she wanted. He was standing in his father's home, inspecting the photos on the mantel: the family after Steve was baptized, a wedding photo of Kim and Steve, Ronnie and Jonah as toddlers. The frames were dusty, untouched in years. He knew that it had been his mother who put them there, and as he stared at them, he wondered what his father thought as he looked at them, or if he even saw them at all, or if he even realized they were there.

"Yes," he finally said. "He told me he loved me."

"I'm glad," she said. Her tone was relieved and satisfied, as though his answer had affirmed something to her about the world. "I know how important that was to you."

Steve grew up in a white ranch-style house, in a neighborhood of white ranch-style houses on the intracoastal side of the island. It was small, with two bedrooms, a single bathroom, and a separate garage that housed his father's tools and smelled permanently of sawdust. The backyard, shaded by a gnarled live oak that held its leaves year-round, didn't get enough sun, so his mother planted the vegetable garden in the front. She grew tomatoes and onions, turnips and beans, cabbage and corn, and in the summers, it was impossible to see the road that fronted the house from the living room. Sometimes Steve would overhear the neighbors grumbling in hushed voices, complaining about declining property values, but the garden was replanted every spring, and no one ever said a word directly to his father. They knew, as well as he did, that it wouldn't have done them any good. Besides, they liked his wife, and they all knew they would need his services one day.

His father was a trim carpenter by trade, but he had a gift for fixing anything. Over the years, Steve had seen him repair radios, televisions, auto and lawn mower engines, leaking pipes, dangling gutters, broken windows, and once, even the hydraulic presses of a small tool-manufacturing plant near the state line. He'd never attended high school, but he had an innate understanding of mechanics and building concepts. At night, when the phone rang, his father always answered, since it was usually for him. Most of the time, he said very little, listening as one emergency or another was described, and then Steve would watch him carefully jot the address on pieces of scratch paper torn from old newspapers. After hanging up, his father would venture to the garage, fill his toolbox, and head out, usually without mentioning where he was going or when he would be back home. In the morning, the check would be tucked neatly beneath the statue of Robert E. Lee that his father had carved from a piece of driftwood, and his mother would rub his back and promise to deposit it at the bank as his father ate his breakfast. It was the only regular affection he noticed between them. They didn't argue and avoided conflict as a rule. They seemed to enjoy each other's company when they were together, and once, he'd caught them holding hands while watching TV; but in the eighteen years Steve had lived at home, he never saw his parents kiss.

If his father had one passion in life, it was poker. On the nights the phone didn't ring, his father went to one of the lodges to play. He was a member of those lodges, not for the camaraderie, but for the games. There, he would sit at the table with other Freemasons or Elks or Shriners or veterans, playing Texas hold 'em for hours. The game transfixed him; he loved computing the probabilities of drawing an outside straight or deciding whether to bluff when all he held was a pair of sixes. When he talked about the game, he described it as a science, as if the luck of the draw had nothing to do with winning. "The secret is to know how to lie," he used to say, "and to know when someone's lying to you." His father, Steve eventually decided, must have known how to lie. In his fifties, with his hands nearly crippled from over thirty years of carpentry, his father stopped installing crown molding and door frames in the custom oceanfront homes that had begun to spring up on the island; he also began to leave the phone unanswered in the evenings. Somehow, he continued to pay his bills, and by the end of his life, he had more than enough in his accounts to pay for the medical care his insurance didn't cover.

He never played poker on Saturday or Sunday. Saturdays were reserved for chores around the house, and while the garden in the front yard may have bothered the neighbors, the interior was a showpiece. Over the years, his father added crown molding and wainscoting; he carved the fireplace corbels from two blocks of maple. He built the cabinets in the kitchen and installed wood floors that were as flat and sure as a billiard table. He remodeled the bathroom, then remodeled it again eight years later. Every Saturday evening, he put on a jacket and tie and took his wife to dinner. Sundays, he reserved for himself. After church, he would tinker in his workshop, while his wife baked pies or canned vegetables in the kitchen.

On Monday, the routine started all over again.

His father never taught him to play the game. Steve was smart enough to learn the basics on his own, and he liked to think he was keen enough to spot someone bluffing. He played a few times with fellow students in college and found out he was simply average, no better or worse than any of the others. After he graduated and moved to New York, he'd occasionally come down to visit his parents. The first time, he hadn't seen them in two years, and when he walked through the door, his mom hugged him fiercely and kissed him on the cheek. His father shook his hand and said, "Your mom's missed you." Apple pie and coffee were served, and after they finished eating, his dad stood, reaching for his jacket and car keys. It was a Tuesday; that meant he was going to the Elks lodge. The game ended at ten and he would be home fifteen minutes later.

"No . . . no go tonight," his mom urged, her European accent as heavy as ever. "Steve just got home."

He remembered thinking that it was the only time he'd ever heard his mom ask his father not to go to the lodge, but if he was surprised, his father didn't show it. He paused at the doorway, and when he turned around, his face was unreadable.

"Or take him with you," she urged.

He draped his jacket over his arm. "Do you want to go?"

"Sure." Steve drummed his fingers on the table. "Why not? That sounds like fun."

After a moment, his father's mouth twitched, exhibiting the tiniest and briefest of smiles. Had they been at the poker table, Steve doubted he would have shown even that much.

"You're lying," he said.

His mom passed away suddenly a few years after that encounter when an artery burst in her brain, and in the hospital, Steve was thinking of her sturdy kindness when his father woke with a low wheeze. He rolled his head and spotted Steve in the corner. At that angle, with shadows playing across the sharp angles of his face, he gave the impression of being a skeleton.

"You're still here."

Steve set aside the score and scooted the chair closer. "Yeah, I'm still here."

"Why?"

"What do you mean, why? Because you're in the hospital."

"I'm in the hospital because I'm dying. And I'd be dying whether you were here or not. You should go home. You have a wife and kids. There's nothing you can do for me here."

"I want to be here," Steve said. "You're my father. Why? Don't you want me here?"

"Maybe I don't want you to see me die."

"I'll leave if you want."

His father made a noise akin to a snort. "See, that's your problem. You want me to make the decision for you. That's always been your problem."

"Maybe I just want to spend time with you."

"You want to? Or did your wife want you to?"

"Does it matter?"

His dad tried to smile, but it came out like a grimace. "I don't know. Does it?"

From his spot at the piano, Steve heard an approaching car. The headlights flashed through the window and raced across the walls, and for an instant he thought that Ronnie might have gotten a ride home. But just as quickly the light shrank to nothing, and Ronnie still wasn't here.

It was after midnight. He wondered whether he should try to find her.

Some years ago, before Ronnie had stopped talking to him, he and Kim had gone to see a marriage counselor whose office was located near Gramercy Park, in a renovated building. Steve remembered sitting beside Kim on a couch and facing a thin, angular woman in her thirties who wore gray slacks and liked to press her fingertips together. When she did, Steve noticed she didn't wear a wedding band.

Steve was uncomfortable; the counseling had been Kim's idea, and she'd already gone alone. This was their first joint session, and by way of introduction, she told the counselor that Steve kept his feelings bottled up inside but that it wasn't his fault. Neither of his parents had been expressive people, she said. Nor had he grown up in a family that discussed their problems. He sought out music as an escape, she went on to say, and it was only through the piano that he learned to feel anything at all.

"Is that true?" the counselor asked.

"My parents were good people," he answered.

"That doesn't answer the question."

"I don't know what you want me to say."

The counselor sighed. "Okay, how about this? We all know what happened and why you're here. I think what Kim wants is for you to tell her how it made you feel."

Steve considered the question. He wanted to say that all this talk of feelings was irrelevant. That emotions come and go and can't be controlled, so there's no reason to worry about them. That in the end, people should be judged by their actions, since in the end, it was actions that defined everyone.

But he didn't say this. Instead, he threaded his fingers together. "You want to know how it made me feel."

"Yes. But don't tell me." She gestured to his wife. "Tell Kim."

He faced his wife, sensing her anticipation.

"I felt . . ."

He was in an office with his wife and a stranger, engaged in the type of conversation he could never have imagined growing up. It was a few minutes past ten o'clock in the morning, and he'd been back in New York for only a few days. His tour had taken him to twenty-some different cities, while Kim worked as a paralegal at a Wall Street law firm.

"I felt . . . ," he said again.

When the clock struck one a.m., Steve went outside to stand on the back porch. The blackness of the night had given way to the purple light of the moon, making it possible to see up and down the beach. He hadn't seen her in sixteen hours and was concerned, if not quite worried. He trusted she was smart and careful enough to take care of herself.

Okay, maybe he was a little worried.

And despite himself, he wondered if she was going to vanish tomorrow, the same way she had today. And whether it would be the same story day after day, all summer.

Spending time with Jonah had been like finding special treasure, and he wanted to spend time with her as well. He turned from the porch and went back inside.

As he took his seat at the piano, he felt it again, the same thing he'd told the marriage counselor as he'd sat on the couch.

He felt empty.

10

....♪....

Ronnie

For a while, a larger group had gathered at Bower's Point, but one by one, they'd taken off until only the five regulars remained. Some of the others had been okay, a couple were even kind of interesting, but then the liquor and beer started taking effect, and everyone but Ronnie thought they were a lot funnier than they really were. After a while, it got kind of boring and familiar.

She was standing alone at the water's edge. Behind her, near the bonfire, Teddy and Lance were smoking, drinking, and occasionally throwing fireballs at each other, Blaze was slurring her words and hanging all over Marcus. It was getting late, too. Not by New York standards—back home, she didn't show up at the clubs until midnight—but considering what time she'd gotten up, it had been a long day. She was tired.

Tomorrow, she was going to sleep in. When she got home, she was going to hang towels or a blanket over the curtain rod; hell, she'd nail them to the wall if she had to. She had no intention of spending the whole summer rising with the farmers, even if she was going to spend the day at the beach with Blaze. Blaze had surprised her with the suggestion, and it actually sounded kind of appealing. Besides, there wasn't much to do otherwise. Earlier, after they'd left the diner, they'd walked through most of the

nearby shops—including the music store, which was very cool—
and afterward, they'd gone to Blaze's house to watch *The Breakfast Club* while her mom was at work. Sure, it was an eighties
movie, but Ronnie still loved it and had seen it at least a dozen
times. Even though it was dated, it felt surprisingly real to her.
More real than what was going on here tonight—especially since
the more Blaze drank, the more she ignored Ronnie and clung
to Marcus.

Ronnie already neither liked nor trusted Marcus. She had
pretty good radar when it came to guys, and she sensed there was
something "off" about him. It was like there was something *missing* in Marcus's eyes when he talked to her. He said the right
things—no more crazy suggestions about heading to Florida, at
least, and by the way, how weird was that?—but the more time
she spent with him, the more he creeped her out. She didn't like
Teddy or Lance, either, but Marcus . . . she got the vibe that acting normal was simply a game he played so he could manipulate
people.

And Blaze . . .

It was strange being in her house earlier, because it seemed so
normal. It stood in a quiet cul-de-sac and had bright blue shutters
and an American flag that fluttered from the porch. Inside, the
walls were painted cheery colors, and a vase of fresh flowers stood
on the dining room table. The place was clean, but not neuroti-
cally so. In the kitchen, there was some money on the table, along
with a note addressed to Blaze. When Ronnie caught Blaze sliding a few bills into her pocket and reading the note, Blaze mentioned that her mom always left money for her. It was how she
knew Blaze was okay when she didn't come home.

Odd.

What she really wanted was to talk to Blaze about Marcus, but
she knew that wouldn't do any good. Lord knows she'd learned
that from Kayla—Kayla lived in denial—but even so, it didn't
make sense. Marcus was bad news, and Blaze was clearly better off

without him. She wondered why Blaze couldn't see that. Maybe tomorrow they'd talk about it at the beach.

"Are we boring you?"

Turning, she saw Marcus standing behind her. He was holding a fireball, letting it roll across the back of his hand.

"I just wanted to come down to the water."

"Do you want me to bring you a beer?"

By the way he asked, she could tell he already knew what she was going to say.

"I don't drink."

"Why?"

Because it makes people act stupid, she could have said. But she didn't. She knew that any explanation she offered would only prolong the conversation. "I just don't. That's all."

"Just say no?" he taunted.

"If you say so."

In the darkness, he wore the ghost of a smile, but his eyes remained shadowy pits. "Do you think you're better than us?"

"No."

"Then c'mon." He gestured to the bonfire. "Sit with us."

"I'm fine."

He glanced over his shoulder. Behind him, Ronnie could see Blaze digging through the cooler for another beer, which was the last thing she needed. She was already unsteady on her feet.

Without warning, he took a step toward her, reaching for her waist. He squeezed, pulling her closer to him. "Let's walk the beach."

"No," she hissed. "I'm not in the mood. And take your hand off me."

It stayed in place. She could tell Marcus was enjoying this. "You worried about what Blaze would think?"

"I just don't want to, okay?"

"Blaze won't care."

She took a step back, increasing the distance between them.

"I do," she said. "And I've got to go."

He continued to stare at her. "Yeah, you do that." Then, after a pause, he spoke up so the others could hear: "No, I'll just stay here. But thanks for asking."

She was too shocked to say anything in response. Instead, she started down the beach, knowing that Blaze was watching, and suddenly thinking she couldn't get away fast enough.

At home, her father was playing the piano, and as soon as she walked in, he peeked at the clock. After what just happened, she wasn't in the mood to deal with him, so she started for the hallway without a word. He must have seen something in her face, however, because he called out to her.

"Are you okay?"

She hesitated. "Yeah, I'm fine," she said.

"You sure?"

"I don't want to talk about it."

He studied her before answering. "Okay."

"Is there anything else?"

"It's almost two a.m.," he pointed out.

"And?"

He bent over the keyboard. "There's some pasta in the fridge if you're hungry."

She had to admit he'd surprised her with that one. No lecture, no orders, no laying down the law. Pretty much the opposite of how Mom would have handled it. She shook her head and walked to the bedroom, wondering if anyone or anything was normal down here.

She forgot to hang blankets over the windows, and the sun lasered into the room, waking her after she'd slept for less than six hours.

Groaning, she rolled over and pulled the pillow on top of her head when she remembered what had happened at the beach the night before. Then she sat up, knowing sleep was out of the question.

Marcus definitely creeped her out.

Her first thought was that she should have said something last night, when he had called out. Something like *What the hell are you talking about?* or *If you think I'd go anywhere alone with you, you're out of your mind!* But she hadn't, and she suspected that simply walking away was the worst thing she could have done.

She really, *really* had to talk to Blaze.

With a sigh, she swung herself out of bed and padded to the bathroom. Quickly, she showered and threw on a bathing suit beneath her clothes, and then filled a tote bag with towels and lotion. By the time she was ready, she could hear her father playing the piano. Again. Even back in the apartment he'd never played this much. Focusing on the music, she realized he was playing one of the pieces she'd performed at Carnegie Hall, the same one on the CD that her mom had been playing in the car.

As if she didn't have enough to deal with right now.

She needed to find Blaze so she could explain what happened. Of course, how to do that without making Marcus out to be a liar might be a problem. Blaze would want to believe Marcus, and who knew what the guy had said after she left. But she'd cross that bridge when she came to it; hopefully, lying in the sun would keep things mellow and she could bring it up naturally.

Ronnie left her bedroom and walked down the hall just as the music from the living room ended, only to be followed by the second piece she'd played at Carnegie Hall.

She paused, adjusting the tote bag on her shoulder. Of course he'd do that. No doubt because he'd heard the shower and knew she was awake. No doubt because he wanted them to find common ground.

Well, not today, Dad. Sorry, but she had things to do. She really wasn't in the mood for this.

She was about to make a dash to the front door when Jonah emerged from the kitchen.

"Didn't I say you were supposed to get something good for you?" she heard her dad ask.

"I did. It's a Pop-Tart."

"I was thinking more along the lines of cereal."

"This has sugar." Jonah wore an earnest expression. "I need my energy, Dad."

She started to walk quickly through the living room, hoping to make it to the door before he tried to talk to her.

Jonah smiled. "Oh, hey, Ronnie!" he said.

"Hi, Jonah. Bye, Jonah." She reached for the door handle.

"Sweetheart?" she heard her dad say. He stopped playing. "Can we talk about last night?"

"I really don't have time to talk right now," she said, adjusting her tote bag.

"I just want to know where you were all day."

"Nowhere. It's not important."

"It is important."

"No, Dad," she said, her voice firm. "It isn't. And I've got things to do, okay?"

Jonah motioned to the door with his Pop-Tart. "What things? Where are you going now?"

This was exactly the conversation she'd hoped to avoid. "It's none of your business."

"How long are you going to be gone?"

"I don't know."

"Will you be back for lunch or dinner?"

"I don't know," she huffed. "I'm leaving."

Her dad started to play the piano again. Her *third* piece from Carnegie Hall. He might as well have been playing Mom's CD.

"We're going to fly kites later. Me and Dad, I mean."

She didn't seem to hear him. Instead, she swiveled toward her dad. "Would you just stop with that?" she snapped.

He stopped playing abruptly. "What?"

"The music you're playing! You don't think I recognize those pieces? I know what you're doing, and I already told you I'm not going to play."

"I believe you," he said.

"Then why do you keep trying to get me to change my mind? Why is it that every time I see you, you're sitting there pounding away?"

He seemed genuinely confused. "It has nothing to do with you," he offered. "It just . . . makes me feel better."

"Well, it makes me feel sick. Don't you get that? I hate the piano. I hate that I had to play every single day! And I hate that I even have to see the damn thing anymore!"

Before her dad could say another word, she turned, snatched Jonah's Pop-Tart out of his hand, and stormed out the door.

It took a couple of hours before she found Blaze in the same music store they'd visited yesterday, a couple of blocks from the pier. Ronnie hadn't known what to expect when they'd first visited the store—it seemed kind of antiquated these days in the age of iPods and downloads—but Blaze had assured her it would be worth it, and it had been.

In addition to CDs, there were actual vinyl record albums— thousands of them, some of them most likely collector's items, including an unopened copy of *Abbey Road* and a slew of old 45s simply hanging on the wall with signatures of people like Elvis Presley, Bob Marley, and Ritchie Valens. Ronnie was amazed that they weren't under lock and key. They had to be valuable, but the guy who managed the place looked like a throwback to the sixties and seemed to know everyone. He had long gray hair pulled back into a ponytail that reached his waist, and his glasses were the same kind John Lennon had favored. He wore sandals and a Hawaiian shirt, and though he was old enough to be Ronnie's grandfather, he knew more about music than anyone she'd ever met, including a lot of recent underground stuff she'd never even heard in New York. Along the back wall were headphones where customers could either listen to albums and CDs or download music onto their iPods. Peeking through the window this morning, she saw Blaze standing with one hand cupping a headphone to an ear, the other tapping the table in rhythm to whatever she was listening to.

In no way was she prepared for a day at the beach.

Ronnie took a deep breath and headed inside. As bad as it sounded—she didn't think Blaze should be getting drunk in the first place—she kind of hoped that Blaze had been so out of it that she'd forgotten what happened. Or even better, that she had been sober enough to know that Ronnie had no interest in Marcus.

As soon as she started down the aisle full of CDs, Ronnie sensed that Blaze had been expecting her. She turned down the volume on the headphones, though she didn't remove them from her ears, and turned around. Ronnie could still hear the music, something loud and angry she didn't recognize. Blaze gathered up the CDs.

"I thought we were friends," she started.

"We are," Ronnie insisted. "And I've been looking all over for you because I didn't want you to have the wrong idea about what went on last night."

Blaze's expression was icy. "You mean about asking Marcus to go for a walk with you?"

"It wasn't like that," Ronnie pleaded. "I didn't ask him. I don't know what his game was . . ."

"His game? *His* game?" Blaze threw down the headphones. "I saw the way you were staring at him! I heard what you said!"

"But I didn't say it! I didn't ask him to walk anywhere—"

"You tried to kiss him!"

"What are you talking about? I didn't try to kiss him . . ."

Blaze took a step forward. "He told me!"

"Then he's lying!" Ronnie snapped, holding her ground. "There's something seriously wrong with that guy."

"No . . . no . . . don't even go there . . ."

"He lied to you. I wouldn't kiss him. I don't even like him. The only reason I was there was because you insisted that we go."

For a long moment, Blaze didn't say anything. Ronnie wondered if she was finally getting through to her.

"Whatever," Blaze said, her tone making her meaning perfectly clear.

She pushed past Ronnie, jostling her as she headed toward the door. Ronnie watched her go, unsure whether she was hurt or angry at the way Blaze had just acted before deciding it was a bit of both. Through the window, she saw Blaze storm off.

So much for trying to make things better.

Ronnie wasn't sure what to do next: She didn't want to go to the beach, but she didn't want to go home, either. She didn't have access to a car, and she knew absolutely no one. Which meant . . . what? Maybe she'd end up spending the summer on some bench where she'd feed the pigeons like some of the weirder denizens of Central Park. Maybe she'd end up naming them . . .

At the exit, her thoughts were brought to a halt by the sudden blaring of an alarm, and she glanced over her shoulder, first in curiosity and then in confusion as she realized what was happening. There was only one way in and out of the store.

The next thing she knew, the ponytailed man was rushing toward her.

She didn't try to run because she knew she'd done nothing wrong; when the ponytailed man asked for her bag, she saw no reason not to give it to him. Obviously, a mistake had been made, and it wasn't until the man removed two CDs and half a dozen of the signed 45s from her tote bag that she realized she'd been right about Blaze expecting Ronnie to find her. The CDs were the ones that Blaze had been holding, and Blaze had taken down the 45s from the wall. In shock, she began to understand that Blaze had planned it all along.

Suddenly dizzy, she barely heard the manager tell her that the police were already on their way.

11

·····♪·····

Steve

After buying the materials he needed, primarily two-by-fours and sheets of plywood, Steve and Jonah spent the morning closing off the alcove. It wasn't pretty—his father would have been mortified—but Steve thought it would do. He knew the cottage would eventually be demolished; if anything, the land was worth more without it. The bungalow was flanked by three-story mini-mansions, and Steve was certain those neighbors considered the place an eyesore that depressed their own property values.

Steve hammered in a nail, hung the photograph of Ronnie and Jonah he'd removed from the alcove, and took a step back to examine his handiwork.

"What do you think?" he asked Jonah.

Jonah wrinkled his nose. "It looks like we built an ugly plywood wall and hung a picture on it. And you can't play the piano anymore, either."

"I know."

Jonah tilted his head from side to side. "I think it's crooked, too. It kind of bends in and out."

"I don't see anything."

"You need glasses, Dad. And I still don't see why you wanted to put it up in the first place."

"Ronnie said she didn't want to see the piano."

"So?"

"There's no place to hide the piano, so I put a wall up instead. Now she doesn't have to see it."

"Oh," Jonah said, thinking. "You know, I really don't like having to do homework. In fact, I don't even like to see it piled on my desk."

"It's summer. You don't have any homework."

"I'm just saying that maybe I should build a wall around the desk in my room."

Steve suppressed a laugh. "You might have to talk to your mom about that."

"Or you could."

Steve gave in to a chuckle. "You hungry yet?"

"You said we were going to go kite flying."

"We will. I just want to know if you want lunch."

"I think I'd rather have some ice cream."

"I don't think so."

"A cookie?" Jonah sounded hopeful.

"How about a peanut butter and jelly sandwich?"

"Okay. But then we're going to fly the kite, right?"

"Yes."

"All afternoon?"

"As long as you want."

"Okay. I'll have a sandwich. But you have to have one, too."

Steve smiled, putting his arm on Jonah's shoulder. "Deal." They headed toward the kitchen.

"You know, the living room is a whole lot smaller now," Jonah observed.

"I know."

"And the wall *is* crooked."

"I know."

"And it doesn't match the other walls."

"What's your point?"

Jonah's face was serious. "I just want to make sure you're not going crazy."

It was perfect kite-flying weather. Steve sat on a dune two houses down from his own, watching the kite zigzag across the sky. Jonah, full of energy as usual, ran up and down the beach. Steve watched him with pride, amazed to recall that when he'd done the same thing as a child, neither of his parents had ever joined him.

They weren't bad people. He knew that. They never abused him, he never went hungry, they never argued in his presence. He visited the dentist and doctor once or twice a year, there was always plenty to eat, and he always had a jacket on cold winter mornings and a nickel in his pocket so he could buy milk at school. But if his father was stoic, his mother wasn't all that different, and he supposed that was the reason they'd stayed married as long as they had. She was originally from Romania; his father had met her while stationed in Germany. She spoke little English when they were married and never questioned the culture in which she'd been raised. She cooked and cleaned and washed the clothes; in the afternoons, she worked part-time as a seamstress. By the end of her life, she'd learned passable English, enough to navigate the bank and grocery store, but even then her accent was heavy enough that it was sometimes difficult for others to understand her.

She was also a devout Catholic, something of an oddity in Wilmington at the time. She went to services every day and prayed the rosary in the evenings, and though Steve appreciated the tradition and ceremony of mass on Sundays, the priest always struck him as a man who was both cold and arrogant, more interested in church rules than what might be best for his flock. Sometimes— many times, actually—Steve wondered how his life would have turned out had he not heard the music coming from the First Baptist Church when he was eight years old.

Forty years later, the details were fuzzy. He vaguely remembered walking in one afternoon and hearing Pastor Harris at the piano. He knew the pastor must have made him feel welcome, since he obviously went back again, and Pastor Harris eventually became his first piano teacher. In time, he began to attend—and then later ditch—the Bible study the church offered. In many ways, the Baptist church became his second home and Pastor Harris became his second father.

He remembered his mother wasn't happy about it. When upset, she would mutter in Romanian, and for years, whenever he left for the church, he would hear unintelligible words and phrases while she made the sign of the cross and forced him to wear a scapular. In her mind, having a Baptist pastor teach him the piano was akin to playing hopscotch with the devil.

But she didn't stop him, and that was enough. It didn't matter to him that she didn't attend meetings with his teachers, or that she never read to him, or that no one ever invited his family to neighborhood barbecues or parties. What mattered was that she allowed him not only to find his passion, but to pursue it, even if she distrusted the reason. And that somehow she kept his father, who ridiculed the idea of earning a living through music, from stopping it as well. And for this, he would always love her.

Jonah continued to jog back and forth, though the kite didn't require it. Steve knew the breeze was strong enough to hold it aloft unaided. He could see the outline of a Batman symbol silhouetted between two dark cumulous clouds, the kind that suggested rain was coming. Although the summer storm wouldn't last long— maybe an hour before the sky cleared again—Steve rose to tell Jonah that it might be a good time to call it a day. He took only a few steps before he noticed a series of faint lines in the sand that led to the dune behind his house, tracks he'd seen more than a dozen times when he was growing up. He smiled.

"Hey, Jonah!" he called out, following the tracks. "Come here! There's something I think you should see!"

Jonah jogged toward him, the kite tugging at his arm. "What is it?"

Steve made his way down the dune to a spot where it merged with the beach itself. Only a few eggs were visible a couple of inches below the surface when Jonah reached his side.

"Whatcha got?" Jonah asked.

"It's a loggerhead nest," Steve answered. "But don't get too close. And don't touch. You don't want to disturb it."

Jonah leaned closer, still holding the kite.

"What's a loggerhead?" he panted, struggling to control the kite.

Steve reached for a piece of driftwood and began etching a large circle around the nest. "It's a sea turtle. An endangered one. They come ashore at night to lay their eggs."

"Behind our house?"

"This is one of the places sea turtles lay their eggs. But the main thing you should know is that they're endangered. Do you know what that means?"

"It means they're dying," Jonah answered. "I watch Animal Planet, you know."

Steve completed the circle and tossed aside the piece of driftwood. As he stood, he felt a flash of pain but ignored it. "Not exactly. It means that if we don't try to help them and we're not careful, the species might become extinct."

"Like the dinosaurs?"

Steve was about to answer when he heard the phone in the kitchen begin to ring. He'd left the back door open to catch any stray breezes, and he alternately walked and jogged through the sand until he'd reached the back porch. He was breathing hard when he answered the phone.

"Dad?" he heard on the other end.

"Ronnie?"

"I need you to pick me up. I'm at the police station."

Steve reached up to rub the bridge of his nose. "Okay," he said. "I'll be right down."

Pete Johnson, the officer, told him what had happened, but he knew Ronnie wasn't ready to talk about it yet. Jonah, however, didn't seem to care.

"Mom is going to be mad," Jonah remarked.

Steve saw Ronnie's jaw clench.

"I didn't do it," she started.

"Then who did?"

"I don't want to talk about it," she said. She crossed her arms and leaned against the car door.

"Mom's not going to like it."

"I didn't do it!" Ronnie repeated, swiveling toward Jonah. "And I don't want you to tell her that I did." She made sure he understood she was serious before turning to face her father.

"I didn't do it, Dad," she repeated. "I swear to God I didn't. You have to believe me."

He heard the desperation in her tone but couldn't help remembering Kim's despair when they'd talked about Ronnie's history. He thought about the way she'd acted since she'd been here and considered the kinds of people she'd chosen to befriend.

Sighing, he felt what little energy he had left dissipate. Ahead, the sun was a hot and furious orange ball, and more than anything, he knew his daughter needed the truth.

"I believe you," he said.

By the time they got home, dusk was setting in. Steve went outside to check on the turtle nest. It was one of those gorgeous evenings typical of the Carolinas—a soft breeze, the sky a quilt of a thousand different colors— and just offshore, a pod of dolphins played beyond the break point. They passed by the house twice a day, and he reminded himself to tell Jonah to watch for them. No doubt he'd want to swim out to see if he could get close enough to touch them; Steve used to try the same thing when he was young, but never once had he been successful.

He dreaded having to call Kim and tell her what happened. Putting it off, he took a seat on the dune beside the nest, staring at what was left of the turtle tracks. Between the wind and the crowds, most of them had been erased entirely. Aside from a small indentation at the spot where the dune met the beach, the nest was practically invisible, and the couple of eggs he could see re-sembled pale, smooth rocks.

A piece of Styrofoam had blown onto the sand, and as he leaned over to pick it up, he noticed Ronnie approaching. She was walking slowly, her arms crossed, head bowed so that her hair hid most of her face. She stopped a few feet away.

"Are you mad at me?" she asked.

It was the first time since she'd been here that she'd spoken to him without a hint of anger or frustration.

"No," he said. "Not at all."

"Then what are you doing out here?"

He pointed toward the nest. "A loggerhead turtle laid her eggs last night. Have you ever seen one?"

Ronnie shook her head, and Steve went on. "They're beautiful creatures. They've got this reddish-brown shell, and they can weigh up to eight hundred pounds. North Carolina is one of the few places they nest. But anyway, they're endangered. I think only one out of a thousand live to maturity, and I don't want the raccoons to get the nest before they hatch."

"How would the raccoons even know that a nest is here?"

"When a female loggerhead lays her eggs, she urinates. The raccoons can smell it, and they'll eat every single one of the eggs. When I was young, I found a nest on the other side of the pier. One day everything was fine, and the next day all the shells had been broken open. It was sad."

"I saw a raccoon on our porch the other day."

"I know. It's been getting into the garbage. And as soon as I go in, I'm going to leave a message with the aquarium. Hopefully, they'll send someone by tomorrow with a special cage that'll keep the critters out."

"What about tonight?"

"I guess we're going to have to have faith."

Ronnie tucked a strand of hair behind her ear. "Dad? Can I ask you something?"

"Anything."

"Why did you say you believed me?"

In profile, he could see both the young woman she was becoming and the little girl he remembered.

"Because I trust you."

"Is that why you built the wall to hide the piano?" She looked at him only indirectly. "When I went inside, it wasn't that hard to miss."

Steve shook his head. "No. I did that because I love you."

Ronnie flashed a brief smile, hesitating before taking a seat beside him. They watched the waves rolling steadily up the shore. High tide would be here soon, and the beach was half-gone.

"What's going to happen to me?" she asked.

"Pete is going to talk to the owner, but I don't know. A couple of those records were real collector's items. They're pretty valuable."

Ronnie felt sick to her stomach. "Have you told Mom yet?"

"No."

"Are you going to?"

"Probably."

Neither of them said anything for a moment. At the water's edge, a group of surfers walked past, holding their boards. In the distance, the swells were slowly rising, forming waves that seemed to collide before immediately re-forming.

"When are you going to call the aquarium?"

"When I head back inside. I'm sure Jonah's getting hungry anyway. I should probably start dinner."

Ronnie stared at the nest. With her stomach in knots, she couldn't imagine eating. "I don't want anything to happen to the turtle eggs tonight."

Steve turned toward her. "So what do you want to do?"

Hours later, after tucking Jonah into bed, Steve stepped out onto the back porch to check on Ronnie. Earlier, after he'd left a message at the aquarium, he'd gone to the store to buy what he thought she needed: a light sleeping bag, a camping lantern, a cheap pillow, and some bug spray.

He wasn't comfortable with the idea of Ronnie sleeping outside, but she was clearly determined and he admired her impulse to protect the nest. She'd been insistent that she would be fine, and to some extent, he trusted she was right. Like most people who grew up in Manhattan, she'd learned to be careful and had seen and experienced enough of the world to know it was sometimes a dangerous place. Moreover, the nest was less than fifty feet from his bedroom window—which he intended to keep open—so he was confident he'd hear something if Ronnie ran into trouble. Because of the shape of the windblown dune and the location of the nest, it wasn't likely that anyone walking on the beach would even know she was there.

Still, she was only seventeen, and he was her father, all of which meant he'd probably end up checking on her every few hours. There wasn't a chance he'd be able to sleep through the night.

The moon was only a sliver, but the sky was clear, and as he moved through the shadows, he thought back on their conversation. He wondered how she felt about the fact that he'd hidden the piano. Would she wake up tomorrow with the same attitude she'd had when she'd first arrived? He didn't know. As he drew near enough to make out Ronnie's sleeping form, the play of starlight and shadow made her appear both younger and older than she really was. He thought again about the years he'd lost and would never get back.

He stayed long enough to gaze up and down the beach. As far as he could tell, no one was out, so he turned and headed back inside. He sat on the couch and turned on the television, flipping through the channels before turning it off. Finally, he went to his room and crawled into bed.

He fell asleep almost immediately but woke an hour later. Tiptoeing outside again, he went to check on the daughter he loved more than life itself.

12

· · · · ♪ · · · ·

Ronnie

Her first thought upon waking was that everything hurt. Her back was stiff, her neck ached, and when she got the courage to sit up, a stabbing pain coursed through her shoulder.

She couldn't imagine anyone ever choosing to sleep outdoors. When she was growing up, some of her friends had extolled the joys of camping, but she'd thought they were deranged. Sleeping on the ground *hurt*.

And so, of course, did the blinding sun. Judging by fact that she'd been waking up with the farmers since she'd arrived, she figured today was no different. It probably wasn't even seven yet. The sun was hanging low over the ocean, and a few people were walking their dogs or jogging near the water's edge. No doubt they'd slept in beds. She couldn't imagine walking, let alone exercising. Right now it was hard enough to breathe without passing out.

Steeling herself, she slowly got to her feet before remembering why she'd been out here in the first place. She checked the nest, noting with relief that it was undisturbed, and ever so slowly, the aches and pains began to subside. She wondered idly how Blaze could tolerate sleeping on the beach, and then all of a sudden she remembered what Blaze had done to her.

Arrested for shoplifting. Serious shoplifting. *Felony* shoplifting.

She closed her eyes, reliving it all: the way the store manager had glared at her until the officer had arrived, Officer Pete's disappointment on the drive to the station, the awful phone call she'd had to make to her dad. She'd felt like throwing up on the car ride home.

If there was one bright spot in all that had happened, it was that her dad hadn't blown a gasket. And even more incredible, he'd said he believed her to be innocent Then again, he hadn't spoken to Mom yet. As soon as that happened, all bets were off. No doubt Mom would scream and shout until Dad gave in, and he'd end up grounding her because he'd promised Mom that he would. After the *Incident*, her mom had grounded her for a month, and this was way, way bigger than just an incident.

She felt sick again. She couldn't imagine having to spend an entire month in her room, a room she had to share, no less, in a place she didn't want to be. She wondered if things could get any worse. As she stretched her arms above her head, she yelped at a stabbing pain in her shoulder. She lowered them slowly, wincing.

She spent the next couple of minutes dragging her things to the back porch. Even though the nest was behind her house, she didn't want the neighbors to guess that she'd slept outside. Based on the grandeur of their houses, she pegged them as the kind of people who wanted everything picture perfect when they stood on their back decks drinking coffee in the mornings. The knowledge that someone had been sleeping beside their house probably didn't fit with their image of perfection, and the last thing she wanted was to have the police to show up again. With her luck, she'd probably get arrested for vagrancy. Felony vagrancy.

It took two trips to get everything—she didn't have the energy to carry it all at once—and then she realized she'd left behind her copy of *Anna Karenina*. She'd intended to read it last night, but she'd been too tired and had set it under a piece of driftwood so the mist wouldn't ruin it. When she went back to get it, she spotted someone wearing a beige jumpsuit advertising Blakelee Brakes, carrying a roll of yellow tape and a bunch of sticks. He seemed to be walking up the beach toward the house.

By the time she'd retrieved her book, the man was closer and hunting around the dune. She started toward him, wondering what he was doing, and then he turned in her direction. When their eyes met, it was one of the few times in her life that she actually felt tongue-tied.

She recognized him immediately, despite the uniform. She flashed on the way he'd looked without a shirt, tan and fit, his brown hair wet with sweat, the macramé bracelet on his wrist. He was the guy at the volleyball court who'd crashed into her, the guy whose friend almost got into a fight with Marcus.

Coming to a halt in front of her, he didn't seem to know what to say, either. Instead, he just stared at her. Although she knew it was crazy, she had the impression that he was somehow pleased to run into her again. She could see it in his dawning recognition, in the way he began to smile at her, none of which made any sense.

"Hey, it's you," he said. "Good morning."

She wasn't sure what to think, other than to question the friendly tone.

"What are you doing here?" she asked.

"I got a call from the aquarium. Someone called last night to report a loggerhead nest, and they asked me to come here to check it out."

"You work for the aquarium?"

He shook his head. "I just volunteer there. I work at my dad's brake shop. You wouldn't happen to have seen a turtle nest around here, would you?"

She felt herself relax a little. "It's over there," she said, pointing.

"Hey, that's great." He smiled. "I was hoping it was near a house."

"Why?"

"Because of storms. If the waves wash over the nest, the eggs won't make it."

"But they're sea turtles."

He raised his hands. "I know. It doesn't make sense to me, either, but that's the way nature works. Last year, we lost a couple of nests when a tropical storm came through. It was really sad. They're endangered, you know. Only one out of a thousand live to maturity."

"Yeah, I know."

"You do?" He sounded impressed.

"My dad told me."

"Oh," he said. He motioned down the beach with a friendly wave. "I take it you live around here?"

"Why do you want to know?"

"Just making conversation," he answered easily. "My name's Will, by the way."

"Hi, Will."

He paused. "Interesting."

"What?"

"Usually when someone introduces himself, the other person does the same."

"I'm not most people." Ronnie crossed her arms, careful to keep her distance.

"I already figured that out." He flashed a quick smile. "I'm sorry about running into you at the volleyball game."

"You already apologized, remember?"

"I know. But you seemed kind of mad."

"My soda went down my shirt."

"That's too bad. But you should really try to pay more attention to what's going on."

"Excuse me?"

"It's a fast-moving game."

She put her hands on her hips. "Are you trying to say it was my fault?"

"Just trying to make sure it doesn't happen again. Like I said, I felt bad about what happened."

With his answer, she got the feeling that he was trying to flirt with her, but she didn't know why. It didn't make sense—she knew she wasn't his type, and frankly, he wasn't her type, either. But at this early hour, she wasn't in the mood to try to figure it out. Instead, she motioned to the items he was holding, thinking it was probably better to get back to the subject at hand. "How is that tape supposed to keep the raccoons away?"

"It doesn't. I'm just here to mark the nest. I run the tape around the dowels so the guys who do put up the cage know where to find the nest."

"When are they going to put it up?"

"I don't know." He shrugged. "Maybe in a couple of days."

She thought about the agony she'd experienced upon waking, and she began to shake her head. "No, I don't think so. You call them and tell them that they have to do something to protect the nest *today*. Tell them I saw a raccoon last night hovering around the nest."

"Did you?"

"Just tell them, okay?"

"As soon as I'm finished, I'll make sure to call. I promise."

She squinted up at him, thinking that was *too* easy, but before she could dwell on it further, her dad stepped onto the back porch.

"Good morning, sweetheart," he called out. "I've got breakfast going if you're hungry."

Will looked from Ronnie to her dad and back again. "You live here?"

Instead of answering, she took a step backward. "Just make sure you tell the people at the aquarium, okay?"

She started back toward the house and had stepped onto the porch when she heard Will call out.

"Hey!"

She turned.

"You didn't tell me your name."

"No," she answered. "I don't suppose I did."

As she headed for the door, she knew she shouldn't look back, but she couldn't help stealing a quick peek over her shoulder.

When he raised an eyebrow, she kicked herself mentally, glad that she hadn't told him her name.

In the kitchen, her dad was standing over a frying pan at the stove, stirring with a spatula. On the counter beside him lay a packet of tortillas, and Ronnie had to admit that whatever he was making smelled terrific. Then again, she hadn't eaten since yesterday afternoon.

"Hey there," he said over his shoulder. "Who was that you were talking to?"

"Just some guy from the aquarium. He's here to mark the nest. What are you making?"

"A vegetarian breakfast burrito."

"You're kidding."

"It has rice, beans, and tofu. It all goes in the tortilla. I hope that's okay. I found the recipe online, so I can't vouch for how it tastes."

"I'm sure it's fine," she said. She crossed her arms, thinking she might as well get this over with. "Have you talked to Mom yet?"

He shook his head. "No, not yet. I did talk to Pete this morning, though. He said he still hadn't been able to talk to the owner yet. She's out of town."

"She?"

"It seems the man who works there is the owner's nephew. But Pete said he knows the owner pretty well."

"Oh," she said, wondering if that would make any difference.

Her dad tapped the spatula on the pan. "Anyway, I just figured that it might be a good idea if I held off calling your mom until I have all the details. I'd hate to have to worry her unnecessarily."

"You mean you might not have to tell her?"

"Unless you want me to."

"No, that's okay," she said quickly. "You're right. It's probably better if we wait."

"Okay," he agreed. After one last stir, he turned off the burner. "I think this is just about ready. Are you hungry?"

"Starved," she confessed.

As she approached, he took down a plate from the cupboard and added a tortilla, then scooped some of the mixings onto it. He offered it to her. "Is that enough?"

"Plenty," she said.

"Do you want coffee? I've got a pot going." He reached for a coffee cup and handed it to her. "Jonah mentioned that sometimes you go to Starbucks, so that's what I bought. It might not be as good as what they make in their stores, but it's the best I can do."

She took the cup, staring at him. "Why are you being so nice to me?"

"Why shouldn't I be?"

Because I haven't been very nice to you, she could have said. But she didn't. "Thanks," she mumbled instead, thinking the whole thing felt like some weird *Twilight Zone* episode, where her dad had somehow completely forgotten the last three years.

She poured herself some coffee and took a seat at the table. Steve joined her a moment later with his own plate and began to roll his burrito.

"How was it last night? Did you sleep okay?"

"Yeah, when I slept. Waking up wasn't so easy."

"I realized too late that I probably should have picked up an air mattress."

"It's okay. But after breakfast, I think I'm going to lie down for a while. I'm still kind of tired. It's been a long couple of days."

"Maybe you shouldn't have coffee."

"It won't matter. Believe me, I'll be out."

Behind them, Jonah walked into the kitchen wearing Transformers pajamas, his hair poking out all over. Ronnie couldn't help smiling.

"Good morning, Jonah," she said.

"Are the turtles okay?"

"They're fine," she said.

"Good job," he said. He scratched his back as he walked to the stove. "What's for breakfast?"

"Breakfast burritos," her dad answered.

Warily, Jonah studied the mixings in the pan, then the items on the counter. "Don't tell me you went over to the dark side, Dad!"

Steve tried to stifle his smile. "It's good."

"It's tofu! It's disgusting!"

Ronnie laughed as she pushed back from the table. "How about I get you a Pop-Tart instead?"

He seemed to be trying to decide if this was some kind of trick question. "With chocolate milk?"

Ronnie glanced at her dad.

"There's plenty in the fridge," he said.

She poured him a glass and set it on the table. Jonah didn't move. "Okay, what's going on?"

"What do you mean?"

"This isn't normal," he said. "Someone should be mad. Someone's always mad in the mornings."

"Are you talking about me?" Ronnie asked. She put two Pop-Tarts in the toaster. "I'm *always* cheerful."

"Yeah, right," he said. He squinted at her. "Are you sure the turtles are okay? 'Cause the two of you are acting like they died."

"They're fine. I promise," Ronnie assured him.

"I'm going to check."

"Go ahead."

He studied her. "After breakfast," he added.

Steve smiled and glanced over at her. "So what's on your agenda today?" he asked. "After your nap?"

Jonah reached for his milk. "You never take naps."

"I do when I'm tired."

"No," he said, shaking his head. "This isn't right." He put the milk back down. "Something weird is going on and I'm not leaving here until I find out what it is."

After she'd finished eating—and once Jonah had been placated—Ronnie retired to her room. Steve followed with some towels that he draped over the curtain rod, not that Ronnie needed them. She fell asleep almost immediately and woke up sweating in mid-afternoon. After a long, cool shower, she stopped by the workshop to tell her dad and Jonah what she was going to do. Still no mention of punishment from her dad.

It was possible, of course, that he'd ground her later, after he talked to the officer or her mom. Or maybe he'd been telling the truth—maybe he'd believed her when she'd said she was innocent.

Wouldn't that be something?

Either way, she had to talk to Blaze, and she spent the next couple of hours searching for her. She checked Blaze's mom's house and the diner, and though she didn't go inside, she peeked through the windows of the music shop, heart thumping, making sure the manager had his back turned. Blaze wasn't there, either.

Standing on the pier, she scanned up and down the beach, without luck. It was possible, of course, that Blaze had gone to Bower's Point; it was a favorite hangout of Marcus's gang. But she didn't want to go there alone. The last thing she wanted was to see him, let alone try to talk some sense into Blaze while he was around.

She was just about ready to give up and go home when she spotted Blaze emerging from between the dunes a little ways down the beach. She raced back to the steps, making sure not to lose sight of her, then hurried down to the beach. If Blaze noticed that Ronnie was walking toward her, she gave no sign of caring. Instead, as Ronnie got close she took a seat on the dune and stared out over the water.

"You have to tell the police what you did," Ronnie said without preamble.

"I didn't do anything. And you're the one who got caught."

Ronnie felt like shaking her. "You put those forty-fives and CDs in my bag!"

"No, I didn't."

"The CDs were the ones you were listening to!"

"And the last time I saw them, they were still by the headphones." Blaze refused to face her.

Ronnie felt the blood beginning to rush to her cheeks. "This is serious, Blaze. This is my life. I can get convicted of a felony! And I told you what happened before!"

"Oh, well."

Ronnie pressed her lips together to keep from exploding. "Why are you doing this to me?"

Blaze got up from her spot, brushing the sand from her jeans. "I'm not doing anything to you," she said. Her voice was cold and flat. "And that's exactly what I told the police this morning."

In disbelief, Ronnie watched Blaze walk off, acting almost as though she actually believed it.

Ronnie walked back to the pier.

She didn't want to return home, knowing that as soon as her dad talked to Officer Pete, he'd learn what Blaze had said. Yeah, maybe he'd still be cool about the whole thing—but what if he didn't believe her?

And why was Blaze doing this? Because of Marcus? Either Marcus talked her into it because he was mad about the way Ronnie had rejected him the other night, or Blaze believed that Ronnie was trying to steal her boyfriend. Right now, she was leaning toward the latter, but in the end, it didn't really matter. Whatever her motivation, Blaze was lying and more than willing to ruin Ronnie's life.

She hadn't eaten since breakfast, but with her stomach in knots, she wasn't hungry. Instead, she sat on the pier until the sun went down, watching the water turn from blue to gray and then finally charcoal. She wasn't alone: Along the pier, people were fishing, though as far as she could tell, nothing much seemed to be biting. An hour ago, a young couple had shown up with sandwiches and a kite. She noticed the tender way they stared at each other. She figured they were in college—they were only a couple of years older than her—but there was an easy affection between them that she had yet to experience in any of her own relationships. Yeah, she'd had boyfriends, but she'd never been in love, and sometimes she doubted whether she ever would be. After her parents divorced, she'd been kind of cynical about the whole thing, as had most of her friends. Most of their parents were divorced as well, so maybe that had something to do with it.

When the last rays of the sun were fading from the sky, she started toward home. She wanted to be back at a decent hour to-night. It was the least she could do to show her dad that she ap-preciated how understanding he'd been. And despite her earlier nap, she was still tired.

When she reached the head of the pier, she opted to walk through the business district instead of along the beach. As soon as she rounded the corner near the diner, she knew she'd made the wrong decision. A shadowy figure leaned against the hood of a car, holding a fireball.

Marcus.

Only this time he was alone. She stopped, feeling her breath catch in her throat.

He pushed off the car and walked toward her, the play of street-lights casting his face half in shadow. He rolled the fireball over the back of his hand, watching her, before the ball ended up back in his fist. He squeezed his hand, extinguishing it, and started toward her.

"Hi, Ronnie," he said. His smile made him seem even creepier.

She stayed in place, wanting him to see that she wasn't afraid of him. Even though she sort of was.

"What do you want?" she demanded, hating the slight quiver in her voice.

"I saw you walking and thought I'd say hello."

"You did," she said. "Bye."

She started to move past him, but he stepped in front of her.

"I hear you're having troubles with Blaze," he whispered.

She leaned back, her skin crawling. "What do you know about it?"

"I know enough not to trust her."

"I'm not in the mood for this."

Again she turned, making her way around him, and this time he let her pass before calling out to her.

"Don't walk away. I came to find you because I wanted you to know that I might just be able to talk her out of what she's doing to you."

Despite herself, Ronnie hesitated. In the dim light, Marcus stared at her.

"I should have warned you she gets pretty jealous."

"Which is why you tried to make it worse, huh?"

"I was just making a joke that night. I thought it was funny. Do you think I had any idea what she would do to you?"

Of course you did, Ronnie thought. And it was exactly what you wanted.

"So fix it," she said. "Talk to Blaze, do whatever you have to do."

He shook his head. "You didn't hear me. I said I *might* be able to talk some sense into her. If . . ."

"If what?"

He closed the gap between them. The streets, she noticed, were quiet. No one else around, no cars in the intersection.

"I was thinking we could be . . . friends."

She felt her cheeks flush again, and the word came out before she could stop it. "What?"

"You heard me. And I can clear all this up."

She realized he was close enough to touch her, and she took a sudden step backward. "Just stay away from me!"

She turned and ran, knowing he would follow, conscious that he knew the area better than she did, terrified that he would catch her. She could feel her heart pounding, she could hear her own frantic breaths.

Her house wasn't far, but she wasn't in shape. Despite the fear and rush of adrenaline, she could feel her legs getting heavier. She knew she couldn't keep it up, and as she made a turn, she chanced a look back over her shoulder.

And realized that she was alone on the street, no one behind her at all.

Back at her house, Ronnie didn't go inside right away. The light was on in the living room, but she wanted to regain her composure before she faced her dad. For whatever reason, she didn't want him to see how scared she'd been, so she took a seat on the steps of the front porch.

Above her, the stars were out in full, the moon floating near the horizon. The scent of salt and brine rode on the mist from the ocean, a vaguely primordial smell. In another context, she might have found something soothing about it; right now, it felt as foreign as everything else.

First Blaze. Then Marcus. She wondered if everyone was crazy down here.

Marcus certainly was. Well, maybe not technically—he was intelligent, cunning, and, as far as she could tell, completely without empathy, the kind of person who thought only about himself and what he wanted. Last fall, in her English class, she'd had to read a novel by a contemporary author, and she'd chosen *The Silence of the Lambs*. In the book, she'd learned that the cen-

tral character, Hannibal Lecter, wasn't psychopathic, he was so-
ciopathic; it was the first time she'd realized there was a difference
between the two. Though Marcus wasn't a murdering cannibal,
she had the feeling he and Hannibal were more similar than
different, at least in the way they viewed the world and their
role in it.

Blaze, though . . . she was just . . .

Ronnie wasn't sure exactly. Controlled by her emotions, certainly. Angry and jealous, too. But in the day they'd spent together,
she'd never gotten the feeling that something was wrong with the
girl, aside from being an emotional wreck, a tornado of hormones
and immaturity that left destruction in her wake.

She sighed and ran a hand through her hair. She really didn't
want to go inside. In her mind, she could already hear the conversation.

Hey, sweetie, how did it go?

*Not too well. Blaze is completely under the spell of a manipulative
sociopath and lied to the cops this morning, so I'm going to jail. And
by the way? The sociopath not only decided he wants to sleep with me,
but he followed me and practically scared me to death. How did your
day go?*

Not exactly the pleasant after-dinner chitchat he probably
wanted to have, even if it was the truth.

Which meant she would have to fake it. Sighing, she heaved
herself up from the porch steps and headed for the door.

Inside, her dad sat on the couch, a dog-eared Bible open in
front of him. He closed it as she walked in.

"Hey, sweetie, how did it go?"

Figured.

She forced a quick smile, trying to act as nonchalant as possible. "I didn't have a chance to talk to her," she said.

* * *

It was hard to act normal, but somehow she pulled it off. As soon as she got inside, her dad had encouraged her to follow him to the kitchen, where he had made another pasta dish—tomatoes, egg-plant, squash, and zucchini over penne. They ate in the kitchen while Jonah put together a Lego *Star Wars* outpost, something that Pastor Harris had brought him when he'd dropped by to say hello earlier.

Afterward, they settled in the living room, and sensing she wasn't in the mood to talk, her dad read his Bible while she read *Anna Karenina*, a book her mom had sworn she would love. Though the book seemed okay, Ronnie couldn't concentrate on it. Not only because of Blaze and Marcus, but because her dad was reading the *Bible*. Thinking back, she realized she'd never seen him do that before. Then again, she thought, maybe he had and she'd just never noticed.

Jonah finished building his Lego contraption and announced he was going to bed. She gave him a few minutes, hoping he'd be asleep before she entered the room, then put aside her book and rose from the couch.

"Good night, sweetheart," her dad said. "I know it hasn't been easy for you, but I'm glad you're here."

She paused before crossing the room toward him. Leaning over, and for the first time in three years, she kissed him on the cheek.

"Good night, Dad."

In the darkened bedroom, Ronnie took a seat on her bed, feeling drained. Though she didn't want to cry—she *hated* when she cried—she couldn't seem to stop the sudden rush of emotions. She drew a ragged breath.

"Go ahead and cry," she heard Jonah whisper.

Great, she thought. Just what she needed.

"I'm not crying," she said.

"You sound like you're crying."

"I'm not."

"It's okay. It doesn't bother me."

Ronnie sniffled, trying to get herself under control, and reached under her pillow for the pajamas she'd stashed earlier. Pressing them close to her chest, she stood up to go to the bathroom to change. On her way, she happened to glance out the window. The moon had ascended in the sky, making the sand glow silver, and when she turned in the direction of the turtle nest, she detected a sudden movement in the shadows.

After sniffing the air, the raccoon started toward the nest, protected only by yellow caution tape.

"Oh, crap!"

She threw down her pajamas and raced out of the bedroom. As she bolted through the living room and kitchen, she vaguely heard her dad shouting, "What's wrong?" But she was already out the door before she could answer. Cresting the dune, she began screaming as she waved her arms.

"No! Stop! Go away!!"

The raccoon raised its head, then quickly scurried away. It vanished over the dune into the saw grass.

"What's going on? What happened?"

Turning, she saw her dad and Jonah standing on the porch.

"They didn't put up the cage!"

13

·····❦·····

Will

The doors of Blakelee Brakes had been open only for ten minutes when Will saw her push through the lobby doors and head directly into the service center.

Wiping his hands on a towel, he started toward her.

"Hey," he said, smiling. "I didn't expect to see you here."

"Thanks for nothing!" she snapped.

"What are you talking about?"

"I asked you to do one simple thing! Just make a call to have the cage put up! But you couldn't even do that!"

"Wait . . . what's going on?" He blinked.

"I told you I saw a raccoon! I told you a raccoon was coming around the nest!"

"Did something happen to the nest?"

"Like you even care. What? Did your volleyball game make you forget?"

"I just want to know if the nest is okay."

She continued to glare at him. "Yeah. It's fine. No thanks to you." She turned on her heels and stormed toward the exit.

"Wait!" he shouted. "Hold on!"

She ignored him, leaving Will shocked and rooted in place as she pounded through the small lobby and out the front door.

"What the hell was that all about?"

Over his shoulder, Will realized Scott was staring at him from behind the lift.

"Do me a favor," Will called to him.

"What do you need?"

He fished his keys out of his pocket and started toward the truck he'd parked out back. "Cover for me. I've got to take care of something."

Scott took a quick step forward. "Wait! What are you talking about?"

"I'll be back as soon as I can. If my dad comes in, tell him I'll be right back. You can get things started while I'm gone."

"Where you going?" Scott called.

This time Will didn't answer, and Scott took a step toward him.

"C'mon, man! I don't want to do this alone! We've got a ton of cars to work on."

Will didn't care, and once out of the bay, he jogged toward his truck, knowing where he needed to go.

He found her at the dune an hour later, standing beside the nest, still as angry as she'd been when she'd shown up at the brake shop.

Seeing him approach, she put her hands on her hips. "What do you want?"

"You didn't let me finish. I did call."

"Sure you did."

He inspected the nest. "The nest is fine. What's the big deal?"

"Yeah, it's fine. No thanks to you."

Will felt a ripple of irritation. "What's your problem?"

"My problem is that I had to sleep outside again last night because the raccoon came back. The same raccoon I told you about!"

"You slept outside?"

"Do you ever listen to anything I say? Yes, I had to sleep outside. Two nights in a row, because *you* won't do your job! If I hadn't been looking out the window at exactly the right moment, the raccoon would have gotten the eggs. He wasn't more than a couple of feet away from the nest when I finally scared him away. And then I had to stay out here because I knew he was going to come back. Which is why I asked you to call in the first place! And I assumed that even a beach bum like yourself could remember to *do your job!*"

She stared at him, hands on her hips again, as if trying to annihilate him with her death ray vision.

He couldn't resist. "One more time, so I have the story straight: You saw a raccoon, then you wanted me to call, then you saw a raccoon again. And you ended up sleeping outside. Is that right?"

She opened her mouth, then closed it. Then, whirling away, she made a beeline for her house.

"They're coming first thing tomorrow!" he called out. "And just to let you know, I did call. Twice, in fact. Once right after I put up the tape, and once more after I got off work. How many times do I have to say this before you'll listen?"

Though she stopped, she still wouldn't face him. He went on, "And then this morning, after you left, I went straight to the director of the aquarium and spoke to him in person. He said that this nest will be their first stop in the morning. That they would have come today, but there are eight nests on Holden Beach."

She slowly turned around and studied him, trying to decide whether he was telling the truth.

"That doesn't help my turtles tonight, does it?"

"Your turtles?"

"Yeah," she said. Her tone was emphatic. "My house. My turtles."

And with that, she turned and went back to her house, this time without caring that he was still there.

He liked her; it was as simple as that.

On his way back to work, he still wasn't sure why he liked her, but never once had he left work to chase after Ashley. Every time he'd seen her, she'd managed to surprise him. He liked the way she said what was on her mind, and he liked how unfazed she was by him. Ironically, he'd yet to leave a good impression. First he'd spilled soda on her, next she'd seen him almost involved in a riot, and then this morning she'd believed him to be either lazy or an idiot.

No problem, of course. She wasn't a friend and he didn't really know her . . . but for whatever reason, he cared what she thought about him. And not only did he care, but crazy as it sounded, he wanted her to have a good impression of him. Because he wanted her to like him, too.

It was an odd experience, a new one for him, and the rest of the day at the shop—working through lunch to make up for the time he'd missed—he found his thoughts returning to her. He felt that there was something genuine in the way she spoke and acted, something caring and kind beneath the brittle facade. Something that let him know that while he'd disappointed her to this point, there was, with her, always a chance for redemption.

Later that night, he found her sitting exactly where he thought she would be, in a beach chair with a book open in her lap, reading by the light of a small lantern.

She looked up as he approached, then went back to her book, acting neither surprised nor pleased.

"I figured you'd be here," he said. "Your house, your turtles, and all."

When she didn't respond, his gaze drifted. It wasn't very late, and shadows were moving behind the curtains of the small house she lived in.

"Any sign of the raccoon?"

Instead of answering, she flipped a page of her book.

"Wait. Let me guess. You're giving me the cold shoulder, right?"

With that, she sighed. "Shouldn't you be with your friends, staring at yourselves in the mirror?"

He laughed. "That's funny. I'll have to remember that."

"I'm not being funny. I'm being serious."

"Oh, because we're so good-looking, right?"

In response, she went back to her book, but Will could tell she wasn't actually reading. He took a seat beside her.

"'Happy families are all alike; every unhappy family is unhappy in its own way,'" he quoted, pointing to her book. "It's the first line in your book. I always thought there was a lot of truth in that. Or maybe that's what my English teacher said. I can't really remember. I read it last semester."

"Your parents must be so proud you can read."

"They are. They bought me a pony and everything when I did a book report on *Cat in the Hat*."

"Was that before or after you claimed to have read Tolstoy?"

"Oh, so you are listening. Just making sure." He spread his arms toward the horizon. "It's a beautiful night, isn't it? I've always loved nights like this. There's something relaxing about waves sounding in the darkness, don't you think?" He paused.

She closed her book. "What's with the full-court press?"

"I like people who like turtles."

"So go hang out with your aquarium friends. Oh, wait, you can't. Because they're saving other turtles, and your other friends are painting their nails and curling their hair, right?"

"Probably. But I just figured you might want some company."

"I'm fine," she snapped. "Now go."

"It's a public beach. I like it here."

"So you're going to stay?"

"I think so."

"Then you won't mind if I go inside?"

He sat up straighter and brought a hand to his chin. "I don't know if that's such a good idea. I mean, how can you trust that I'll stay out here all night? And with that pesky raccoon . . ."

"What do you want with me?" she demanded.

"For starters, how about your name?"

She grabbed a towel, spreading it over her legs. "Ronnie," she said. "It's short for Veronica."

He reclined a little, propping his arms behind him. "All right, Ronnie. What's your story?"

"Why do you care?"

"Gimme a break," he said, turning to face her. "I'm trying, okay?"

He wasn't sure what she thought about that, but as she collected her hair into a loose ponytail, she seemed to accept the idea that she wasn't going to be able to easily run him off.

"All right. My story: I live in New York with my mom and little brother, but she shipped us here to spend the summer with our dad. And now I'm stuck babysitting turtle eggs while a volleyball player slash grease monkey slash aquarium volunteer tries to hit on me."

"I'm not hitting on you," he protested.

"No?"

"Believe me, you'd know if I was hitting on you. You wouldn't be able to stop yourself from succumbing to my charms."

For the first time since he'd arrived, he heard her laugh. He took that as a good sign and went on.

"Actually, I came here because I felt bad about the cage, and I didn't want you to be out here alone. Like I said earlier, it's a public beach and you never know who might come walking up."

"Like you?"

"It's not me you should be worried about. There are bad people everywhere. Even here."

"And let me guess. You'd protect me, right?"

"If it came down to that, I'd protect you in a heartbeat."

She didn't respond, but he had the feeling he'd surprised her. The tide was coming in, and together they watched the waves flare silver whenever they rolled and washed toward the shore. Through the windows, the curtains fluttered, as though someone were watching them.

"All right," she finally said, breaking the silence. "Your turn. What's your story?"

"I'm a volleyball player slash grease monkey slash aquarium volunteer."

He heard her laugh again, liking its unfettered energy. It felt contagious.

"Are you okay if I stay with you for a while?"

"It's a public beach."

He motioned toward the house. "Do you need to tell your dad I'm out here?"

"I'm sure he already knows you're here," she said. "Last night, he must have checked on me every other minute."

"He sounds like a good dad."

She seemed to consider something before shaking her head. "So you love volleyball, huh?"

"It keeps me in shape."

"That doesn't really answer the question."

"I enjoy it. I don't know if I love it, though."

"But you do like crashing into people, right?"

"That depends on who I crash into. But a few days ago, I guess I'd have to say it turned out pretty well."

"You think drenching me is a good thing?"

"If I hadn't soaked you, I might not be here now."

"And I could be enjoying a quiet, peaceful night at the beach instead."

"I don't know." He smiled. "Quiet, peaceful nights are over-rated."

"I guess I'm not going to find out tonight, huh?"

He laughed. "Where do you go to school?"

"I don't," she said. "I graduated a couple of weeks ago. You?"

"I just graduated from Laney High School. It's where Michael Jordan went."

"I'll bet everyone in your high school says that."

"No," he corrected. "Not everyone. Just the ones who graduated."

She rolled her eyes. "All right. So what's next for you? Are you going to keep working for your dad?"

"Just through the summer." He scooped up some sand and let it slip through his fingers.

"And then?"

"I'm afraid I can't tell you."

"No?"

"I don't know you well enough to trust you with that information."

"How about a hint?" she prodded.

"How about you go first? What's next for you?"

She thought about it. "I'm strongly considering a career in guarding turtle nests. I seem to have a knack for it. I mean, you should have seen the way that raccoon took off. It was like it thought I was the Terminator."

"You sound like Scott," he said. Seeing her blank expression, he explained. "He's my volleyball partner, and the guy is the king of movie references. It's like he can't complete a sentence without one of them. Of course, he usually works some sexual innuendo in as well."

"That sounds like a special talent."

"Oh, it is. I could get him to give you a personal demonstration."

"No, thank you. I don't need any sexual innuendos."

"You might like it."

"I think not."

He held her gaze as they bantered, noting that she was prettier than he remembered. Funny and smart, too, which was even better.

Near the nest, saw grass bent in the breeze and the steady sound of the waves surrounded them, making him feel as if they were in a cocoon. Up and down the beach, lights glowed in the ocean-front houses.

"Can I ask you a question?"

"I'm not sure I could stop you."

He pushed his feet back and forth in the sand. "What's with you and Blaze?"

In the silence, she stiffened slightly. "What do you mean?"

"I was just wondering why you were hanging out with her the other night."

"Oh," she said. Though he had no idea why, she seemed relieved. "Actually, we met when she spilled my soda on me. Right after I finished cleaning up what you did."

"You're kidding."

"Nope. As far as I can tell, dumping soda on people is the equivalent of 'Hi, it's nice to meet you' in this part of the world. Frankly, I think standard greetings work better, but what do I know?" She drew a long breath. "Anyway, she seemed cool and I didn't know anyone else, so we just . . . ended up hanging out for a while."

"Did she stay here with you last night?"

She shook her head. "No."

"What? Didn't she want to save the turtles? Or at least keep you company?"

"I didn't tell her about this."

He could tell she didn't want to say more, so he let it drop. Instead, he motioned to the beach.

"Do you want to go for a walk?"

"Do you mean a romantic walk, or just a walk?"

"I'm going to say . . . just a walk."

"Good choice." She clapped her hands together. "But just so you know, I don't want to go too far, being that the aquarium volunteers weren't concerned about the raccoon and the eggs are still exposed."

"They were definitely concerned. I have it on good authority that an aquarium volunteer is helping to guard the nest right now."

"Yes," she said. "But the real question is why?"

They walked the beach in the direction of the pier, passing a dozen oceanfront mansions, each with massive decks and staircases that led down to the beach. A few houses down, one of the neighbors was hosting a small gathering; all the lights on the third floor were on, and three or four couples leaned against the railing, watching the moonlit waves.

They didn't talk much, but for some reason, the silence didn't feel uncomfortable. Ronnie kept just enough distance so they wouldn't accidentally brush against each other, sometimes studying the sand and at other times staring ahead. There were moments when he thought he saw a fleeting smile cross her features, as though she remembered a humorous story she hadn't yet shared with him. Every now and then, she stopped and bent over to retrieve seashells that were half-buried in the sand, and he noted her concentration as she examined them in the moonlight before tossing most of them aside. The others she slipped into her pocket.

There was so much he didn't know about her—in many ways she remained a cipher to him. In that, she was the complete opposite of Ashley. Ashley was nothing if not safe and predictable; he knew thoroughly what he was getting, even if it wasn't what he really wanted. But Ronnie was different, no doubt about it, and when she offered him an unguarded and unexpected smile, he had the sense she was intuiting his thoughts. The realization warmed him, and when they finally turned around and made their way back toward their spot near the turtle nest, there was an instant when he imagined himself walking beside her on the beach each and every night into a distant future.

* * *

When they reached the house, Ronnie went inside to talk to her dad while Will unpacked his truck. He set up his bedroll and supplies on the side of the turtle nest, wishing Ronnie could have stayed near the nest with him. But she'd already told him there wasn't a chance that her dad would agree. At the very least, though, he was glad she'd be able to sleep in her own bed tonight.

Getting comfortable, he lay down, thinking that today had been a start, if nothing else. Anything might happen from here. But when she turned, smiling as she waved a final good night from the porch, he felt something leap inside at the notion that she just might imagine it was the beginning of something, too.

"Who's the stiff?"

"Nobody. Just a friend. Go away."

As the words drifted through the hazy corridors of his mind, Will struggled to remember where he was. Squinting into the sun, he realized he was face-to-face with a little boy.

"Oh, hey," Will mumbled.

The boy rubbed his nose. "What are you doing here?"

"Waking up."

"I can see that. But what were you doing here last night?"

Will smiled. The kid acted as serious as a coroner, which seemed comical given his age and stature. "Sleeping."

"Uh-huh."

Will pushed back, giving himself room to sit up, and noticed Ronnie standing off to the side. She was dressed in a black T-shirt and torn jeans and wore the same amused expression he'd seen the night before.

"I'm Will," he offered. "And you are?"

The boy nodded toward Ronnie. "I'm her roommate," he said. "We go back a long way."

Will scratched his head, smiling. "I see."

Ronnie took a step forward, her hair still damp from her shower. "This is my nosy brother, Jonah."

"Oh?" Will asked.

"Yeah," Jonah answered. "Except for the nosy part."

"Good to know."

Jonah continued to stare at him. "I think I know you."

"I don't think so. I feel like I would have remembered meeting you."

"No, I do remember," Jonah said, beginning to smile. "You were the guy who told the police officer that Ronnie went to Bower's Point!"

The memory of that night came surging back, and Will turned to Ronnie, watching with dread as her expression changed from curiosity to puzzlement and finally to understanding.

Oh, no.

Jonah was still going on. "Yeah, Officer Pete brought her home, and she and Dad had this big fight the next morning . . ."

Will saw Ronnie's mouth tighten. Muttering, she turned and stormed into the house.

Jonah stopped in midsentence, wondering what he'd said.

"Thanks for that," Will growled, then hopped to his feet and sprinted after Ronnie.

"Ronnie! Wait! C'mon. I'm sorry! I didn't mean for you to get into trouble."

He reached for her arm as he caught up with her. When his fingers grazed her T-shirt, she whirled to face him.

"Go away!"

"Just listen to me for a second—"

"You and I have nothing in common!" she snapped. "Get it?"

"Then what was last night about?"

Her cheeks were red. "Leave. Me. Alone."

"Your act doesn't work on me," he said. For some reason, his words kept her quiet long enough to go on. "You stopped the fight, even though everyone else wanted blood. You were the only one who even noticed the kid who started to cry, and I saw the way you smiled when he went off with his mom. You read Tolstoy in your spare time. And you like sea turtles."

Though she raised her chin defiantly, he sensed he'd struck a nerve. "So what?"

"So I want to show you something today." He paused, relieved that she didn't immediately say no. But she hadn't said yes, either, and before she could decide one way or the other, he took a small step forward.

"You'll like it," he said. "I promise."

Will pulled into the empty parking lot of the aquarium and followed a small service drive that led around back. Ronnie sat beside him in the truck but hadn't said much on the drive over. As he walked her toward the employees entrance, he could tell that even though she'd agreed to come, she hadn't yet made up her mind about whether or not to still be angry with him.

He held open the door for her, feeling the cool draft as it mingled with the hot, humid air outside. He led her down a long corridor, then pushed through yet another door that led into the aquarium itself.

There were a handful of people working in their offices, although the aquarium wouldn't open to the public for another hour. Will loved being here before it opened; the dim lights from the tanks and absence of sound made it feel like a secret hideaway. Often, he would find himself mesmerized by the poisoned spines of the lionfish as they moved in saltwater loops, skimming the glass. He wondered whether they realized their habitat had shrunk in size, and if they even knew he was there.

Ronnie walked next to him, observing the activity. She seemed content to stay quiet as they passed a massive ocean tank, home to a smaller replica of a sunken German submarine from World War II. When they reached the tank of slowly undulating jellyfish that glowed fluorescent beneath a black light, she stopped and touched the glass in wonder.

"*Aurelia aurita*," Will said. "Also known as moon jellies."

She nodded, returning her gaze to the tank, transfixed by their slow-motion movement. "They're so delicate," she said. "It's hard to believe the stings can be so painful."

Her hair had dried curlier than it had the day before, making her appear a bit like an unruly tomboy.

"Tell me about it. I think I've been stung at least once a year since I was a kid."

"You should try to avoid them."

"I do. But they find me anyway. I think they're attracted to me."

She smiled faintly, then turned and faced him directly. "What are we doing here?"

"I told you I wanted to show you something."

"I've seen fish before. And I've been to an aquarium, too."

"I know. But this is special."

"Because no one else is here?"

"No," he answered. "Because you're going to see something that the public doesn't see."

"What? You and me alone near a fish tank?"

He grinned. "Even better. C'mon."

In a situation like this, he normally wouldn't hesitate to take a girl's hand, but he couldn't bring himself to try it with her. He motioned with his thumb toward a corner hallway, tucked neatly away so as to be practically unnoticeable. At the end of the hallway, he paused before the door.

"Don't tell me they gave you an office," she teased.

"No," he said, pushing open the door. "I don't work here, remember? I'm just a volunteer."

They entered a large cinder-block room crisscrossed by air ducts and dozens of exposed pipes. Fluorescent lights hummed overhead, but the sound was drowned out by the enormous water filters that lined the far wall. A giant open tank, filled nearly to the top with ocean water, lent the air a tang of salt and brine.

Will led the way onto a steel-grated platform that circled the tank and climbed down the industrial steps. On the far side of the tank was a medium-size Plexiglas window. The lights above provided enough illumination to make out the slowly moving creature.

He watched Ronnie as she eventually recognized what she was seeing.

"Is that a sea turtle?"

"A loggerhead, actually. Her name is Mabel."

As the turtle glided past the window, the scars on her shell became apparent, as did the missing flipper.

"What happened to her?"

"She was hit by a boat propeller. She was rescued about a month ago, barely alive. A specialist from NC State had to amputate part of her front flipper."

In the tank, unable to stay completely upright, Mabel swam at a slight angle and bumped into the far wall, then began her circuit again.

"Is she going to be okay?"

"It's a miracle she's lived this long, and I hope she'll make it. She's stronger now than she was. But no one knows if she can survive in the ocean."

Ronnie watched as Mabel bumped into the wall again before correcting her course, then turned to face Will.

"Why did you want me to see this?"

"Because I thought you'd like her as much as I do," he said. "Scars and all."

Ronnie seemed to wonder at his words, but she said nothing. Instead, she turned to watch Mabel in silence for a while. As Mabel vanished into the back shadows, he heard Ronnie sigh.

"Aren't you supposed to be at work?" she asked.

"It's my day off."

"Working for Dad has its perks, huh?"

"You might say that."

She tapped the glass, trying to get Mabel's attention. After a moment, she turned to him again. "So what do you usually do on your day off?"

"Just a good old southern boy, huh? Going fishing, watching the clouds. I feel like you should be wearing a NASCAR hat and chewing tobacco."

They'd spent another half hour at the aquarium—Ronnie was especially delighted by the otters—before Will had taken her to a bait shop to pick up some frozen shrimp. From there, he'd brought her to an undeveloped lot on the intracoastal side of the island, where he'd pulled out the fishing gear he kept stored in the truck box. Then he'd led her to the edge of a small dock, and they sat, their feet dangling just a couple of feet above the water.

"Don't be a snob," he chided her. "Believe it or not, the South is great. We have indoor plumbing and everything. And on weekends, we get to go mudding."

"Mudding?"

"We drive our trucks in the mud."

Ronnie faked a dreamy expression. "That sounds so . . . intellectual."

He nudged her playfully. "Yeah, tease me if you want. But it's fun. Muddy water spraying all over the windshield, getting stuck, spinning your wheels to soak the guy behind you."

"Believe me, I'm giddy just thinking about it," Ronnie said, deadpan.

"I take it that's not how you spend your weekends in the city."

She shook her head. "Uh . . . no. Not exactly."

"I'll bet you never even leave the city, do you?"

"Of course I leave the city. I'm here, aren't I?"

"You know what I mean. On the weekends."

"Why would I want to leave the city?"

"Maybe just to be alone now and then?"

"I can be alone in my room."

"Where would you go if you wanted to sit beneath a tree and read?"

"I'd go to Central Park," she countered easily. "There's this great knoll behind Tavern on the Green. And I can buy a latte just around the corner."

He shook his head in mock lament. "You're such a city girl. Do you even know how to fish?"

"It's not that hard. Bait the hook, cast the line, then hold the pole. How am I doing so far?"

"Okay, if that's all there was to it. But you have to know where to cast and be good enough to cast exactly where you want. You have to know what bait and lures to use, and those depend on everything from the type of fish to the weather to the clarity of the water. And then, of course, you have to set the hook. If you're too early or too late, you'll miss the fish."

Ronnie seemed to consider his comment. "So why did you choose to use shrimp?"

"Because it was on sale," he answered.

She giggled, then brushed lightly against him. "Cute," she said. "But I guess I deserved that."

He could still feel the warmth of her touch on his shoulder. "You deserve worse," he said. "Believe me, fishing is like a religion to some folks around here."

"You included?"

"No. Fishing is . . . contemplative. Gives me time to think without interruption. And besides, I enjoy watching the clouds while I wear my NASCAR hat and chew tobacco."

She wrinkled her nose. "You don't really chew tobacco, do you?"

"No. I kind of like the idea of not losing my lips to mouth cancer."

"Good," she said. She swung her legs back and forth. "I'd never date anyone who chewed tobacco."

"Are you saying we're on a date?"

"No. This definitely isn't a date. This is fishing."

"You've got so much to learn. I mean, this . . . is what life's all about."

She picked at a sliver of wood on the dock. "You sound like a beer commercial."

An osprey glided over them just as the line ducked once and then a second time. Will jerked the rod upward as the line went tight. He scrambled to his feet as he began to reel it in, the rod already bending. It happened so fast that Ronnie barely had time to figure out what was happening.

"Did you get one?" she asked, jumping up.

"Come closer," he urged, continuing to reel. He forced the rod toward her. "Here!" he shouted. "Take it!"

"I can't!" she squealed, backing away.

"It's not hard! Just take it and continue to turn the reel!"

"I don't know what to do!"

"I just told you!" he said. Ronnie edged forward, and he practically forced the rod into her hands. "Now keep turning the reel!"

She watched the rod bob lower as she began to turn the crank. "Hold it up! Keep the line tight!"

"I'm trying!" she cried.

"You're doing great!"

The fish splashed near the surface—a small red drum, he noticed—and Ronnie screamed, making a scene. When he burst out laughing, she started laughing, too, hopping on one foot. When the fish splashed again, she screamed a second time, jumping even higher, but this time with an expression of fierce determination.

It was, he thought, one of the funniest things he'd seen in a long time.

"Just keep doing what you're doing," he encouraged. "Get it

closer to the dock and I'll take care of the rest." Holding the net, he got down on his belly, stretching his arm over the water as Ronnie continued to reel. With a quick motion, he was able to scoop the fish into the net, then he stood. As he inverted the net, the fish dropped onto the dock, flopping as it hit the surface. Ronnie continued to hold the reel, dancing around the fish as Will grabbed for the line.

"What are you doing?" she shrieked. "You've got to put it back into the water!"

"It'll be fine—"

"It's dying!"

He squatted and grabbed the fish, pinning it to the dock. "No, it isn't!"

"You've got to get the hook out!" she shrieked again.

He reached for the hook and began to pry it out. "I'm trying! Just give me a second!"

"It's bleeding! You hurt it!" She danced around him frantically.

Ignoring her, he began to work the hook out. He could feel the tail moving back and forth, flopping against the back of his hand. It was small, maybe three or four pounds, but surprisingly strong.

"You're taking too long!" Ronnie fretted.

He carefully freed the hook but held the fish pinned against the dock. "You sure you don't want to bring it home for dinner? You should be able to get a couple of fillets out of it."

Her mouth opened and closed in disbelief, but before she could say anything, Will tossed the fish back into the water. With a splash, it dove and vanished. Will reached for a hand towel and wiped the blood from his fingers.

Ronnie continued to stare at him accusingly, her cheeks flushed with excitement. "You would have eaten it, wouldn't you? If I weren't here?"

"I would have thrown it back."

"Why don't I believe you?"

"Because you're probably right." He smiled at her before reaching for the rod. "Now, do you want to bait the next hook or should I?"

"So Mom's been going crazy trying to plan my sister's wedding and make the whole thing perfect," Will said. "It's been a little . . . tense at the house."

"When's the wedding?"

"August ninth. It doesn't help matters that my sister wants to have it at our house. Which, of course, only adds to my mom's stress."

Ronnie smiled. "What's your sister like?"

"Smart. Lives in New York. A bit of a free spirit. Pretty much like another older sister I know."

That seemed to please her. As they strolled the beach, the sun was setting and Will could tell that Ronnie was feeling more relaxed. They'd ended up catching and releasing three more fish before he drove her to downtown Wilmington, where they'd enjoyed lunch on a deck that overlooked the Cape Fear River. Drawing her eyes to a spot on the opposite bank, he'd pointed out the USS *North Carolina,* a decommissioned battleship from World War II. Watching Ronnie inspect it, Will was struck by how easy it was to spend time with her. Unlike other girls he knew, she said what she meant and didn't play stupid games. She had a quirky sense of humor that he liked, even when it was directed at him. In fact, he liked everything about her.

As they approached her house, Ronnie ran ahead to check on the nest tucked into the base of the dune. She paused at the cage— it was made of chicken wire and secured into the sandy dune by extralong stakes—and when he joined her at the dune, she turned to him doubtfully.

"This is going to keep the raccoon away?"

"That's what they say."

She studied it. "How do the turtles get out? They can't fit through the holes, can they?"

Will shook his head. "The aquarium volunteers remove the cage before the eggs hatch."

"How do they know when they'll hatch?"

"They've got it down to a science. The eggs take around sixty days to incubate before they hatch, but that can vary slightly depending on the weather. The hotter the temperature is all summer, the quicker they'll hatch. And keep in mind that this isn't the only nest on the beach, and it wasn't the first one, either. Once the first nest clears, the others usually follow within a week or so."

"Have you ever seen a nest hatch?"

He nodded. "Four times."

"What's it like?"

"It's a little crazy, actually. As the time approaches, we remove the cages, and then we dig a shallow trench from the nest to the water's edge, making it as smooth as possible, but high enough on the sides so the turtles can only go in one direction. And it's weird, because at first only a couple of eggs are moving, but it's like their movement is enough to set the whole nest going, and before you know it, the nest is like a crazy beehive on steroids. The turtles are climbing over each other to get out of the hole, and then they hit the sand and head toward the water in this little crablike parade. It's amazing."

As he described it, he got the sense Ronnie was trying to picture the scene. Then she noticed her dad stepping onto the back porch, and she waved.

Will motioned to the house. "I take it that's your dad?" he asked.

"Yup."

"Don't you want to introduce me?"

"Nope."

"I promise to have good manners."

"That'd be good."

"So why won't you introduce me?"

"Because you haven't taken me to meet your parents yet."

"Why do you have to meet my parents?"

"Exactly," she said.

"I'm not sure I follow what you mean."

"Then how on earth did you ever make it through Tolstoy?"

If he wasn't confused before, he was completely baffled now. She started walking slowly down the beach, and he took a few quick steps to catch up with her.

"You're not exactly easy to figure out."

"And?"

"And nothing. Just noting it for the record."

She smiled to herself, glancing toward the horizon. In the distance, a shrimp trawler was making its way to port. "I want to be here when it happens," she offered.

"When what happens?"

"When the turtles hatch. What did you think I was talking about?"

He shook his head. "Oh, we're back to that. Well, okay, when do you leave for New York?"

"Late August."

"That's cutting it close. Just hope for a long hot summer."

"It's off to a good start. I'm boiling."

"That's because you're wearing black. And jeans."

"I didn't realize I'd be spending most of the day outside."

"Otherwise you would have worn a bikini, right?"

"I don't think so," she said.

"You don't like bikinis?"

"Of course I do."

"Just not around me?"

She tossed her head. "Not today."

"What if I promise to take you fishing again?"

"You're not helping yourself."

"Duck hunting?"

That stopped her. When she finally found her voice, it was disapproving. "Tell me you don't really kill ducks?"

When Will said nothing, Ronnie went on, "Cute, sweet little

feathered creatures, flying toward their little duck pond, just minding their own business? And you blow them out of the sky?"

Will considered the question. "Only in the winter."

"When I was a little girl, my favorite stuffed animal was a duck. I had duck wallpaper. I had a hamster named Daffy. I *love* ducks."

"I do, too." he said.

She didn't bother to hide her skepticism. Will responded by counting on the tips of his fingers as he continued, "I love them fried, roasted, broiled, with a side of sweet-and-sour sauce—"

She gave him a shove, knocking him off balance for a step or two. "That's terrible!"

"It's funny!"

"You're just a mean man."

"Sometimes," he said. He motioned toward the house. "So if you don't want to go home yet, do you want to come with me?"

"Why? Are you planning to show or tell me about yet another way you kill small animals?"

"I've got a volleyball game soon and I want you to come. It's fun."

"Are you going to spill soda on me again?"

"Only if you bring a soda."

She debated for an instant, then fell into step with him in the direction of the pier. He nudged her and she nudged him back.

"I think you have problems," she told him.

"What problems?"

"Well, for starters, you're an evil duck killer."

He laughed before catching her eye. She looked down at the sand, then up the beach, then finally toward him. She shook her head, unable to suppress a smile, as if marveling at what was happening between them and enjoying every moment.

14

·····♪·····

Ronnie

If he weren't so damn cute, none of this would have happened.

As she watched Will and Scott scramble around the court, she reflected on the series of events that had brought her here. Had she really gone fishing earlier today? And watched a wounded turtle swim around a tank at eight o'clock in the morning?

She shook her head, trying not to focus on Will's lean body and visible muscles as he chased the ball across the sand. Tough to ignore, since he wasn't wearing a shirt.

Maybe the rest of the summer wouldn't be so terrible after all.

Of course, she'd thought the same thing after meeting Blaze, and look how *that* had turned out.

He wasn't really her type, but as she watched him play, she began to wonder whether that was such a bad thing. She hadn't had the best luck when it came to choosing guys in the past, Rick being the prime example. Lord knows Will was smarter than any of the other guys she'd dated, and more than that, he seemed to be doing something with his life. He worked, he volunteered, he was a pretty good athlete; he even got along with his family. And even though he liked to play things off in an "*aw, shucks*" sort of way, he wasn't a pushover. When she tested him, he called her on it—more than once, in fact—and she had to admit she sort of liked it.

If there was one thing about him that gave her pause, it was this: She didn't know why he liked her. She wasn't anything like the girls she'd seen him with the night of the carnival—and in all honesty, she wasn't even sure he'd want to see her again after today. She watched him jog back to the service line, then glance in her direction, obviously pleased she'd come. He moved easily through the sand, and when he got ready to serve the ball, he signaled something to Scott, who seemed to play the game as though his life depended on it. As soon as Scott turned toward the net, Will rolled his eyes, making it plain that he found his friend's intensity a bit over the top. *It's only a game*, he seemed to say, and she found that heartening. Then, after tossing the ball in the air and serving hard, he raced toward the side of the court to keep the volley going. When he sacrificed his body by diving for the ball and sending a plume of sand in the air, she wondered whether what she'd seen a moment earlier had been only an illusion—but after his shot went wide and Scott threw up his hands in frustration with an angry glare, Will ignored him. After winking at Ronnie, he readied himself for the next shot.

"You and Will, huh?"

Mesmerized, Ronnie hadn't realized someone had taken a seat beside her. Turning, she recognized the blonde who had been hanging out with Will and Scott on the night of the carnival.

"Excuse me?"

The blonde ran a hand through her hair and flashed her perfect teeth. "You and Will. I saw the two of you walk up."

"Oh," Ronnie said. Her instincts told her that it was best not to say much.

If the blonde took notice of Ronnie's wary reaction, she didn't show it. Tossing her head with practiced skill, she flashed those teeth again. She definitely had to be a bleacher, Ronnie decided. "I'm Ashley. And you're . . ."

"Ronnie."

Ashley continued to stare at her. "And you're on vacation?" When Ronnie glanced at her, she smiled again. "I would have known if you were from around here. I've known Will since we were kids."

"Uh-huh," Ronnie said again, trying to sound noncommittal.

"I guess you two met when he made you spill your soda, huh? Knowing him, he probably did it on purpose."

Ronnie blinked. "What?"

"It's not the first time I've seen him do it. And let me guess. He just took you fishing, right? On that little dock on the other side of the island?"

This time, Ronnie couldn't mask her surprise.

"That's what he always does when he starts getting to know a girl. Well, either that or he brings her to the aquarium."

As Ashley went on, Ronnie stared at her in disbelief, feeling the world around her suddenly begin to narrow.

"What are you talking about?" she croaked out, her voice deserting her.

Ashley roped her arms around her legs. "New girl, new conquest? Don't be mad at him," she said. "It's just the way he is. He can't help it."

Ronnie felt the blood drain from her face. She told herself not to listen, not to believe it, that Will wasn't that way. But the words kept echoing in her mind . . .

Let me guess. He took you fishing, right?

Either that or he brings her to the aquarium . . .

Had she really misjudged him? It seemed like she was wrong about everyone she'd met down here. Which made sense, considering she'd never wanted to come down here at all. When she drew a long breath, she noticed that Ashley was studying her.

"Are you okay?" she asked, her perfectly shaped eyebrows knitted together in concern. "Did I say something to upset you?"

"I'm fine."

"Because you looked like you were about to get sick."

"I said I'm fine," Ronnie snapped.

Ashley's mouth opened and closed before her expression softened. "Oh, no. Don't tell me you were actually falling for it?"

New girl, new conquest? It's just the way he is . . .

The words kept ringing through her head, and Ronnie still didn't answer—couldn't answer. In the silence, Ashley went on, her voice sympathetic. "Well, don't feel too bad, because he's pretty much the most charming guy in the world when he wants to be. Trust me, I know, because I fell for it, too." She nodded at the crowd. "And so have half the other girls you see around here."

Ronnie instinctively surveyed the crowd, taking in the sight of half a dozen pretty girls in bikinis, all of their gazes fixed on Will. She felt incapable of speech. Meanwhile, Ashley was going on.

"I just figured you'd be able to see through it . . . I mean, you seem a little more sophisticated than the other girls around here. I guess I thought—"

"I've got to go," Ronnie announced, her tone steadier than her nerves. She felt her legs shaking slightly as she stood. On the court, Will must have seen her stand because he turned toward her, smiling, acting . . .

Like the most charming guy in the world . . .

She turned away, angry at him, but even angrier at herself for being so stupid. She wanted nothing more than to get the hell out of this place.

In her bedroom, she tossed the suitcase on the bed and was shoving clothes inside when the door opened behind her. Over her shoulder, she saw her dad standing in the doorway. She hesitated only briefly before crossing to the dresser and grabbing more of her things.

"Tough day?" her dad asked. His voice was soft, but he didn't wait for an answer. "I was in the workshop with Jonah when I saw you come up the beach. You looked pretty mad."

"I don't want to talk about it."

Her dad stayed in place, keeping his distance. "Going somewhere?"

She drew a furious breath as she continued to pack. "I'm out of here, okay? I'm calling Mom and I'm going home."

"That bad, huh?"

She turned toward him. "Please don't make me stay. I don't like it here. I don't like the people here. I don't fit in here. I don't belong here. I want to go home."

Her dad said nothing, but she saw the disappointment in his face.

"I'm sorry," she added. "And it's not you, okay? If you call, I'll talk to you. And you can come see me in New York and we'll spend time together, okay?"

Her dad continued to watch her in silence, which made her feel even worse. She surveyed the contents of her suitcase before adding the rest of her things.

"I'm not sure I can let you go."

She knew this was coming, and inwardly she tensed. "Dad . . ."

He raised his hands. "It's not for the reason you think. I'd let you go if I could. I'd call your mom right now. But given what happened the other day at the music store . . ."

With Blaze, she heard herself answer. *And the arrest . . .*

Her shoulders sagged. In her anger, she'd forgotten about the stolen goods.

Of course she'd forgotten about them. She hadn't stolen them in the first place! Her energy suddenly evaporated and she turned around, plopping down on the bed. This wasn't fair. None of this was fair.

Her dad still hadn't moved into the room.

"I can try to reach Pete—Officer Johnson—and see if it would be okay. I might not be able to reach him until tomorrow, though, and I don't want you to get into any more trouble. But if he says it's okay and you still want to go, I won't make you stay."

"Do you promise?"

"Yeah," he said. "Even though I'd rather you stay, I promise."

She nodded, pressing her lips together. "Will you come to New York to see me?"

"If I can," he said.

"What does that mean?"

Before her dad could answer, there was a sudden knocking on the door, loud and insistent. Her dad glanced over his shoulder. "I think that's probably the boy you were with today." She wondered how he knew, and reading her expression, he added, "I saw him heading this way when I came in the house to find you. Do you want me to handle it?"

Don't be mad at him. It's just the way he is. He can't help it.

"No," she said. "I'll handle it."

Her dad smiled, and for an instant, she thought he looked older than he had just the day before. As though her request had somehow aged him.

But even so, she didn't belong here. This was his place, not hers.

The knocking at the door sounded again.

"Hey, Dad?"

"Yeah?"

"Thanks," she said. "I know you really want me to stay, but I can't."

"It's okay, sweetheart." Though he smiled, the words came out wounded. "I understand."

She tugged at the seam on her jeans before rising from the bed. As she reached the door, he placed a hand on her back and she paused. Then, steeling herself, she went to the door and pulled it open, noting that Will's hand was hanging in the air. He seemed surprised that she'd opened it.

She stared at him, wondering how she could have been so stupid to trust him. She should have listened to her instincts.

"Oh, hey . . . ," he said, lowering his hand. "You're here. For a second there—"

She slammed the door, only to hear him immediately begin knocking again, his voice pleading.

"C'mon, Ronnie! Wait! I just want to know what happened! Why'd you leave?"

"Go away!" she shouted back.

"What did I do?"

She swung the door open again. "I'm not going to play your game!"

"What game? What are you talking about?"

"I'm not stupid. And I don't have anything to say to you."

Again, she slammed the door. Will began pounding on it.

"I'm not leaving until you talk to me!"

Her dad motioned to the door. "Trouble in paradise?"

"It's not paradise."

"So it seems," he said. "Do you want me to take care of it?" he offered again.

The pounding started up again.

"He won't stay long. It's better to just ignore him."

After a moment, he seemed to accept that and motioned to the kitchen. "Are you hungry?"

"No," she said automatically. Then, putting her hands on her stomach, she changed her mind. "Well, maybe a little."

"I found another good recipe online. This one has onions, mushrooms, and tomatoes cooked in olive oil, served over pasta, and tossed with Parmesan cheese. Does that sound okay?"

"I don't think Jonah will like it."

"He wanted a hot dog."

"Now there's a surprise."

He smiled just as the knocking sounded again. When it continued, he must have seen something in her face because he opened his arms.

Without thinking, Ronnie walked toward him and felt him hold her close. There was something . . . gentle and forgiving in his embrace, something she'd missed for years. It was all she could do to stop the tears from coming before she pulled back.

"How about I give you a hand with dinner?"

Ronnie tried once again to absorb the contents of the page she'd just read. The sun had set an hour ago, and after surfing restlessly through a handful of channels on her dad's TV, she had shut it off and picked up her book. But try as she might, she couldn't seem to make it through a single chapter, because Jonah had been standing near the window for almost an hour . . . which forced her to think about what was outside the window, or rather *who* was outside.

Will. It had been four hours, and the guy still hadn't left. He'd stopped knocking a long time ago and simply perched himself just beyond the crest of the dune, his back to the house. Technically, he was on the public beach, so neither she nor her father could do anything except ignore him. Which was what she and her dad—who, oddly, was reading the Bible again—were trying to do.

Jonah, on the other hand, simply couldn't ignore him. He seemed to find Will's vigil transfixing, like a UFO landing near the pier or Bigfoot trudging through the sand. Though he was wearing his Transformers pajamas and should have gone to bed half an hour earlier, he'd begged his dad to let him stay up for a little while, because, in his words, "if I go to bed too early, I might wet the bed."

Right.

He hadn't wet his bed since he was a toddler, and she knew her dad didn't believe a word of it. His acquiescence probably had to do with the fact that it was the first full evening they'd all spent together since she'd arrived and—depending on what Officer Johnson told them tomorrow—maybe their last. She figured her dad simply wanted to prolong the experience.

Which was understandable, of course, and sort of made her feel bad about the whole wanting-to-leave thing. Making dinner with him had been more fun than she'd thought it would be, since he hadn't laced his questions with insinuations the way her mom did lately. Still, she had no intention of staying any longer than she had to, even if it was hard on her dad. The least she could do was try to make tonight enjoyable.

Which was impossible, of course.

"How long do you think he's going to sit out there?" Jonah mumbled. By her reckoning, he'd asked the same question at least five times, even though neither she nor her dad had answered. This time, however, her dad set aside his Bible.

"Why don't you go ask him," he suggested.

"Yeah, right," Jonah snorted. "He's not my boyfriend."

"He's not my boyfriend, either," Ronnie added.

"He's acting like your boyfriend."

"He's not, okay?" She flipped to a new page.

"Then why is he sitting out there?" He cocked his head, trying to solve the riddle. "I mean, it's just weird, don't you think? Sitting out there for hours, waiting for you to talk to him. I mean, we're talking about my sister. My *sister*."

"I can hear you," Ronnie said. In the last twenty minutes, she figured she had reread the same paragraph six times.

"I'm just saying it's weird," Jonah mused, sounding like a baffled scientist. "Why would he wait outside for *my sister*?"

Ronnie glanced up, watching as her dad tried and failed to stifle a smile.

She returned to her book and began working through the same paragraph with renewed determination, and for the next couple of minutes there was silence in the room.

Aside from the sound of Jonah fidgeting and muttering by the window.

She tried to ignore him. She scooted herself down, perched her feet on the end table, and forced herself to concentrate on the words. For a minute or so, she was able to block out everything around her and was on the verge of slipping back into the story when she heard Jonah's little voice again.

"How long do you think he's going to sit out there?" Jonah mumbled.

She slammed the book shut. "Fine!" she cried, thinking again that her brother knew precisely what buttons to push to drive her crazy. "I get it! I'll go!"

A strong breeze was blowing, carrying with it the scent of salt and pine, as Ronnie stepped off the porch and headed toward Will. If he heard the door close, he gave no indication; instead, he seemed content to toss tiny seashells at the spider crabs that were scurrying to their holes.

A layer of marine haze screened out the stars, making the night seem colder and darker than before. Ronnie crossed her arms, trying to keep the chill away. Will, she noticed, was in the same pair of shorts and T-shirt he'd worn all day. She wondered whether he was cold, then forced the thought away. It wasn't important, she reminded herself as he turned toward her. In the dark, she couldn't read his expression, but as she stared at him, she realized that she was less angry at him than exasperated by his persistence.

"You've got my brother completely wigged out," Ronnie stated in what she hoped was an authoritative voice. "You should go."

"What time is it?"

"It's after ten."

"It took you long enough to get out here."

"I shouldn't have had to come out here at all. I told you to leave earlier." She glared at him.

His mouth tensed into a flat line. "I want to know what happened," he said.

"Nothing happened."

"Then tell me what Ashley said to you."

"She didn't say anything."

"I saw the two of you talking!" he accused.

This was why she hadn't wanted to come out here in the first place; this was what she'd wanted to avoid. "Will—"

"Why did you run off after talking to her? And why did it take you four hours to come outside to finally talk to me?"

She shook her head, refusing to admit how burned she felt. "It's not important."

"In other words, she told you something, didn't she? What did she say? That we were still seeing each other? Because we're not. It's over between us."

It took a moment for Ronnie to realize what he meant. "She was your girlfriend?"

"Yeah," he answered. "For two years."

When Ronnie said nothing, he stood up and took a step closer to her. "What exactly did she say to you?"

But Ronnie barely heard his voice. Instead, she thought back to the first time she'd seen Ashley, the first time she'd seen Will. Ashley, with her perfect bikini-clad figure, staring at Will . . .

Vaguely, she heard Will going on. "What? You're not even going to talk to me? You make me sit out here for hours and you won't even dignify my question with a simple answer?"

But Ronnie barely heard it. Instead, she remembered the way Ashley had looked that day on the sidelines. Posing prettily, clapping . . . wanting Will to notice her?

Why? Because Ashley was trying to win him back? And she feared Ronnie might get in the way?

With that, things began to click in place. But before she could think of what to say, Will shook his head.

"I thought you were different. I just thought . . ." He stared at her, his face a mixture of anger and disappointment, before suddenly turning away and heading for the beach. "Hell, I don't know what I thought," he tossed over his shoulder.

She took a step forward and was about to call after him when she noticed a flicker of light down the beach near the water's edge. The light rose and fell, as if someone were tossing a . . .

Fireball, she realized.

She felt her breath catch in her throat, knowing Marcus was there, and took an involuntary step backward. She had a sudden image of him sneaking toward the nest while she slept outside. She wondered how close he might have come. Why wouldn't he leave her alone? Was he stalking her?

She'd seen stories on the news and heard about things like this. Though she liked to think she would know what to do and could handle herself in almost any situation, this was different. Because Marcus was different.

Because Marcus scared her.

Will was already a couple of houses down the beach, his figure vanishing in the night. She thought about calling him back and telling him everything, but the last thing she wanted was to stay outside any longer than she had to. Nor did she want Marcus to connect her to Will. In any case, there was no her and Will. Not anymore, anyway. Now it was just her.

And Marcus.

Panicking, she took another step back, then forced herself to stop. If he knew she was scared, it might make things worse. Instead, she forced herself into the circle of the porch light and deliberately turned to stare in Marcus's direction.

She couldn't see him—only the flicker of light as it bobbed up and down. Marcus, she knew, wanted her to be scared, which set something off inside her. Continuing to stare at him, she put her hands on her hips and raised her chin defiantly in his direction. Her blood pounded in her chest, but she held her position even as the fireball settled in his hand. A moment later, the light went out and she knew Marcus had closed his fist over it, announcing his approach.

Still, she refused to move. She wasn't certain what she'd do if he suddenly appeared only a few yards away, but as the seconds became one minute and then another, she knew he'd decided it was best to stay away. Tired of waiting and satisfied that she'd conveyed her message, she turned and headed back inside.

It was only as she leaned against the door after closing it that she realized her hands were shaking.

15

.... ♪ ....

Marcus

I want to get something to eat at the diner before it closes," Blaze pleaded.

"Then go," Marcus said. "I'm not hungry."

Blaze and Marcus were at Bower's Point, along with Teddy and Lance, who'd picked up two of the ugliest girls Marcus had ever seen and were in the process of getting them drunk. Marcus had been annoyed to find them here in the first place, and then Blaze had been hounding him for the past hour, asking where he'd been all day.

He got the feeling she knew it had something to do with Ronnie, because Blaze wasn't stupid. Blaze had known all along that Marcus was interested in her, which explained why she'd planted those CDs in Ronnie's bag. It was the perfect solution to get Ronnie to keep her distance . . . which meant that Marcus wouldn't have a chance to see Ronnie either.

That pissed him off. And then to find her here, whining about being hungry and hanging all over him and pestering him with questions . . .

"I don't want to go alone," she whined again.

"Didn't you hear me?" he snarled. "Do you ever listen to a single thing I say? I said I'm not hungry."

"I'm not saying you have to eat anything . . . ," Blaze mumbled, subdued.

"Would you just shut up about it?"

That stopped her. At least for a few minutes, anyway. He could tell by the way she was pouting that she wanted him to apologize for something. Yeah, well, it wasn't going to happen.

Turning toward the water, he lit his fireball, angry at the fact that she was still here. Angry that Teddy and Lance were here, when he wanted some peace and quiet. Angry at the fact that Blaze had run Ronnie off and especially angry that he was angry about any of it. It wasn't like him, and he hated the way it made him feel. He wanted to hit something or someone, and when he glanced at Blaze and saw her pouting, she was tops on the list. He turned away, wishing he could drink his beer and turn up the music and just think in private for a while. Without all these people crowding him.

Besides, he wasn't really angry at Blaze. Hell, when he'd first heard what she'd done, he'd been kind of pleased about it, thinking it might smooth the road between him and Ronnie. You scratch my back, I scratch yours, that kind of thing. But when he'd suggested it to Ronnie, she'd reacted like he had some kind of disease, like she'd rather die than come near him. But he wasn't the type to give up, and he figured she'd eventually come to realize it was her only way out of this mess. So he'd gone to her house for a little visit, hoping for a chance to talk. He'd decided he would tone down the act and instead listen sympathetically when she talked about the awful thing that Blaze did. They might have gone for a walk and maybe ended up under the pier, and then whatever happened, happened. Right?

But when he got to her house, Will was there. Of all people, Will, just sitting there on that dune, waiting to talk to her. And Ronnie eventually did come outside and talk with him. Actually, they seemed to argue, but by the way they were acting, there was plainly something between them, which pissed him off, too.

Because it meant they knew each other. Because it meant they were probably an item.

Which meant he'd been reading her all wrong.

And then? Oh, that was the kicker. After Will left, Ronnie realized that she had two visitors, not just one. When she noticed him watching her, he knew one of two things was going to happen. Either she'd come out and talk to him in the hopes of getting Blaze to tell the truth, or she'd act all scared like she had earlier and run inside. He liked the fact that he could scare her. He could use it to his advantage.

But she did neither of those things. Instead, she stared in his direction as if to say, *Bring it on*. She stood on the porch, her body language signaling angry defiance, until finally she went back into the house.

No one did that to him. Especially girls. Who in the hell did she think she was? Tight little body or not, he didn't like it. He didn't like it at all.

Blaze interrupted his thoughts. "Are you sure you don't want to come?"

Marcus turned toward her, feeling the sudden urge to clear his mind, to cool off. He knew just what he needed and who would give it to him.

"Come here," he said. He forced a smile. "Sit next to me. I don't want you to go just yet."

16

$\cdots\cdots\int\cdots\cdots$

Steve

Steve looked up as Ronnie came back inside. Though she flashed a smile, trying to assure him that nothing was wrong, he couldn't help noticing her expression as she grabbed her book and made for her bedroom.

Something was definitely wrong.

He just wasn't sure what. He couldn't tell whether she was sad or angry or scared, and while he debated the idea of trying to talk to her, he was pretty certain that whatever was going on, she wanted to handle it alone. He supposed that was normal. He may not have spent much time recently with her, but he'd taught teenagers for years, and he knew that it was when your kids wanted to talk to you—when they had something important to say—that your stomach should clench with worry.

"Hey, Dad," Jonah said.

While Ronnie had been outside, he'd forbidden Jonah from watching through the window. It seemed like the right thing to do, and Jonah had sensed it was best not to argue. He'd found *SpongeBob* on one of the channels and had been watching happily for the last fifteen minutes.

"Yes?"

Jonah stood up, his expression serious. "What has one eye, speaks French, and loves cookies before bedtime?"

Steve considered the question. "I have no idea."

Jonah reached up and covered one eye with his hand. "*Moi.*"

Steve laughed as he rose from the couch, putting down his Bible. The kid made him laugh a lot. "Come on. I have some Oreos in the kitchen." They headed that way.

"I think Ronnie and Will had a fight," Jonah said, pulling up his pajamas.

"Is that his name?"

"Don't worry. I checked him out."

"Ah," Steve said. "Why do you think they had a fight?"

"I could hear them. Will sounded mad."

Steve frowned at him. "I thought you were watching cartoons."

"I was. But I could still hear them," Jonah said matter-of-factly.

"You shouldn't listen in on other people's conversations," Steve chided.

"But sometimes they're interesting."

"It's still wrong."

"Mom tries to listen in on Ronnie when she's talking on the phone. And she sneaks Ronnie's phone when she's in the shower and checks her text messages."

"She does?" Steve tried not to sound too surprised.

"Yeah. How else would she keep track of her?"

"I don't know . . . maybe they could talk," he suggested.

"Yeah, right," Jonah snorted. "Even Will can't talk to her without arguing. She drives people crazy."

When Steve was twelve, he had few friends. Between attending school and practicing the piano, he had little free time, and the person he most often found himself talking to was Pastor Harris.

By that point in his life, the piano had become an obsession, and Steve would often practice for four to six hours a day, lost in his own world of melody and composition. By that point, he'd won numerous local and state competitions. His mother had attended only the first one, and his father never made it to any. Instead, he would often find himself in the front seat of the car with Pastor Harris as they traveled to Raleigh or Charlotte or Atlanta or Washington, D.C. They spent long hours talking, and though Pastor Harris was a religious man and worked the blessings of Christ into most conversations, it always sounded as natural as someone from Chicago commenting on the endless futility of the Cubs during the pennant race.

Pastor Harris was a kind man who led a harried life. He took his calling seriously, and on most evenings he would tend to his flock, either at the hospital or at a funeral home or at the homes of congregation members he had come to consider friends. He performed weddings and baptisms on the weekends, he had fellowship on Wednesday nights, and on Tuesdays and Thursdays he worked with the choir. But every evening in the hour before dusk and no matter what the weather, he reserved for himself an hour to walk the beach alone. When he returned, Steve often found himself thinking that the hour of solitude had been just what the pastor needed. There was something settled and peaceful in his expression whenever he returned from those walks. Steve had always assumed that it was the pastor's way of reclaiming a bit of solitude—until he'd asked him about it.

"No," Pastor Harris had replied. "I don't walk the beach to be alone, because that's not possible. I walk and talk with God."

"You mean pray?"

"No," Pastor Harris said again. "I mean talk. Never forget that God is your friend. And like all friends, He longs to hear what's been happening in your life. Good or bad, whether it's been full of sorrow or anger, and even when you're questioning why terrible things have to happen. So I talk with him."

"What do you say?"

"What do you say to your friends?"

"I don't have friends." Steve gave a wry smile. "At least any that I can talk to."

Pastor Harris laid a reassuring hand on his shoulder. "You have me." When he didn't respond, Pastor Harris gave his shoulder a squeeze. "We talk in the same way that you and I do."

"Does He answer?" Steve was skeptical.

"Always."

"You hear Him?"

"Yes," he said, "but not with my ears." He put a hand to his chest. "This is where I hear the answers. This is where I feel His presence."

After kissing Jonah on the cheek and tucking him in bed, Steve paused just inside the door to study his daughter. Surprising him, Ronnie was asleep when they entered the room, and whatever had been bothering her when she came back inside was no longer in evidence. Her face was relaxed, her hair cascaded over her pillow, and she had both arms tucked close to her chest. He debated whether or not to kiss her good night but decided to leave her be, allowing her dreams to drift without interruption, like snowmelt flowing downstream, to the places they were meant to go.

Still, he couldn't bring himself to leave just yet. There was something calming about watching both of his children sleep, and as Jonah rolled to the side, away from the hall light, he wondered how long it had been since he'd kissed Ronnie good night. In the year or so before he'd separated from Kim, Ronnie had reached the age where she found such things embarrassing. He distinctly remembered the first night that he said he'd come tuck her in, only to hear her respond, "You don't have to. I'll be okay." Kim had looked at him then with an expression of eloquent sorrow: She'd known that Ronnie was growing up, but even so, the passing of childhood left an ache in her heart.

Unlike Kim, Steve didn't begrudge Ronnie the fact that she

was growing up. He thought back to his life at the same age and remembered making his own decisions. He remembered forming his own ideas about the world, and his years as a teacher only reinforced the idea that change not only was inevitable, but usually brought its own rewards. There were times when he would find himself in a classroom with a student, listening as the student told him about his struggles with his parents, about how his mother tried to be his friend or how his father tried to control him. Other teachers in the department seemed to feel that he had a natural rapport with students, and often, when the students left, he was surprised to discover that many students felt the same way. He wasn't sure why. Most of the time, he either listened in silence or simply reframed their questions, forcing the students to reach their own conclusions and trusting that in most situations, they were often the right ones. Even when he felt the need to say something, he usually volunteered only the most generic comments typical of armchair psychologists. "Of course your mom wants to be your friend," he might offer, "she's beginning to think of you more as an adult she wants to know." Or, "Your dad knows he made mistakes in his life, and he doesn't want you to make the same ones." Ordinary thoughts from an ordinary man, but to his amazement, the student would sometimes turn toward the window in silence, as if absorbing something profound. Sometimes he'd even receive a call from the student's parents afterward, thanking him for talking to their child and noting that he seemed to be in a better mood lately. When he hung up the phone, he would try to remember what he'd said in the hope that he had been more insightful than he realized, but he always came up empty.

In the silence of the room, Steve heard Jonah's breathing begin to slow. He knew his son had already fallen asleep; the sun and endless fresh air seemed to exhaust him in ways that Manhattan never could. As for Ronnie, he was relieved that sleep had erased the tension of the last few days. Her face was serene, almost angelic, and somehow reminded him of the way Pastor Harris looked after his walks on the beach. He watched her in the utter stillness of that room, longing again for a sign of God's presence. Tomorrow Ronnie might be leaving, and at the thought, he took a hesitant step toward her. Moonlight drifted through the window, and he heard the steady drone of ocean waves beyond the glass. The tender fire of distant stars flickered a heavenly affirmation, as if God were announcing His presence somewhere else. Suddenly he felt tired. He was alone, he thought; he would always be alone. He bent and kissed Ronnie gently on the cheek, feeling again the undertow of his love for her, a joy as intense as pain.

Just before dawn, his waking thought—more of a sensation, really—was that he missed playing the piano. As he winced at the predictable flash of pain in his stomach, he felt the urge to rush to the living room and lose himself in his music.

He wondered when he would have an opportunity to play again. He now regretted not making the acquaintance of others in town; there had been moments since he'd boarded up the piano when he fantasized about approaching a friend with the request to play the seldom used piano in his living room, the one his imaginary friend regarded as decoration. He could see himself taking a seat on the dusty bench as his friend watched from the kitchen or the foyer—he wasn't quite clear on this—and all at once, he would begin to play something that would move his friend to tears, something he'd been unable to accomplish during all those long months on tour.

He knew it was a ridiculous fantasy, but without music he felt aimless and adrift. Rising from the bed, he forced those dark thoughts away. Pastor Harris had told him that a new piano had been ordered for the church, a gift from one of its members, and that Steve was welcome to play it as soon as it arrived. But that wouldn't be until sometime in late July, and he wasn't sure he could make it until then.

Instead, he took a seat at the kitchen table and placed his hands on the top. With enough concentration, he should be able to hear the music in his mind. Beethoven composed the *Eroica* when he was mostly deaf, hadn't he? Perhaps he could hear it all in his head, the way Beethoven had. He chose the concerto that Ronnie had played at her performance at Carnegie Hall, and closing his eyes, he concentrated. The strains were faint at first as he began to move his fingers. Gradually, the notes and chords became clearer and more distinct, and though it wasn't as satisfying as actually playing the piano, he knew it would have to do.

With the final phrases of the concerto reverberating in his mind, he slowly opened his eyes again and found himself sitting in the semidark kitchen. The sun would be poking over the horizon in just a few minutes, and for some reason, he heard the sound of a single note, a B flat, hanging long and low, beckoning him. He knew he'd only imagined it, but the sound of the note lingered, and he found himself scrambling for pen and paper.

He quickly sketched out some rough musical bars and jotted down the notes before pressing his finger to the table once more. Again it sounded, but this time it was followed by a few more notes, and he scribbled those down as well.

He'd written music throughout much of his life, but even he regarded the melodies as figurines compared with the statues he generally preferred to play. This might not amount to much, either, but he felt himself warming to the challenge. What if he was able to compose something . . . inspired? Something that would be remembered long after he was forgotten?

The fantasy didn't last long. He'd tried and failed in the past, and he had no doubt he would fail again. But even so, he felt good about what he'd done. There was something transporting about the act of creating something from nothing. Though he hadn't gotten very far on the melody—after much work, he'd reverted to the first few notes he'd written and had decided to start over—he somehow felt satisfied.

As the sun crested the dunes, Steve reflected on his thoughts of the night before and decided to go for a walk on the beach. More than anything, he wanted to return to the house with the same look of peace that he'd seen on Pastor Harris's face, but as he trudged through the sand, he couldn't help feeling like an amateur, someone who searched for God's truths like a child searching for seashells.

It would have been nice if he'd been able to spot an obvious sign of His presence—a burning bush, perhaps—but he tried instead to focus on the world around him: the sun risen out of the sea, the trill of morning birdsong, the lingering mist atop the water. He strove to absorb the beauty without conscious thought, trying to feel the sand beneath his feet and the breeze as it caressed his cheek. Despite his efforts, he didn't know if he was getting any closer to his answer than when he'd started.

What was it, he wondered for the hundredth time, that enabled Pastor Harris to hear the answers in his heart? What did he mean when he said he felt God's presence? Steve supposed he could ask Pastor Harris directly, but he doubted that would do any good. How could anyone explain such a thing? It would be like describing colors to someone blind from birth: The words might be understood, but the concept would remain mysterious and private.

It was odd for him to think such thoughts. Until recently, he'd never been plagued by such questions, but he figured his daily responsibilities had always kept him busy enough to avoid thinking about them, at least until he'd returned to Wrightsville Beach. Here, time had slowed with the pace of his life. As he continued to walk the beach, he reflected again on the fateful decision he'd made to try his luck as a concert pianist. It's true that he'd always wondered whether he could succeed, and yes, he had felt that time was running out. But how had those thoughts acquired such urgency at the time? Why had he been so willing to leave his family for months at a time? How, he wondered, could he have been so selfish? In retrospect, it hadn't proved to be a wise decision for any of them. He'd once thought that his passion for music had forced the decision, but he now suspected that he'd really been searching for ways to fill the emptiness he sometimes felt inside him.

And as he walked, he began to wonder whether it was in this realization that he would eventually find his answer.

17

·····♪·····

Ronnie

When Ronnie woke, she glanced at the clock, relieved that for the first time since she'd arrived, she'd managed to sleep in. It wasn't late, but as she climbed out of bed, she actually felt somewhat refreshed. She could hear the television in the living room, and leaving the bedroom, she immediately spotted Jonah. He was lying on the couch on his back, his head dangling off the cushion as he stared intently at the screen. His neck, exposed as if in preparation for the guillotine, was sprinkled with Pop-Tarts crumbs. She watched as he took another bite, scattering more crumbs on himself and the rug.

She didn't want to ask. She knew the answer wouldn't make sense, but she couldn't help it.

"What are you doing?"

"I'm watching TV upside down," he answered. He was watching one of those irritating Japanese cartoons with big-eyed creatures that she never did understand.

"Why?"

"Because I want to."

"And again I ask, why?"

"I don't know."

She knew she shouldn't have asked. Instead, she glanced toward the kitchen. "Where's Dad?"

"I don't know."

"You don't know where Dad is?"

"I'm not his babysitter." He sounded annoyed.

"When did he leave?"

"I don't know."

"Was he here when you got up?"

"Uh-huh." His gaze never wavered from the TV. "We talked about the window."

"And then . . ."

"I don't know."

"Are you saying he just vanished into thin air?"

"No. I'm saying that after that, Pastor Harris came by and they went outside to talk." He made it sound as though the answer were obvious.

"Then why didn't you say that?" Ronnie threw up her hands in exasperation.

"Because I'm trying to watch my show while I'm *upside down*. It's not easy to talk to you with the blood rushing to my head."

He'd set himself up for any number of snappy comebacks— *Maybe you should be upside down more often, then,* for instance— but she didn't give in to temptation. Because she was in a better mood. Because she'd slept in. And best of all, because she heard a little voice inside her whisper, *You might be going home today.* No more Blaze, no more Marcus or Ashley, no more early mornings.

No more Will, either . . .

The thought gave her pause. All in all, he hadn't been so bad. Actually, she'd had a good time with him yesterday, up until the end, anyway. She really should have told him what Ashley had said; she should have explained herself. But with Marcus showing up . . .

She really, really wanted to get as far away from this place as possible.

Pulling aside the curtains, she peeked out the window. Her dad and Pastor Harris were standing in the driveway, and she realized she hadn't seen the pastor since she was a little girl. He'd changed little since then; though he now leaned on a cane, the thick white hair and eyebrows were as memorable as ever. She smiled, remembering how nice he'd been after her grandfather's funeral. She knew why her dad liked him so much; there was something infinitely kind about him, and she recalled that after the service, he'd offered her a glass of fresh lemonade that was sweeter than any soda. They seemed to be talking to someone else in the drive, someone she couldn't see. She walked to the door and opened it to get a better view. It took only an instant to recognize the squad car. Officer Pete Johnson was standing just inside the open front car door, plainly getting ready to leave.

She could hear the engine idling, and as she descended the porch steps, her dad offered a tentative wave. Pete swung the door shut, leaving Ronnie with a sinking feeling.

When she reached her dad and Pastor Harris, Officer Pete was already backing out of the drive, which only confirmed her sense that bad news was coming.

"You're up," her dad said. "I just checked in on you a little while ago and you were dead to the world." He motioned with his thumb. "Do you remember Pastor Harris?"

Ronnie offered her hand. "I remember. Hi again. It's good to see you."

When Pastor Harris took it, she noticed the shiny scars covering his hands and arms. "I can't believe this is the same young lady I had the good fortune of meeting so long ago. You're all grown up now." He smiled. "You look like your mother."

She'd heard that a lot lately, but she still wasn't sure what to make of it. Did it mean she looked old? Or that her mom looked young? It was hard to tell, but she knew he meant it as a compliment. "Thank you. How's Mrs. Harris doing?"

He adjusted his cane. "She's keeping me in line, just like she always has. And I'm sure she'd love to see you as well. If you find a chance to swing by the house, I'll make sure she has a jar of homemade lemonade for you."

It figured that he'd remember. "I might just take you up on that."

"I hope so." He turned to Steve. "Thank you again for offering to make the window. It's coming along beautifully."

He waved off the thanks. "You don't have to thank me . . ."

"Of course I do. But I really have to be going. I've got the Towson sisters leading Bible study this morning, and if you knew them, you'd understand why it's imperative that I don't leave them to their own devices. They're quite the fire-and-brimstone types. They love Daniel and Revelation, and seem to forget that Second Corinthians is even a chapter in the good book." He turned to Ronnie. "It was wonderful to see you again, young lady. I hope your father isn't causing you too much trouble these days. You know how parents can be."

She smiled. "He's okay."

"Good. But if he causes you any trouble, you come talk to me, and I'll do my best to set him straight. He was quite the mischievous child at times, so I can only imagine how frustrated you must get."

"I wasn't mischievous," her dad protested. "All I did was play the piano."

"Remind me to tell you about the time he put red dye in the baptismal well."

Her dad seemed mortified. "I never did that!"

Pastor Harris seemed to be enjoying himself. "Maybe not, but my point stands. No matter how he presents himself, your dad wasn't perfect."

With that, he turned and started up the drive. Ronnie watched him go, amused. Anyone who could make her dad squirm—in a harmless way, of course—was someone she definitely wanted to get to know a little better. Especially if he had stories to tell about her dad. Fun stories. *Good* stories.

Her dad's expression as he watched him go was inscrutable. When he turned back to her, however, he seemed to have reverted to the dad she knew, and she remembered again that Officer Pete had been here only a couple of minutes earlier.

"What was that all about?" she asked. "With Officer Pete."

"Why don't we have breakfast first? I'm sure you're probably starved. You barely had any dinner."

She reached for his arms. "Just tell me, Dad."

Her dad hesitated, struggling to find the right words, but there was no way he could candy-coat the truth. He sighed. "You're not going to be able to go back to New York, at least until you're arraigned next week. The store's owner intends to press charges."

Ronnie sat on the dune, less angry than frightened at the thought of what was happening inside the house. It had been an hour since her dad had told her what Officer Pete had said, and she'd been sitting out here ever since. She knew her dad was inside talking to her mom on the phone, and Ronnie could only imagine how her mom was reacting. It was the only good thing about being here at all.

Except for Will . . .

Ronnie shook her head, wondering why on earth she kept thinking about him. They were already over, assuming that they had ever really begun. Why had he been interested in her? He'd been together with Ashley for a long time, which meant he liked her type. If there was one thing she'd learned, it was that people didn't change. They liked what they liked, even if they didn't understand why. And she was nothing like Ashley.

No discussion, no debate. Because if she was like Ashley, she might as well just start swimming toward the horizon until all hope of rescue was gone. She might as well end it now.

Still, that wasn't what bothered her most. What bothered her was her mom. Her mom was no doubt hearing about the arrest, since her dad was on the phone *right now*. The idea made her cringe. Her mom was blowing a gasket, no doubt *screaming*. As soon as she hung up with Dad, she would probably call her sister or her own mom and spread the news about the latest horrible thing Ronnie had done. She was into rehashing all sorts of personal stuff, usually with just enough exaggeration to make Ronnie seem as guilty as possible. Her mom always neglected the nuances, of course. In this case, the most important nuance was that *she hadn't done it!*

But did that matter? Of course not. She could *feel* her mom's rage, and the whole thing made her sick to her stomach. Maybe it was a good thing she wasn't going home today.

Behind her, she heard her dad approach. When she glanced over her shoulder, he hesitated. She knew he was trying to figure out whether she wanted to be alone, before he gingerly took a seat beside her. He didn't say anything right away. Instead, he seemed to be watching a distant shrimp trawler anchored near the horizon.

"Was she mad?"

She already knew the answer, but she couldn't help asking.

"A little," he admitted.

"Just a little?"

"I'm pretty sure she Godzilla'd the kitchen while we were talking."

Ronnie closed her eyes, imagining the scene. "Did you tell her what really happened?"

"Of course I did. And I made sure to tell her that I was certain you were telling the truth." He put an arm around her shoulder and gave her a hug. "She'll get over it. She always does."

Ronnie nodded. In the silence, she could feel her dad studying her.

"I'm sorry you can't go home today," he said. His tone was soft and apologetic. "I know how much you hate it here."

"I don't hate it here," she said automatically. Surprising herself, she realized that as much as she'd been trying to convince herself otherwise, she was telling the truth. "It's just that I don't belong here."

He gave her a melancholy smile. "If it's any consolation, when I was growing up, I didn't feel like I belonged here, either. I dreamed about going to New York. But it's strange, because when I finally escaped this place, I ended up missing it more than I thought I would. There's something about the ocean that just calls to me."

She turned toward him. "What's going to happen to me? Did Officer Pete say anything more?"

"No. Just that the owner feels like she has to press charges, since the items were valuable and she's had a lot of problems with shoplifting lately."

"But I didn't do it!" Ronnie cried.

"I know," he said, "and we'll work it out. We'll find a good lawyer and take it from there."

"Are lawyers expensive?"

"Good ones are," he said.

"Can you afford that?"

"Don't worry. I'll figure something out." He paused. "Can I ask you something? What did you do that made Blaze so mad? You never told me."

Had her mom asked, she probably wouldn't have answered. Nor would she have answered her dad even a couple of days earlier. Now, she couldn't see any reason not to. "She has this weird, scary boyfriend, and she thinks I was trying to steal him away from her. Or something like that."

"What do you mean by weird and scary?"

She paused. At the water's edge, the first of the families were arriving, loaded with towels and beach toys. "I saw him last night," she said in a low voice. She pointed down the beach. "He was standing over there while I was talking to Will."

Her dad didn't try to hide his concern. "But he didn't come any closer."

She shook her head. "No. But there's something . . . off about him. Marcus . . ."

"Maybe you should keep your distance from those two. Blaze and Marcus, I mean."

"Don't worry. I wasn't planning to talk to either one of them again."

"Do you want me to call Pete? I know you haven't had a good experience with him . . ."

Ronnie shook her head. "Not yet. And believe it or not, I'm not mad at Pete at all. He was just doing his job, and actually, he was pretty understanding about the whole thing. I think he felt sorry for me."

"He told me he believes you. Which is why he talked to the owner."

She smiled, thinking how nice it was to talk to her dad like this. For an instant, she wondered how different her life would have been had he never moved away. She hesitated, scooping up a handful of sand and letting it sift through her fingers.

"Why did you leave us, Dad?" she asked. "I'm old enough for the truth, okay?"

Her dad stretched his legs out, obviously buying time. He seemed to be wrestling with something, trying to figure out how much to tell her and where to begin, before he started with the obvious. "After I stopped teaching at Juilliard, I did every show that I could. It was my dream, you know? Be a famous concert pianist? Anyway . . . I guess I should have thought more about the reality of the situation before I made the decision. But I didn't. I didn't realize how hard it was going to be on your mom." He fixed her with a serious gaze. "In the end, we just sort of . . . drifted apart."

She watched her dad as he answered, trying to read between the lines.

"There was someone else, wasn't there," she said. Her voice held no inflection.

Her dad didn't answer, and his gaze fell away. Ronnie felt something plummet inside her.

When he finally answered, he sounded tired. "I know I should have tried harder to save the marriage, and I'm sorry about that. More sorry than you'll ever know. But I want you to know something, okay? I never once stopped believing in your mom, I never once stopped believing in the endurance of our love. Even though it didn't work out in the end the way you or I wanted it to, I see you and Jonah and I think how lucky I am to have you as children. In a lifetime of mistakes, you two are the greatest things that have ever happened to me."

When he finished, she scooped up another handful of sand and let it trickle through her fingers, feeling tired again. "What am I going to do?"

"You mean about today?"

"I mean about everything."

She felt him lay a gentle hand on her back. "I think maybe your first step should be to go talk to him."

"Who?"

"Will," he said. "Do you remember when you walked past the house yesterday? When I was standing on the porch? I was watching you, thinking how natural the two of you seemed together."

"You don't even know him," Ronnie said, her voice a mixture of wonder and surprise.

"No," he said. He smiled, his expression tender. "But I know you. And you were happy yesterday."

"What if he won't talk to me?" she fretted.

"He will."

"How do you know?"

"Because I was watching, and he was happy, too."

* * *

Standing outside the lobby of Blakelee Brakes, she could only think, *I don't want to do this.* She didn't want to face him, except she also sort of wanted to and knew she had no other choice. She knew she hadn't been fair to him, and at the very least, he deserved to know what Ashley had said to her. He'd waited outside her house for hours, right?

Besides, she had to admit her father was right. She'd had a lot of fun with Will, or at least as much fun as she could have in a place like this. And there was something about him that set him apart from any of the guys she'd known. Not so much that he played volleyball and had the body of an athlete, or even that he was smarter than he let on. He wasn't afraid of her. Too many guys simply rolled over these days, thinking that being nice was all that mattered. And it did matter, but not if the guy equated being nice with being a doormat. She liked the fact that he'd taken her fishing, even though she hadn't been enthusiastic about it. It was his way of telling her, *This is who I am, and this is what I enjoy, and of all the people I know right now, I want to enjoy this experience with you.* Too often, when a guy asked her out, he picked her up without the slightest idea of what to do or where to go, eventually forcing her to come up with the plan. There was something so wishy-washy and clueless about that. Will was anything but wishy-washy, and she couldn't help liking him for that.

Which meant, of course, that she had to fix things. Steeling herself in case he was still angry, she entered the lobby. In the bay, Will and Scott were working beneath a lifted car. Scott said something to Will, who turned and saw her, but he didn't smile. Instead, he wiped his hands on a rag and started toward her.

He stopped a few feet away. Up close, his expression was unreadable. "What do you want?"

Not exactly the opening she'd hoped for, but it wasn't entirely unexpected, either.

"You were right," she said. "Yesterday, I left the game because Ashley said that I was just your latest project. She also implied that

I wasn't the first, that our day together—all the things we did and places you took me—were tricks you use with every new girl."

Will continued to stare at her. "She lied."

"I know."

"Then why did you leave me sitting outside for hours? And why didn't you say anything yesterday?"

She tucked a strand of her hair behind her ear, feeling shame well up in her chest but trying not to let it show. "I was angry and upset. And I was going to tell you, but you left before I had the chance."

"You're saying it was my fault?"

"No, not at all. There's a lot of stuff that was going on that doesn't have anything to do with you. It's been . . . difficult for the past few days." She ran a nervous hand through her hair. It felt so hot in the garage.

Will took a moment to absorb what she'd said. "Why would you believe her in the first place? You don't even know her."

She closed her eyes. Why? she wondered. *Because I'm an idiot. Because I should have trusted my instincts about her.* But she didn't say those things. She simply shook her head. "I don't know."

When she didn't seem willing to add anything else, he tucked his thumbs into his pockets. "Is that all you came to say? Because I've got to get back to work."

"I also wanted to apologize," she said, her voice subdued. "I'm sorry. I overreacted."

"Yeah, you did," Will shot back. "You were completely irrational. Anything else?"

"And I also wanted you to know that I had a really good time yesterday. Well, up until the end, anyway."

"Okay."

She wasn't sure what his answer meant, but when he flashed a brief smile, she felt herself begin to relax.

"'Okay?' That's it? That's all you're going to say after I came all the way down here to apologize? 'Okay'?"

Instead of answering, Will took a step toward her, and all at once, everything happened too quickly to even make sense of it. One second he was standing three feet away from her, and in the next he had a hand on her hip and was pulling her close. Leaning in, he kissed her. His lips were soft, and he was surprisingly gentle. Maybe it was simply that he'd caught her by surprise, but even so, she found herself kissing him back. The kiss didn't last long, and it wasn't the kind of earthshaking, soul-destroying kiss common in movies these days; but even so, she was glad it happened, and for whatever reason, she realized it was exactly what she'd wanted him to do.

When he pulled back, Ronnie could feel the blood flood her cheeks. His expression was kind but serious, and there was absolutely nothing wishy-washy about it.

"The next time you're mad at me, talk to me," he said. "Don't shut me out. I don't like playing games. And by the way, I had a great time, too."

Ronnie still felt a little off balance as she walked back home. Replaying their kiss a hundred times, she still wasn't sure how it happened.

But she liked it. She liked it a lot. All of which begged the question as to why she'd simply left afterward. It felt as though they should have made plans to see each other again, but with Scott in the background staring at them with his mouth hanging open, it seemed easier to give him another quick kiss and let him get back to work. But somehow she was certain they'd see each other again, probably sooner rather than later.

He liked her. She wasn't sure why or how it happened, but he did. The thought was amazing, and she wished Kayla were here so she could talk to her about it. She supposed she could call her, but it wouldn't be the same, and besides, she wasn't even sure what she would say. She supposed she just wanted someone to listen.

As she approached the house, the door to the workshop swung

open. Jonah stepped out into the sunlight and headed toward the house.

"Hey, Jonah!" she called out.

"Oh, hey, Ronnie!" Jonah turned and started jogging toward her. When he got close, he seemed to study her. "Can I ask you a question?"

"Sure."

"Do you want a cookie?"

"What?"

"A cookie. Like an Oreo. Do you want one?"

She had no idea where this was going, for the simple reason that her brother's brain ran on tracks perpendicular, not parallel, to her own. She answered with caution. "No."

"How can you not want a cookie?"

"I just don't."

"Okay, fine," he said, waving it off. "Let's say you did want a cookie. Let's say you were *dying* for a cookie, and there were cookies in the cupboard. What would you do?"

"I'd eat a cookie?" she suggested.

Jonah snapped his fingers. "Exactly. That's all I'm saying."

"What are you saying?"

"That if people want cookies, they should get a cookie. It's what people do."

Aha, she thought. Now it makes sense. "Let me guess. Dad won't let you have a cookie?"

"No. Even though I'm practically starving to death, he won't even consider it. He says I have to have a sandwich first."

"And you don't think that's fair."

"You just said you'd get a cookie if you wanted one. So why can't I? I'm not a little kid. I can make my own decisions." He stared at her earnestly.

She brought a finger to her chin. "Hmm. I can see why this bothers you so much."

"It's not fair. If he wants a cookie, he can have one. If you want a cookie, you can have one. But if I want a cookie, the rules don't count. Like you said, it's not fair."

"So what are you going to do?"

"I'm going to eat a sandwich. Because I have to. Because the world isn't fair to ten-year-olds."

He trudged off without waiting for a response. She had to smile as she watched him go. Maybe later, she thought, she'd take him out for an ice cream. For a moment, she debated whether or not to follow him into the house, then she changed her mind and headed to the workshop. She figured it was probably time to see the window that she'd heard so much about.

From the door, she could see her dad soldering some lead together.

"Hey, sweetheart. Come on in."

Ronnie stepped inside, really taking in the workshop for the first time. She wrinkled her nose at the weird animals on the shelves and eventually wandered to the table, where she saw the window. As far as she could tell, they still had a long way to go; it wasn't even a quarter complete, and if the pattern was any indication, there were probably hundreds of pieces to go.

After finishing with the piece, her dad stood straighter and rolled his shoulders. "The table's a little low for me. It gets to me after a while."

"Do you need some Tylenol?"

"No, I'm just getting old. Tylenol can't do much to fix that."

She smiled before walking away from the table. Tacked to the wall, next to a newspaper article describing the fire, was a photograph of the window. She leaned in closer to get a better look before she turned to face him. "I talked to him," she said. "I went over to the garage where he works."

"And?"

"He likes me."

Her dad shrugged. "He should. You're a catch."

Ronnie smiled, feeling a surge of gratitude. She wondered, but couldn't quite remember, if he'd always been this nice. "Why are you making the window for the church? Because Pastor Harris is letting you stay in the house?"

"No. I would have made one anyway . . ." He trailed off. In the silence, Ronnie was looking at him expectantly. "It's a long story. Are you sure you want to hear it?"

She nodded.

"I was maybe six or seven when I first wandered into Pastor Harris's church. I took refuge there to get out of the rain—I mean, it was pouring and I was soaked. When I heard him playing the piano, I remember thinking that he'd tell me I couldn't stay. But he didn't. Instead, he brought me a blanket and a cup of soup, and he called my mom so she could come pick me up. But before she got there, he let me play the piano. I was just a little kid, banging on the keys, but . . . anyway, I ended up going back the next day and he eventually became my first piano teacher. He had this great love of music. He used to tell me that beautiful music was akin to angels singing, and I just got hooked. I went to the church every day and I'd play for hours beneath the original window, with this heavenly light cascading around me. That's the image I always see when I recall the hours I spent there. This beautiful flood of light. And a few months ago, when the church burned . . ."

He motioned to the article on the wall. "Pastor Harris almost died that night. He was inside doing a last minute rewrite on his sermon, and he barely got out. The church . . . it went up in minutes and the whole place burned to the ground. Pastor Harris was in the hospital for a month, and since then he's been holding services in an old warehouse that someone is letting him use. It's dingy and dark, but I figured it was only temporary until he told me that the insurance covered only half the damage, and there was no way they could afford a new window. I just couldn't imagine that. The church wouldn't be the same place I remember, and it wouldn't be right. So I'm going to finish it." He cleared his throat. "I need to finish it."

As he spoke, Ronnie found herself trying to picture her dad as a child at the church piano, her gaze flitting from him to the photograph to the partly constructed window on the table.

"You're doing a good thing."

"Yeah, well . . . we'll see how it turns out at the end. But Jonah seems to like working on it."

"Oh, about Jonah. He's pretty bitter about the fact you wouldn't let him have a cookie."

"He needed lunch first."

She smirked. "I'm not arguing. I just thought it was funny."

"Did he tell you he already had two cookies today?"

"I'm afraid he didn't mention that."

"I figured." He stacked his gloves on the table. "You want to have lunch with us?"

She nodded. "Yeah. I think I do."

They headed toward the door. "By the way," he said, trying to sound casual, "am I ever going to have a chance to meet the young man who likes my daughter?"

She slid past him, into the sunlight. "Probably."

"How about inviting him over for dinner. And maybe afterwards we can . . . you know, do what we used to do," her dad said tentatively.

Ronnie thought about it. "I don't know, Dad. It can get kind of heated."

"I'll tell you what. I'll let you decide, okay?"

18

. . . . ♪ . . . .

Will

C'mon, man. You've got to keep your head in the game. If you do that, we'll crush Landry and Tyson in the tournament."

Will tossed the ball from one hand to the other as he and Scott stood in the sand, still sweating from the final volleys. It was late afternoon. They'd finished up at the garage at three and had raced over to the beach for a scrimmage against a couple of teams from Georgia that were spending the week in the area. They were all preparing for the southeastern tournament later that August, which was going to be held at Wrightsville Beach.

"They haven't lost yet this year. And they just won the junior nationals," Will pointed out.

"So? We weren't there. They beat a bunch of scrubs."

In Will's humble opinion, the competition at the junior national tournament weren't scrubs. In Scott's world, however, anyone who lost was a scrub.

"They beat us last year."

"Yes, but last year you were even worse than you are now. I had to carry the entire load."

"Thanks."

"I'm just saying. You're inconsistent. Like yesterday? After that chick from the Lost Boys stormed off? You played the rest of the game like you were blind."

"She's not the chick from the Lost Boys. Her name is Ronnie."

"Whatever. Do you know what your problem is?"

Yes, Scott, please tell me my problem, Will thought. I'm dying to hear what you think. Scott went on, oblivious to Will's thoughts.

"Your problem is that you're not *focused*. One little thing happens, and you're off in never-never land. Oh, I spilled Elvira's soda on her, so I'll miss the next five digs. Oh, Vampira got mad at Ashley, so I better miss the next two serves—"

"Would you stop?" Will interrupted.

Scott seemed confused. "Stop what?"

"Stop calling her names."

"See! That's exactly what I'm talking about! I'm not talking about her. I'm talking about you and your lack of *focus*. Your inability to concentrate on the game."

"We just won two straight sets, and they only scored seven points total! We crushed them," Will protested.

"But they shouldn't have even had five points. We should have shut them out."

"Are you serious?"

"Yeah, I'm serious. They're not very good."

"But we won! Isn't that enough?"

"Not if you could win by more. We could have broken their spirit, so that when they meet us in the tournament, they'd give up before the game even starts. It's called psychology."

"I think it's called running the score up."

"Well, that's just because you're not thinking straight, or you never would have ended up mashing faces with Cruella de Vil."

Elvira, Vampira, and now Cruella. At least, Will thought, he wasn't recycling any material.

"I think you're jealous," Will said.

"No. Personally, I think you should go out with Ashley, so I can go out with Cassie."

"You're still thinking about that?"

"Hello? Who else would I be thinking about? You should have seen her in her bikini yesterday."

"So ask her out."

"She won't go." Scott frowned in consternation. "It's like a package deal or something. I don't understand it."

"Maybe she thinks you're ugly."

Scott glared at him before forcing out a fake laugh. "Ha-ha! That is so funny. You should really try booking yourself on *Letterman*." His glare remained fixed on Will.

"I'm just saying."

"Well, don't, okay? And what is it with you and . . ."

"Ronnie?"

"Yeah. What was that about? Yesterday, you spent your whole day off with her, and then she shows up this morning and you kiss her? Are you, like . . . serious about her or something?"

Will remained silent.

Scott shook his head as he raised a finger, emphasizing his point. "See, here's the thing. The last thing you need is to get serious with a girl. You need to concentrate on what's important. You've got a full-time job, you volunteer trying to save the dolphins or whales or turtles or whatever, and you know how much we have to practice to get ready for the tournament. You don't have enough time as it is!"

Will said nothing, but he could see Scott growing more panicked with every passing second.

"Ah, come on, man! Don't do this to me. What on earth do you see in her?"

Will said nothing.

"No, no, no," Scott repeated like a mantra. "I knew this was going to happen. That's why I told you to go out with Ashley! So you wouldn't get serious again. You know what's going to happen.

You're going to turn into a hermit. You're going to blow off your friends so you can hang out with her. Trust me, the last thing you need is to get serious with . . ."

"Ronnie," Will filled in.

"Whatever," Scott snapped. "You're missing the point."

Will smiled. "Did you ever realize you have more opinions about my life than your own life?"

"That's because I don't mess things up like you do."

Will gave an involuntary twitch, flashing back to the night of the fire and wondering if Scott was really so clueless.

"I don't want to talk about it," Will said, but he realized that Scott wasn't listening. Instead, his gaze was focused over Will's shoulder, on a spot down the beach.

"You've got to be kidding," Scott mumbled.

Will turned around and saw Ronnie approaching. In jeans and a dark T-shirt, of course, looking as out of place as a crocodile in Antarctica. A huge grin spread over his face.

He started toward her, drinking in the sight of her, wondering again what she was thinking. He loved the fact that he couldn't completely figure her out.

"Hey," he said, reaching for her.

She stopped, just out of reach. Her expression was serious. "Don't kiss me. Just listen, okay?"

Sitting beside him in the truck, Ronnie remained as enigmatic as ever. She stared out the window, smiling faintly, seemingly content to watch the scenery.

Ronnie brought her hands together in her lap. "I want you to know my dad won't care that you're wearing shorts and a tank top."

"It's only going to take a few minutes."

"But it's supposed to be a casual dinner."

"I'm hot and sweaty. I'm not going to come to your house for dinner with your dad dressed like a bum."

"But I just said he won't care."

"I care, though. Unlike some people, I like to make a good impression."

Ronnie bristled. "Are you saying I don't?"

"Of course not. For instance, everyone I know loves to meet people with purple hair."

Though she knew he was teasing, her eyes widened and then narrowed suddenly. "You don't seem to have a problem with it."

"Yes, but that's because I'm special."

She crossed her arms and stared at him. "Are you going to be like this all night?"

"Like what?"

"Like someone with no shot of ever, ever kissing me again?"

He laughed and turned toward her. "I apologize. I didn't mean it. And actually, I like the purple streaks. It's . . . who you are."

"Yeah, well, you'll just have to learn to be more careful with what you say next time." As she spoke, she opened his glove compartment and began sifting through it.

"What are you doing?"

"Just looking. Why? Are you hiding something?"

"Feel free to sort through all of it. And while you're at it, maybe you could straighten it up a bit."

She pulled out a bullet and held it up so he could see. "I suppose this is what you use to kill ducks, right?"

"No, that's for deer. It's too big for a duck. The duck would be shredded to pieces if I shot it with that."

"You have serious problems, you know."

"So I've heard."

She giggled before settling into silence. They were on the intracoastal side of the island, and between the ever-growing sprawl of houses, the sun was glinting off the water. She closed the glove compartment and lowered the visor. Noticing a photograph of a lovely blonde, she pulled it out and examined it.

"She's pretty," Ronnie commented.

"Yeah, she is."

"Ten bucks says you posted this on your Facebook page."

"You lose. That's my sister."

He watched as her gaze flickered from the photo to his wrist, eyeing the macramé wristband.

"What's with the matching bracelets?" she asked.

"My sister and I make them."

"To support a worthy cause, no doubt."

"No," he said, and when he said nothing else, he was impressed that she seemed to intuit that he didn't want to say anything more. Instead, she carefully tucked the photo back in place and lifted the visor again.

"How far away do you live?" Ronnie asked.

"We're almost there," Will assured her.

"If I'd known it was this far away, I would have walked home. Since we're heading farther and farther away from my house, I mean."

"But you would have missed my scintillating conversation."

"Is that what you call it?"

"Do you plan on insulting me some more?" He glanced at her. "I just need to know whether or not to turn up the music so I don't have to hear it."

"You know you shouldn't have kissed me earlier. It wasn't exactly romantic," Ronnie shot back.

"I thought it was very romantic."

"We were in a garage, you had grease on your hands, and your buddy was gawking."

"A perfect setting," he said.

As he slowed the car, he flipped down his visor. Then, after making a turn, he came to a stop as he pressed the remote. Two wrought-iron gates slowly slid open, and the truck rolled forward again. Excited at the prospect of having dinner with Ronnie's family later that evening, Will didn't seem to notice that Ronnie had gone quiet.

19

....✦....

Ronnie

Okay, she thought, this was ridiculous. Not just the grounds with the sculptured rose gardens and hedges and marble statues, or the massive Georgian mansion supported by elegant columns, or even the overpriced exotic cars that were being waxed by hand in an area reserved for such things—but all of it.

It wasn't just ridiculous. It was beyond ridiculous.

Yeah, she knew there were rich people in New York with twenty-three-room apartments on Park Avenue and houses in the Hamptons, but it wasn't as if she'd ever spent time with those people or been invited to those homes. The closest she'd ever come to seeing a place like this was in magazines, and even then, most of those had been flyover shots taken by paparazzi.

And here she was, wearing a T-shirt and torn jeans. Nice. At the very least, he could have warned her.

She continued to stare at the house as the truck zipped up the drive, turning in to the roundabout in front of the house. He came to a stop directly in front of the entrance. She turned to him and was about to ask whether he actually lived here, then realized it was a stupid question. Obviously he lived here. By then, he was already getting out of the truck.

Following suit, she opened her door and stepped outside. The two men washing the cars glanced at her before quickly going back to work.

"Like I said, I'm just going to rinse off. It won't take long."

"Fine," she said. Really, there wasn't anything else she could think to say. It was the largest house she'd ever seen in her life.

She followed him up the steps that led to the porch and paused briefly at the door, just long enough to see a small brass plaque posted near the door that read, "*The Blakelees.*"

As in Blakelee Brakes. As in the national automotive chain. As in Will's dad didn't simply own an individual franchise but had probably started the entire business.

She was still trying to process that simple fact as Will pushed open the door and led her into a massive foyer centerpieced by a grand staircase. A dark-paneled library beckoned on her right, while some kind of music room opened to the left. Directly ahead lay a huge, sun-filled open room, and beyond that, she saw the sparkling waters of the Intracoastal Waterway.

"You didn't tell me your last name was Blakelee," Ronnie mumbled.

"You didn't ask." He gave an indifferent shrug. "Come on in."

He led her past the staircase toward the great room. At the back of the house, she saw a massive covered veranda; near the water, she caught sight of what could only be described as a mid-size yacht parked at the dock.

Okay, she admitted it. She felt out of place here, and the fact that everyone probably felt out of place the first time they came here was no consolation. She might as well have landed on Mars.

"Can I get you something to drink while I get ready?"

"Um, no, I'm okay. Thanks," she said, trying not to gawk at her surroundings.

"You want me to show you around first?"

"I'm fine."

Somewhere ahead and off to the side, she heard a voice calling out.

"Will? Did I hear you come in?"

Ronnie turned to see an attractive woman in her early fifties, wearing an expensive linen pantsuit and holding a wedding magazine, step into view.

"Hey, Mom," he said. He tossed his truck keys into a bowl perched on the entry table, right next to the vase of fresh-cut lilies. "I brought someone over. This is Ronnie. And this is my mom, Susan."

"Oh. Hello, Ronnie," Susan said coolly.

Though Susan tried to hide it, Ronnie could tell she wasn't pleased about having been surprised by Will's unexpected guest. Her displeasure, Ronnie couldn't help but think, had less to do with the *unexpected* part than the *guest* part. Namely, her.

But if Ronnie noticed the tension, Will obviously didn't. Maybe, Ronnie thought, it was a woman thing to be able to sense things like that, because Will went on chatting with his mom with casual ease.

"Is Dad around?" he asked.

"I believe he's in his office."

"Before I go, I need to talk to him."

Susan shifted the magazine from one hand to the other. "You're leaving?"

"I'm having dinner with Ronnie's family tonight."

"Oh," she said. "That's wonderful."

"You'll like this. Ronnie's a vegetarian."

"Oh," Susan said again, turning to scrutinize Ronnie. "Is that right?"

Ronnie felt as if she were shrinking. "Yes."

"Interesting," Susan said. While Ronnie could see that it was anything but interesting to Susan, Will remained oblivious.

"Okay, so I'm just going to pop upstairs for a few minutes. I'll be right back."

Though Ronnie felt like telling him to *hurry*, she didn't. "Okay," she offered instead.

With a couple of long, loping steps, he was heading up the stairs, leaving Ronnie and Susan facing each other. In the ensuing silence, Ronnie was acutely conscious of the fact that as little as they had in common, they were united in their unhappiness at being left alone with each other.

Ronnie felt like strangling Will. The least he could have done was warn her.

"So," Susan said, forcing a smile. She looked almost plastic. "You're the one with the turtle nest behind your house?"

"That's me."

Susan nodded. She'd obviously run out of things to say, so Ronnie struggled to fill the silence. She motioned toward the foyer. "You have a beautiful home."

"Thank you."

With that, Ronnie was at a loss for words, and for a long moment, they faced each other awkwardly. She had no idea what would have happened if the two of them had remained alone. But thankfully they were joined by a man in his fifties or early sixties, dressed casually in Dockers and a polo.

"I thought I heard someone come in," he said, walking toward them. His demeanor was friendly, almost jocular, as he approached. "I'm Tom, aka Will's dad, and you're Ronnie, right?"

"It's a pleasure to meet you," she responded.

"I'm glad I finally have a chance to meet the girl he's been talking about."

Susan cleared her throat. "Will is going to be joining Ronnie and her family for dinner."

Tom turned toward Ronnie. "I hope you don't make anything fancy. The kid lives on pepperoni pizza and burgers."

"Ronnie is a vegetarian," Susan added. Ronnie couldn't help noticing that Susan said it in the same way another person might have said she was a *terrorist*. Or maybe not. Ronnie couldn't exactly tell. Will really, really should have warned her about what to expect, so she could have at least been prepared. But Tom, like Will, didn't seem to notice.

"No kidding? That's great. At least he'll eat healthy for a change." He paused. "I know you're waiting for Will, but do you have a few minutes? I want to show you something."

"I'm sure she's not interested in your airplane, Tom," Susan protested.

"I don't know. Maybe she is," he said. Turning to Ronnie, he asked, "Do you like airplanes?"

Of course, she thought, why wouldn't the family have an airplane? Let's just add *that* to the equation. This whole mess was Will's fault. She was going to *kill* him as soon as she got out of here. But what choice did she have?

"Yeah," she said. "Of course I like airplanes."

She supposed she had an image in mind—a Learjet or Gulfstream parked in a personal hangar on the far side of the property—but it was a fuzzy image, since the only private jets she'd ever seen were in photographs. Still, this wasn't what she'd expected at all: the sight of someone older than her father flying a remote-control toy airplane and concentrating on the controls.

The plane whined as it skirted over the trees, swooping low over the Intracoastal Waterway.

"I've always wanted one of these things, and I finally broke down and got one. Actually, this is the second one. The first one accidentally ended up in the water."

"That's too bad," Ronnie sympathized.

"Yeah, but it taught me that I should probably read all the directions next time."

"Did you crash it?"

"No, it ran out of gas." He glanced at her. "Do you want to try?"

"I'd better not," Ronnie demurred. "I'm not good at things like that."

"It's not too hard," Tom assured her. "This is one of the beginner planes. It's supposed to be idiot-proof. Of course, the last one was, too, so what does that tell you?"

"That maybe you should have read the directions?"

"Right," he said. There was something about the way he said it that made him sound just like Will.

"Did you and Susan talk about the wedding?" he asked.

Ronnie shook her head. "No. Will mentioned something about it, though."

"I had to spend two hours today at the florist's looking at flower arrangements. Have you ever spent two hours looking at flower arrangements?"

"No."

"Consider yourself lucky."

Ronnie giggled, relieved to be out here with him. Just then Will came up behind her, freshly showered and dressed neatly in a polo shirt and shorts. Both name brand, but she supposed she should have expected that.

"You'll have to forgive my dad. He sometimes forgets he's an adult," Will quipped.

"At least I'm honest. And I didn't see you racing home to help."

"I had a volleyball game."

"Yeah, I'm sure that was the reason. And I gotta tell you, Ronnie here is a whole lot prettier than you let on."

Though Ronnie smiled with pleasure, Will cringed. "Dad . . ."

"It's true," Tom added quickly. "Don't be embarrassed." After making sure the plane was flying straight again, he glanced at Ronnie. "He gets embarrassed a lot. He used to be the shyest kid in the world. He couldn't even sit near a pretty girl without his cheeks turning bright red."

Will, meanwhile, was shaking his head in disbelief. "I can't believe you're saying this, Dad. Right in front of her."

"What's the problem?" Tom looked at Ronnie. "Does that bother you?"

"Not at all."

"See?" He tapped Will's chest, as if he'd proved his point. "She doesn't care."

"Thanks for that." He grimaced.

"What are dads for? Hey, you want to give this thing a whirl?"

"I really can't. I'm supposed to bring Ronnie home so we can have dinner."

"Listen to me. Even if they serve you eggplant on rutabaga with tofu, I want you to eat what they put in front of you and then make sure you compliment them on the meal," Tom admonished.

"It'll be probably just be pasta," Ronnie said, grinning.

"Really?" Tom seemed disappointed. "He'll eat that."

"What? You don't want me to eat?"

"It's always good to experience new things. How'd it go at the shop today?"

"That's what I needed to talk to you about. Jay said there's a problem with the computer or the software—everything keeps double printing."

"Just at the flagship or everywhere?"

"I don't know."

Tom sighed. "I suppose I'd better check it out, then. Assuming, of course, I can land this thing. And you two have a good time, okay?"

A few minutes later, after getting into the truck, Will jingled his keys before starting his engine.

"Sorry about all that. My dad sometimes says the craziest things."

"Don't be sorry. I like him."

"And I wasn't that shy, by the way. My cheeks never turned bright red."

"Of course they didn't."

"I'm serious. I was always smooth."

"I'm sure you were," she said, reaching over to pat his knee. "But listen. About tonight. My family has this weird tradition."

* * *

"You're lying!" Will shouted. "You've been lying all night and I'm sick and tired of it."

"Don't even go there!" Ronnie shouted back. "You're the one who's lying!"

The dishes from dinner had long ago been cleared—Dad had served spaghetti and marinara sauce, as predicted, with Will making sure to clean his plate—and they were now sitting at the kitchen table holding playing cards to their foreheads in a game of liar's poker. Will was holding an eight of hearts, Steve a three of hearts, and Jonah a nine of spades. Piles of change were stacked in front of each of them, and the pot in the middle overflowed with nickels and dimes.

"You're both lying," Jonah added. "Neither of you knows how to tell the truth."

Will offered Jonah his game face and reached into his pile of change. "A quarter says you don't know what you're talking about."

Her dad started shaking his head. "Bad move, young man. It's over. I'm going to have to raise you fifty cents."

"I'll see that!" Ronnie cried. Both Jonah and Will immediately followed suit.

They paused, all of them eying one another before slapping their cards down on the table. Ronnie, seeing that she'd been holding an eight, surmised that they'd all lost to Jonah. Again.

"You're all liars!" he said. His winnings, she noticed, were twice as much as anyone else's, and as she watched her brother drag the change pile toward him, she observed that at least to this point, the evening had gone pretty well. She hadn't known what to expect when she'd brought Will over, since it was the first time she'd ever brought a boy to meet her father. Would he try to give them space by hiding out in the kitchen? Would he try to become buddies with Will? Would he do or say something that embarrassed her? On the drive to her house, she'd already begun thinking of escape plans she could use as soon as they finished dinner.

As soon as they stepped inside, however, she had a good feeling. For starters, the house was picked up, Jonah was obviously under orders not to cling to their sides or question Will like a prosecutor, and her dad met Will with a simple handshake and an easygoing, "It's a pleasure to meet you." Will was on his best behavior, of course, answering questions with "Yes, sir" and "No, sir," which struck her as endearing in a southern kind of way. The dinner conversation was easy; her dad asked some questions about the work Will did at the garage and at the aquarium, and Jonah went so far as to put his napkin in his lap. Best of all, her father didn't say anything embarrassing, and though he brought up the fact that he used to teach at Juilliard, he didn't volunteer that he'd been her teacher or that she'd once played at Carnegie Hall or that they'd written songs together, nor had he mentioned the fact that until a few days ago, he and Ronnie had been completely estranged. When Jonah asked for cookies after he'd finished, both Ronnie and her dad burst out laughing, making Will wonder what was so funny. Together, the four of them pitched in to clean up the table, and when Jonah suggested that they play liar's poker, Will had agreed enthusiastically.

As for Will, he was just the kind of guy her mom wanted Ronnie to date: polite, respectful, intelligent, and best of all, sans tattoos . . . It might have been nice to have her mom there, if only to assure her that her daughter hadn't gone completely off the deep end. On the other hand, her mom probably would have been so excited about the whole thing that she would have either tried to adopt Will on the spot or gushed to Ronnie a million times after he was gone about what a nice young man he was, which only would have made Ronnie want to end the whole thing before her mom got too carried away. Her dad would do none of those things—he seemed to trust Ronnie's judgment and was content to let her make her own decisions without inserting his own opinions.

Which was really weird, considering he was only just starting to get to know her again, and also kind of sad at the same time, because she was beginning to think she'd made a big mistake by avoiding him for the past three years. It might have been nice to talk to him when her mom was driving her crazy.

All in all, she was glad she'd invited Will over. It certainly was easier for him to meet her dad than it had been for Ronnie to meet Susan. The woman scared the living daylights out of her. Well, maybe that was an exaggeration, but she was definitely intimidated. The woman had made it abundantly clear that she either didn't like Ronnie or didn't like the fact that her son liked Ronnie.

Normally, she wouldn't have cared what someone's parent thought of her, and she wouldn't have given a second thought to the way she'd been dressed. She was who she was, after all . . . This was the first time in what seemed like forever that she'd felt she didn't measure up, and it had bothered her far more than she'd thought it would.

As darkness fell and the game of liar's poker began to wind down, she sensed Will watching her. She returned his gaze with a smile.

"I'm almost out," he announced, fingering his pile of change.

"I know. I am, too."

He glanced toward the window. "Do you think it would be okay if we went for a walk?"

This time, she knew with certainty that he was asking because he wanted to spend some time alone with her—because he cared about her, even if he was unsure whether she felt the same way.

She met his eyes directly. "I'd love to go for a walk."

20

.... ♪ ....

Will

The beach stretched for miles, separated from Wilmington by the bridge over the Intracoastal Waterway. It had changed, of course, since Will was a kid—growing more congested in the summers, small bungalows like the one where Ronnie was living replaced by imposing oceanfront mansions—but he still loved the ocean at night. When he was young, he used to ride his bike over to the beach, in the hope of seeing something interesting, and he was almost never disappointed. He'd seen large sharks washed up on the beach, sand castles so intricate they could have won any national competition, and once he'd even spotted a whale, not fifty yards from shore, rolling in the water just beyond the surf.

Tonight, the place was deserted, and as he and Ronnie strolled barefoot through the breaking surf, he was struck by the thought that this was the girl with whom he'd like to face the future.

He knew he was too young for such thoughts and was under no illusion that he was even considering marriage, but somehow he felt that if he met Ronnie ten years from now, she might be the one. He knew Scott wouldn't understand the concept—Scott seemed unable to imagine a future that stretched past the upcoming weekend—but then Scott wasn't so different from most of his peers. It was as if their minds ran on separate tracks: He wasn't into one-night stands, he wasn't into scoring to see if he could, he wasn't into acting just charming enough to get what he wanted before cutting someone loose in favor of someone new and attractive. He just wasn't like that. He would never be like that. When he met a girl, the first question he asked himself wasn't whether she was good for a few dates; it was whether she was the kind of girl he could imagine spending time with over the long haul.

He supposed that had partly to do with his parents. They'd been married for thirty years, started out struggling as many couples did, and over the years had built the business and raised a family. Through it all, they had loved each other well, celebrating their successes and supporting each other during tragedy. Neither of them was perfect, but he'd grown up certain that they were a team, and eventually, he'd absorbed that lesson.

It was easy to think that he'd spent two years with Ashley because she was beautiful and rich, and though he'd be lying if he said that her beauty was irrelevant, it was less important than the things he thought he saw in her. She'd listened to him just as he'd listened to her, he'd believed he could tell her anything, and vice versa. But over time, he'd felt increasingly disappointed in her, especially when she'd tearfully admitted that she'd made out at a party with some guy from the local college. Things were never the same after that. Not because he worried that she'd do something like that again—everyone made mistakes, and it had only been a kiss—but somehow the incident helped crystallize his thoughts about what he wanted from the people he was closest to. He began to notice the way she treated other people, and he wasn't sure he liked what he saw. Her ceaseless gossiping—once something he considered harmless—began to annoy him, as did the long waits she made him endure while she readied herself to go out at night. He felt bad about eventually breaking up with her but consoled himself with the fact that he'd only been fifteen when he first started dating her, and she was the first girlfriend he'd ever had. In the end, he felt he had no other choice. He knew who he was and what was important to him, and he didn't see any of that reflected in Ashley. He figured it was better just to end the relationship before things got any harder.

His sister, Megan, was like him that way. Beautiful and smart, she'd intimidated most of the boys she'd ever dated. For a long time, she had flitted from one guy to the next, but not out of vanity or flightiness. When he'd asked why she seemed unable to settle down, her answer had been straightforward: "There are guys who grow up thinking they'll settle down some distant time in the future, and there are guys who are ready for marriage as soon as they meet the right person. The former bore me, mainly because they're pathetic; and the latter, quite frankly, are hard to find. But it's the serious ones I'm interested in, and it takes time to find a guy like that whom I'm equally interested in. I mean, if the relationship can't survive the long term, why on earth would it be worth my time and energy for the short term?"

Megan. He smiled, thinking about her. She lived her life by her own rules. She had driven Mom crazy during the last six years with her attitude, of course, since she'd quickly eliminated pretty much every guy in town who hailed from the kind of family of which his mother approved. But he had to admit, he thought Megan had gotten it right, and thankfully, she'd been able to meet a guy in New York who satisfied all her criteria.

In a strange way, Ronnie reminded him of Megan. She was an oddball, a freethinker, and stubbornly independent, too. On the surface, she was unlike anyone he could ever imagine finding attractive, but . . . her dad was great, her brother was a hoot, and she was just about as smart and caring as anyone he'd ever met. Who else would camp out all night to protect a turtle nest? Who else would stop a fight to help a little kid? Who else read Tolstoy in her spare time?

And who else, at least in this town, would fall for Will before knowing anything about his family?

That, he had to admit, was important to him, too, as much as he wished it weren't. He loved his dad and his family name, and he was proud of the business his dad had built. He appreciated the advantages that his life had brought him, but . . . he wanted to be his own person, too. He wanted people to know him first as *Will*, not *Will Blakelee*, and there wasn't another person in the world he could talk to about it, other than his sister. It wasn't as if he lived in Los Angeles, where celebrity kids could be found in every school, or was at a place like Andover, where practically everyone knew someone who came from a famous family. It wasn't so easy in a place like this, where everyone knew everybody, and as he'd grown older, he'd grown somewhat cautious about his friendships. He was willing to talk to almost anyone, but he'd learned to put up an invisible wall, at least until he was certain his family had nothing to do with the new acquaintance or was the reason a girl seemed to be interested in him. And if he hadn't known for certain that Ronnie knew nothing about his family, he'd been convinced when he'd pulled up in front of his house.

"What are you thinking about?" he heard her ask. A light breeze rippled through her hair, and she tried in vain to collect the strands into a loose ponytail. "You've been kind of quiet."

"I was thinking about how much I enjoyed coming over."

"To our little house? It's a bit different from what you're used to."

"Your house is great," he insisted. "And so is your dad and Jonah. Even though he crushed me in liar's poker."

"He always wins, but don't ask me how. I mean, ever since he was little. I think he cheats, but I haven't figured out how."

"Maybe you just need to lie better."

"Oh, you mean like you telling me you work for your dad?"

"I do work for my dad," Will said.

"You know what I mean."

"Like I told you, I didn't think it mattered." He stopped walking and turned to her. "Does it?"

She seemed to choose her words carefully. "It's interesting and it helps explain a few things about you, but if I told you that my mom worked as a paralegal at a Wall Street law firm, would you feel any different about me?"

This, he knew, he could answer with complete honesty. "No. But it's different."

"Why?" she asked. "Because your family is rich? A statement like that only makes sense to someone who thinks that money is all that matters."

"I didn't say that."

"Well, what did you mean?" she challenged, then shook her head. "Look, let's get one thing straight. I don't care if your dad is the sultan of Brunei. You happened to be born into a privileged family. What you do with that truth is completely up to you. I'm here because I want to be with you. But if I didn't, all the money in the world wouldn't have changed my feelings about you."

As she spoke, he watched her growing more animated. "Why do I get the feeling you've given that speech before?"

"Because I *have* said it before." She stopped walking and turned to face him. "Come to New York, and you'll understand why I've learned to say what I mean. In some clubs, all you meet are snobs, and they're so into who their family is or how much their family makes . . . it bores me. I stand there, and all I want to say is, *It's great that others in your family have done something, but what have you done?* But I don't, because they don't get it. They think they're the chosen ones. It's not even worth getting mad about, because the whole idea is so ridiculous. But if you think I invited you over because of who your family is—"

"I didn't," he said, cutting her off. "I never thought that for a second."

In the darkness, he knew she was considering whether he was telling the truth or simply saying what she wanted to hear. Hoping to put an end to the discussion, he turned and motioned behind them, toward the workshop near the house.

"What's that place?" he asked.

She didn't answer right away, and he sensed she was still trying to decide whether she believed him.

"It came with the house," she said at last. "My dad and Jonah are making a stained-glass window this summer."

"Your dad makes stained-glass windows?"

"He does now."

"Is that what he's always done?"

"No," she answered. "Like he told you at dinner, he used to teach piano." She paused to brush something from her feet, then changed the subject. "What's next for you? Are you going to keep working for your dad?"

He swallowed, resisting the temptation to kiss her again. "I will until the end of August. I'm going to Vanderbilt in the fall."

From one of the houses up the beach drifted the faint strains of music; squinting into the distance, Will could see a group congregated on the back deck. The song was something from the eighties, though he couldn't pinpoint it.

"That should be fun."

"I guess."

"You don't sound very excited."

Will took her hand and they began to stroll again. "It's a great school, and the campus is beautiful," he recited a little awkwardly.

She studied him. "But you don't want to go there?"

Ronnie seemed to intuit his every feeling and thought, which was both disconcerting and a source of relief. At least he could tell her the truth.

"I wanted to go somewhere else, and I got accepted at a school that has this incredible environmental science program, but my mom really wanted me to go to Vanderbilt." He could feel the sand sliding between his toes as he walked.

"Do you always do what your mom wants?"

"You don't understand," he said, shaking his head. "It's a family tradition. My grandparents went there, my parents went there,

my sister went there. My mom is on the board of trustees, and
. . . she . . ."

He struggled to find the right words. Beside him, he could sense
Ronnie watching him, but he couldn't meet her gaze.

"I know that she can be kind of . . . distant when people meet
her for the first time. But once you get to know her, she's the truest
person in the world. She would do anything—I mean *anything*—
for me. But the last few years have been really hard for her."

He stopped to pick out a seashell from the sand. After examin-
ing it, he sent it arcing toward the waves. "Do you remember
when you asked about the bracelet?"

Ronnie nodded, waiting for him to go on.

"My sister and I wear the bracelets in honor of our little brother.
His name was Mike, and he was a great little guy . . . the kind of
kid who was happiest when he was with other people. He had this
real infectious laugh, and you couldn't help but laugh along with
him when something funny happened." He paused, looking over
the water. "Anyway, four years ago, Scott and I had a basketball
game and it was my mom's turn to drive, so like always, Mike
came along with us. It had been raining all day, and a lot of the
roads were slick. I should have been paying more attention, but
Scott and I started playing mercy in the backseat. You know that
game? Where you try to bend each other's wrists in the wrong
direction until one of you gives in?"

He hesitated, trying to summon his strength for the rest of
what he had to say.

"We were really trying to get each other—wiggling and kicking the back of the seat—and my mom kept telling us to stop, but
we ignored her. In the end, I got Scott just where I wanted and I
really gave it my all and I made him scream. My mom turned
around to see what happened, and that was all it took. She lost
control of the car. And . . ." He swallowed, feeling the words
choke him. "Anyway, Mike didn't make it. Hell, without Scott,
my mom and I probably wouldn't have made it either. We went

through the guardrail and into the water. The thing is, Scott's an amazing swimmer, grew up at the beach and all that—and he managed to pull the three of us out, even though he was only twelve at the time. But Mikey . . ." Will pinched the bridge of his nose. "Mikey died on impact. He hadn't even finished his first year of kindergarten."

Ronnie reached for his hand. "I'm so sorry."

"Me, too." He blinked back the tears that still came when he thought of that day.

"You know it was an accident, right?"

"Yeah, I know. And my mom does, too. But even so, she blames herself for losing control of the car, just like I know there's a part of her that blames me, too." He shook his head. "Anyway, after that, she's always felt the need to control things. Including me. I know she's just trying to keep me safe, to keep bad things from happening, and I think part of me believes that, too. I mean, look what happened. My mom just completely lost it at the funeral, and I hated myself for doing that to her. I felt responsible. And I promised myself I would try to somehow make it up to her. Even though I knew that I couldn't."

As he spoke, he began to twist the macramé bracelet.

"What do the letters mean? IMTF?"

"In my thoughts forever. It was my sister's idea, as a way to remember him. She told me about it right after the funeral, but I barely heard her. I mean, it was just so awful to be in the church that day. With my mom screaming and my little brother in the casket, and my dad and sister crying . . . I swore that I'd never go to another funeral."

For once, Ronnie seemed at a loss for words. Will straightened up, knowing it was a lot to take in and wondering why he'd even told her. "I'm sorry. I shouldn't have told you all that."

"It's okay," she said quickly, squeezing his hand. "I'm glad you did."

"It's not the perfect life you probably imagined, is it."

"I never assumed your life was perfect."

He said nothing, and Ronnie impulsively leaned forward and kissed him on the cheek. "I wish you didn't have to go through all that."

He drew a long breath and resumed walking down the beach. "Anyway, it was important to my mom that I go to Vanderbilt. So that's where I'm going."

"I'm sure you'll have fun. I've heard it's a great school."

He laced his fingers through hers, thinking how soft they felt next to his callused skin. "Now it's your turn. What don't I know about you?"

"There's nothing like what you just told me," she said, shaking her head. "It doesn't even compare."

"It doesn't have to be important. It just has to explain who you are."

She glanced back at the house. "Well . . . I didn't talk to my dad for three years. Actually, I started talking to him only a couple of days ago. After he and my mom separated, I was . . . angry with him. I honestly never wanted to see him again, and the last thing I wanted was to spend the summer down here."

"How about now?" He noticed the moonlight shining in her eyes. "Are you glad you came?"

"Maybe," she answered.

He laughed and gave her a playful nudge. "What were you like when you were a kid?"

"Boring," she said. "All I did was play the piano."

"I'd like to hear you play."

"I don't play anymore," she said quickly, a stubborn edge to her voice.

"Ever?"

She shook her head, and though he knew there was more, she clearly didn't want to talk about it. Instead, he listened as she went on to describe her friends in New York and how she usually spent her weekends, smiling at her stories about Jonah. It felt so natural to spend time with her, so easy and true. He'd told her things he'd never discussed even with Ashley. He supposed he wanted her to know the real him, and somehow he trusted she'd know how to respond.

She wasn't like anyone he'd met before. He was sure he wanted never to let go of her hand; their fingers seemed to fit together in just the right way—effortlessly clasped, like perfect complements.

Aside from the house that was hosting the party, they were completely alone. The strains of music were soft and distant, and when he looked up, he caught the brief flash of a shooting star passing overhead. When he turned to Ronnie, he knew by her expression that she'd seen it as well.

"What did you wish for?" she asked, her voice a whisper. But he couldn't answer. Instead, he raised her hand and slipped his other arm around her back. He stared at her, knowing with certainty that he was falling in love. He pulled her close and kissed her beneath a blanket of stars, wondering how on earth he'd been lucky enough to find her.

21

·····⚜·····

Ronnie

Okay, she admitted that she could get used to living like this: lounging on the diving board in the backyard pool, an ice cold glass of sweet tea by her side, a fruit tray in the cabana, which had been served by the chef, along with real silverware and a fancy mint garnish.

Still, she couldn't imagine what it must have been like for Will to grow up in a world like this. Then again, since he'd never known anything different, he probably didn't notice it anymore. As she sunned herself on the diving board, she took in the sight of him standing on the roof of the cabana, getting ready to jump. He'd climbed it like a gymnast, and even from a distance, she could see the muscles flexing in his arms and stomach.

"Hey," he shouted. "Watch me do a flip."

"A flip? That's it? You climb all the way up there and you're only going to do one flip?"

"What's wrong with doing a flip?" he demanded.

"I'm just saying that anyone can do one flip," she taunted. "Even I could do one flip."

"I'd like to see that." He sounded skeptical.

"I don't want to get wet."

"But I invited you over here to swim!"

"This is how girls like me swim. It's also known as tanning."

He laughed. "Actually, it's probably a good idea you're getting some sun. I guess the sun doesn't shine in New York, huh?"

"Are you saying I'm pale?" She frowned.

"No," he said, shaking his head. "That's not the word I'd use. I think 'pasty' is a bit more accurate."

"Wow, what a charmer. It makes me wonder what I used to see in you."

"Used to?"

"Yes, and I must say that if you keep using words like *pasty* when it comes to describing me, I'm not seeing much of a future for us, either."

He seemed to evaluate her. "How about if I do two flips? Will you forgive me?"

"Only if you end the flips with a perfect dive. But if two flips and a big clumsy entry is all you can do, I'll pretend to be amazed, as long as you don't get me wet."

He raised an eyebrow before retreating a few steps and then taking one big step to launch himself in the air. He pulled himself into a tight tuck, spun twice, and went into the water arms first and body straight, almost without a ripple.

Now that, she thought, was impressive, if not completely surprising, given the graceful way he moved on the volleyball court. When he surfaced at the edge of the diving board, treading water, she knew he was pleased with himself.

"That was okay," she said.

"Just okay?"

"I'd give it a four point six."

"Out of five?"

"Out of ten," she said.

"That was at least an eight!"

"Of course you think that. That's why I'm the judge."

"How do I appeal?" he said, reaching up to latch on to the edge of the board.

"You can't. It's official."

"What if I'm not happy?"

"Then maybe you'll think twice about using the word *pasty*."

He laughed and began to pull himself up. Ronnie gripped the diving board.

"Hey . . . stop . . . don't do that . . . ," she warned.

"You mean . . . this?" he said, pulling down even harder.

"I told you I don't want to get wet!" she shrieked.

"And I want you to come swimming with me!" Without warning, he seized her arm and gave a tug. Squealing, she plunged into the water. As soon as she came up for air, he tried to kiss her, but she backed away.

"*No!*" she cried out, laughing, relishing the briskness of the water and the silky sensation of his skin against hers. "I don't forgive you!"

As she struggled playfully with him, she noticed Susan watching from the veranda. From the expression on her face, she was definitely not happy.

Later that afternoon, as they were heading back to the beach to check on the turtle nest, they stopped for ice cream. Ronnie walked beside Will, licking her fast-melting ice-cream cone, thinking how amazing it was that they'd kissed for the first time only yesterday. If last night had been almost perfect, then today had been even better. She loved how easily they shifted from serious to lighthearted and that he was as good at teasing her as he was at being teased.

Of course, he *had* pulled her into the pool, which was why she needed to time her reaction perfectly. It wasn't that hard since he didn't know it was coming, but as soon as he raised his own ice-cream cone to his lips, she gave the cone a sharp nudge, smearing ice cream on his face. Giggling, she skipped off around the corner . . . directly into the arms of Marcus.

Blaze was with him, as were Teddy and Lance.

"Well, isn't this a nice surprise," Marcus drawled, tightening his grip.

"Let me go!" she cried, hating the sudden panic in her voice.

"Let her go," Will added from behind her. His voice was unwavering. Serious. "Now."

Marcus seemed almost amused. "You should watch where you're going, Ronnie."

"Now!" Will demanded, sounding angry, moving into view.

"Take it easy, Richie Rich. She slammed into me—I was just keeping her from falling. And by the way, how's Scott doing? Has he been playing with any bottle rockets lately?"

To Ronnie's surprise, Will froze. Smirking, Marcus turned his gaze back to her. He squeezed her arms harder before finally releasing her. As Ronnie took a quick step back, Blaze lit a fireball, her expression nonchalant.

"I'm glad I was able to keep you from stumbling," Marcus said. "It wouldn't look good to be all bruised when you go to court on Tuesday, would it? You don't want the judge to think you're violent, in addition to being a thief."

Ronnie could only stare at him, speechless, until Marcus turned away. As they walked off, she saw Blaze toss him the fireball, which he caught with ease and threw back to her.

Seated on the dune outside her house, Will remained quiet as she recounted everything that had happened since she arrived, including the events at the music store. When she finished, she twisted her hands together in her lap.

"And that's all of it. As for the shoplifting I did back in New York, I don't even know why I took that stuff. It wasn't like I needed it. It was just something to do because my friends were doing it. When I went to court, I admitted everything because I knew I was wrong and that I wasn't ever going to do it again. And I didn't—not there, and not here. But unless the charges are dropped or Blaze admits what she did, I'm not only going to get in big trouble here, but I'm going to be in trouble back home, too. I know it sounds crazy and I'm sure you don't believe me, but I swear I'm not lying."

He covered her clasped hands with his own. "I believe you," he said. "And trust me—nothing surprises me about Marcus. He's been crazy since he was a kid. My sister had him in a class and she told me that the teacher once found a dead rat in her drawer. Everyone knew who did it, even the principal, but they couldn't prove anything, you know? And he's still up to his usual tricks, but now he has Teddy and Lance to do his bidding. I've heard some scary things about him. But Galadriel . . . she used to be the nicest girl. I've known her since I was a little kid, and I don't know what's been going on with her lately. I know her mom and dad got divorced, and I heard she took it really hard. I don't know what she sees in Marcus, though, or why she's so intent on ruining her life. I used to feel bad for her, but what she's doing to you is wrong."

Ronnie suddenly felt tired. "I have to go to court next week."

"Do you want me to come?"

"No. I don't want you to see me standing in front of the judge."

"It doesn't matter—"

"It will if your mom finds out. I'm pretty sure she doesn't like me."

"Why do you say that?"

Because I saw the way she was looking at me earlier, she could have said. "It's just a feeling."

"Everyone feels like that when they first meet her," he assured her. "Like I said, once you get to know her, she'll loosen up."

Ronnie wasn't so sure. Behind her, the sun was dropping, turning the sky a bright shade of orange. "What's going on with Scott and Marcus?" she asked.

Will stiffened. "What do you mean?"

"Do you remember that night at the festival? After he did his show, Marcus seemed all hyped up about something, so I tried to keep my distance from him. It was like he was scanning the crowd, and when he spotted Scott, he got this . . . weird look on his face, like he found what he needed. Next thing I know, he had balled up his cup of French fries and hurled it at him."

"I was there, too, remember?"

"But remember what he said? It was odd. He asked if Scott was going to shoot a bottle rocket at him. And when he said almost the same thing to you just a little while ago, you sort of froze."

Will looked away. "It's nothing," he insisted, squeezing her hands. "And I wouldn't have let anything happen to you." He leaned back, propping himself on his elbows. "May I ask you a question? Totally different subject?"

Ronnie lifted an eyebrow, unsatisfied by his answer but deciding to let it go.

"Why is there a piano behind a plywood wall at your house?" When she seemed surprised, he shrugged. "You can see it through the window, and the plywood wall doesn't exactly match the rest of the interior."

It was Ronnie's turn to look away. She disengaged her hands and buried them in the sand. "I told my dad that I didn't want to see the piano anymore, so he put up the wall."

Will blinked. "You hate the piano that much?"

"Yes," she answered.

"Because your dad was your teacher?" She looked up in surprise as Will went on. "He used to teach at Juilliard, right? It only makes sense that he'd teach you to play. And I'd be willing to bet that you were great at it, if only because you have to love something before you can hate it."

For a grease monkey slash volleyball player, he was pretty perceptive. Ronnie dug her fingers deeper into the sand, where the layers felt cool and heavy.

"He taught me to play from the time I was able to walk. I played for hours, seven days a week, for years. We even did some composing together. It's what we shared, you know? It was something for just the two of us, and when he moved out of the apartment . . . I felt like he hadn't only betrayed the family. I felt like he'd betrayed me personally, and I was just so angry about all of it that I swore I'd never play or write another song again. So when I first got down here and saw the piano and heard him playing it every time I was around, I couldn't help feeling that he was trying to pretend that what he'd done didn't matter. Like he thought we could just start over. But we couldn't. You can't undo the past."

"You seemed friendly with him the other night," Will observed.

Ronnie slowly pulled her hands from the sand. "Yeah, we've been getting along better in the last few days. But that doesn't mean I want to play again," she said.

"It's not my business, but if you were that good, then you're only hurting yourself. It's a gift, right? And who knows? Maybe you could go to Juilliard."

"I know I could. They still write me. They've promised me they'll make room if I change my mind." She felt a surge of irritation.

"Then why don't you go?"

"Does it matter that much to you?" She glared at him. "That I'm not just who you thought I was? That I have some special talent? Does that make me good enough for you?"

"Not at all," he said. "You're still the person I thought you were. From the first moment we met. And there's no way you could ever be a better fit for me."

As soon as he'd said it, she felt ashamed of her outburst. She heard the sincerity in his tone and knew he meant what he'd said.

She reminded herself that they'd known each other for only a few days, and yet . . . he was kind and smart and she already knew he loved her. As if sensing her thoughts, he sat up and scooted closer. Leaning in, he kissed her softly on lips, and she was suddenly certain that she wanted nothing more than to spend hours and hours wrapped in his arms, just like this.

22

·····🖋·····

Marcus

Marcus watched them from a distance. *So that's the way it's going to be, huh?*

Screw it. Screw her. It was time to party.

Teddy and Lance had picked up the booze, and people were already arriving. Earlier, he'd seen a family of vacationers packing up their piece-of-crap minivan with their ugly dog and even uglier kids at one of the houses not three or four down from Ronnie's own piece-of-crap house. He'd been around long enough to know that the next rental wouldn't start until tomorrow, after the cleaners came, which meant that all he had to do was get inside and the place would be theirs for the night.

Not so hard, considering he had the key and the security code. Vacationers never locked the door when they went to the beach. Why should they? It's not like they ever brought anything but food and maybe a few video games to the beach, since most of them stayed for only a week. And the out-of-town owners—probably from someplace like Charlotte and tired of fielding calls from the security company when the idiots who rented the place set off the alarm in the middle of the night—had been kind enough to post the code right above the security pad in the kitchen. Smart. Real smart. With enough patience, he'd always been able to find a house or two to host a party, but the secret was not to abuse their opportunities. Teddy and Lance always wanted to party in these kinds of places, but Marcus knew that if he did it too often, the management companies would get suspicious. They'd send the managers by to check things out, they'd tell the police to make frequent rounds, and they'd warn the vacationers and owners. Then where would they be? Stuck down at Bower's Point, like they usually were.

Once a year. Once a summer. That was his rule, and that was enough, unless he burned the house down afterward. He smiled. Do that and the problem was solved. No one would even suspect there'd been a party at all. There was nothing like a big fire, because fires were *alive*. Fires, especially big ones, moved and danced and destroyed and devoured. He remembered setting fire to a barn when he was twelve and watching it burn for hours, thinking he'd never seen anything more incredible. So he'd lit another one, this time at an abandoned warehouse. Over the years, he'd set a bunch of them. There was nothing better; nothing made him higher than the power he felt with a lighter in his hands.

But he wouldn't do that. Not tonight, because his past wasn't something he wanted either Teddy or Lance to know about. Besides, the party was going to be something. Booze and drugs and music. And girls. Drunk girls. He'd have Blaze first and then maybe a couple of others after that, if he got Blaze ripped enough to pass out. Or maybe he'd hook up with some dumb little hottie, even if Blaze was sober enough to realize what was happening. That might be fun, too. Oh, he knew she'd make a scene, but he'd just ignore her and have Teddy or Lance kick her out. He knew she'd come back. She always came back, begging and crying.

She was so damn predictable. And she whined all the damn time.

Not like Miss Tight Little Body just down the beach.

He'd been trying hard not to think about Ronnie. So she didn't like him, so she wanted to spend time with Richie Rich, the brake shop prince. She probably wasn't going to put out anyway. She was probably a frigid little tease. Even so, he couldn't figure out where he'd gone wrong with her or how she'd seemed to see right through him.

He was better off without her. He didn't need her. He didn't need anyone, which made him wonder why he continued to watch her or cared in the slightest that she was hanging out with Will.

Of course, that made the whole thing a little more interesting, if only because he knew all about Will's weak spot.

He could have some fun with that. Just like he was going to have fun tonight.

23

.... ♪ ....

Will

For Will, the summer was passing way too quickly. Between working at the garage and spending most of his remaining free time with Ronnie, the days seem to fly by. As August approached, he found himself growing increasingly anxious at the thought that in a few weeks she'd be heading back to New York and he'd be off to Vanderbilt.

She'd become part of his life—in many ways, the best part. Even though he didn't always understand her, their differences somehow seemed to make their relationship stronger. They had argued over his request to accompany her to court, which she had adamantly refused, but he remembered her surprise when she found him waiting for her outside the courthouse with a bouquet of flowers. He knew she was upset that the charges had not been dropped—her next court appearance was scheduled on August 28, three days after he'd leave for college—but knew he'd done the right thing by showing up when she accepted the bouquet with a shy kiss.

She surprised him by getting a part-time job at the aquarium. She didn't tell him about her plans beforehand or ask if he could put in a good word for her. Frankly, he hadn't even realized she'd wanted a job. When he'd asked her about it afterward, she'd explained, "You're working during the day, and my dad and Jonah are making a stained-glass window. I needed something to do, and besides, I want to pay for the lawyer myself. It's not like my dad has a lot of money." When he picked her up after her first day of work, however, he noticed her skin had an almost greenish tint to it. "I had to feed the otters," she confessed. "Have you ever stuck your hand into a bucket of dead, slimy fish? It's disgusting!"

They talked, endlessly. There didn't seem to be enough time in the world to share everything they wanted to. Sometimes it was simply talk to fill the quiet moments—when they debated their favorite movies, for instance, or when she told him that even though she was a vegetarian, she still hadn't decided whether eggs or milk counted. But at other times the conversation turned serious. She told him more about her memories of playing the piano and her relationship with her dad; he admitted that he sometimes resented the fact that he felt a responsibility to be the kind of person his mom insisted he be. They talked about her brother, Jonah, and his sister, Megan, and speculated and dreamed about where they'd end up in life. For him, the future seemed tidily planned: Four years at Vanderbilt, and after graduation he'd gain some experience working for another firm before coming back to run his dad's business. Yet even as he recited the plan, he could hear his mom's voice whispering her approval, and he found himself wondering whether it was what he really wanted. As for Ronnie, she admitted that she wasn't sure what the following year or two would bring. The uncertainty didn't seem to frighten her, though, which made him admire her even more. Later, when he reflected on their respective plans, he was struck by the realization that of the two of them, she was more in charge of her own destiny than he was.

Despite the cages that had been built to guard the turtle nests up and down the beach, raccoons had burrowed beneath the wire mesh and destroyed six nests. As soon as Ronnie learned what happened, she insisted they take turns guarding the nest behind her house. There was no reason for both of them to be there all night, but they spent most nights holding each other, kissing, and talking quietly until long after midnight.

Scott, of course, couldn't understand it at all. More than once, Will was late for practice and he'd arrive to see Scott pacing in agitation, wondering what had gotten into his friend. At work, in the rare instances that Scott asked how things were going with Ronnie, Will didn't volunteer much—he knew Scott wasn't asking because he was truly interested. Scott did his best to keep Will's attention focused on the upcoming beach volleyball tournament, usually pretending either that Will would come to his senses soon or that Ronnie didn't exist.

Ronnie had been right about his mom, though. While she hadn't said anything directly to him about his new relationship, he read her disapproval in the way she had to force a smile at the mention of Ronnie's name and in the almost formal demeanor she adopted when he brought Ronnie to the house. She never asked about Ronnie, and when he said something about her— about how much fun they'd had or how smart she was or how she understood him better than anyone—his mom would say things like, "You're going to be at Vanderbilt soon, and long-distance relationships are hard" or would even wonder aloud if he thought they were "spending too much time together." He hated when she said those things. It was all he could do not to snap at her, because he knew she was being unfair. Unlike practically everyone else Will knew, Ronnie didn't drink or curse or gossip, and they hadn't gone any further than kissing, but he knew intuitively those things wouldn't matter to his mom. She was locked into her prejudices, so any attempt to change her opinion of Ronnie would be pointless. Frustrated, he started making excuses to stay away from the house as much as possible. Not only because of the way his mom felt about Ronnie, but because of the way he was beginning to feel about his mom.

And about himself, of course, for failing to call her on it.

Other than Ronnie's preoccupation with her upcoming court

appearance, the only blemish on their largely idyllic summer was the continuing presence of Marcus. Though they'd mostly been able to avoid him, it was sometimes impossible. When they did run into him, Marcus always seemed to find a way to provoke Will, usually with a reference to Scott. Will felt paralyzed. If he overreacted, Marcus might go to the police; if he did nothing, he felt ashamed. Here he was, dating a girl who'd stood in court and admitted her guilt, and the fact that he couldn't summon the courage to do the same had started to torment him. He'd tried talking to Scott about coming clean and going to the police, but Scott had rejected the idea. And in his own indirect way, he never let Will forget what he'd done for him and his family that horrible day when Mikey died. Will admitted Scott been heroic, but as the summer wore on, he began to wonder whether a previous good deed meant a later bad one should be completely overlooked—and, in his darkest moments, whether he could bear the true cost of Scott's friendship.

One night in early August, Will agreed to take Ronnie out to the beach to hunt for spider crabs.

"I told you I don't like crabs!" Ronnie squealed, grabbing hold of Will's arm.

He laughed. "They're just spider crabs. They won't hurt you."

She squinched up her nose. "They're like creepy, crawly bugs from outer space."

"You're forgetting that doing this was your idea."

"No, it was Jonah's idea. He said it was fun. Which serves me right for listening to someone who learns about life by watching cartoons."

"I would think someone who feeds slimy fish to otters wouldn't be bothered by a few harmless crabs on the beach." He swept his flashlight across the ground, illuminating the fast-moving creatures.

She scanned the sand frantically, lest another crab dart near her foot. "First off, there aren't a few harmless crabs. There are hundreds of them. Second, if I'd known that this is what happens to the beach at night, I would have made you sleep by the turtle nest every night. So I'm a little angry at you for hiding this fact. And third, even though I work at the aquarium, it doesn't mean that I enjoy having crabs run over my feet."

He did his best to keep a straight face, but it was too hard. When she looked up, she caught his expression.

"Stop smirking. It's not funny."

"Yes, it is . . . I mean, there must be twenty little kids and their parents out here, doing the same thing we are."

"It's not my fault if their parents lack common sense."

"Do you want to go back?"

"No, it's fine," she said. "You've already lured me out here into the middle of the infestation. I might as well put up with it."

"You do know we've been walking the beach a lot lately."

"I know. So again, thank you for bringing the flashlight and ruining the memories."

"Fine," he said, turning it off.

She dug her nails into his arm. "What are you doing? Turn it back on!"

"You've made it perfectly clear you don't like the flashlight."

"But if you turn it off, then I won't see them!"

"Right."

"Which means they might be surrounding me right now. Turn it back on," she pleaded.

He did, and as they started down the beach, he laughed. "One day, I'm going to figure you out."

"I don't think so. If you haven't done it yet, it just might be beyond you."

"That could be true," he admitted. He draped an arm around her. "You still haven't told me if you're going to come to my sister's wedding."

"That's because I haven't decided yet."

"I want you to meet Megan. She's great."

"It's not your sister I'm worried about. I just don't think your mom wants me to come."

"So? It's not her wedding. My sister wants you there."

"You've talked to her about me?"

"Of course."

"What did you say?"

"The truth."

"That you think I'm pasty?"

He squinted at her. "Are you still thinking about that?"

"No. I've forgotten all about it."

He snorted. "Okay, to answer your question. No, I didn't say you were pasty. I said you *used to be* pasty."

She elbowed him in the ribs, and he pretended to beg for mercy. "I'm kidding, I'm kidding . . . I would never say that."

"What did you tell her, then?"

He stopped, turning her to face him. "Like I said, I told her the truth. That you're smart and funny and easy to be with and beautiful."

"Oh, well, that's okay, then."

"You're not going to say that you love me, too?"

"I'm not sure I can love such a needy guy," she teased. She slipped her arms around him. "Or you can take that comment as payback for letting crabs run over my toes. Of course I love you."

They kissed before resuming their walk. They'd almost reached the pier and were about to turn around when they saw Scott, Ashley, and Cassie approaching from the other direction. Ronnie tensed under his arm as Scott veered off to intercept them.

"There you are, man," Scott called out when he was close. He stopped in front of them. "I've been texting you all night."

Will drew his arm tighter around Ronnie. "Sorry. I left my phone at Ronnie's. What's up?"

As he answered, he could feel Ashley staring at Ronnie from a distance.

"I got calls from five of the teams that are going to be in the

tournament, and they want to do some pre-tournament scrim-
maging. They're all pretty good, and they want to put a mini–
boot camp together to get everyone ready to face Landry and
Tyson. Lots of practice, lots of drills, lots of games. We're even
thinking about switching up the teams now and then to improve
our reaction times, since we all have different styles."

"When are they coming?"

"Whenever we're ready, but we were thinking this week."

"How long are they going to be here?"

"I don't know. Three or four days? Pretty much right up until
the tournament. I know you've got wedding stuff and rehearsals,
but we can work around all that."

He thought again about the fact that his time with Ronnie
would soon be coming to an end. "Three or four days?"

Scott frowned. "Come on, man. This is just what we need to do
to get ready."

"Don't you think we're ready now?"

"What's gotten into you? You know how many coaches from
the West Coast are coming to watch the tournament." He pointed
a finger at Will. "You might not need a volleyball scholarship to
go to college, but I do. And this is the only chance they'll get to
see me play."

Will hesitated. "Let me think about it, okay?"

"You want to *think* about it?"

"I have to talk to my dad first. I can't just agree to take off work
for four days on such short notice without asking him. And I
don't think you can, either."

Scott glanced at Ronnie. "Are you sure that work is what this
is all about?"

Will recognized the challenge but didn't want to get into it
with Scott right then. Scott, too, seemed to think better of it and
took a step back. "All right, fine. Talk to your dad. Whatever," he
said. "Maybe you'll find a way to squeeze it into your schedule."

With that he turned away, walking off without a backward

glance. Will, unsure what else to do, started leading Ronnie back to her house. They were out of earshot of Scott when Ronnie wrapped her arm around his waist and asked, "Was he talking about the tournament you told me about?"

Will nodded. "Next weekend. The day after my sister's wedding."

"On a Sunday?"

He nodded. "It's a two-day tournament, but the women play on Saturday."

Ronnie thought about that. "And he needs a volleyball scholarship to go to college?"

"It would definitely help."

She pulled him to a stop. "Then make time for this boot camp thing. Practice and drill. Do whatever you have to do to get ready. He's your friend, right? We'll still find time to be together. Even if both of us have to sit out by the turtle nest. I can go to work tired."

As she spoke, Will could only think how beautiful she was and how much he was going to miss her.

"What's going to happen to us, Ronnie? At the end of the summer?" He searched her face.

"You're going to go to college," Ronnie answered, looking away. "And I'll go back to New York."

He tilted her face up to his. "You know what I mean."

"Yes," she said, "I know perfectly what you mean. But I don't know what you want me to say. I don't know what either of us can say."

"How about, I don't want it to end?"

Her eyes were sea green, tender in apology. "I don't want it to end," she repeated softly.

Though it was what he'd wanted to hear and she obviously meant it, he realized what she'd already known: that speaking the words, even if true, had little power to change the inevitable or even make him feel much better.

"I'm going to come to New York to visit," he promised.

"I hope you do."

"And I want you to come to Tennessee."

"I suppose I could handle another trip down south if I had a good reason to go."

He smiled as they began moving down the beach. "I'll tell you what. I'll do everything Scott wants to get ready for the tournament if you agree to come with me to my sister's wedding."

"In other words, you're going to do what you should be doing anyway, and in exchange, you get what you want."

It wasn't quite the way he would have phrased it. But she had a point. "Yeah," he said, "I guess that's it."

"Anything else? Since you're driving such a hard bargain?"

"Now that you mention it, there is. I want you to try to talk some sense into Blaze."

"I've already tried to talk to her."

"I know, but that was what? Six weeks ago? She's seen us together, so she knows you're not interested in Marcus. And she's had time to get over it."

"She's not going to tell the truth," Ronnie countered. "That means she'd get in trouble."

"How? What would she be charged with? The point is, I don't want you to get in trouble for something you didn't do. The owner isn't listening, the DA isn't listening, and I'm not saying that Blaze is going to listen, either, but I don't see what other choice you have if you want to get out from under this thing."

"It's not going to work," Ronnie insisted.

"Maybe not. But I think it's worth a try. I've known her a long time, and she wasn't always like this. Maybe there's still something deep down inside her that knows she's doing the wrong thing and all she needs is a good reason to try to make it better."

Though she didn't agree, she didn't disagree, either, and they walked back toward the house in relative silence. When they got close, Will could see light flooding out the open door of the workshop.

"Is your dad still working on the window tonight?"

"It looks that way," she said.

"May I see it?"

"Why not?"

Together, they headed toward the ramshackle building. Once inside, Will saw a bare light bulb dangling from an extension cord, over a large worktable in the center of the room.

"I guess he's not here," Ronnie said, looking around.

"Is that the window?" Will asked, approaching the worktable. "It's huge."

Ronnie moved to his side. "It's amazing, isn't it? It's for the church they're rebuilding down the street."

"You didn't tell me that." His voice sounded strained, even to his own ears.

"I didn't think it was important," she said automatically. "Why? Is it important?"

Will forced his mind away from images of Scott and the fire. "Not really," he said quickly, pretending to inspect the glass. "I just didn't realize your dad had the ability to make something so intricate."

"I didn't either. Neither did he, until he started, anyway. But he told me it was important to him, so maybe that has something to do with it."

"Why was it so important to him?"

As Ronnie related the story her dad had told her, Will stared at the window, remembering what Scott had done. And, of course, what *he* hadn't done. She must have seen something in his face because when she finished, she seemed to be studying him.

"What are you thinking about?"

He ran his hand over the glass before he answered. "Do you ever wonder what it means to be a friend?"

"I'm not sure what you mean."

He looked over at her. "How far would you go to protect a friend?"

She hesitated. "I suppose that depends on what the friend did. And how serious it was." She put a hand on his back. "What aren't you telling me?"

When he didn't answer, she scooted closer to him. "In the end, you should always do the right thing, even if it's hard. I know that might not help you and that the right thing isn't always so easy to figure out. At least on the surface, anyway. But even when I was justifying to myself that stealing was no big deal, I knew it was wrong. It was making me feel . . . dark inside." She brought her face close to his, and he caught the scent of sand and sea on her skin. "I didn't fight the charges because something inside me knew that what I'd been doing was wrong. Some people can live with that, as long as they get away with it. They see shades of gray where I see black and white. But I'm not that kind of person . . . and I don't think you are, either."

Will's gaze slid away from hers. He wanted to tell her, longed to tell her everything since he knew she was right, but he couldn't seem to find the words. She understood him in ways that no one else ever had. He could learn from her, he thought. He would be a better person with her by his side. In many ways, he needed her. When he forced himself to nod, she rested her head against his shoulder.

When they finally left the shed, he reached out to stop her before she headed back to her house. He pulled her close and began to kiss her. First her lips, then her cheek, and then her neck. Her skin was like fire, as if she'd been lying in the sun for hours, and when he kissed her lips again, he felt her fold her body into his. He buried his hands in her hair, continuing to kiss her as he slowly backed her against the wall of the workshop. He loved her, he wanted her, and as they continued to kiss, he could feel her arms moving over his back and shoulders. Her touch was electric against his skin, her breath hot against his, and he felt himself slipping away to a place governed only by his senses.

His hands were roving over her back and stomach when he finally felt Ronnie place her hands on his chest and push him away.

"Please," she breathed, "we've got to stop."

"Why?"

"Because I don't want my dad to catch us. He might be watching us from the window right now."

"We're just kissing."

"Yeah. And we just sort of like each other, too." She laughed.

A languid smile spread over his face. "What? We weren't just kissing?"

"I'm just saying that it felt like . . . what we were doing was leading up to something more," she said, straightening her shirt.

"And the problem is?"

Her expression told him to stop playing games, and he knew she had a point, even if it wasn't what he wanted. "You're right." He sighed, dropping his hands into a loose circle around her waist. "I'll try to control myself."

She kissed him on the cheek. "I have complete confidence in you."

"Gee, thanks," he groaned.

She winked. "I'm going to go check on my dad, okay?"

"Okay. I've got to be at work early tomorrow anyway."

She smiled. "Too bad. I don't have to be at work until ten."

"Are they still having you feed the otters?"

"They'd starve without me. I'm pretty much indispensable now."

He laughed. "Have I told you that I think you're a keeper?"

"I don't think anyone's ever said that to me. But just so you know, you're not so bad to have around, either."

24

······*······

Ronnie

Ronnie watched Will walk off before making her way back to the house, thinking about the things he'd said and wondering if he was right about Blaze. The upcoming court date had been weighing on her all summer: She sometimes wondered whether the anticipation of the possible punishment was worse than the punishment itself. As the weeks had rolled by, she'd been waking up in the middle of the night and finding it impossible to go back to sleep. It wasn't that she was terrified of going to prison—she doubted that she'd be locked up—but she fretted that these crimes would follow her forever. Would she have to reveal her history to a college she might attend? Did she have to tell her future employers? Would she be able to get a job teaching? She didn't know whether she'd attend college or even wanted to become a teacher, but the fear remained. Would this haunt her forever?

Her lawyer didn't think so, but she wouldn't promise anything.

And the wedding. It was easy for Will to ask her to come, to assume it was no big deal. But she knew that Susan didn't want her there, and the last thing she wanted was to be some sort of distraction. This was supposed to be Megan's day.

Reaching the back porch, she was about to step inside when

she heard the rocking chair squeak. She jumped back in terror, only to see Jonah watching her.

"That. Was. So. Gross."

"What are you doing out here?" she demanded, her heart still racing.

"Watching you and Will. Like I said, that was really gross." He made a point to shiver.

"You were spying on us?"

"It was kind of hard not to. You were right there by the workshop with Will. It looked like he was practically squishing you to death."

"He wasn't," Ronnie assured him.

"I'm just saying how it looked."

She smiled. "You'll understand when you're a little older."

Jonah shook his head. "I understand exactly what you were doing. I've seen movies. I just think it's gross."

"You've already said that," she pointed out.

That seemed to stop him for a second. "Where's he going?"

"Home. He's got to work tomorrow."

"Are you going to watch the turtle nest tonight? Because you don't have to. Dad said that we could watch it tonight."

"You convinced Dad to sleep outside?"

"He wants to. He thinks it'll be fun."

I doubt it, she thought. "It's fine with me."

"I've already got my stuff ready. Sleeping bag, lantern, juices, sandwiches, a box of Ritz crackers, marshmallows, potato chips, cookies, and a tennis racket."

"You're going to play tennis?"

"In case the raccoon comes. You know. If it tries to attack us."

"It's not going to attack you."

"Really?" He sounded almost disappointed.

"Well, maybe it is a good idea," Ronnie agreed. "Just in case. You never know."

He scratched his head. "That's what I thought, too."

She pointed toward the workshop. "The window looks beautiful, by the way."

"Thanks," Jonah said. "Dad wants to make sure every single piece is perfect. He makes me do some pieces two or three times. But I'm getting pretty good."

"It looks like it."

"But it gets hot. Especially when he runs the kiln. It's like an oven."

It is an oven, she thought. But she didn't correct him. "That's too bad. How's the whole cookie war going?"

"It's fine. I just have to eat them when he's napping."

"Dad doesn't nap."

"He does now. Every afternoon, for a couple of hours. Sometimes I have to shake him pretty hard to wake him up."

She stared at her brother before peering through the window into the house. "Where is Dad, by the way?"

"He's at the church. Pastor Harris came by earlier. He's been coming by a lot lately. Him and Dad like to talk."

"They're friends."

"I know. But I think he just used that as an excuse. I think Dad went to play the piano."

"What piano?" Ronnie asked, puzzled.

"It got delivered to the church last week. Dad's been going over there to play."

"He has, huh?"

"Hold on," he said. "I'm not sure I was supposed to tell you that. Maybe you should forget I said it."

"Why shouldn't you tell me?"

"Because you might yell at him again."

"I'm not going to yell at him," Ronnie protested. "When was the last time I yelled at him?"

"When he was playing the piano. Remember?"

Oh, yeah, she thought. The kid had an amazing memory. "Well, I'm not going to yell at him."

"Good. Because I don't want you to yell at him. We're supposed to go to Fort Fisher tomorrow, and I want him to be in a good mood."

"How long has he been at the church?"

"I don't know. It feels like hours. That's why I was out here. I was waiting for him. And then you showed up with Will and started making out."

"We were just kissing!"

"No, I don't think so. You were definitely making out," Jonah said with conviction.

"Have you had any dinner yet?" she asked, eager to change the subject.

"I was waiting for Dad."

"Do you want me to make you a couple of hot dogs?"

"With ketchup only?" he pressed.

She sighed. "Sure."

"I thought you didn't even like to touch them."

"You know, it's funny, but I've been handling a lot of dead fish lately, so a hot dog doesn't strike me as all that disgusting anymore."

He smiled. "Will you bring me to the aquarium one time so I can watch you feed the otters?"

"If you want, I might even be able to let you feed them."

"Really?" Jonah's voice rose with excitement.

"I think so. I'll have to ask, of course, but they let some of the student groups do it, so I don't think it would be a problem."

His little face lit up. "Wow. Thanks." Then, getting up from the rocking chair, he added, "Oh, by the way, you owe me ten bucks."

"For what?"

"Hello? For not telling Dad about what Will and you were doing. Duh."

"Are you serious? Even though I'm going to make you dinner?"

"Come on. You work and I'm poor."

"You obviously think I earn far more than I do. I don't have ten dollars. Everything I've earned has gone to help pay for my lawyer."

He thought about that. "How about five, then?"

"You'd take five dollars from me even though I just told you I don't even have ten dollars to my name?" Ronnie feigned outrage.

He thought about that. "How about two?"

"How about one?"

He smiled. "Deal."

After making Jonah his dinner—he wanted the hot dogs boiled, not microwaved—Ronnie headed down the beach, toward the church. It wasn't far, but it lay in the opposite direction from the route she usually walked, and she'd barely noticed it the few times she'd passed it.

As she approached, she saw the outlines of the spire silhouetted against the evening sky. Other than that, the church disappeared into its surroundings, mostly because it was so much smaller than either of the homes flanking it and had none of the expensive details. The walls were made of clapboard siding, and despite the new construction, the place already looked weathered.

She had to climb over the dune to reach the parking lot on the street side, and here there was more evidence of recent activity: an overflowing Dumpster, a fresh stack of plywood by the door, and a large work van parked near the entrance. The front door was propped open, illuminated by a soft cone of light, though the rest of the building looked dark.

She walked toward the entrance and stepped inside. Looking around, she could see that the place had a long way to go. The floor was concrete, the drywall looked only half-complete, and there were no seats or pews. Dust coated every exposed two-by-four, yet straight ahead, where Ronnie could imagine Pastor Harris preaching on Sundays, her father was sitting behind a new piano that looked utterly out of place. An old aluminum lamp attached to an extension cord provided the only illumination.

He hadn't heard her come in, and he continued to play, though she didn't recognize the song. It seemed almost contemporary, unlike the music he usually played, but even to her ears it sounded . . . unfinished somehow. Her dad seemed to realize the same thing because he stopped for a moment, appeared to think of something new, and started over from the beginning.

This time, she heard the subtle variations he made. They were an improvement, but the melody still wasn't right. She felt a rush of pride that she still had the ability not only to interpret music, but to imagine possible variations. When she was younger, it was this talent above all else that had amazed her father.

He started over again, making further changes, and as she watched him, she knew he was happy. Though music wasn't part of her life anymore, it had always been part of his, and she suddenly felt guilty for taking that away from him. Looking back, she remembered being angry at the thought that he was trying to get her to play, but had he really been trying to do that? Had it really been about her? Or had he played because it was an essential aspect of who he was?

She wasn't sure, but watching him, she felt moved by what he'd done. The serious way he considered every note and the ease with which he made changes made her realize how much he'd given up as a result of her childish demand.

As he played, he coughed once, then again, before stopping the song. He coughed some more, the sound thick and mucousy, and when it continued unabated, she broke into a run to reach him.

"Dad?" she cried. "Are you okay?"

He looked up, and for some reason, the coughing began to subside. By the time she bent down next to him, he was only wheezing slightly.

"I'm okay," he said, his voice weak. "There's so much dust in here—it just gets to me after a while. It happens every time."

She stared at him, thinking he looked a little pale. "Are you sure that's it?"

"Yeah, I'm sure." He patted her hand. "What are you doing here?"

"Jonah told me you were here."

"I guess you caught me, huh?"

She waved it off. "It's okay, Dad. It's a gift, right?"

When he didn't respond, she motioned to the keyboard, remembering all the songs they'd written together. "What was that you were playing? Are you writing a new song?"

"Oh, that," he said. "Trying to write one is more like it. It's just something I've been working on. No big deal."

"It was good . . ."

"No, it wasn't. I don't know what's wrong with it. You might—you were always better at composing than I was—but I just can't seem to get it right. It's like I'm doing everything backwards."

"It was good," she insisted. "And it was . . . more modern than what you usually play."

He smiled. "You noticed that, huh? It didn't start out that way. To be honest, I don't know what's happening to me."

"Maybe you've been listening to my iPod."

He smiled. "No, I can assure you that I haven't."

She looked around her. "So when's the church going to be finished?"

"I don't know. I think I told you that the insurance didn't cover all the damage—it's stalled for the time being."

"What about the window?"

"I'm still going to finish it." He pointed to a plywood-covered opening in the wall behind him. "That's where it'll go, even if I have to install it myself."

"You know how to do that?" Ronnie asked in disbelief.

"Not yet."

She smiled. "Why is there a piano here? If the church isn't finished? Aren't you worried it's going to get stolen?"

"It wasn't supposed to be delivered until the church was finished, and technically, it's not supposed to be in here. Pastor Harris hopes to find someone who's willing to store it, but with no completion date in sight, it's not as easy as it sounds." He turned to peek out the doorway and seemed surprised that night had fallen. "What time is it?"

"It's a little after nine."

"Oh, geez," he said, starting to rise. "I didn't realize the time. I'm supposed to camp out with Jonah tonight. And I should probably get him something to eat."

"Already taken care of."

He smiled, but as he gathered up his sheet music and turned out the light in the church, she was struck by how tired and frail he looked.

25

. . . . ♪ . . . .

Steve

Ronnie was right, he thought. The song was definitely modern.

He hadn't been lying when he'd told her that it hadn't started out that way. In the first week, he'd tried to approximate something by Schumann; for a few days after that, he'd been inspired more by Grieg. After that, it was Saint-Saëns he heard in his head. But in the end nothing felt right; nothing he did captured the same feeling he'd had when he'd recorded those first simple notes on a scrap of paper.

In the past, he worked to create music that he fantasized would live for generations. This time, he didn't. Instead, he experimented. He tried to let the music present itself, and little by little, he realized he'd stopped trying to echo the great composers and was content to finally trust himself. Not that he was there yet, because he wasn't. It wasn't right and there was a possibility that it would never be right, but somehow this felt okay to him.

He wondered if this had been his problem all along—that he'd spent his life emulating what had worked for others. He played music written by others hundreds of years earlier; he searched for God during his walks on the beach because it had worked for Pastor Harris. Here and now, with his son sitting beside him on a dune outside his house and staring through a pair of binoculars, despite the fact he most likely wouldn't see a thing, he wondered if he'd made those choices less because he thought others had the answers and more because he was afraid to trust his own instincts. Perhaps his teachers had become his crutch, and in the end, he had been afraid to be himself.

"Hey, Dad?"

"Yeah, Jonah."

"Are you going to come visit us in New York?"

"Nothing would make me happier."

"Because I think Ronnie will talk to you now."

"I would hope so."

"She's changed a lot, don't you think?"

Steve put down the binoculars. "I think we've all changed a lot this summer."

"Yeah," he said. "I think I've gotten taller, for one thing."

"You definitely have. And you've learned how to make a stained-glass window."

He seemed to think about that. "Hey, Dad?"

"Yeah?"

"I think I want to learn to stand on my head."

Steve hesitated, wondering where on earth that came from. "Can I ask why?"

"I like being upside down. I don't know why. But I think I'll need you to hold my legs. At least in the beginning."

"I'd be glad to."

They were silent for a long time. It was a balmy, starlit night, and as he reflected on the beauty of his surroundings, Steve felt a sudden rush of contentment. About spending the summer with his kids, about sitting on the dune with his son and talking about nothing important. He'd gotten used to days like these and dreaded the thought that they would soon be ending.

"Hey, Dad?"

"Yeah, Jonah?"

"It's kind of boring out here."

"I think it's peaceful," Steve responded.

"But I can barely see anything."

"You can see the stars. And hear the waves."

"I hear them all the time. They sound the same every day."

"When do you want to start practicing standing on your head?"

"Maybe tomorrow."

Steve put his arm around his son. "What's wrong? You sound kind of sad."

"Nothing." Jonah's voice was barely audible.

"Are you sure?"

"Can I go to school here?" he asked. "And live with you?"

Steve knew he'd have to tread carefully. "What about your mom?"

"I love Mom. And I miss her, too. But I like it here. I like spending time with you. You know, making the window, flying kites. Just hanging out. I've had so much fun. I don't want it to end."

Steve drew him close. "I love being with you, too. The best summer of my life. But if you're in school, it's not as if we'd be together like we are now."

"Maybe you could homeschool me."

Jonah's voice was soft, almost scared, and to Steve, he actually sounded his age. The realization made his throat tighten. He hated what he had to say next, even though he had no choice. "I think your mom would miss you if you stayed with me."

"Maybe you could move back. Maybe you and Mom could get married again."

Steve took a deep breath, hating this. "I know this is hard and doesn't seem fair. I wish there were a way I could change that, but I can't. You need to be with your mom. She loves you so much, and she wouldn't know what to do without you. But I love you, too. I never want you to forget that."

Jonah nodded as though he'd expected Steve's response. "Are we still going to Fort Fisher tomorrow?"

"If you want to. And afterwards, maybe we can go to the waterslides."

"There are waterslides there?"

"No. But there's a place not too far from there. We just have to remember to bring our suits."

"Okay," Jonah said, sounding more animated.

"Maybe we'll go to Chuck E. Cheese's, too."

"Really?"

"If you want to. We can make it happen."

"Okay," he said. "I want to."

Jonah was quiet again before finally reaching for the cooler. When he pulled out a plastic bag of cookies, Steve knew enough not to say anything.

"Hey, Dad?"

"Yeah?"

"Do you think the turtles will hatch tonight?"

"I don't think they're quite ready yet, but it shouldn't be long."

Jonah brought his lips together but said nothing, and Steve knew his son was thinking about leaving again. He squeezed him a little closer, but inside he felt something break, something he knew would never quite heal.

Early the next morning, Steve stared down the beach, knowing that if he walked, he would do so simply to enjoy the morning.

God, he came to realize, wasn't there. At least for him, anyway. But that made sense, now that he thought about it. If pinpointing God's presence were really that simple, then he supposed the beaches would be more crowded in the mornings. They would be filled with people on their own quests, instead of people jogging or walking their dogs or fishing in the surf.

The search for God's presence, he understood now, was as much of a mystery as God himself, and what was God, if not mystery?

Funny, though, that it took him so long to see it that way.

* * *

He spent the day with Jonah, just as they'd planned the night before. The fort was probably more interesting to him than Jonah, since he understood some of the history of the War Between the States and knew that Wilmington was the last major functioning port in the Confederacy. The waterslides, however, were far more exciting for Jonah than they were for Steve. Everyone was responsible for carrying his own mat up to the top, and while Jonah was strong enough the first couple of times, Steve soon had to take over.

He honestly felt as though he were going to die.

Chuck E. Cheese's, a pizza parlor with dozens of video games, kept Jonah occupied for another couple of hours. They played three games of air hockey, accumulated a few hundred game tickets, and, after cashing in the tickets, walked out with two squirt guns, three bouncy balls, a packet of colored pencils, and two erasers. He didn't even want to think about how much it had cost him.

It was a good day, a day of laughter, but wearying. After spending some time with Ronnie, he went to bed. Exhausted, he fell asleep within minutes.

26

. . . . ♪ . . . .

Ronnie

After her dad and Jonah had taken off for the day, Ronnie went to look for Blaze, hoping to catch her before she was due at the aquarium. She figured she had nothing to lose. The worst that could happen was that Blaze would blow her off or reject her out of hand, which would leave her in the same position she was already in. She didn't expect Blaze to suddenly change her mind and didn't want to get her hopes up, but it was hard not to. Will had a point: Blaze wasn't anything like Marcus, who had no conscience at all, and she had to be feeling just a little guilty, right?

It didn't take long to find her. Blaze was sitting on the dune near the pier, watching the surfers. She said nothing as Ronnie walked up.

Ronnie wasn't even sure where to start, so she began with the obvious.

"Hi, Blaze," she said.

Blaze said nothing, and Ronnie collected herself before going on.

"I know you probably don't want to talk to me . . ."

"You look like an Easter egg."

Ronnie glanced at the outfit she was required to wear at the aquarium: turquoise shirt with the aquarium logo, white shorts, and white shoes.

"I tried to get them to change the uniform to black, but they wouldn't let me."

"Too bad. Black's your color." Blaze flashed a quick smile. "What do you want?"

Ronnie swallowed. "I wasn't trying to pick up Marcus that night. He came on to me, and I don't know why he said what he did, other than because he wanted to make you jealous. I'm sure you don't believe me, but I want to let you know I never would have done something like that to you. I'm not that kind of person." It had all come out in a rush, but she had said it now.

Blaze paused, then said, "I know."

It wasn't the answer Ronnie had expected. "Then why did you put those things in my bag?" she blurted out.

Blaze squinted up at her. "I was mad at you. Because it was obvious he liked you."

Ronnie bit back a response that would have put an immediate end to the conversation, giving Blaze the opportunity to go on. Blaze focused on the surfers again. "I see you've been spending a lot of time with Will this summer."

"He said the two of you used to be friends."

"Yeah, we were," she said. "A long time ago. He's nice. You're lucky." She wiped her hands on her pants. "My mom's going to marry her boyfriend. After she told me, we got in this really big fight and she kicked me out of the house. She changed the locks and everything."

"I'm sorry to hear that," Ronnie said, and she was.

"I'll survive."

Her comment made Ronnie think about the similarities in their lives—divorce, anger, and rebellion, a parent's remarriage—yet despite those things, they were no longer the same at all. Blaze had changed since the beginning of the summer. Gone was the zest for life Ronnie had noticed when they first met, and Blaze seemed older, too, as if she'd aged years instead of weeks. But not in a good way. There were bags under her eyes, and her skin was sallow. She'd lost weight, too. A lot of weight. In a strange way, it was as if Ronnie were seeing the person she might have become, and she didn't like what she saw.

"What you did to me was wrong," Ronnie said. "But you can still make it right."

Blaze shook her head slowly. "Marcus won't let me. He said he wouldn't talk to me again."

Listening to her robotic tone made Ronnie want to shake her. Blaze seemed to sense what Ronnie was thinking, and she sighed before going on.

"I don't have anywhere else to go. My mom called all the relatives and told them not to take me in. She told them that it's hard for her, but what I need is 'tough love' right now. But I don't have any money to eat, and unless I want to sleep on the beach every night for the rest of my life, I have to do what Marcus tells me. When he's mad at me, he won't even let me shower at his place. And he won't give me any money from the shows we do, so I can't eat, either. He treats me like a dog sometimes, and I hate it. But who else do I have?"

"Have you tried talking to your mom?"

"What's the point? She thinks I'm a lost cause, and she hates me."

"I'm sure she doesn't hate you."

"You don't know her like I do."

Ronnie flashed back on the time she had visited Blaze's house and seen the money tucked into the envelope. It didn't sound like the same mother, but Ronnie didn't want to say that. In the silence, Blaze pushed herself up and stood. Her clothes were dirty and rumpled, as though she'd been wearing them for a week straight. Which was probably true.

"I know what you want me to do," Blaze said. "But I can't. And it's not because I don't like you. I do. I think you're nice, and I shouldn't have done what I did. But I'm as trapped as you are. And I don't think Marcus is done with you, either."

Ronnie stiffened. "What do you mean?"

Blaze stood. "He's been talking about you again. And not in a good way. I'd stay away from me if I were you."

Before Ronnie could respond, Blaze started walking off.

"Hey, Blaze," she called out.

Blaze slowly turned around.

"If you ever need something to eat or a place to stay, you know where I live."

For an instant, Ronnie thought she saw not only a flash of gratitude, but something that reminded her of the smart, lively girl she'd first met in June.

"And one more thing," Ronnie added. "That fire stuff you're doing with Marcus is crazy."

Blaze gave her a sad smile. "Do you really think it's crazier than anything else in my life right now?"

The following afternoon, Ronnie stood in front of her closet, knowing she had absolutely nothing to wear. Even if she was going to the wedding—which she still wasn't certain about—she didn't have anything remotely appropriate, unless it was a wedding with Ozzy Osbourne and his clan.

But this was a formal, black-tie wedding: Tuxedos and gowns were required for *guests*, not just the wedding party. She'd never imagined attending something like this when she was packing for the summer back in New York. She hadn't even brought along the pair of black pumps her mom had purchased for her last Christmas, the ones that were still in the box.

She really didn't understand why Will wanted her to come. Even if she found a way to look presentable, it wasn't as though she'd have anyone to talk to. Will was in the wedding party, which meant tons of pictures while she went to the reception, and he had to sit at the head table, so they wouldn't even be together for the meal. She'd probably end up sitting at a table with the governor or a senator or some family that had flown in on a private jet . . . talk about awkward. Add in the fact that Susan hated her, and the whole thing was a bad idea. A really bad idea. Horrible in every conceivable way.

On the other hand . . .

When would she ever be invited to a wedding like this again? Supposedly, the house had undergone a major transformation in the last couple of weeks: A new, temporary deck had been erected over the pool, tents had been raised, tens of thousands of flowers had been planted, and not only had lights been rented from one of the film studios in Wilmington, but the crew had come in and set up everything using stand-ins. The catering—everything from caviar to Cristal champagne—was being supplied by three different restaurants in Wilmington, and overseeing the whole operation was a chef Susan knew from Boston, who was supposedly once considered for the position of head chef at the White House. It was completely over the top, certainly nothing she would ever want for her own wedding—something beachside in Mexico with a dozen people in attendance was more her style—but she supposed that was part of the appeal of attending. She'd never go to another wedding like it for as long as she lived.

Assuming, of course, she could find something to wear. Honestly, she didn't even know why she was searching her closet. She couldn't wave a magic wand and turn a pair of her jeans into a dress or pretend that a new part in her hair would make someone overlook one of her concert T-shirts. The only halfway decent outfit she owned, the only one that Susan might not find repugnant if she'd simply stopped by on her way to a movie, was the outfit she wore to the aquarium, the one that made her look like an Easter egg.

"What are you doing?"

Jonah stood in the doorway, staring at her.

"I need to find something to wear," she said.

"Are you going out?"

"No. I meant to wear to the wedding."

He tilted his head. "You're getting married?"

"Of course not. Will's sister is getting married."

"What's her name?"

"Megan."

"Is she nice?"

Ronnie shook her head. "I don't know. I've never met her."

"Then why are you going to her wedding?"

"Because Will asked me to go. That's the way it works," she explained. "He can bring a guest to the wedding. I'm supposed to be the guest."

"Oh," he said. "What are you going to wear?"

"Nothing. I don't have anything."

He motioned toward her. "What you're wearing is nice."

The Easter egg outfit. Figures.

She tugged at her shirt. "I can't wear this. It's a formal wedding. I'm supposed to wear a gown."

"Do you have a gown in the closet?"

"No."

"Then why are you standing there?"

Right, she thought, closing the door. She flopped down on her bed.

"You're right," she said. "I can't go. It's as simple as that."

"Do you want to go?" Jonah asked curiously.

In an instant, her thoughts flashed from *Absolutely not* to *Kind of* and, finally, to *Yeah, I do*. She tucked her legs up under her. "Will wants me to go. It's important to him. And it would be something to see."

"Then why don't you buy a gown?"

"Because I don't have any money," she said.

"Oh," he said. "That's easy to fix." He went to his collection of toys in the corner. Wedged in at one end was a model of an airliner; he picked it up and brought it over, unscrewing the nose of the plane. As he began dumping the contents on her bed, Ronnie's jaw dropped at the sight of all the cash he'd accumulated. There had to be at least a few hundred dollars.

"It's my bank," he said. He wiped his nose. "I've been saving for a while."

"Where did you get all this?"

Jonah pointed to a ten-dollar bill. "This one was for not telling Dad I saw you that night at the carnival." He pointed to a single. "This one was for not telling Dad that you were making out with Will." He continued to point at various bills. "This one was for the guy with blue hair, and this was from liar's poker. This one was for that time you snuck out after your curfew—"

"I get it," she said. But still . . . She blinked. "You saved it all?"

"What else was I supposed to do with it?" he answered. "Mom and Dad buy me everything I need. All I have to do is beg long enough. It's pretty easy to get what I want. You just have to know how to work it. Mom needs me to cry, but Dad needs me to explain why I deserve it."

She smiled. Her brother, the blackmailer slash psychologist. Amazing.

"So I don't really need it. And I like Will. He makes you happy."

Yeah, she thought, he does.

"You're a pretty good little brother, you know?"

"Yeah, I know. And you can have it all, on one condition."

Here it comes, she thought. "Yes?"

"I'm not going to go dress shopping with you. It's boring."

It didn't take long for her to make a decision. "Deal."

Ronnie stared at herself, hardly able to recognize the image in the mirror. It was the morning of the wedding, and she had spent the past four days trying on pretty much every appropriate gown in the city, walking back and forth in various pairs of new shoes, and sitting for hours in the hair salon.

It had taken her almost an hour of curling and blowing to do her hair the way the girl at the salon had taught her. As Ronnie sat in the chair, she'd also asked advice about makeup, and the girl had given her some suggestions that Ronnie had followed carefully. The dress—there weren't all that many good choices despite the number of stores she'd visited—featured a deep V-neck and black sequins, a far cry from anything she'd ever imagined wearing. The night before, she'd filed and painted her nails on her own, taking her time, pleased that she hadn't smeared any of the polish.

I don't know you, Ronnie told her reflection, turning this way and that. *I've never seen you before.* She tugged at her dress, adjusting it slightly. She looked pretty good, she had to admit. She smiled. And definitely good enough for the wedding.

She slipped into her shoes on the way out the door and headed down the hallway to the living room. Her dad was reading his Bible again, and Jonah was watching cartoons, as usual. When her dad and brother looked up, they did visible double takes.

"Holy crap," Jonah said.

Her dad turned to glare at him. "You shouldn't say that word."

"What word?" Jonah asked.

"You know the word I'm talking about."

"Sorry, Dad," he said, chastised. "I meant jiminy crap," he tried again.

Ronnie and her dad laughed, and Jonah turned from one to the other. "What?"

"Nothing," her dad said. Jonah moved nearer to inspect her more closely.

"What happened to the purple in your hair?" he asked. "It's gone."

Ronnie bobbed her curls. "Temporarily," she said. "Is it okay?"

Before her dad could answer, Jonah piped up. "You look normal again. But you don't look like my sister."

"You look wonderful," her dad said quickly.

Surprising herself, Ronnie breathed a sigh of relief. "Is the dress okay?"

"It's perfect," her dad answered.

"And my shoes? I'm not sure they go with the dress."

"They're just right."

"I tried to do my makeup and my nails . . ."

Before she even finished, her dad shook his head. "You've never been more beautiful," he said. "In fact, I don't know if there's anyone more beautiful in the entire world."

He'd said the same thing a hundred times before. "Dad—"

"He means it," Jonah interrupted. "You look awesome. I'm being honest. I barely recognize you."

She frowned at him in mock indignation. "So you're saying you don't like the way I usually look?"

He shrugged. "No one likes purple hair except weirdos."

When she laughed, she caught her dad smiling at her.

"Wow" was all he could say.

Half an hour later, she was pulling through the gates of the Blakelee estate, her heart racing. They had just run the gauntlet of Highway Patrol officers stationed along the road to check IDs, and now they were being stopped by men in suits who wanted to park their car. Her dad tried calmly to explain that he was simply dropping her off, but his response made no sense to any of the three valets—they couldn't seem to grasp the fact that a guest at the wedding didn't even have her own car.

And the improvements . . .

Ronnie had to admit the place was as spectacular as a movie set. There were flowers everywhere, the hedge was trimmed to perfection, and even the brick-and-stucco wall that surrounded the property had been freshly painted.

When they were finally able to make their way to the central roundabout, her dad stared at the house, which was growing larger in the foreground. Eventually, he turned to her. She wasn't used to seeing her father surprised by anything, but she could hear it in his voice.

"This is Will's house?"

"This is it," she said. She knew what he'd say: that it was huge, or he didn't realize how wealthy the family was, or did she feel like she belonged in a place like this? Instead, he smiled at her without a trace of self-consciousness.

"What a lovely place for a wedding."

He drove carefully, thankfully drawing no extra attention to the old car they were driving. It was actually Pastor Harris's car, an old Toyota sedan with a boxy style that was out of date as soon as it came off the production line in the 1990s; but it ran, and right now that was good enough. Her feet were already aching. How some women wore pumps every day was beyond her. Even when she was seated, they felt like instruments of torture. She should have wrapped her toes in Band-Aids. And her dress obviously hadn't been designed to wear while sitting; it was digging into her ribs, making it hard to breathe. Then again, maybe she was just too nervous to breathe.

Her dad made his way around the circle drive, his gaze fixed on the house just as hers had been the first time she'd seen it. Even though she should have been used to it by now, the place still felt overwhelming to her. Add in the guests—she'd never seen so many tuxedos and formal gowns in her life—and she couldn't help but feel out of place already. She really didn't belong here.

Up ahead, a dark-suited man was signaling to the cars, and before she knew it, it was her turn to get out. As the man swung open her door and offered his hand to help her out, her father reached out to pat her leg.

"You can do this." He smiled. "And have fun."

"Thanks, Dad."

She peeked in the mirror one last time before emerging from the car. Once she was out, she adjusted her dress, thinking it was easier to breathe now that she was standing. The porch railings were decorated with lilies and tulips, and as she made her way up the steps toward the door, it suddenly swung open.

In his tuxedo, Will looked nothing like the shirtless volleyball player she'd first encountered or the easygoing southern boy who'd taken her fishing; in a way, it was like glimpsing the successful, sophisticated man he would be a few years from now. Somehow, she hadn't expected him to seem so . . . *refined*, and she was about to make a joke about how "he cleaned up pretty good" before she realized he hadn't even said hello.

For a long time, all he could do was stare at her. In the extended silence, the butterflies in her stomach began to feel like birds, and all she could think was that she'd done something wrong. Maybe she'd arrived too early, or maybe she'd overdone it with her dress and makeup. She wasn't sure what to think and was beginning to imagine the worst when Will finally began to smile.

"You look . . . incredible," he said, and at those words, she felt herself relax. Well, a little bit, anyway. She still hadn't seen Susan, and until then, she wasn't out of the woods. Still, she was pleased that Will liked what he saw.

"You don't think it's too much?" she asked.

Will stepped toward her and placed his hands on her hips. "Definitely not."

"But not too little, right?"

"Just right," he whispered.

She reached up, straightened his bow tie, then slipped her arms around his neck. "I must admit you don't look half bad yourself."

It wasn't as bad as she'd thought it would be. It turned out they'd already taken most of the bridal pictures before the guests arrived, so she and Will were able to spend some time together before the ceremony. Mostly they walked around the grounds, Ronnie gawking at all the arrangements. Will hadn't been kidding: The back of the house had been completely restyled, and the pool had been covered with a temporary deck that looked anything but temporary. Scores of white chairs fanned across the surface, facing a white trellis where Megan and her fiancé would exchange their vows. New walkways had been constructed in the yard, making it easy to access the few dozen tables where they'd eventually dine, beneath the vault of a massive white tent. There were five or six intricately carved ice sculptures, large enough to hold their form for hours, but what really drew her interest were the flowers: The grounds were a sea of brilliant gladiolus and lilies.

The crowd was pretty much what she'd expected. Aside from Will, the only guests she knew were Scott, Ashley, and Cassie, and none of them were particularly thrilled to see her. Not that it mattered much. Once people took their seats, everyone, with the possible exception of Will, was focused on Megan's imminent appearance. Will seemed content to fix his eyes on Ronnie from his spot near the trellis.

She wanted to remain as unobtrusive as possible, so she chose a seat about three rows from the back and away from the aisle. So far, she hadn't seen Susan, who was probably fussing over Megan, and she prayed she wouldn't notice Ronnie until after the ceremony. If she had her way, Susan wouldn't notice her then, either, but that was probably unlikely, since she would be spending so much time with Will.

"Excuse me," she heard someone say. Looking up, she saw an older man and his wife trying to slip past her to the empty seats on the far side of her.

"It's probably easier if I scoot down," she offered.

"Are you sure?"

"It's no problem at all," she said, moving over to the last empty seat to make room. The man seemed vaguely familiar to her, but the only thing that came to mind, the only possible connection, was the aquarium, and that didn't feel quite right.

Before she could dwell on it further, a string quartet started the first strains of the "Wedding March." She looked over her shoulder toward the house, along with everyone around her. She heard an audible gasp when Megan appeared at the top of the veranda stairs. As she began to move down the steps toward her father waiting at the bottom, Ronnie made the instantaneous decision that Megan was without doubt the most dazzling bride she'd ever seen.

Captivated by the sight of Will's sister, she barely registered the fact that the elderly man beside her seemed more interested in scrutinizing her than Megan.

The ceremony was elegant and yet surprisingly intimate. The pastor read from Second Corinthians, and then Megan and Daniel recited vows they'd written together. They promised patience when it was easy to be impatient, candor when it was easier to lie, and in their own ways, each recognized the fact that real commitment could be proven only through the passage of time.

As Ronnie watched them exchange rings, she appreciated that they'd decided on an outdoor wedding. It was less traditional than the church weddings she'd been to, but somehow still formal, and the setting was picture perfect.

She also knew that Will was right: She was going to like Megan. In the weddings she'd been to, she always had the sense that the brides were intent on pulling off an act, and more than once, she'd seen brides get upset if anything deviated from the script. Megan, on the other hand, seemed to be genuinely enjoying herself. As her father walked her up the aisle, she winked at some friends and stopped to give her grandmother a hug. When the ring bearer— barely a toddler and cute as a bug in his little tuxedo—stopped halfway up the aisle and crawled into his mother's lap, Megan laughed in delight, defusing the momentary tension.

Afterward, Megan was less interested in staging more magazine-worthy wedding photos than in visiting with her guests. She was, Ronnie thought, either incredibly confident or utterly clueless about all the stress her mother had incurred over every last wedding detail. Even from a distance, Ronnie could tell that nothing was going quite the way Susan had envisioned.

"You owe me a dance," she heard Will whisper.

Turning, she was struck anew by how handsome he was. "I don't believe that was part of our deal," she said. "You said you just wanted me to attend the wedding."

"What? You don't want to dance with me?"

"There's no music."

"I mean later."

"Oh," she said. "Well, in that case, I might consider it. But shouldn't you be posing for pictures?"

"I've been doing that for hours. I needed a break."

"Too much smiling hurts your cheeks?"

"Something like that. Oh, I'm supposed to tell you that you're going to be eating at table sixteen with Scott, Ashley, and Cassie."

Bummer. "Great," she said.

He laughed. "It won't be as bad as you think. They'll be on their best behavior. Otherwise my mom would probably lop off their heads."

It was Ronnie's turn to laugh. "Tell your mom she did a wonderful job getting all this organized. It's beautiful here."

"I will," he said. He continued to stare at her until both of them heard his name being called. When they turned, Ronnie thought Megan showed a trace of amusement at her brother having wandered off. "I have to get back," he said. "But I'll come find you at dinner. And don't forget about our dance later."

He really was heartbreakingly handsome, she thought again. "I should warn you that my feet are already hurting."

He put one hand over his heart. "I promise not to make fun of you if you limp."

"Gee, thanks."

He leaned in and kissed her. "Have I told you how beautiful you look tonight?"

She smiled, still tasting his lips on hers. "Not for at least twenty minutes. But you better go. You're needed elsewhere, and I don't want to get in trouble."

He kissed her before rejoining the rest of the wedding party. Feeling a rush of contentment, she turned around, only to see the elderly man she'd made room for at the ceremony watching her again.

At dinner, Scott, Cassie, and Ashley made little attempt to include her in their conversation, but she found she didn't really care. She wasn't in the mood to talk to them, nor was she hungry. Instead, after nibbling a few bites, she excused herself and headed toward the veranda. The porch gave her a panoramic view of the festivities, which somehow were even more enchanting in the dark. Under the moon's silvery spell, the tents seemed to be glowing. She could hear strains of conversation blending with the music from the band, which was now playing, and she found herself wondering what she would have been doing back home tonight had she stayed in New York. As the summer had progressed, she'd spoken to Kayla less and less often. Though she still considered her a friend, she realized that she didn't miss the world she'd left behind. She hadn't thought about going to a club in weeks, and when Kayla talked about the latest, greatest guy she'd met, Ronnie found her thoughts wandering to Will. She knew that whomever Kayla was fixated on was absolutely nothing like Will.

She didn't talk much about Will to Kayla. Kayla knew they were still seeing each other, but every time she mentioned the things they'd done—whether it was fishing or mudding or walking the beach—she had the feeling that Kayla was on another wavelength entirely. Kayla wasn't able to grasp the fact that Ronnie was happy simply being with Will, and Ronnie couldn't help wondering what that would mean for their friendship when she returned to New York. She knew she'd changed in the weeks she'd been down here, while Kayla, it seemed, hadn't changed at all. Ronnie realized she had no interest in going to clubs anymore.

Thinking back, she wondered why she'd been so interested in them in the first place—the music was loud, and everyone was on the make. And if everything was supposed to be so great, why did everyone drink or do drugs in the hope of enhancing their experience? It didn't make sense to her, but as the ocean sounded in the distance, she suddenly knew that it never had.

She also wanted a better relationship with her mom. At the very least, her dad had taught her that parents could be okay. Though she was under no illusions that her mom trusted her the way her dad did, she knew the tension cut both ways in their relationship. Maybe if she tried talking to her mom in the same way she talked to her dad, things would begin to improve between them.

Strange, what being forced to slow down could do to a person.

"It's going to end, you know," said a voice behind her.

Absorbed in her own thoughts, she hadn't heard Ashley approach, but she recognized her voice.

"Excuse me?" Warily, she turned to face the blonde.

"I mean, I'm glad Will invited you to the wedding. You should have your fun now because it's not going to last. He leaves in a couple of weeks. Have you thought about that yet?"

Ronnie appraised her. "I don't see how it's any of your business."

"Even if you two make plans to see each other, do you honestly think Will's mom is ever going to accept you?" Ashley went on. "Megan was engaged twice before this, and her mom ran both of them off. And she's going to do the same to you whether you like it or not. But even if she doesn't, you're leaving and he's leaving and it's not going to last."

Ronnie tensed, hating Ashley for giving voice to her darkest thoughts. Still, she was getting tired of this girl, and she had just about reached her limit.

"Hey, Ashley," she said, sidling up closer to her, "I'm going to tell you something, okay? And I want you to pay attention, so

I'm going to be perfectly clear." She took another step forward, until their faces were almost touching. "I'm getting sick and tired of listening to your crap, so if you ever try to talk to me again, I'm going to punch those bleached teeth right out of your mouth. Got it?"

Something in her face must have convinced Ashley that Ronnie was serious, because she turned quickly without another word and retreated to the safety of the tent.

Standing on the dock later, Ronnie was glad she'd finally managed to shut Ashley down, but the spiteful blonde's words still nagged at her. Will would be leaving for Vanderbilt in two weeks, and she'd most likely be leaving a week after that. She wasn't sure what was going to happen to them, aside from one simple truth: Things were going to change.

How could they not? Their relationship had been sustained by seeing each other every day, and try as she might, she couldn't imagine what it would be like to communicate by phone or text. She knew there were other options—using the camera on her computer, for instance—but she was under no illusions that it would resemble what they had now.

Which meant . . . what?

Behind her, the reception was in full swing. The chairs had been cleared from the temporary deck to create a dance floor, and from her vantage point on the dock, she'd seen Will dance at least twice with the six-year-old flower girl, as well as once with his sister, making Ronnie smile. A few minutes after her confrontation with Ashley, she'd watched Megan and Daniel cut the cake. The music started up again as Tom danced with Megan, and when Megan tossed her bouquet, Ronnie was sure that even distant neighbors must have heard the scream from the young woman who caught it.

"There you are," Will said, breaking into her reverie. He was coming down the walkway toward her. "I've been looking all over for you. It's time for our dance."

She watched him close the distance between them, trying to imagine what some of the girls he'd meet in college would think if they were in her shoes right now. Probably the same thing she was thinking: *Wow*.

He skipped down the last steps toward her, and she turned away. Studying the movement of the water seemed easier than facing him.

He knew her well enough to recognize something was amiss. "What's wrong?"

When she didn't answer right away, he gently brushed aside a strand of her hair. "Talk to me," he murmured.

She closed her eyes briefly before facing him. "Where are we going with all this? With you and me."

Will frowned in concern. "I'm not sure what you mean."

Her smile was melancholy. "Yes, you do," she said, and as soon as he lowered his hand from her hair, she knew he understood. "It's not going to be the same."

"That doesn't mean it has to end . . ."

"You make it sound so easy."

"It's not hard to get from Nashville to New York. It's, what . . . a two-hour flight? It's not like I'd have to walk there."

"And you'll come see me?" Ronnie heard the tremulousness of her own voice.

"I was planning on it. And I was hoping you'd come to Nashville, too. We can go to the *Grand Ole Opry*."

She laughed despite the ache she felt inside.

He put his arms around her. "I don't know why all of this is coming up now, but you're wrong. I mean, I know it's not going to be the same, but that doesn't mean it can't be better in some ways, too. My sister lives in New York, remember? And it's not as though school goes year-round. There are breaks in the fall and spring, another around Christmas, and then it's summer. And like I said, it's an easy enough trip if we just wanted to make a weekend out of it."

Ronnie wondered what his parents would think about that, but she said nothing.

"What's going on?" he asked. "Don't you even want to try?"

"Of course I want to try."

"Then we'll find a way to make it work, okay?" He paused. "I want to be with you as much as possible, Ronnie. You're smart and funny and you're honest. I trust you. I trust us. Yeah, I'm leaving and you're going back home. But neither of those things changes the way I feel about you. And my feelings aren't going to change simply because I'm going to Vanderbilt. I love you more than I've ever loved anyone."

She knew he was sincere, but a nagging voice inside her asked how many summer romances actually withstood the test of time. Not many, and it had nothing to do with feelings. People changed. Interests changed. All she had to do was glance in the mirror to recognize that.

Yet losing him seemed unbearable. He was the one she loved, the one she would always love, and as he leaned in to kiss her, she gave herself over to him. While he held her close, she ran her hands over his shoulders and back, feeling the strength in his arms. She knew he'd wanted more in their relationship than she'd been willing to offer, but here and now, she suddenly knew she had no other choice. There was only this moment, and it was theirs.

When he spoke, his voice was at once tentative and urgent. "Do you want to come with me to my dad's boat?"

She could feel herself trembling, uncertain whether she was ready for what was coming next. At the same time, she felt a powerful urge to move forward. "Okay," she whispered.

Will squeezed her hand, and she had the impression that he was as nervous as she felt as he led her toward the boat. She knew she could still change her mind, but she didn't want to stop. She wanted her first time to mean something, to happen with someone she cared deeply about. As they drew near the boat, she only vaguely registered her surroundings; the air was cooling, and from the corner of her eye, she could see guests moving on the dance floor. Off to the side, she saw Susan talking to the elderly man who'd been watching her earlier and was again struck by the nagging thought that she knew him from somewhere.

"That was such a sweet speech, I wish I could have recorded it," she heard someone drawl.

Will flinched. The voice came from the far side of the dock. Though he remained hidden in the darkness, Ronnie knew exactly who it was. Blaze had warned her something like this might be coming. Marcus stepped out from behind a pole and lit a fireball.

"I mean it, Richie Rich. You really charmed the pants off her." He grinned. "Almost, anyway."

Will took a step forward. "Get the hell out of here."

Marcus moved the fireball, rotating it between his fingers. "Or what? You'll call the cops? I know you better than that."

Will tensed. Marcus had somehow struck a nerve, though she didn't know why.

"This is private property," Will said, but he didn't sound as sure of himself as he should have.

"I love this part of town, don't you? Everyone down here is so country club chummy, they built this nice walkway that follows the water from one house to the next. I just love coming out here, you know? To enjoy the views, I mean."

"This is my sister's wedding," Will hissed.

"I always thought your sister was beautiful," Marcus said. "I even asked her out once. But the tramp turned me down. Can you believe that?" He didn't give Will a chance to respond before he motioned to the crowd. "I saw Scott earlier, up there acting like he doesn't have a care in the world. You gotta wonder about his conscience, huh? Then again, yours isn't so clear, either, is it? I'll bet you haven't even told your mommy that your little hooker girlfriend here is probably going to jail."

Will's body felt as taut as a bowstring.

"I'll bet the judge is setting her straight, though, huh?"

The judge . . .

Suddenly, Ronnie knew why the older man had looked so familiar . . . and now the judge was talking to Susan . . .

She felt her own breath catch in her throat.

Oh . . . God . . .

The realization came in the same instant that Will let go of her hand. As he charged toward Marcus, Marcus threw the fireball at him and leapt from the dock to the walkway. He scrambled up into the yard, near the corner of the tent, but he was no match for Will. Will easily closed the distance, but when Marcus glanced over his shoulder, Ronnie saw something in his face that told her this was exactly what he'd wanted from Will.

She had barely a split second to wonder why before she saw Marcus diving toward the ropes that supported the tent . . .

She lunged forward. "Don't, Will! Stop!" she screamed, but it was already too late.

Will crashed into Marcus, entwining them both in the ropes as the pegs tore loose from the ground. Ronnie watched in horror as a corner of the tent began to collapse.

People began to scream, and she heard a sickening crash as one of the ice sculptures toppled over, the guests scattering and screaming. Will and Marcus were struggling on the ground before Marcus was finally able to extricate himself. Instead of continuing to fight, he burst free from the commotion and leapt back onto the walkway, vanishing from sight behind the neighbor's house.

In the ensuing pandemonium, Ronnie found herself wondering whether anyone would even remember seeing Marcus there at all.

They certainly remembered her. Sitting in the study, she felt as if she were twelve years old. All she wanted to do was get as far away from the house as possible and crawl under her covers at home.

As she heard Susan shouting from the next room, she couldn't stop replaying the image of the collapsing tent.

"She ruined your sister's wedding!"

"No, she didn't!" Will shouted back. "I told you what happened!"

"You expect me to believe that some stranger crashed the party and you tried to stop him?"

"That's what happened!"

Why Will never mentioned Marcus by name, Ronnie didn't know, but there was no way on earth she was going to add her two cents. Any second she expected to hear a chair go crashing through the window. Or for the two of them to come charging into the study, so that Susan could berate her.

"Will, please . . . even assuming your story is true, why was he here? Everyone knows about all the security we have! Every judge in town was at the wedding. The sheriff was monitoring the road out front, for goodness' sake. It had to have something to do with that girl! Don't give me that . . . I can tell by your face that I'm right . . . And what were you doing with her at your dad's boat, anyway?"

The way she said "that girl" made Ronnie sound like something disgusting Susan had stepped in and couldn't scrape off her shoe.

"Mom—"

"Stop! Don't even try to make excuses! It was Megan's wedding, Will, don't you get that? Her *wedding*! You know how important this was to all of us. You know how hard your father and I worked to get everything ready!"

"I didn't mean for it to happen—"

"It doesn't matter, Will." Ronnie heard Susan let out an explosive sigh. "You knew what was going to happen if you brought her here. You know she's not like us . . ."

"You haven't even given her a chance—"

"Judge Chambers *recognized* her! He told me she's going to court later this month for felony shoplifting! So either you didn't know and she's been lying to you, or you did know and you've been lying to me!"

There was a tense silence, and despite herself, Ronnie found herself straining to hear Will's response. When he did speak, he sounded subdued.

"I didn't tell you because I knew you wouldn't understand."

"Will, honey . . . don't you get that she's not good enough for you? You've got your whole future ahead of you, and the last thing you need in your life is someone like her. I've been waiting for you to figure it out on your own, but obviously you're too emotionally involved to see the obvious. She's not good enough for you. She's low-class. Low! Class!"

As the voices escalated, Ronnie felt physically sick; it was all she could do not to vomit. Susan wasn't right about everything, but she had guessed right about one thing: Ronnie was the reason Marcus had come. If only she had trusted her instincts and stayed home! She didn't belong here.

"Are you okay?" Tom asked. He was standing in the doorway, holding his car keys.

"I'm really sorry, Mr. Blakelee," she blurted out. "I didn't mean to cause any problems."

"I know you didn't," he said. Despite his sympathetic response, she knew he had to be upset as well. How could he not be? Though no one was seriously hurt, two guests who'd been knocked over during the commotion had been taken to the hospital. He was in control of his emotions, and she was thankful for that. Had he even raised his voice, she would have burst into tears.

"Would you like me to drive you home? It's pretty chaotic out there right now. Your dad might have trouble getting to the house."

Ronnie nodded. "Yes, please." She straightened her dress as she stood, hoping she could make it home without throwing up. "Would you please tell Will that I said good-bye? And that I won't be seeing him anymore?"

Tom nodded. "Yeah," he said. "I can do that."

* * *

She didn't throw up and didn't cry, but she didn't say anything in what had to be the longest car ride of her life. Nor did Tom, though that wasn't exactly surprising.

The house was quiet when she got home; the lights were off, and both Jonah and her dad were sound asleep. From the hallway, she could hear her father breathing; it was deep and heavy, as though he'd had a long, hard day. But all she could think as she crawled into bed and began to cry was that no day could have been longer and harder than the one she'd just endured.

Her eyes were still puffy and sore as she felt someone shaking her awake. Squinting up, she saw Jonah sitting on the bed beside her.

"You've got to get up."

The images from the night before and the things Susan had said came surging back, making her suddenly feel nauseated.

"I don't want to get up."

"You don't have a choice. There's someone here."

"Will?"

"No," he said. "Someone else."

"Ask Dad if he can handle it," she said, pulling the covers over her head.

"I would, except that he's still sleeping. And besides, she asked for you."

"Who?"

"I don't know, but she's waiting for you outside. And she's hot."

After throwing on a pair of jeans and a shirt, Ronnie stepped cautiously onto the porch. She hadn't known what to expect, but this certainly wasn't it.

"You look terrible," Megan said without preamble.

She was dressed in shorts and a tank top, but Jonah was right: Up close, she was even prettier than she'd been at the wedding yesterday. She also radiated a self-confidence that made Ronnie instantly feel years younger.

"I'm really sorry about ruining your wedding . . . ," Ronnie began.

Megan held up a hand. "You didn't ruin the wedding," she said with a wry smile. "You made the reception . . . memorable . . ."

At Megan's comment, Ronnie felt tears beginning to form.

"Don't cry," Megan said gently. "I don't blame you. If it was anyone's fault, it was Marcus's."

Ronnie blinked.

"Yeah, I know what happened. Will and I talked after my mom was finally finished with him. I think I'm pretty clear on everything. So like I said, I don't blame you. Marcus is insane. He always has been."

Ronnie swallowed. Though Megan was being ridiculously forgiving about the whole thing—or maybe *because* she was being so understanding—her feelings of mortification only intensified.

"Umm . . . if you're not here to yell at me, then why did you come?" Ronnie asked.

"Partly because I talked to Will. But the main reason I came is because I want to know something. And I want you to tell me the truth."

Ronnie felt her stomach roiling. "What do you want to know?"

"I want to know if you love my brother."

Ronnie wasn't sure she'd heard right, but Megan's gaze was unwavering. Yet what did she have to lose? Their relationship was over. Distance would make sure of that, if Susan didn't do it first.

Megan had asked for the truth, and in light of the kindness she'd shown, Ronnie knew she had no choice.

"Yes, I do."

"It's not a summer fling?"

Ronnie shook her head fiercely. "Will and I . . ." She trailed off, not trusting herself to speak, knowing that words were inadequate to describe it.

Studying her face, Megan slowly began to smile. "Okay," she said. "I believe you."

Ronnie frowned in consternation, and Megan laughed. "I've been around. I've seen that look before. Like this morning when I looked in the mirror. I feel the same way about Daniel, but I have to say it's a little odd to see that look on you. When I was seventeen, I don't think I even knew what love was. But when it's right, it's right, and you just know it."

As Ronnie registered her words, she decided that Will hadn't been fair when he'd described his sister. She wasn't great, she was . . . way, way better than that. She was the kind of person Ronnie wanted to be in a few years, in practically every way. In a matter of minutes, Megan had become her hero.

"Thank you," she murmured, unable to think of a better response.

"Don't thank me. This isn't about you. This is about my brother, and he's still crazy about you," she said with a knowing smile. "Anyway, my point is that since you're in love with him, then you shouldn't worry about what happened at the reception. All you did was give my mom a story she's going to tell for the rest of her life. Believe me, she'll get a lot of mileage out of it. In time, she'll get over this. She always does."

"I don't know . . ."

"That's because you don't know her. Oh, she's tough, don't get me wrong. And protective. But once you get to know her, there's no one better in the world. She'll do anything for anyone she cares about."

Her words echoed Will's description, but so far, Ronnie hadn't seen that side of Susan.

"You should talk to Will," Megan said, lowering her sunglasses into place as she prepared to leave. "Don't worry. I'm not suggesting you go to the house. And besides, he's not there."

"Where is he?"

She motioned over her shoulder, toward the pier in the distance. "He's at the tournament. Their first game starts in forty minutes."

The tournament. In the wild rush of all that had happened, she'd forgotten about it.

"I was just there, but when I left him, he was really out of it. He was so upset, I don't think he slept at all. Especially after what you told my dad. You need to make things right." Her voice was firm.

Megan was about to step off the porch when she turned to face Ronnie again. "And just so you know? Daniel and I postponed our honeymoon for a day so we could watch my little brother play in the tournament. It would be great if his head was in the game. He might have downplayed it, but doing well in the tournament is important to him."

After showering and dressing, Ronnie raced down the beach. The area around the pier was thronged, much as it had been on her first night in town.

Temporary bleachers that sandwiched two courts had been set up on the far side of the pier, jammed with at least a thousand spectators. Even more were massed along the pier, which provided a bird's-eye view of the game. The beach itself was so packed, she could barely make her way through the crowd. There was no way she'd be able to find Will in time, she fretted.

No wonder winning the tournament was so important.

She searched the crowd, catching sight of some of the other teams, which only made her feel more frantic. As far as she could tell, there wasn't a special area reserved for the players, and she despaired of ever locating him with so many people around.

With only ten minutes until the game began, she was about to give up when she suddenly spotted him walking with Scott near some paramedics who were leaning against their truck. As Will pulled off his shirt, he vanished behind the truck.

She plunged through the crowd, calling out hurried apologies to the people she pushed. It took her less than a minute to reach the spot where she'd last seen him, but he was nowhere in sight. She moved forward again, and this time she thought she saw Scott—he was hard to make out in the ocean of blondes. Just as she let out a frustrated sigh, she saw Will standing by himself in the shade of the bleachers, taking a long drink from a bottle of Gatorade.

Megan had been right. She could tell by the slump of his shoulders that he was exhausted, and she couldn't see evidence of any pre-game adrenaline.

She scooted around some bystanders, breaking into a jog as she got closer. For an instant, she thought she saw surprise in his face, but he quickly turned away and she knew his dad had given him her message.

She read the pain and confusion in his reaction. She would have talked it all through with him, but with the game only minutes away, she didn't have time. As soon as she was close, she threw her arms around him and kissed him as passionately as she could. If he was surprised, he recovered quickly and began to kiss her back.

When they finally separated, he spoke. "About what happened yesterday . . ."

Ronnie shook her head, placing a gentle finger over his lips. "We'll talk about that later, but just so you know, I didn't mean what I said to your dad. I love you. And I need you to do something for me."

When he cocked his head questioningly, she went on.

"Play today like you've never played before."

27

. . . . ⚡ . . . .

Marcus

Kicking at the sand at Bower's Point, Marcus knew he should be enjoying the havoc he'd wreaked the previous evening. Everything had turned out exactly the way he'd planned it. The house had been decorated precisely as the endless newspaper articles had detailed, and loosening the tent pegs—not all the way, just enough to ensure they'd pull free when he slammed into the ropes—had been easy to do when everyone was eating dinner. He'd been thrilled to see Ronnie wander down to the dock, Will in tow; they hadn't let him down. And good old reliable Will had played his part perfectly; if there was a guy more predictable in the entire world, Marcus would be shocked. Push button X and Will would do one thing; push button Y and Will would do another. If it hadn't been so much fun, it would have been boring.

Marcus wasn't like other people; he'd known that for a long time. Growing up, he never felt guilty about anything, and he liked that about himself. There was power in the ability to do whatever he wanted, whenever he wanted to do it, but the pleasure was usually short-lived.

Last night, he'd felt more alive than he had in months; the rush had been incredible. Usually after he pulled off one of his "projects," as he liked to think of them, he would be satisfied for weeks. A good thing, too, since his urges, left unchecked, would eventually get him caught. He wasn't dumb. He knew how things worked, which was why he was always very, very careful.

Now, however, he was plagued by the feeling that he'd made a mistake. Perhaps he'd pushed his luck too far in making the Blakelees the target of his latest project. They were the closest thing to royalty in Wilmington, after all—they had power, they had connections, and they had money. And he knew that if they discovered he was involved, they'd stop at nothing to put him away for as long as possible. So he was left with a nagging doubt: Will had covered for Scott in the past, but would he do so even at the expense of his sister's wedding?

He didn't like this feeling. It felt almost like . . . *fear*. He didn't want to go to prison, no matter how short the sentence. He *couldn't* go to prison. He didn't belong there. He was *better* than that. He was *smarter* than that, and he couldn't imagine being locked in a cage and being ordered around by a bunch of prison guard flunkies or becoming the love interest of a three-hundred-pound neo-Nazi or eating food sprinkled with roach crap or any of the other horrors he could easily imagine.

The buildings he'd burned and the people he'd hurt meant absolutely nothing to him, but the thought of prison made him . . . sick. And never once had the fear felt closer than it had since last night.

So far, things were calm, he reminded himself. Obviously Will hadn't identified him, because if he had, Bower's Point would be crawling with cops. Still, he needed to lay low for a while. Real low. No parties at beach houses, no fires in warehouses, and he wouldn't go anywhere near either Will or Ronnie. It went without saying that he wouldn't utter a single word to Teddy or Lance or even Blaze. It was better to let people's memories fade.

Unless Will changed his mind.

The possibility hit him like a physical blow. Where he'd once had complete power over Will, their roles had suddenly been reversed . . . or at least equalized.

Maybe, he thought, it would be best if he just left town for a while. Head south to Myrtle Beach or Fort Lauderdale or Miami until the little wedding brouhaha faded away completely.

It felt like the right decision, but for that, he needed money. A lot of money. And soon. Which meant he needed to do some shows in front of some very large crowds. Luckily, the beach volleyball tournament was starting today. Will would be competing, no doubt, but there was no reason he had to go anywhere near the courts. He'd do his show on the pier . . . a big show.

Behind him, Blaze was sitting in the sun, wearing only jeans and her bra; her shirt lay balled up near the campfire.

"Blaze," he called out, "we're going to need nine fireballs today. There's going to be a big crowd and we need to make some money."

She didn't answer him, but her audible sigh set his teeth on edge. He was sick and tired of her. Since her mom had kicked her out, she'd been nothing but glum day in and day out. He watched her rise from her spot and grab the bottle of lighter fluid. Good. At least she was working a little to earn her keep.

Nine fireballs. Not all at the same time, of course; they normally used six in the course of a show. But adding one more here and there, something unexpected, might be enough to raise the cash he needed. In a couple of days, he'd be in Florida. Just him. Teddy and Lance and Blaze would be on their own for a while, which was fine with him. He was sick of all of them.

Already planning his trip, he barely noticed as Blaze soaked several cloth balls in lighter fluid, directly above the shirt she would later wear in the show.

28

·····✦·····

Will

Winning their first-round game was remarkably easy; Will and Scott barely broke a sweat. In round two, their game was even easier, their opponents scoring only a single point. In the third round, both he and Scott had to work hard. Though the score appeared lopsided, Will walked off the court thinking that the team they had just beaten was a lot better than the score indicated.

They started the quarterfinals at two p.m.; the final was scheduled for six. As Will rested his hands on his knees, waiting for the opposing team's service, he knew his game was on today. They were down five to two, but he wasn't worried. He felt good, he felt quick, and every shot he placed sent the ball flying to exactly the spot he wanted. Even as his opponent tossed the ball in the air to begin his serve, Will felt unassailable.

The ball came arcing over the net with a heavy topspin; anticipating its drop, he scrambled forward and set up the ball perfectly. With flawless timing, Scott rushed up and leapt before spiking the ball crosscourt, returning the serve to their side. They won the next six points in a row before the other team got the serve back, and as he settled into position, he quickly scanned the stands for Ronnie. She was sitting in the bleachers opposite his parents and Megan—probably a good idea.

He'd hated that he couldn't tell his mom the truth about Marcus, but what could he do? If his mom knew who'd done it, she would go for blood . . . which could only lead to retribution. He was certain the first thing Marcus would do if arrested would be to get his sentence reduced in exchange for "useful information" about another, more serious crime—Scott's. It would cause problems for Scott at a critical time in his scholarship search, not to mention hurt Scott's parents—who also happened to be close friends of his own parents. So he'd lied, and unfortunately his mom had chosen to blame the whole thing on Ronnie.

But she'd shown up this morning and told him that she loved him nonetheless. They'd talk later, she'd promised. And she'd told him that more than anything, she wanted him to play his best in the tournament, which was exactly what he was going to do.

As the opponents served again, Will raced across court to make the shot; Scott followed with a perfect set, and Will spiked it home. From that point on, their opponents scored only one more point before the game ended; in the next game, they scored only twice.

He and Scott advanced to the semifinals, and in the stands, he could see Ronnie cheering for him.

The semifinal match was their toughest yet; they'd won the first game easily, only to lose the second game in a tiebreaker.

Will was standing on the service line, waiting for the official to signal the beginning of the third game, when his gaze wandered first to the bleachers and then to the pier, noting that the crowd was three times larger than it had been the year before. Here and there, he saw clusters of people he'd known in high school and others he'd known growing up. There wasn't an open seat in the stands.

At the referee's signal, Will tossed the ball high in the air and took a series of quick steps. Launching himself into the air, he sent a driving serve down the baseline, aiming for a spot about three-

quarters of the way back. He landed, ready to scramble into position, but he already knew it wasn't necessary. By splitting the
court, both of his opponents had frozen for an instant too long;
the hard-driving ball sent up a plume of sand before skating off
the court.

One to zero.

Will served seven times in a row, putting Scott and him com-
fortably ahead, and they ended up alternating points from then
on, leading to a relatively easy victory.

Walking off the court, Scott slapped his back.

"It's over," he said. "We're on fire today, so let Tyson and Landry bring it on!"

Tyson and Landry, a pair of eighteen-year-olds from Hermosa
Beach, California, were the dominant junior team in the world.
A year ago, they'd ranked eleventh in the world overall, which
would have been good enough to represent virtually every other
country in the Olympic Games. They'd been playing together
since they were twelve years old and hadn't lost so much as a
game in two years. Scott and Will had met them only once before
in last year's semifinal of the same tournament, and they'd walked
off the court with their tails between their legs. They hadn't even
made a game of it.

But today was a different story: They won the first game by
three points; Tyson and Landry won the next game by exactly the
same margin; and in the final game, they found themselves tied at
seven.

Will had been outside in the sun for nine hours. Despite the
liters of water and Gatorade he'd consumed, the sun and heat
should have worn him down at least a little, and maybe it had.
But he didn't feel it. Not now. Not when he realized they actually
had a chance to win the whole thing.

They had the serve—always a disadvantage in beach volleyball, since points were scored with every volley and the team re-

turning the serve had the chance to set and spike the ball—but Scott sent a knuckleball serve over the net that forced Tyson out of position. Tyson was able to reach the ball in time, but he sent it flying in the wrong direction. Landry charged and somehow got his hand on the ball, but that only made matters worse; it soared into the crowd, and Will knew it would be at least another minute until the ball was back in play. When that happened, he and Scott would be leading by a point.

As usual, he turned first toward Ronnie and saw her wave at him; then, facing the other set of bleachers, he smiled and nodded at his family. Beyond them on the pier, he could see the crowd packed in the area closest to the courts, but it was clear just a little farther away. He wondered about that until he saw a fireball arc through the air.

The score was tied at twelve when it happened.

The ball had soared into the crowd again, this time because of Scott, and as Will returned to his spot on the court, he found himself gazing up at the pier, because he knew Marcus was there.

The fact that Marcus was so close made him tense with the same anger he'd felt the night before.

He knew he should let it go, just as Megan had advised him. He knew he shouldn't have troubled her with the whole story last night; it was her wedding, after all, and his parents had booked a suite at the historic Wilmingtonian Hotel for her and Daniel. But she'd insisted, and he'd unburdened himself. Though she didn't criticize his decision, he knew she'd been disappointed that he'd remained silent about Scott's crime. She'd been unequivocally supportive this morning nonetheless, and as he waited for the referee to blow his whistle, he knew he was playing as much for his sister as for himself.

On the pier, he caught sight of fireballs dancing in the air; the crowd had cleared near the railing, and he could just make out Teddy and Lance break-dancing as usual. What surprised him was the sight of Blaze juggling the fireballs with Marcus. She would catch one, then send it flying back toward Marcus. To Will's eye, the fireballs were moving back and forth faster than usual. Blaze was retreating slowly, probably trying to slow things down, until her back finally hit the railing of the pier.

The jolt probably made her lose concentration, even as the fireballs continued to fly her way, because she misjudged the trajectory of one of them and ended up catching it against her shirt. With another fireball following quickly, she reached for that one while pinning the former to her body. Within seconds, the front of her shirt became a sheet of fire, fueled by excess lighter fluid.

Panicking, she tried to bat out the flames, obviously forgetting that she still held the fireball . . .

A moment later, her hands were on fire as well, and her screams drowned out all other noise in the stadium. The crowd surrounding the fire show must have been in shock, because no one made a move toward her. Even from a distance, Will could see the flames consuming her like a cyclone.

Instinctively, he sprinted off the court, racing through the sand toward the pier. Feeling his feet slip, he lifted his knees to increase his speed, Blaze's screams splitting the air.

He barreled through the crowd, zigzagging from one opening to the next and quickly reaching the steps; he took them three at a time, grabbing hold of one of the pilings so he wouldn't slow down, then whipped around as soon as he'd reached the pier.

He shoved through the crowd, unable to see Blaze until he reached the clearing. By then, a man was squatting beside her writhing, screaming figure; there was no sign of Marcus or Teddy or Lance . . .

Will stopped short at the sight of Blaze's shirt, melted into her raw, blistered skin. She was sobbing and screaming incoherently now, yet no one around her seemed to have the slightest idea what to do next.

Will knew he had to do something. An ambulance would take

at least fifteen minutes to get across the bridge and over to the beach, even without the massive crowd. When Blaze cried out in agony once more, he bent over and scooped her gently into his arms. His truck was close by; he'd been one of the first to arrive in the morning, and he began carrying her in that direction. Stunned at what they'd just witnessed, no one tried to stop him.

Blaze was fading in and out of consciousness, and he moved as fast as he could, careful not to jolt her unnecessarily. Ronnie came bounding up the steps as he was carrying Blaze past; he had no idea how she'd been able to get down from the bleachers and reach him so fast, but he was relieved to see her.

"The keys are on the back tire!" he shouted. "We need to stretch her out on the backseat—and when we're driving, call the emergency room and tell them we're on our way so they can be expect us!"

Ronnie raced ahead to the truck and was able to get the door open before Will arrived. It wasn't easy to maneuver Blaze into the seat, but they managed it, and then Will jumped behind the wheel. Peeling out, he floored it for the hospital, already certain he was going to violate a few dozen traffic laws along the way.

The emergency room at the hospital was packed. Will was seated near the door, staring out into the darkening evening. Ronnie sat beside him. His parents, along with Megan and Daniel, had shown up briefly but had left hours earlier.

In the past four hours, Will had told the story multiple times to countless different people, including Blaze's mom, who was in the back with Blaze now. When she'd rushed into the waiting room, Will had clearly seen the raw fear written on her face before one of the nurses had led her away.

Aside from learning that she'd been rushed into surgery, Will hadn't heard anything yet. The night stretched out ahead of them, but he couldn't imagine leaving. His memories kept taking him back to how she'd looked when they sat beside each other in third grade and then forward to the image of the ravaged creature he'd carried in his arms earlier that day. She was a stranger now, but she'd been a friend once, and that was enough for him.

He wondered if the police would come back. They'd arrived with his parents, and he'd told them what he knew, but they'd been more interested in why he'd brought Blaze to the hospital instead of allowing the paramedics to do so. Will had been truthful—he hadn't remembered they were on-site, and he could see she needed to get to the hospital immediately—and thankfully, they'd understood that. He thought he'd even seen Officer Johnson nod slightly, and Will had the sense that in the same situation, Officer Johnson would have done the same thing.

Every time the door beyond the nurses' station opened, Will searched for one of the nurses who'd been there to receive Blaze. In the car, Ronnie had somehow been able to get through to the hospital, and a trauma team was waiting; within a minute, Blaze was on a gurney and being led away. It was almost ten minutes before either he or Ronnie could think of anything to say to each other. Instead they sat motionless, holding hands, trembling at the memory of Blaze screaming in the truck.

The hospital door opened again, and Will recognized Blaze's mom as she walked toward them.

Both Will and Ronnie stood. When she was close, Will could see the tension lines around her mouth.

"One of the nurses told me you were still out here. I wanted to come down to thank you for what you did."

Her voice cracked, and Will swallowed, realizing his throat had gone dry.

"Is she going to be okay?" he managed to croak out.

"I don't know yet. She's still in surgery." Blaze's mom focused on Ronnie. "I'm Margaret Conway. I don't know if Galadriel ever mentioned me."

"I'm really sorry, Mrs. Conway." Ronnie gently reached out to touch her arm.

The woman sniffed, trying and failing to stay composed. "I am, too," she began. Her voice became more ragged as she went on. "I told her a hundred times to stay away from Marcus, but she just wouldn't listen, and now my little girl—"

She broke off, unable to contain her sobs. Will watched, paralyzed, as Ronnie stepped forward to hold her, both of them crying in each other's arms.

As Will drove the streets of Wrightsville Beach, everything stood out in glittering focus. He was driving fast but knew he could drive even faster. In a split-second glance, he was able to notice details that ordinarily would have escaped him: the soft, misty halo around the streetlamps, an overturned garbage can in the alley beside the Burger King, the small dent near the license plate of a cream-colored Nissan Sentra.

Beside him, Ronnie was watching him anxiously but hadn't said anything. She hadn't asked where they were going, but she didn't have to. As soon as Blaze's mom had left the waiting room, Will had stood without a word and stalked furiously back to the truck. Ronnie had followed and climbed into the passenger seat.

Up ahead, the traffic light turned yellow, but instead of slowing the car, Will floored it. The engine revved and the truck shot forward, toward Bower's Point.

He knew the quickest route and navigated the turns easily; leaving the business district, the truck roared past quiet ocean-front homes. The pier was next, and then Ronnie's house; he didn't so much as slow down. Instead, he pushed the truck to the limits of safety.

Next to him, Ronnie was holding on to the handgrip as he made the final turn into a gravel parking lot almost hidden by the trees. The truck skidded to a halt on the gravel as Ronnie finally found the nerve to speak.

"Please don't do this."

Will heard her and knew what she wanted, but he hopped out of the truck anyway. Bower's Point wasn't far. Accessed only by the beach, it lay just around the corner, a couple of hundred meters past the lifeguard stand.

Will broke into a jog. He *knew* Marcus would be here; he felt it. He began to run flat out, images flashing through his mind: the fire at the church, the night at the carnival, the way he'd grabbed Ronnie by the arms . . . and Blaze, going up in flames.

Marcus hadn't tried to help her. He'd run away when she needed him, when she could have died.

Will didn't care what might happen to him. He didn't care what might happen to Scott. He was beyond that now. This time, Marcus had gone too far. As he rounded the corner, he spotted them in the distance, seated on pieces of driftwood around a small campfire.

Fire. Fireballs. *Blaze* . . .

He sped up, steeling himself for what was coming next. He drew close enough to make out the empty beer bottles scattered around the fire, but he knew that the darkness prevented them from seeing him.

Marcus was raising a bottle of beer to his lips as Will lowered his shoulder and slammed into him from the back, just below his neck. He felt Marcus's back whiplash under the impact, the only sound a painful gasp as Will drove him forward into the sand.

Will knew he had to move quickly, in order to reach Teddy before he or his brother could react. The sight of Marcus suddenly being driven to the ground seemed to paralyze them, though, and after Will drove a knee into Marcus's back, he lunged toward Teddy, his legs moving like pistons, driving him back over the driftwood. Will landed on top of Teddy, but instead of using his fists, he reared back and slammed his forehead down onto Teddy's nose.

He felt it crunch as it was flattened under the impact. Will rose quickly, ignoring the sight of Teddy rolling on the ground, hands to his face and blood spurting between his fingers, his screams partially muffled by the sound of him gagging.

Lance was already on the move and charging as Will took one large step back, keeping his distance. Lance was almost on him and going low when Will suddenly drove his knee upward, feeling as it connected with Lance's face. Lance's head whipped back and he was unconscious before he hit the ground.

Two down, one to go.

By then, Marcus was staggering to his feet. He grabbed a piece of driftwood and backed away as Will moved forward. But the last thing Will wanted was for Marcus to be able to position his feet before swinging. Will charged. Marcus swung the wood, but the strike was weak and Will batted it aside before smashing into Marcus's chest. He wrapped his arms around him, locking them and lifting, using the momentum to drive Marcus back. It was a picture-perfect football tackle, and Marcus was slammed onto his back.

Will brought his full weight down on top of Marcus, and as he'd done with Teddy, he head-butted Marcus as hard as he could.

He felt the same crunching of bone, but this time he didn't stop there. Instead, he smashed Marcus with his fist. He hit him again and again, giving in to the rage, unleashing his fury at the impotence he'd felt ever since the fire. He hit Marcus in the ear, then hit his ear again. Marcus's screams only enraged him further. He swung again, this time aiming for the nose he'd already broken—when suddenly he felt someone seize his arm.

He turned, ready for Teddy, but it was Ronnie holding his arm, a terrified expression on her face.

"Stop! He's not worth going to jail for!" she screamed. "Don't ruin your life for him!"

He barely heard her, but he registered her tugging as she began trying to pull him off.

"Please, Will," she said, her voice shaking. "You're not like him. You have a future. Don't throw it all away."

As she gradually loosened her grip, he felt his energy drain away. He struggled to stand, the adrenaline leaving him shaky and off balance. Ronnie slipped an arm around his waist, and they slowly began walking back to the truck.

The next morning, he went to work with his hand aching, only to find Scott waiting for him in the small locker room. As Scott pulled up his coverall, he glared at Will before shrugging the one-piece over his shoulders.

"You didn't have to quit the match," he said, pulling up the zipper. "The paramedics were there the whole time."

"I know," Will said. "I wasn't thinking. I'd seen them earlier, but I forgot. I'm sorry about having to forfeit the match."

"Yeah, well, so am I," Scott snapped. He reached for a rag and tucked it into his belt. "We could have won it all, but you had to rush off to play hero."

"Scott, man, she needed help—"

"Yeah? And why did it have to be you? Why couldn't you wait for help? Why didn't you call 911? Why did you have to haul her off in your truck?"

"I told you—I forgot the paramedics were there. I thought it would take too long for an ambulance to arrive . . ."

Scott slammed his fist against the locker. "But you don't even like her!" he shouted. "You don't even know her anymore! Yeah, if it was Ashley or Cassie or even Ronnie, I could understand it. Hell, if it was a stranger, I could understand it. But Blaze? *Blaze?* The same chick who's gonna send your girlfriend to jail? The chick that hangs out with *Marcus?*" Scott took a step toward him. "Do you think for a second she would have done the same for you? If you were hurt and you needed help? Not a chance!"

"It's just a game," Will objected, feeling his own anger begin to surface.

"To you!" Scott screamed. "To you it's a game! But for you, everything's a game! Don't you get that? Because nothing matters to you! You don't need to win things like this, because even if you lose, you still get life handed to you on a silver platter! But I needed this! It's my *future* on the line, man!"

"Yeah, well, it was a girl's *life* on the line," Will lashed back. "And if you could stop being so self-centered for once, you'd see that saving someone's life is more important than your precious volleyball scholarship!"

Scott shook his head in disgust. "You've been my friend for a long time . . . but you know, it's always been on your terms. Everything has always been what *you* want. *You* want to break up with Ashley, *you* want to hang out with Ronnie, *you* want to blow off practice for weeks on end, *you* want to play hero. Well, you know what? *You* were wrong. I talked to the paramedics. They told me you were wrong. That by hauling her to the truck the way you did, you might have made things worse. And what did you get? Did she thank you? No, of course she didn't. And she won't. But you're perfectly willing to screw a friend over because what *you* want to do is most important."

Scott's words were like blows to his stomach, but they only stoked his anger. "Get over yourself, Scott," Will said. "This time, it's not all about you."

"You owed me!" Scott screamed, slamming the locker again. "I asked for this one simple thing! You know how much it meant to me!"

"I don't owe you anything," Will said with quiet fury. "I've been covering for you for the past eight months. I'm tired of Marcus playing us. You need to do the right thing. You need to tell the truth. Things have changed."

Will turned and strode to the door. As he pushed it open, he heard Scott behind him.

"What did you do?"

Will turned, holding the door half-open and meeting Scott's gaze with steely intent. "Like I said, you need to tell the truth."

He waited until Scott absorbed his words, then stepped out, letting the door slam shut behind him. As he made his way past the cars on lifts, he could hear Scott calling after him.

"You want to ruin my life? You want me to go to jail for an accident? I'm not going to do that!"

Even as he neared the lobby, he could still hear Scott slamming his hand into the lockers.

29

.... ♪ ....

Ronnie

The next week was tense for both of them. Ronnie wasn't comfortable with the violence she'd seen Will display, nor was she entirely comfortable with the way it had made her feel. She didn't like fights, she didn't like to see people get hurt, and she knew that it rarely improved a situation. Yet she couldn't force herself to be angry at Will for what he'd done. As much as she didn't want to condone what happened, watching Will completely *dismantle* the three of them made her feel just a bit safer when she was with him.

But Will was stressed. He was certain that Marcus would report what happened and that the police would come knocking at his door any minute, but Ronnie sensed that something else was bothering him, something he wasn't letting on. For some reason he and Scott weren't on speaking terms, and she wondered whether that had something to do with Will's unease.

Then, of course, there was the family. Particularly Will's mother. Ronnie had seen her twice since the wedding: once as she waited in the truck at Will's house while Will ran inside to pick up a clean shirt, and once at a restaurant in downtown Wilmington when Will took her out. As they'd taken their seats, Susan had walked in with a group of her friends. Ronnie had a perfect view of the entrance, but Will was facing in the other direction. On both occasions, Susan had pointedly turned her back to Ronnie.

She hadn't told Will about either incident. While Will was lost in his own world of retribution and worry, Ronnie noticed that Susan seemed to believe Ronnie was somehow personally responsible for the tragedy that had befallen Blaze.

As she stood in her bedroom, she watched Will's sleeping figure from a distance. He was curled up near the turtles' nest; because a few of the other nests had begun to hatch, they'd removed the cage this afternoon, and the nest was completely exposed. Neither of them felt good about leaving it unattended for the night, and because Will was spending less and less time at home anyway, he'd volunteered to watch it.

She didn't want to think about their newfound troubles, but she found herself replaying all that had happened this summer. She could barely remember the girl she'd been when she'd first arrived at the beach. And the summer wasn't over yet; in a couple of days, she'd turn eighteen, and after one last weekend together, Will would be leaving for college. Her next court appearance was scheduled a few days after that, and then she'd have to go back to New York. So much already done and so much left to do.

She shook her head. Who was she? And whose life was she leading? More than that, where would it take her?

These days, none of it and all of it felt real, more real than anything she'd known: her love for Will, her growing bond with her father, the way her life had slowed down, so simply and completely. All of it sometimes seemed to be happening to someone else, someone she was still getting to know. Never in a million years would she have considered the idea that a sleepy beach town somewhere in the South would have been filled with so much more . . . *life* and *drama* than Manhattan.

Smiling, she had to admit that with a few exceptions, it hadn't been all that bad, either. She was sleeping in a quiet bedroom beside her brother, separated only by glass and sand from the young man she loved, a young man who loved her back. She wondered whether there could be anything greater in life. And despite all that had happened, maybe because of it, she knew she would never forget the summer they'd spent together, no matter what the future might bring.

Lying in bed, she began to drift off to sleep. Her last conscious thought was that there was more coming. Although that sensation often foretold the worst, she knew that couldn't be possible, not after all they'd been through.

In the morning, however, she awoke feeling anxious. As always, she was acutely conscious of the fact that another day had passed, meaning one less day left with Will.

But as she lay there, trying to make sense of the unease she felt, she realized it wasn't just that. Will was heading off to college next week. Even Kayla was heading off to college. Yet she still had no idea what was coming for her. Yeah, she'd turn eighteen, and yeah, she'd deal with whatever the court decided, but then what? Was she going to live with her mom forever? Should she apply for a job at Starbucks? For an instant she flashed on a image of herself holding a shovel and following behind elephants at the zoo.

It was the first time she'd confronted the future so directly. She'd always held to the breezy belief that everything would turn out okay, no matter what she decided. And it would, she knew . . . for a while. But did she still want to be living with her mom at nineteen? Or twenty-one? Or, God forbid, twenty-five?

And how on earth was someone supposed to earn enough on her own—and afford to live in Manhattan—without a college degree?

She didn't know. All she knew for certain was that she wasn't ready for the summer to end. She wasn't ready to go back home. She wasn't ready to think about Will wandering the green quads at Vanderbilt, walking beside coeds in cheerleader outfits. She didn't want to think about any of it.

* * *

"Is everything okay? You've been kind of quiet," Will said.

"I'm sorry," she said. "It's just that I've got a lot on my mind."

They were sitting at the pier, sharing bagels and coffee, which they'd picked up on the way. Usually the pier was crowded with people fishing, but this morning they had the place to themselves. A nice surprise, considering he had the day off.

"Have you given any thought to what you want to do?"

"Anything that doesn't involve elephants and shovels."

He balanced his bagel on the Styrofoam cup. "Do I want to know what you're talking about?"

"Probably not," she said, grimacing.

"Okay." He nodded. "But I was talking about what you wanted to do for your birthday tomorrow."

Ronnie shrugged. "It doesn't have to be anything special."

"But you're turning eighteen. Face it—that's a big deal. You'll legally be an adult."

Great, she thought. Yet another reminder that time was running out to figure out what she was going to do with her life. Will must have read her expression because he reached over to put a hand on her knee.

"Did I say something wrong?"

"No. I don't know. I'm just feeling weird today."

In the distance, a pod of porpoises broke the water beyond the swells. The first time she'd seen them, she'd been amazed. Even the twentieth. Now, they were a regular part of the scenery, but even so, she'd miss them when she was back in New York, doing whatever it was she was going to do. She'd probably end up addicted to cartoons like Jonah and insist on watching them upside down.

"How about I take you out to dinner?"

No, scratch that. She'd probably end up addicted to Game Boy. "Okay."

"Or maybe we'll go dancing."

Or maybe Guitar Hero. Jonah liked to play that for hours. And so had Rick, now that she thought about it. Pretty much everyone without a life was addicted to that game. "Sounds fine."

"Or how about this? We paint our faces and try to summon ancient Incan goddesses."

Addicted to those lousy games, she'd probably still be living at home when Jonah went off to college in eight years. "Whatever you want."

The sound of Will's laughter was enough to bring her attention back to him. "Did you say something?"

"Your birthday. I was trying to figure out what you want for your birthday, but obviously you're out in never-never land. I'm leaving on Monday, and I want to do something special for you."

She thought about it before turning toward the house, noticing again how out of place it was along this stretch of beach. "You know what I really, really want?"

It didn't happen on her birthday, but two nights later, Friday, August 22, was close enough. The staff at the aquarium really did have the whole thing down to a science; earlier that afternoon, workers and volunteers from the aquarium had begun to prepare the area so the turtles could reach the water safely.

She and Will had helped smooth the sand in the shallow trench that led to the ocean; others had put up caution tape to keep the crowd at a safe distance. Most of the crowd, anyway. Her dad and Jonah had been allowed inside the taped area, and they were standing off to the side, out of the way of the bustling workers.

Ronnie didn't have any idea what she was supposed to do, other than make sure no one got too close to the nest. It wasn't as if she were an expert, but when she wore the Easter-egg-colored aquarium outfit, people assumed she knew everything. She must have answered a hundred questions in the last hour. She was pleased that she'd been able to remember the things Will had first told her about the turtles and also relieved that she'd taken a few minutes to review the loggerhead fact card the aquarium had printed up for onlookers. Pretty much everything that people wanted to know was already there in black and white, but she supposed it was easier to ask her than glance at the card they held in their hands.

It also helped to pass the time. They'd already been out here for hours, and though they'd been reassured that the nest might begin to hatch any minute, Ronnie wasn't so certain. The turtles didn't care that some of the little kids might be getting tired or that someone might have to get up early to go to work the next morning.

Somehow she'd imagined that there would be only half a dozen people out here, not the hundreds massing all along the caution tape. She wasn't sure she liked it; it kind of made the whole thing feel like a circus.

As she took a seat on the dune, Will came over to her.

"What do you think?" he asked, gesturing at the scene.

"I'm not sure yet. Nothing's happened so far."

"It's not going to be long now."

"So I keep being told."

Will took a seat beside her. "You need to learn patience, young grasshopper."

"I am patient. I just want the hatching to happen sooner rather than later."

He laughed. "My mistake."

"Shouldn't you be working?"

"I'm just a volunteer. You're the one who actually works at the aquarium."

"Yes, but I'm not being paid for my time, and technically, since you're a volunteer, I think you should man the caution tape for a while."

"Let me guess—half the people ask what's going on, and the

other half ask questions that are answered on the card you hand them."

"Pretty much."

"And you're tired of that?"

"Let's just say that it wasn't as much fun as dinner the other night."

He'd taken her out to a cozy little Italian place for her birthday; he'd also bought her a silver necklace with a silver turtle pendant, which she loved and had been wearing ever since.

"How do you know when it's almost time?"

He pointed to the head of the aquarium and one of the biologists on staff. "When Elliot and Todd start getting excited."

"Sounds pretty scientific."

"Oh, it is. Trust me."

"Mind if I join you?"

After Will had gone off to retrieve some extra flashlights from the truck, her dad had walked over.

"You don't have to ask, Dad. Of course you can."

"I didn't want to bother you. You looked sort of preoccupied."

"I'm just waiting, like everyone else," she said. She moved over, making room as he took a seat beside her. The crowd had grown even larger in the last half hour, and she was glad her dad had been allowed inside the caution tape. Lately, he looked so tired.

"Believe it or not, growing up, I never saw a nest hatch."

"Why not?"

"It just wasn't the big deal it is now. I mean, I'd sometimes stumble across a nest and think it was neat, but I never thought much about it. The closest I ever came to seeing an actual hatching was coming across a nest the day after it happened. I saw all the broken shells around the nest, but it was just part of life around here. In any case, I'll bet this isn't what you expected, huh? All these people around?"

"What do you mean?"

"Between you and Will, you watched that nest every night, keeping it safe. And now that the exciting part is about to happen, you have to share it with everyone."

"That's okay. I don't mind."

"Even a little?"

She smiled. It was amazing how well her dad had come to know her. "How's your song coming?"

"It's a work in progress. I've probably written a hundred variations of it so far, but it's still not right. I know it's kind of a pointless exercise—if I haven't figured it out yet, I probably never will—but it gives me something to do."

"I saw the window this morning. It's almost done."

Her dad nodded. "It's getting close."

"Have they figured out when they're going to install it?"

"No," he said. "Still waiting for the money for the rest of the church. They don't want to put it in until the place is being used. Pastor Harris is worried some vandals might throw rocks at it. The fire has made him a lot more cautious about everything."

"I'd probably be cautious, too."

Steve straightened his legs out on the sand, then drew them back in, wincing.

"Are you okay?" she asked.

"Just been standing too much these last few days. Jonah wants to finish the window before he leaves."

"He's had a good time this summer."

"Yeah?"

"He told me the other night that he doesn't want to go back to New York. That he wants to stay with you."

"He's a sweet kid," he said. He hesitated before turning toward her. "I guess the next question is whether you had a good time this summer."

"Yeah, I did."

"Because of Will?"

"Because of everything," she said. "I'm glad we spent time together."

"Me, too."

"So when's your next trip to New York?"

"Oh, I don't know. We'll play that by ear."

She smiled. "Too busy these days?"

"Not hardly," he said. "But you want to know something?"

"What's that?"

"I think you're a terrific young lady. I never want you to forget how proud I am of you."

"What brought that up?"

"I wasn't sure I'd told you that lately."

She rested her head on his shoulder. "You're okay, too, Dad."

"Hey," he said, motioning to the nest. "I think it's starting."

She turned toward the nest, then scrambled to her feet. As Will had predicted, Elliot and Todd were moving around with great excitement while a hush came over the crowd.

It unfolded the way Will had originally described it, except that words didn't really do it justice. Because she was able to get so close, she could see it all: the first egg beginning to crack open, followed by another and then another, all the eggs seemingly wiggling on their own until the first turtle actually emerged and began to scramble over the wiggling eggs and out of the nest.

Still, it was what followed that was most amazing: first a little movement, then some movement, and then so much movement that it was impossible for the eye to capture it all as five and then ten and then twenty and then too many turtles to count joined in a massive frenzy of activity.

Like a crazy beehive on steroids . . .

And then there was the sight of the tiny, prehistoric-looking turtles trying to escape the hole; clawing their way up and slipping back down, crawling over the tops of one another . . . until one finally got out, followed by a second, and then a third, all moving along the sandy trench toward the light Todd was holding as he stood in the surf.

One by one, Ronnie watched them crawling past, thinking them so incredibly small that survival seemed almost inconceivable. The ocean would simply swallow them up, making them disappear, which was exactly what happened as they reached the water and were tossed and rolled in the surf, bobbing briefly to the surface before vanishing from sight.

She'd stood beside Will, squeezing his hand tightly, immensely happy that she'd spent all those nights by the nest and that she'd played some small part in this miracle of new life. It was incredible to think that after weeks of absolutely nothing happening, everything she'd been waiting for would be over in a matter of minutes.

As she stood beside the boy she loved, she knew she'd never shared anything more magical with anyone.

An hour later, after excitedly reliving the hatching in detail, Ronnie and Will said good night to the others from the aquarium as they headed toward their cars. Aside from the trench, all evidence of what had happened was gone. Even the shells were nowhere in sight; Todd had gathered them up because he wanted to study the thickness of the shells and test for the possible presence of chemicals.

As she walked beside him, Will slipped his arm around her. "I hope that was all you thought it would be."

"It was even better," she said. "But I keep thinking about the baby turtles."

"They'll be okay."

"Not all of them."

"No," he admitted. "Not all of them. When they're young, the odds are stacked against them."

They walked a few steps in silence. "That makes me sad."

"It's the circle of life, right?"

"I don't need philosophy from *The Lion King* right now," she sniffed. "I need you to lie to me."

"Oh," he said easily. "In that case . . . They're all going to make it. All fifty-six of them. They'll grow larger and mate and make little baby turtles and eventually pass away from old age after living far longer than most turtles, of course."

"Do you really think so?"

"Of course," he said confidently. "They're our babies. They're special."

She was still laughing when she saw her dad step out onto the back porch with Jonah.

"Okay, after all the ridiculous buildup," Jonah started, "and watching the whole thing from start to finish, I just have one thing to say."

"What's that?" Will prompted.

Jonah grinned broadly. "That. Was. So. Cool."

Ronnie laughed, remembering. At Will's puzzled expression, she just shrugged. "Private joke," she said, and in that instant, her dad coughed.

It was a loud, wet cough, sounding . . . sick . . . but just as had happened in the church, it didn't stop with one cough. He coughed again and again, one racking sound followed by another.

She watched as her dad grabbed the rail to keep his balance; she could see Jonah's brow furrowing with worry and fear, and even Will was frozen in place.

She watched her father try to stand straighter, arching his back, struggling to control the hacking. He brought both hands to his mouth and coughed one more time, and when at last he drew a ragged breath, it sounded almost as if he were breathing through water.

He gasped again, then lowered his hands. For what seemed like the longest few seconds of her life, Ronnie was frozen in place, suddenly more scared than she'd ever been. Her father's face was covered in blood.

30

.... ♪ ....

Steve

He received his death sentence in February, while sitting in a doctor's office, only an hour after giving his last piano lesson.

He'd started teaching again when he'd first moved back to Wrightsville Beach, after failing as a concert pianist. Pastor Harris, without consulting him, had brought a promising student to the house a few days after Steve had moved in and asked that Steve do him "a favor." It was just like Pastor Harris to realize that by returning home, Steve was broadcasting the fact that he was lost and alone and that the only way to help him was to bring a sense of purpose back into his life.

The student was Chan Lee. Both her parents taught music at UNC Wilmington, and at seventeen she was a wonderful technician, but she somehow lacked the ability to make the music her own. She was both serious and engaging, and Steve took to her immediately; she listened with interest and worked hard at incorporating his suggestions. He looked forward to her visits, and for Christmas, he gave her a book on the construction of classical pianos, something he thought she would enjoy. But despite the joy he felt in teaching again, he found himself increasingly tired. The lessons drained him when they should have given him energy. For the first time in his life, he began to take regular naps.

Over time, he began to take longer naps, up to two hours at a time, and when he woke, he often felt pain in his stomach. One evening while cooking chili for dinner, he suddenly felt a sharp, stabbing pain and doubled over, knocking the pan from the stove, strewing tomatoes and beans and beef across the kitchen floor. As he tried to catch his breath, he knew something was seriously wrong.

He made an appointment with a doctor, then went back to the hospital for scans and X-rays. Afterward, while Steve watched the vials fill with the blood necessary for the recommended tests, he thought of his father and the cancer that had eventually killed him. And he suddenly knew what the doctor would tell him.

On the third visit to the doctor, he found out he was right.

"You have stomach cancer," the doctor said. He took a long breath. "And from the scans, it's metastasized to your pancreas and lungs." His voice was neutral, but not unkind. "I'm sure you have a lot of questions, but let me start by saying it's not good."

The oncologist was compassionate and yet was telling Steve that there was nothing he could do. Steve knew this, just as he knew the doctor wanted him to ask specific questions, in the hope that talking might somehow make things easier.

When his dad was dying, Steve had done his research. He knew what it meant when cancer metastasized, he knew what it meant to have cancer not only in his stomach, but also in his pancreas. He knew the odds of surviving were next to nil, and instead of asking anything, he turned toward the window. On the ledge, a pigeon was settled near the glass, oblivious to what was going on inside. *I've been told that I'm dying,* he thought while staring at it, *and the doctor wants me to talk about it. But there's nothing really to say, is there?*

He waited for the bird to coo in agreement, but of course, there was no response from the bird at all.

I'm dying, he thought again.

Steve remembered clasping his hands together, amazed that they weren't shaking. If ever they should shake, he thought, it would be at a time like this. But they were as steady and still as a kitchen sink.

"How much time do I have?"

The doctor seemed relieved that the silence had been broken at last. "Before we start going into that, I want to talk about some of your options."

"There are no options," Steve said. "You and I both know that."

If the doctor was surprised by his response, he didn't show it. "There are always options," he said.

"But none that can cure it. You're talking about quality of life."

The doctor set aside his clipboard. "Yes," he said.

"How can we discuss quality if I don't know how much time I have? If I only have a few days, it might mean that I should start making phone calls."

"You have more than a few days."

"Weeks?"

"Yes, of course . . ."

"Months?"

The doctor hesitated. He must have seen something in Steve's face that signaled he would continue to press until he knew the truth. He cleared his throat. "I've been doing this a long time, and I've come to learn that predictions don't mean much. Too much lies outside the realm of medical knowledge. A lot of what happens next comes down to you and your specific genetics, your attitude. No, there's nothing we can do to stop the inevitable, but that's not the point. The point is that you should try to make the most of the time you have left."

Steve studied the doctor, aware that his question hadn't been answered.

"Do I have a year?"

This time, the doctor didn't respond, but his silence gave him away. Leaving the office, Steve took a deep breath, armed with the knowledge that he had less than twelve months to live.

The reality hit him later as he was standing on the beach.

He had advanced cancer, and there was no known cure. He would be dead within the year.

On his way out of the office, the doctor had given him some information. Little pamphlets and a list of websites, useful for a book report but good for little else. Steve had tossed them in the garbage on the way to the car. As he stood beneath the winter sun on the deserted beach, he tucked his hands into his coat, staring at the pier. Though his vision wasn't what it once was, he could see people moving about or fishing by the rails, and he marveled at their normalcy. It was as if nothing extraordinary had happened.

He was going to die, and sooner rather than later. With that, he realized that so many of the things he'd spent time worrying about no longer mattered. His 401(k) plan? *Won't need it.* A way to make a living in his fifties? *Doesn't matter.* His desire to meet someone new and fall in love? *Won't be fair to her, and to be frank, that desire ended with the diagnosis anyway.*

It was over, he repeated to himself. In less than a year, he was going to die. Yes, he'd known something was wrong, and perhaps he'd even expected the doctor to deliver the news he had. But the memory of the doctor speaking the actual words began to recur in his mind, like an old-fashioned record skipping on a turntable. On the beach, he began to shake. He was scared and he was alone. Head lowered, he put his face into his hands and wondered why it had happened to him.

The following day, he called Chan and explained that he could no longer teach piano. Next he met with Pastor Harris to tell him the news. At that time, Pastor Harris was still recovering from the injuries he'd suffered in the fire, and though Steve knew it was selfish to burden his friend during his convalescence, he could think of no one else to talk to. He met him at the house, and as they sat on the back porch, Steve explained his diagnosis. He tried to keep the emotion out of his voice, but he failed, and in the end, they cried together.

Afterward, Steve walked the beach, wondering what to do with the little time he had remaining. What, he wondered, was most important to him? Passing by the church—at that point, the repairs hadn't been started, but the blackened walls had been torn down and hauled away—he stared at the gaping hole that once housed the stained-glass window, thinking of Pastor Harris and the countless mornings he'd spent in the halo of sunlight as it streamed through the window. It was then that he knew he had to make another.

A day later, he called Kim. When he told her the news, she broke down on the phone, weeping into the receiver. Steve felt a tightness in the back of his throat, but he didn't cry with her, and somehow he knew he would never cry about his diagnosis again.

Later, he called her again to ask whether the kids could spend the summer with him. Though the idea frightened her, she consented. At his request, she agreed not to tell them about his condition. It would be a summer filled with lies, but what choice did he have if he wanted to get to know them again?

In the spring, as the azaleas were blooming, he began to muse more often on the nature of God. It was inevitable, he supposed, to think about such things at a time like this. Either God existed or He didn't; he would either spend eternity in heaven, or there would be nothing at all. Somehow he found comfort in turning the question over in his mind; it spoke to a longing deep inside him. He eventually came to the conclusion that God was real, but he also wanted to experience God's presence in this world, in mortal terms. And with that, he began his quest.

It was the last year of his life. Rain fell almost daily, making it one of the wettest springs on record. May, however, was absolutely dry, as if somewhere the faucet had been turned off. He purchased the glass he needed and began to work on the window; in June, his children arrived. He'd walked the beach and searched for God, and somehow, he realized, he'd been able to mend the fraying ropes that had tethered him to his children. Now, on a dark night in August, baby turtles were skimming the surface of the ocean, and he was coughing up blood. It was time to stop lying; it was time to tell the truth.

His children were scared, and he knew they wanted him to say or do something to take their fear away. But his stomach was being pierced by a thousand twisting needles. He wiped the blood from his face using the back of his hand and tried to sound calm.

"I think," he said, "I need to go to the hospital."

31

·····✦·····

Ronnie

Her dad was hooked up to an IV in a hospital bed when he told her. She immediately began to shake her head. It wasn't true. It couldn't be true.

"No," she said, "this isn't right. Doctors make mistakes."

"Not this time," he said, reaching for her hand. "And I'm sorry you had to find out like this."

Will and Jonah were downstairs in the cafeteria. Her dad wanted to talk to each of his children separately, but Ronnie suddenly wanted nothing to do with any of it. She didn't want him to say anything else, not one more word.

Her mind flashed on a dozen different images: Suddenly she knew why her dad had wanted her and Jonah to come to North Carolina. And she understood that her mom had known the truth all along. With so little time left together, he had no desire to argue with her. And his ceaseless work on the window now made perfect sense. She recalled his coughing fit in the church and the times he'd winced in pain. In hindsight, the pieces all fit together. Yet everything was falling apart.

He would never see her married; he would never hold a grandchild. The thought of living the rest of her life without him was almost too much to bear. It wasn't fair. None of this was fair at all.

When she spoke, her words sounded brittle. "When were you going to tell me?"

"I don't know."

"Before I left? Or after I was back in New York?"

When he didn't answer, she could feel the blood rising in her cheeks. She knew she shouldn't be angry, but she couldn't help it. "What? Were you planning to tell me on the phone? What were you going to say? 'Oh, sorry I didn't mention this when we were together last summer, but I have terminal cancer. How's it going with you?'"

"Ronnie—"

"If you weren't going to tell me, why did you bring me down here? So I could *watch* you die?"

"No, sweetie. Just the opposite." He rolled his head to face her. "I asked you to come so I could watch you live."

At his answer, she felt something shake loose inside, like the first pebbles skittering downhill before an avalanche. In the corridor, she heard two nurses walking past, their voices hushed. The fluorescent lights hummed overhead, casting a bluish pall over the walls. The IV dripped steadily—normal scenes from any hospital, but there was nothing normal about any of this. Her throat felt as thick and sticky as paste, and she turned away, willing the tears not to come.

"I'm sorry, sweetheart," he continued. "I know I should have told you, but I wanted a normal summer, and I wanted you to have a normal summer. I just wanted to get to know my daughter again. Can you forgive me?"

His plea cut her to the core, and she let out an involuntary cry. Her father was dying, and he wanted her forgiveness. There was something so pitiful in that, and she didn't know how to respond. As he waited, he reached over and she took his hand.

"Of course I forgive you," she said, and it was then she began to cry. She leaned toward him, resting her head on his chest, and noticed how thin he'd become without her even being aware of it.

She could feel the sharp outline of the bones in his chest, and she suddenly realized that he had been wasting away for months. It broke her heart to know she hadn't been paying attention; she'd been so caught up in her own life that she hadn't even noticed.

When her dad put his arm around her, she began to cry harder, conscious that there would soon be a time when this simple act of affection would no longer be possible. Despite herself, she remembered the day she'd arrived at his house and the anger she'd felt toward him; she remembered storming off, the thought of touching him as alien to her as space travel. She'd hated him then and she loved him now.

She was glad she finally knew his secret, even as she wished she didn't. She felt him running his fingers through her hair. There would come a time when he would no longer be able to do this, when he would no longer be around, and she squeezed her eyelids shut, trying to block out the future. She needed more time with him. She needed him to listen as she whined; she needed him to forgive her when she made mistakes. She needed him to love her the way he had this summer. She needed all of it forever, and she knew it wouldn't happen.

She allowed her dad to hold her and wept like the child she no longer was.

Later, he answered her questions. He told her about his father and the history of cancer in his family, he told her about the pains he'd begun to feel as the New Year rolled in. He told her that radiation was not an option, because the disease was present in so many of his organs. As he spoke the words, she imagined the malignant cells moving from one spot in his body to the next, a marauding army of evil that left destruction in its wake. She asked about chemotherapy, and again his answer was the same. The cancer was aggressive, and while chemotherapy might help slow the disease, it couldn't stop it, and it would leave him feeling worse than if he'd done nothing at all. He explained the concept of quality of life, and as he did, she hated him for not telling her earlier. Yet she knew he'd made the right decision. Had she known, the summer would have unfolded differently. Their relationship would have taken a different course, and she didn't want to think of what it might have become.

He was pale, and she knew the morphine was making him sleepy.

"Does it still hurt?" she asked.

"Not like it did. It's better," he assured her.

She nodded. She tried again not to think about the malignant cells invading his organs.

"When did you tell Mom?"

"In February, right after I found out. But I asked her not to tell you."

Ronnie tried to remember how her mom had acted back then. She had to have been upset, but either Ronnie couldn't remember or she hadn't been paying attention. As usual, she'd been thinking only about herself. She wanted to believe she was different now, but she knew that wasn't completely true. Between work and spending time with Will, she'd spent relatively little time with her dad, and time was the one thing she could never get back.

"But if you'd told me, I would have been around more. We could have seen each other more, I could have helped you so you wouldn't be so tired all the time."

"Just knowing you were here was more than enough."

"But maybe you wouldn't have ended up in the hospital."

He reached for her hand. "Or maybe watching you enjoy a carefree summer while you fell in love was what kept me out of the hospital in the first place."

Though he didn't say as much, she knew he didn't expect to live much longer, and she tried to imagine life without him.

If she hadn't come to stay with him, if she hadn't given him a chance, it might have been easier to let him go. But she had, and nothing about what was happening was going to be easy. In the eerie quiet, she was able to hear his labored breathing, and she noticed again how much weight he'd lost. She wondered whether he would live until Christmas, or even long enough for her to visit again.

She was alone and her father was dying, and there was absolutely nothing she could do to stop it.

"What's going to happen?" she asked him. He hadn't slept long, maybe ten minutes, before he'd rolled to her.

"I'm not sure what you mean."

"Will you have to stay in the hospital?"

It was the one question she'd been afraid to ask. While he'd dozed, she'd held his hand, imagining that he would never leave this place. That he'd spend the rest of his life in this room that smelled of disinfectant, surrounded by nurses who were no more than strangers.

"No," he said. "I'll probably be home in a few days." He smiled. "At least I hope so."

She squeezed his hand. "And then what? Once we're gone?"

He thought about it. "I suppose I'd like to see the window completed. And finish the song I started. I still think there's something . . . special there."

She scooted her chair closer. "I mean who's going to make sure you're okay?"

He didn't answer right away but tried to sit up a little in the bed. "I'll be fine," he said. "And if I need something, I can call Pastor Harris. He lives only a couple of blocks away."

She tried to imagine Pastor Harris, with his burned hands and his cane, trying to aid her father if he needed help getting into the car. He seemed to know what she was thinking.

"Like I said, I'll be okay," he murmured. "I've known this was coming, and if worse comes to worst, there's a hospice associated with the hospital."

She didn't want to imagine him there, either. "A hospice?"

"It's not as bad as you think. I've been there."

"When?"

"A few weeks ago. And I went back again last week. They'll be ready for me whenever I need it."

Yet another thing she didn't know, yet another secret revealed. Yet another truth portending the inevitable. Her stomach roiled, nausea settling in.

"But you'd rather be at home, wouldn't you?"

"I will be," he said.

"Until you can't?"

His expression was almost too sad to bear. "Until I can't."

She left her father's room, heading for the cafeteria. It was time, her dad said, for him to talk to Jonah.

She was dazed as she walked the corridors. It was almost midnight now, but the emergency room was as busy as always. She passed by rooms, most of them with open doors, and saw crying children accompanied by anxious parents and a woman who couldn't stop vomiting. Nurses bustled around the main station, reaching for charts or loading up carts. It amazed her that so many people could be sick this late at night, yet she knew that most of them would be gone by tomorrow. Her dad, on the other hand, was scheduled to be moved to a room upstairs; they were only waiting for the paperwork to go through.

She weaved through the crowded waiting room toward a door that led to the main area of the hospital lobby and the cafeteria. As the door swung shut behind her, the noise level dropped. She could hear the sound of her footfalls, could almost hear herself thinking, and as she moved, she felt waves of exhaustion and nausea coursing through her. This was the place where sick people came; this was the place where people came to die, and she knew her father would see this place again.

She could barely swallow as she reached the cafeteria. She

rubbed her gritty, swollen eyes, promising herself that she was going to keep it together. The grill was closed at this hour, but there were vending machines on the far wall, and a couple of nurses sat in the corner, sipping coffee. Jonah and Will were seated at a table near the door, and Will looked up as she approached. On the table stood a half-empty bottle of water and milk and a packet of cookies for Jonah. Jonah turned around to look at her.

"That took you long enough," he said. "What's going on? Is Dad okay?"

"He's doing better," she said. "But he wants to talk to you."

"About what?" He put down his cookie. "I'm not in trouble, am I?"

"No, nothing like that. He wants to tell you what's going on."

"Why can't you tell me?" He sounded anxious, and Ronnie felt her heart contract with dread.

"Because he wants to talk to you alone. Like he did with me. I'll walk you over there and wait outside the door, okay?"

He got up from his seat and headed for the door, leaving her to trail after him. "Cool," he said as he passed her, and Ronnie suddenly wanted to run away. But she had to stay with Jonah.

Will continued to sit, unmoving, his eyes fixed on Ronnie.

"Give me a second, okay?" she called to Jonah.

Will stood up from the table, looking frightened for her. He knows, she suddenly thought. Somehow he already knows.

"Can you wait for us?" Ronnie began. "I know you probably—"

"Of course I'll wait," he said quietly. "I'll be right here for as long as you need me."

Relief rushed through her, and she gave him a grateful look, then turned and followed Jonah. They pushed open the door and headed into the otherwise empty corridor, toward the hustle and bustle of the emergency room.

No one close to her had ever died. Though her dad's parents had died and she remembered attending the funerals, she'd never known them well. They weren't the kind of grandparents that visited. They were strangers in a way, and even after they'd passed away, she'd never remembered missing them.

About the closest she'd ever come to something like this was when Amy Childress, her seventh-grade history teacher, was killed in a traffic accident the summer after Ronnie had finished taking her class. She'd heard about it first from Kayla, and she remembered feeling less sad than shocked, if only because Amy was so young. Ms. Childress was still in her twenties and had been teaching only a few years, and Ronnie remembered how surreal it had felt. She was always so friendly; she was one of the few teachers Ronnie ever had that used to laugh aloud in class. When she returned to school in the fall, she wasn't sure what to expect. How did people react to something like this? What did the other teachers think? She walked the halls that day, searching for signs of anything different, but aside from a small plaque that had been mounted on the wall near the principal's office, she saw nothing out of the ordinary. Teachers taught their classes and socialized in the lounge; she saw Mrs. Taylor and Mr. Burns—two of the teachers Ms. Childress often ate lunch with—smiling and laughing as they walked down the halls.

She remembered that it bothered her. Granted, the accident had occurred over the summer and people had already mourned, but when she went by Ms. Childress's classroom and saw that it was now being used to teach science, she realized she was angry, not only that Ms. Childress had died, but that her memory had been erased so entirely in such a short period of time.

She didn't want that to happen to her dad. She didn't want him forgotten in a matter of weeks—he was good man, a good father, and he deserved more than that.

Thinking along those lines made her realize something else, too: She'd never really known her dad when he was healthy. She'd last spent time with him when she was a freshman in high school. Now, she was technically an adult, old enough to vote or join the army, and over the summer, he'd harbored his secret. Who would he have been had he not known what was happening to him? Who was he, really?

She had nothing to judge him by, other than memories of him as her piano teacher. She knew little about him. She didn't know the novelists he liked to read, she didn't know his favorite animal, and if pressed, she couldn't begin to guess his favorite color. They weren't important things and she knew they didn't really matter, but somehow she was troubled by the thought that she would probably never learn the answers.

Behind the door, she heard the sounds of Jonah crying, and she knew he'd learned the truth. She heard her brother's frantic denials and the answering murmurs of her father. She leaned against the wall, aching for Jonah and for herself.

She wanted to do something to make this nightmare go away. She wanted to turn back the clock to the moment the turtles had hatched, when all was right with the world. She wanted to stand beside the boy she loved, her happy family by her side. She suddenly remembered Megan's radiant expression when she'd danced with her father at the wedding, and she felt a piercing ache at the knowledge that she and her dad would never share that special moment.

She closed her eyes and put her hands over her ears, trying to block out the sound of Jonah's cries. He sounded so helpless, so young . . . so scared. There was no way he could understand what was happening, there was no way he would ever really recover. She knew he'd never forget this awful day.

"Can I get you a glass of water?"

She barely heard the words but somehow knew they were directed at her. Looking up through her tears, she saw Pastor Harris standing before her.

She couldn't answer, but she was somehow able to shake her head. His expression was kind, but she could see his anguish in the stoop of his shoulders, in the way he gripped the cane.

"I'm very sorry," he said. His voice sounded weary. "I can't imagine how hard this is for you. Your dad is a special man."

She nodded. "How did you know he was here? Did he call you?"

"No," he said. "One of the nurses called me. I'm here two or three times a week, and when you brought him in, they thought I'd want to know. They know I think of him as my son."

"Are you going to talk to him?"

Pastor Harris eyed the closed door. "Only if he wants to see me." By his pained expression, she knew he could hear Jonah's cries. "And after talking to the two of you, I'm sure he will. You have no idea how much he was dreading this moment."

"You've talked about it?"

"Many times. He loves the two of you more than life itself, and he didn't want to hurt you. He knew the time would come, but I'm sure he didn't want you to find out like this."

"It doesn't matter. It's not like it changes anything."

"But everything has changed," Pastor Harris countered.

"Because I know?"

"No," he said. "Because of the time you've spent together. Before the two of you came down, he was so nervous. Not about being sick, but because of how much he wanted to spend time with you, and wanted everything to go well. I don't think you realize how much he missed you, or how much he really loves you and Jonah. He was literally counting the days. When I'd see him, he'd say, 'Nineteen days,' or, 'Twelve days.' And the day before you arrived? He spent hours cleaning the house and putting new sheets on the beds. I know the place isn't much, but if you'd seen it before, you'd understand. He wanted the two of you to have a summer to remember, and he wanted to be part of that. Like all parents, he wants you to be happy. He wants to know that you're going to be okay. He wants to know that you'll make good decisions. That's what he needed this summer, and that's what you've given him."

She squinted up at him. "But I haven't always made good decisions."

Pastor Harris smiled. "All that shows is that you're human. He never expected perfection. But I do know how proud he is of the young woman you've become. He told me that just a few days ago, and you should have seen him when he spoke about you. He was so . . . proud, so happy, and that night, when I prayed, I thanked God for that. Because your dad really struggled when he moved back here. I wasn't sure he'd ever be happy again. And yet, despite everything that's happened, I now know that he is."

She felt the lump in her throat. "What am I supposed to do?"

"I'm not sure there's anything you can do."

"But I'm scared," she said. "And my dad . . ."

"I know," he said. "And though both of you have made him very happy, I know your dad is scared, too."

That night, Ronnie stood on the back porch. The waves were as steady and rhythmic as always, and the stars were flickering with pinprick intensity, but everything else about the world around her seemed different. Will was talking with Jonah in the bedroom, so there were three people here as usual, but somehow the house felt emptier.

Pastor Harris was still with her dad. Pastor Harris told her he planned to stay through the night, so she could bring Jonah back home, but she felt guilty nonetheless for leaving. Tomorrow, her dad had tests scheduled during the day and another meeting with his doctor. In between those things, he would be tired and she knew he'd need his rest. But she wanted to be there, she wanted to be at his side, even if he was asleep, because she knew the time would come when she couldn't.

Behind her, she heard the back door squeak open; Will closed it gently behind him. As he approached her, she continued to gaze out over the sandy beach.

"Jonah's finally asleep," he said. "But I don't think he really understands what's happening. He told me he's pretty sure the doctor will make his dad all better, and he kept asking when his dad could come home."

She remembered his cries from the hospital room, and all she could do was nod. Will slipped his arms around her.

"Are you okay?" he asked.

"How do you think I'm doing? I just found out my father is dying and that he probably won't live to see Christmas."

"I know," he said gently. "And I'm sorry. I know how hard this is for you." She could feel his hands on her waist. "I'll stay tonight so if anything happens and you have to go, someone can be with Jonah. I can stay around here as long as you need me to. I know I'm supposed to be leaving in a couple of days, but I can call the dean's office and explain what's happening. Classes don't start until next week."

"You can't fix this," she said. Though she could hear the sharpness in her tone, she couldn't help it. "Don't you get that?"

"I'm not trying to fix it—"

"Yes, you are! But you can't!" Her heart suddenly felt as if it were going to explode. "And you can't understand what I'm going through, either!"

"I've lost someone, too," he reminded her.

"It's not the same!" She squeezed the bridge of her nose, trying to stifle her tears. "I was so mean to him. I quit the piano! I blamed him for everything, and I didn't say more than a few words to him for three years! Three years! And I can't get those years back. But maybe if I hadn't been so angry, he might not have gotten sick. Maybe I caused that extra . . . stress that did all this. Maybe it was me!" She pulled away from Will.

"It's not your fault."

Will tried to take her back into his arms, but it was the last thing she wanted, and she tried to push him away. When he didn't let go, she pounded his chest.

"Let me go! I can handle this alone!"

But still he held her, and when she realized he wasn't going to let go, she finally collapsed into him. And for a long time, she let him hold her as she cried.

Ronnie lay in her darkened bedroom, listening to the sound of Jonah breathing. Will was sleeping on the couch in the living room. She knew she should try to rest, but she kept waiting for the phone to ring. She imagined the worst: that her father had begun to cough again, that he'd lost more blood, that there was nothing anyone could do . . .

Beside her, on the bedstand, was her father's Bible. Earlier, she'd glanced through it, unsure what she would find. Had he underlined passages or folded down pages? As she flipped through the book, she'd found few traces of her father, other than a well-worn feel to the pages that suggested a deep familiarity with nearly every chapter. She wished that he'd done something to make it his own, something that left behind clues about himself, but there was nothing even to suggest that he'd found one passage more interesting than another.

She'd never read the Bible, but somehow she knew that she would read this one, searching for whatever meaning her father had found within the pages. She wondered if the Bible had been given to him by Pastor Harris or whether he'd bought it on his own, and how long it had been in his possession. There was so much she didn't know about him, and she wondered now why she'd never bothered to ask him.

But she would, she decided. If she soon would have only memories, then she wanted as many as she could collect, and as she found herself praying for the first time in years, she begged God for enough time to make it possible.

32

.....♪.....

Will

Will didn't sleep well. Throughout the night, he'd heard Ronnie tossing and turning and pacing in her room. He recognized the shock she was feeling; he remembered the numbness and guilt, the disbelief and anger, after Mikey had died. The years had dulled the emotional intensity, but he could remember the conflicting desire for company and the need to be left alone.

He felt sadness for Ronnie and also for Jonah, who was too young to grasp it at all. And even for himself. During the summer, Steve had been incredibly kind to him, as they'd spent a lot more time at Ronnie's than they had at his house. He liked the quiet way he cooked in the kitchen and the easy familiarity he shared with Jonah. He'd often seen the two of them out on the beach, flying kites or playing catch near the waves, or working on the stained-glass window in quiet concentration. While most fathers liked to see themselves as the kind of men who made time for their kids, it seemed to Will that Steve was the real thing. In the short time he'd known him, he'd never once seen Steve get angry, never heard him raise his voice. He supposed that it could have had something to do with the fact that he knew he was dying, but Will didn't think that explained everything. Ronnie's dad was just . . . a good man at peace with himself and others; he loved his kids and somehow trusted that they were usually smart enough to make the right decisions.

As he lay on the couch, he reflected that he wanted to be the same kind of father someday. Though he loved his dad, he hadn't always been the easygoing man Ronnie had met. There were long stretches of Will's life during which he hardly remembered seeing his father as he worked to grow his business. Add in his mom's occasional volatility and the death of Mikey, which sent the entire family into depression for a couple of years, and there had been times when he wished he'd been born into a different family. He knew he was lucky, and it was true that things had been a lot better lately. But growing up hadn't been all cupcakes and parties, and he could remember wishing for a different life.

But Steve was an altogether different kind of parent.

Ronnie had told him that he would sit with her for hours as she learned to play the piano, but in all the time he'd been at the house, he'd never heard Steve talk about it. He hadn't even mentioned it in passing, and though at first Will thought it odd, he began to see it as a powerful indication of his love for Ronnie. She didn't want to talk about it, so he didn't, even though it had been a major part of their life together. He'd even boarded up the alcove because she didn't want to be reminded of it.

What kind of person would do that?

Only Steve, a man he'd grown to admire, a man he'd learned from, and the kind of man he himself hoped to be as he grew older.

He was awakened by the morning sunlight streaming through the living room windows, and he stretched before rising to his feet. Peeking down the hall, he saw that the door to Ronnie's room was open, and he knew that she was already awake. He found her on the porch in the same spot as the night before. She didn't turn around.

"Good morning," he said.

Her shoulders sagged as she turned toward him. "Good morning," she said, offering the slightest of smiles. She opened her arms, and he wrapped himself around her, grateful for the embrace.

"I'm sorry about last night," she said.

"There's no reason to be sorry." He nuzzled her hair. "You didn't do anything wrong."

"Mmmm," she said. "But thanks anyway."

"I didn't hear you get up."

"I've been up for a while." She sighed. "I called the hospital and talked to my dad. Though he didn't say as much, I could tell he's still in a lot of pain. He thinks they might keep him for a couple of days after his tests are done."

In almost any other situation, he would have assured her that everything would be fine, that it would all work out. But in this case, they both knew the words would mean nothing. Instead, he leaned forward, resting his forehead against hers.

"Were you able to get any sleep? I heard you wandering around last night."

"Not really. I finally crawled in bed with Jonah, but my brain just wouldn't shut off. But not just because of what's going on with my dad." She paused. "It was because of you, too. You're leaving in a couple of days."

"I already told you I could postpone it. If you need me to stay, I will . . ."

She shook her head. "I don't want you to. You're about to start a whole new chapter of your life, and I can't take that away from you."

"But I don't have to go now. Classes don't start right away—"

"I don't want you to," she said again. Her voice was soft but implacable. "You're going off to college, and it's not your problem. I know that might sound harsh, but it isn't. He's my dad, not yours, and that will never change. And I don't want to think about what you might be giving up, in addition to everything else that's going on in my life. Can you understand that?"

Her words had the ring of truth to them, even if he wished she were wrong. After a moment, he untied his macramé bracelet and held it out to her.

"I want you to have this," he whispered, and by her expression, he could tell that she understood how much her acceptance meant to him.

She flashed a small smile as she closed her hand around it. He thought she was about to say something when both of them heard the workshop door suddenly bang open. For an instant, Will thought someone had broken in. Then he saw Jonah clumsily dragging a broken chair outside. With enormous effort, he lifted it up and tossed it over the dune near the workshop. Even from this distance, Will could see the fury in Jonah's expression.

Ronnie was already moving off the porch.

"Jonah!" she screamed, breaking into a run.

Will leapt after her, almost bumping into her as she reached the workshop door. Looking past her, he saw Jonah trying to push a heavy crate across the floor. He was struggling mightily, oblivious to their sudden appearance.

"What are you doing?" Ronnie cried. "When did you come out here?"

Jonah continued to push at the crate, grunting with the effort.

"Jonah!" Ronnie shouted.

Her cry broke through his tunnel-like focus, and he turned toward Will and his sister, surprised by their presence. "I can't reach it!" he cried, angry and on the verge of tears. "I'm not tall enough!"

"Can't reach what?" she asked before taking a sudden step forward. "You're bleeding!" she said, panic rising in her voice.

Will noticed the torn jeans and blood on Jonah's leg as Ronnie rushed toward him. Driven by his own demons, Jonah pushed frantically at the crate, and the corner of the box smashed into one of the shelves. The half-squirrel/half-fish creature toppled off, landing on Jonah just as Ronnie reached him.

His face was tight and red. "Go away! I can do this by myself! I don't need you!" he screamed.

He tried to move the crate again, but it was pinned by the shelf, locked in place. Ronnie tried to help him, but Jonah shoved her away. By now, Will could see the tears on his cheeks.

"I told you to go away!" he shouted at her. "Dad wants me to finish the window! Me! Not you! That's what we were doing all summer!" His words came out in broken gasps, angry and terrified. "This was what we did! All you ever cared about were the turtles! But I was with him every day!"

As he shouted through his tears, his voice cracked.

"And now I can't reach the middle part of the window! I'm too short! But I have to finish it, because maybe if I finish it, then Dad will get better. He has to get better, so I tried to use the chair to reach the middle of the window, but it broke and I fell into the glass and I got mad and then I wanted to use the crate, but it's too heavy—"

By then, he could barely get the words out, and he suddenly rocked back and collapsed onto the ground. Wrapping his arms around his knees and lowering his head, he began to sob, his shoulders convulsing.

Ronnie took a seat on the floor beside him. She slipped an arm around his shoulder and pulled him toward her as he continued to cry. As Will watched, he could feel a lump in the back of his throat, knowing he didn't belong here.

Still, he stayed while Ronnie held her brother as he cried, not trying to hush him or assure him that everything was going to be okay. She just held him wordlessly until his sobs began to subside. Finally he looked up, his eyes red through his glasses, his face blotchy with tears.

When Ronnie spoke, her voice was gentle—as kind as he had ever heard her.

"Can we go in the house for a few minutes? I just want to check the cut on your leg."

Jonah's voice was still quavering. "What about the window? It has to be finished."

Ronnie met Will's eyes, then returned her gaze to Jonah. "Can we help?"

Jonah shook his head. "You don't know how."

"Show us."

After Ronnie cleaned Jonah's leg and put some Band-Aids on it, Jonah led them back to the workshop.

The window was nearly complete—all of the detailed etchings of the faces were finished, and the reinforcing bars were already in place. The work that remained consisted of adding hundreds of intricate pieces to form the heavenly glow in the sky.

Jonah showed Will how to cut the lead strips and taught Ronnie how to solder; Jonah cut the glass, as he'd been doing most of the summer, and slid them into the lead strips before making room for Ronnie to set the pieces in place.

It was hot and crowded in the workshop, but eventually the three of them fell into a rhythm of sorts. At lunchtime, Will ran out to pick up some burgers and a salad for Ronnie; they took a short break while they ate but were soon back at their task. As the afternoon rolled on, Ronnie called the hospital three times, only to learn that her dad was either in tests or sleeping but doing well. By the time dusk settled in, they'd finished about half the work; Jonah's hands were getting tired, and they took another break to eat before moving some lamps from the living room to add additional light to the workshop.

Darkness fell, and Jonah was yawning steadily by ten; when they went inside to relax for a few minutes, Jonah fell asleep almost immediately. Will carried him to his room and put him in bed. By the time he returned to the living room, Ronnie was already back at the workshop.

Will took over the glass cutting; he'd seen Jonah doing it all day, and though he made some mistakes in the beginning, he quickly got the hang of it.

They worked through the night, and by the time dawn began to break, both of them were dead on their feet. On the table in front of them lay the completed window. Will wasn't sure how Jonah would feel knowing he hadn't had a hand in finishing the final pieces, but he figured Ronnie would know how to handle it.

"You two look like you've been up all night," said a voice behind them. Turning around, Will saw Pastor Harris standing in the doorway.

Pastor Harris was leaning on his cane. He was wearing a suit—probably for his Sunday church service—but Will noticed the horrific scars on the backs of his hands and knew immediately that they extended up his arms. Thinking back to the fire at the church and the secret he'd kept all these months, he found it impossible to meet the pastor's eyes.

"We've been finishing the window," Ronnie said hoarsely.

Pastor Harris motioned toward the window. "May I?"

Ronnie nodded. "Of course."

Pastor Harris stepped into the workshop, moving slowly. His cane tapped against the wooden floor as he approached. At the table, his expression changed from curiosity to wonderment. Leaning on his cane, he ran a knobby, scarred hand over the glass.

"It's incredible," he breathed. "It's more beautiful than I would have imagined possible."

"My dad and Jonah did all the real work," Ronnie said. "We just helped to finish it."

He smiled. "Your father will be so pleased."

"How's the church coming? I know my dad would love to see the window in place."

"From your mouth to God's ears." He shrugged. "The church isn't as popular as it once was, so there aren't as many members. But I have faith that it will work out."

From her anxious expression, Will knew Ronnie was wondering whether or not the window would be installed in time but was afraid to ask.

"Your dad is doing well, by the way," Pastor Harris said. "He should be out of the hospital soon, and you should be able to visit him this morning. You didn't miss much yesterday. I spent most of the day sitting in his room alone while they were running tests."

"Thanks for staying with him."

"No, sweetheart," he said. He glanced at the window again. "Thank you."

It was quiet in the workshop as Pastor Harris made his way out. Will watched him go, unable to shake the image of his scarred hands.

In the silence, he studied the window, struck by the work that had been necessary to make a new one, a window that shouldn't have had to be replaced. He thought of the pastor's words and the possibility that Ronnie's dad might not even live to see the window installed.

Ronnie was lost in her own thoughts as he turned to her.

He felt something collapse inside him, like a house of cards. "There's something I need to tell you."

As they sat on the dune, Will told her everything from the beginning. When he finished, Ronnie seemed confused.

"You're saying that Scott started the fire? And that you've been protecting him?" Her voice rang with disbelief. "You've been lying for him?"

Will shook his head. "It's not like that. I told you it was an accident."

"It doesn't matter." Ronnie's eyes searched his. "Accident or not, he needs to take responsibility for what he did."

"I know. I told him to go to the police."

"But what if he doesn't? Are you going to keep covering for him forever? You're going to let Marcus keep controlling your life? It's wrong."

"But he's my friend . . ."

Ronnie leapt to her feet. "Pastor Harris almost died in that fire! He spent weeks in the hospital. Do you know how painful burns are? Why don't you ask Blaze how it feels? And the church . . . you know he can't even rebuild it . . . and now my dad's never going to see the window where it belongs!"

Will shook his head, trying to stay calm. He could see that it was all too much for Ronnie—her dad, his impending departure, her upcoming court date. "I know it was wrong," he said quietly. "And I've felt guilty about it. I can't tell you how many times I've wanted to go to the police."

"So what?" she demanded. "That doesn't mean anything! Didn't you hear me when I told you about admitting in court what I had done? Because I knew what I did was wrong! Truth only means something when it's hard to admit! Don't you get that? That church was Pastor Harris's life! It was my dad's life! And now it's gone and the insurance won't cover the damage and they have to hold services in a warehouse . . ."

"Scott's my friend," he protested. "I can't just . . . throw him to the wolves."

She blinked, wondering if he could even hear what he was saying. "How can you be so selfish?"

"I'm not being selfish—"

"That's exactly what you are, and if you can't understand that, then I don't want to talk to you!" she said. She turned and started toward the house. "Just go! Leave!"

"Ronnie!" he called out, getting up to follow her. She sensed his movement and whirled to face him.

"It's over, okay?"

"It's not over. C'mon, be reasonable . . ."

"Reasonable?" She waved her hands. "You want me to be reasonable? You haven't just been lying for Scott, you've been lying to me, too! You knew why my dad was making the window! You stood right next to me and you never said anything about it!"

Her words seemed to clarify something in her mind, and she took another step backward. "You're not who I thought you were! I thought you were better than this!"

He flinched, unable to think of a response, but when he took a step forward, she retreated.

"Go! You're leaving anyway, and we're never going to see each other again. Summers always come to an end. We can talk and pretend all we want, but we can't change that, so let's just end it here and now. I can't handle all this right now, and I can't be with someone I don't trust." Her eyes glittered with unshed tears. "I don't trust you, Will. You need to go."

He couldn't move, couldn't speak.

"Leave!" she shouted, and ran back to the house.

That night, his last night in Wrightsville Beach, Will sat in the den, still trying to make sense of everything that had happened. He looked up when his dad walked in.

"You okay?" Tom asked. "You were kind of quiet at dinner."

"Yeah," Will answered. "I'm okay."

His dad wandered to the couch and took a seat across from him. "Are you nervous about leaving tomorrow?"

Will shook his head. "No."

"Are you all packed?"

Will nodded and felt his dad studying him. His dad leaned forward.

"What's going on? You know you can talk to me."

Will took his time before answering, suddenly nervous. Finally, he met his father's eyes. "If I asked you to do something important for me, something big, would you do it? No questions asked?"

Tom leaned back, still studying him, and in the silence, Will knew what the answer would be.

33

·····✦·····

Ronnie

Y ou really finished the window?"

Ronnie watched her dad as he talked to Jonah in the hospital room, thinking he seemed better. He still looked tired, but his cheeks had a bit more color and he was moving with greater ease.

"It's awesome, Dad," Jonah said. "I can't wait for you to see it."

"But there were still so many pieces left."

"Ronnie and Will helped a little," Jonah admitted.

"Yeah?"

"I had to show them how. They didn't know anything. But don't worry, I was patient even when they made mistakes."

Her dad smiled. "That's good to hear."

"Yeah, I'm a pretty good teacher."

"I'm sure you are."

Jonah wrinkled his nose. "It smells kinda funny in here, doesn't it?"

"A little."

Jonah nodded. "I thought so." He motioned toward the television. "Have you been watching any movies?"

Her dad shook his head. "Not too many."

"What does that do?"

Her dad glanced at the IV bag. "It's got some medicine in it."

"Will it make you better?"

"I'm feeling better now."

"So you're coming home?"

"Pretty soon."

"Today?"

"Maybe tomorrow," he said. "But you know what I could use?"

"What?"

"A soda. Do you remember where the cafeteria is? Down the hall and around the corner?"

"I know where it is. I'm not a little kid. What kind do you want?"

"A Sprite or a Seven-Up."

"I don't have any money, though."

When her dad glanced at her, Ronnie took it as a cue to reach into her back pocket. "I've got some," she said. She pulled what she thought he'd need from her pocket and handed it to him as he headed out the door. As soon as he was gone, she could feel her dad staring at her.

"The lawyer called this morning. They've postponed your court date until late October."

Ronnie's gaze flickered to the window. "I can't think about that right now."

"I'm sorry," he said. He was quiet for a moment, and she could feel him watching her. "How's Jonah really holding up?" he asked.

Ronnie gave a half shrug. "Lost. Confused. Scared. Barely holding it together." *Like me*, she wanted to say.

Her dad motioned for her to come over. She took a seat in the chair that Jonah had been using. He reached for her hand and squeezed it. "I'm sorry I wasn't strong enough to stay out of the hospital. I never wanted you to see me like this."

She was already shaking her head. "Never, ever apologize for that."

"But—"

"No buts, okay? I needed to know. I'm glad I know."

He seemed to accept that. But then he surprised her.

"Do you want to talk about what happened with Will?"

"What makes you say something like that?" she asked.

"Because I know you. Because I know when something else is on your mind. And because I know how much you cared for him."

Ronnie sat up straighter, not wanting to lie to him. "He went home to pack," she said.

She could feel her dad studying her.

"Did I ever tell you my dad was a poker player?"

"Yeah, you told me. Why? Do you want to play poker?"

"No," he said. "I just know there's more to what happened with Will than what you're saying, but if you don't want to talk about it, that's okay, too."

Ronnie hesitated. She knew he'd be understanding, but she wasn't ready yet. "Like I said, he's leaving," she said instead. And with a nod, her dad let it go.

"You look tired," he said. "You should go home and take a nap later."

"I will. But I want to stay here for a while."

He adjusted his hand in hers. "Okay."

She glanced at the IV bag Jonah had asked about before. But unlike her brother, she knew that it wasn't medicine to make him better.

"Does it hurt?" she asked.

He paused before answering. "No," he answered. "Not too much."

"But it has hurt?"

Her dad started to shake his head. "Sweetheart . . ."

"I want to know. Did it hurt before you got here? Tell me the truth, okay?"

He scratched at his chest before answering. "Yes."

"How long?"

"I don't know what you mean—"

"I want to know when it started hurting," Ronnie said, leaning over the bedrail. She willed him to meet her eyes.

Again, he shook his head. "It's not important. I'm feeling better. And the doctors know what to do to keep helping me."

"Please," she said. "When did it start hurting?"

He looked down at their hands, clasped so tightly on the bed. "I don't know. March or April? But it wasn't every day—"

"When it hurt before," she went on, determined to hear the truth, "what did you do?"

"It wasn't so bad before," he answered.

"But it still hurt, right?"

"Yes."

"What did you do?"

"I don't know," he protested. "I tried not to think about it. I focused on other things."

She could feel the tension in her shoulders, hating what he might say but needing to know. "What did you focus on?"

Her dad smoothed out a wrinkle in the bedsheet with his free hand. "Why is this so important to you?"

"Because I want to know whether you focused on other things by playing the piano."

As soon as she said it, she knew she was right. "I saw you playing that night in the church, the night you had that coughing fit. And Jonah said you'd been sneaking over there as soon as the piano came in."

"Honey—"

"Do you remember when you said that playing the piano made you feel better?"

Her dad nodded. He could see what was coming, and she was sure he wouldn't want to answer. But she had to know.

"Did you mean that you didn't feel the pain as much? And

please tell me the truth. I'll know if you're lying." Ronnie would not be deflected, not this time.

He closed his eyes briefly, then met her gaze. "Yes."

"But you built the wall around the piano anyway?"

"Yes," he said again.

With that, she felt her fragile composure give way. Her jaw began to quiver as she lowered her head to her dad's chest.

Her dad reached out to her. "Don't cry," he said. "Please don't cry . . ."

But she couldn't help it. The memories of how she'd acted back then and the knowledge of what he had been going through drained whatever energy she had left. "Oh, Daddy . . ."

"No, baby . . . please don't cry. It wasn't so bad back then. I thought I could handle it, and I think I did. It wasn't until the last week or so that . . ." He touched a finger to her jaw, and when she looked into his eyes, what she saw there almost broke her heart. She had to look away.

"I could handle it then," he repeated, and she knew by his voice that he meant it. "I promise. It hurt, but it wasn't the only thing I thought about, because I could escape it in other ways. Like working on the window with Jonah, or just enjoying the kind of summer I dreamed about when I asked your mom to let both of you stay with me."

His words seared her, his forgiveness more than she could bear. "I'm so sorry, Daddy . . ."

"Look at me," he said, but she couldn't. She could think only about his need for the piano, something she'd taken away from him. Because she'd thought only about herself. Because she'd wanted to hurt him. Because she hadn't cared.

"Look at me," he said again. His voice was soft but insistent. Reluctantly, she raised her head.

"I had the most wonderful summer of my life," he whispered. "I got to watch you save the turtles, and I had the chance to see you fall in love, even if it doesn't last forever. And most of all, I got to know you as a young woman, not a little girl, for the first time ever. And I can't tell you how much joy those things gave to me. That's what got me through the summer."

She knew his words were sincere, which only made her feel worse. She was about to say something when Jonah burst through the door.

"Look who I found," he said, motioning with the can of Sprite.

Ronnie looked up to see her mom standing behind Jonah.

"Hey, sweetie," she said.

Ronnie turned to her dad.

He shrugged. "I had to call her," he explained.

"Are you doing okay?" her mom asked.

"I'm okay, Kim," her dad answered.

Her mom took that as an invitation to step into the room. "I think we all need to talk," she announced.

The following morning, Ronnie had made up her mind and was waiting in her room when her mom walked in.

"Have you finished packing yet?"

She fixed her mom with a calm but determined stare. "I'm not going back to New York with you."

Kim put her hands on her hips. "I thought we discussed this."

"No," Ronnie said evenly. "You discussed this. But I'm not coming with you."

Her mom ignored her comment. "Don't be ridiculous. Of course you're coming home."

"I'm not going back to New York." Ronnie crossed her arms but didn't raise her voice.

"Ronnie . . ."

She shook her head, knowing she'd never been more serious in her life. "I'm staying and I'm not going to discuss it. I'm eighteen now and you can't force me to go back with you. I'm an adult and I can do what I want."

As she absorbed Ronnie's words, her mom shifted uncertainly from one foot to the other.

"This . . . ," she finally said, motioning toward the living room, trying to sound reasonable. "This isn't your responsibility."

Ronnie took a step toward her. "No? Then whose is it? Who's going to take care of him?"

"Your dad and I have talked about that . . ."

"Oh, you mean about Pastor Harris?" Ronnie demanded. "Oh yeah, like he can take care of dad if he collapses or starts vomiting blood again. Pastor Harris can't physically do it."

"Ronnie . . . ," her mother began again.

Ronnie threw up her hands, her frustration and resolve growing. "Just because you're still mad at him doesn't mean that I have to be mad at him, okay? I know what he did and I'm sorry he hurt you, but this is about my dad. He's sick and he needs my help, and I'm going to be here for him. I don't care that he had an affair, I don't care that he left us. But I do care about him."

For the first time, her mom seemed genuinely taken aback. When she spoke again, her voice was soft. "What exactly did your dad tell you?"

Ronnie was about to protest that it didn't matter, but something stopped her. Her mother's expression was so strange, almost . . . *guilty*. As if . . . *as if* . . .

She stared at her mom, recognition dawning even as she spoke. "It wasn't Dad who had the affair, was it?" she said slowly. "It was you."

Her mother's posture didn't change, but she looked stricken. The realization hit Ronnie with an almost physical force.

Her mom had the affair, not her dad. And . . .

The room suddenly felt suffocating as the implications became clear. "That's why he left, isn't it? Because he found out. But you let me believe all along that it was all his fault, that he walked out for no good reason. You *pretended* it was him, when it was you all along. How could you do that?" Ronnie could barely breathe.

Her mom seemed unable to speak, and Ronnie found herself wondering whether she'd ever known her mom at all.

"Was it with Brian?" she suddenly demanded. "Were you cheating on Dad with Brian?"

Her mom stayed silent, and again Ronnie knew she was right.

Her mom had let her believe it was her dad who had left for no reason at all. *And I didn't talk to him for three years because of it . . .*

"You know what?" Ronnie snapped. "I don't care. I don't care what happened between the two of you, I don't care what happened in the past. But I'm not leaving my dad, and you can't make me—"

"Who's not leaving?" Jonah interrupted. He'd just walked into the room, holding a glass of milk, and he turned from their mom to her. She could hear the panic in his voice.

"Are you staying here?" he asked.

It took a moment for Ronnie to answer as she wrestled her anger under control. "Yeah," she said, hoping she sounded calmer than she felt. "I'm staying."

He put his glass of milk on the dresser. "Then I'm staying, too," he announced.

Her mom looked suddenly helpless, and though Ronnie could still feel the sharp edge of her anger, there was no way she was going to let Jonah watch his father die. She crossed the room and squatted down.

"I know you want to stay, but you can't," she said gently.

"Why not? You're staying."

"But I don't have school."

"So what? I can go to school here. Dad and I talked about it."

Their mom moved toward them. "Jonah . . ."

Jonah suddenly backed away, and she could hear the panic rising in his voice as he realized he was outnumbered. "I don't care about school! That's not fair! I want to stay here!"

34

·····❧·····

Steve

He wanted to surprise her. That had been his plan, anyway.

He'd played a concert in Albany; his next performance was scheduled in Richmond two days later. Normally, he never went home while on tour; it was easier to maintain a kind of rhythm as he traveled from city to city. But because he had a bit of extra time and hadn't seen his family in two weeks, he caught a train and arrived in the city as the lunch crowd came streaming out of their office towers in search of something to eat.

It was pure coincidence that he saw her at all. Even now, the odds seemed so remote as to be impossible. It was a city of millions and he was near Penn Station, and he was walking past a restaurant that was already nearly full.

His first thought, when he saw her, was that the woman looked exactly like his wife. She was seated at a small table wedged against the wall, across from a gray-haired man who appeared to be a few years older than her. She was dressed in a black skirt and a red silk blouse and was running a finger over the rim of her wineglass. He captured all of that and did a quick double take. It actually was Kim, he realized, and she was dining with a man that he'd never seen before. Through the window, he watched as she laughed, and with a sinking certainty, he knew he'd seen that laugh before. He remembered it from years ago, back when things were better between them. When she rose from the table, he watched as the man stood and placed his hand on the small of her back. The man's touch was tender, almost familiar, as though he'd done it hundreds of times before. She probably liked the way he touched her, Steve thought as he watched the stranger kiss his wife on the lips.

He wasn't sure what to do, but thinking back, he couldn't remember feeling much of anything. He knew they'd been distant with each other, he knew they'd been arguing too much, and he supposed that most men would have gone into the restaurant and confronted the two of them. Perhaps even made a scene. But he wasn't like most men. So he shifted the small carry bag he'd packed the night before to his other hand, turned around, and headed back in the direction of Penn Station.

He caught a train two hours later and arrived in Richmond late that evening. As always, he picked up the phone to call his wife, and she answered on the second ring. He could hear the television in the background as she said hello.

"You finally made it, huh?" she asked. "I was wondering when you were going to call."

As he sat on the bed, he pictured the stranger's hand on the small of her back. "I just got in," he said.

"Anything exciting happen?"

He was in a budget hotel, and the comforter was fraying slightly at the edges. There was an air conditioner beneath the window, and it rattled, making the curtains move. He could see dust coating the top of the television set.

"No," he said. "Nothing exciting at all."

In the hospital room, he remembered those images with a clarity that surprised him. He supposed it was because he knew Kim would be arriving soon, along with Ronnie and Jonah.

Ronnie had called him earlier to tell him that she wasn't going back to New York. He knew it wasn't going to be easy. He remembered his dad's shrunken, emaciated figure toward the end, and he didn't want his daughter to see him that way. But her mind was made up, and he knew he wouldn't be able to change it. But it scared him.

Everything about this scared him.

He'd been praying regularly in the last couple of weeks. Or, at least, that's how Pastor Harris had once described it. He didn't clasp his hands or bow his head; he didn't ask to be healed. He did, however, share with God the concerns he had regarding his children.

He supposed he wasn't much different from most parents in his worries for them. They were still young, they both had long lives ahead of them, and he wondered what would become of them. Nothing fancy: He would ask God whether He thought they would be happy, or continue to live in New York, or whether they would ever get married and have children. The basics, nothing more, but it was then, at that moment, that he finally understood what Pastor Harris had meant when he said he walked and talked with God.

Unlike Pastor Harris, however, he'd yet to hear the answers in his heart or experience God's presence in his life, and he knew he didn't have much time.

He glanced at the clock. Kim's plane was leaving in less than three hours. She would leave from the hospital to go straight to the airport with Jonah sitting beside her, and the realization was terrifying.

In just a little while, he would hold his son for the last time; today, he would say good-bye.

Jonah was in tears as soon as he rushed into the room, racing straight for the bed. Steve had just enough time to open his arms before Jonah fell into them. His birdlike shoulders were shuddering, and Steve felt his own heart breaking. He concentrated on how his son felt against him, trying to memorize the sensation.

Steve loved his children more than life itself, but more than that, he knew that Jonah needed him, and once more, he was struck by the realization that he was failing as a father.

Jonah continued to cry inconsolably. Steve held him close, wanting never to let go. Ronnie and Kim stood in the doorway, keeping their distance.

"They're trying to send me home, Daddy," Jonah whimpered. "I told them I could stay with you, but they're not listening. I'll be good, Daddy. I promise I'll be good. I'll go to bed when you tell me to and I'll clean my room and I won't eat cookies when I'm not supposed to. Tell them I can stay. I promise to be good."

"I know you'd be good," Steve murmured. "You've always been good."

"Then tell her, Dad! Tell her you want me to stay! Please! Just tell her!"

"I do want you to stay," he said, hurting for himself and for his son. "I want that more than anything, but your mom needs you, too. She misses you."

If Jonah had held out any hope, it ended then and there, and he began to cry again.

"But I'm never going to see you again . . . and it's not fair! It's just not fair!"

Steve tried to talk through the tightness in his throat. "Hey . . . ," he said. "I want you to listen to me, okay? Can you do that for me?"

Jonah forced himself to look up. Though he tried not to, Steve knew he was beginning to choke on his words. It took everything he had not to break down in front of his son.

"I want you to know that you're the best son a dad could hope to have. I've always been so proud of you, and I know you're going to grow up and do wonderful things. I love you so much."

"I love you, too, Daddy. And I'm going to miss you so much."

From the corner of his eye, Steve could see Ronnie and Kim, tears running down their faces.

"I'm going to miss you, too. But I'm always going to watch over you, okay? I promise. Do you remember the window we made together?"

Jonah nodded, his little jaw quivering.

"I call it God Light, because it reminds me of heaven. Every time the light shines through the window we built or any window at all, you'll know I'm right there with you, okay? That's going to be me. I'll be the light in the window."

Jonah nodded, not even bothering to wipe away his tears. Steve continued to hold his son, wishing with all his heart that he could make things better.

35

·····♪·····

Ronnie

Ronnie went outside with her mom and Jonah to see them off, and to speak with her mom alone before she left, asking her to do something for her as soon as she got back to New York. Then she returned to the hospital and sat with her dad, waiting until he fell asleep. For a long time he remained silent, staring out the window. She held his hand, and they sat together without speaking, both of them watching the clouds drifting slowly beyond the glass.

She wanted to stretch her legs and get some fresh air; her dad's good-bye to Jonah had left her drained and shaky. She didn't want to picture her brother on the plane or entering their apartment; she didn't want to think about whether he was still crying.

Outside, she walked along the sidewalk in front of the hospital, her mind wandering. She was almost past him when she heard him clear his throat. He was seated on a bench; despite the heat, he wore the same kind of long-sleeved shirt he always did.

"Hi, Ronnie," Pastor Harris said.

"Oh . . . hi."

"I was hoping to visit with your father."

"He's sleeping," she said. "But you can go up there if you want."

He tapped his cane, buying time. "I'm sorry for what you're going through, Ronnie."

She nodded, finding it hard to concentrate. Even this simple conversation seemed impossibly arduous.

Somehow, she got the sense he felt the same way.

"Would you pray with me?" His blue eyes held a plea. "I like to pray before I see your dad. It . . . helps me."

Her surprise gave way to an unexpected sense of relief.

"I'd like that very much," she answered.

She began to pray regularly after that, and she found that Pastor Harris was right.

Not that she believed her dad would be cured. She'd spoken to the doctor and seen the scans, and after their conversation, she'd left the hospital and gone to the beach and cried for an hour while her tears dried in the wind.

She didn't believe in miracles. She knew that some people did, but she couldn't force herself to think that her dad was somehow going to make it. Not after what she'd seen, not after the way the doctor had explained it. The cancer, she'd learned, had metastasized from his stomach to his pancreas and lungs, and holding out hope seemed . . . dangerous. She couldn't imagine having to come to terms a second time with what was happening to him. It was hard enough already, especially late at night when the house was quiet and she was alone with her thoughts.

Instead she prayed for the strength she needed to help her dad; she prayed for the ability to stay positive in his presence, instead of crying every time she saw him. She knew he needed her laughter and he needed the daughter she'd recently become.

The first thing she did after bringing him home from the hospital was to take him to see the stained-glass window. She watched as he slowly approached the table, his eyes taking in everything, his expression one of shocked disbelief. She knew then that there had been moments when he'd wondered whether he would live long enough to see it through. More than anything, she wished Jonah had been there with them, and she knew her dad was thinking the same thing. It had been their project, the way they'd spent their summer. He missed Jonah terribly, he missed him more than anything, and though he turned away so she couldn't see his face, she knew there were tears in his eyes as he made his way back to the house.

He called Jonah as soon as he got back inside. From the living room, Ronnie could hear her dad's assurances that he was feeling better, and though Jonah would likely misinterpret that, she knew her dad had done the right thing. He wanted Jonah to remember the happiness of the summer, not dwell on what was coming next.

That night, as he sat on the couch, he opened the Bible and began to read. Ronnie now understood his reasons. She took a seat beside him and asked the question she'd been wondering about since she'd examined the book herself.

"Do you have a favorite passage?" she asked.

"Many," he said. "I've always enjoyed the Psalms. And I always learn a lot from the letters of Paul."

"But you don't underline anything," she said. When he raised an eyebrow, she shrugged. "I looked through it while you were gone and I didn't see anything."

He thought about his answer. "If I tried to underline something important, I'd probably end up underlining almost everything. I've read it so many times and I always learn something new."

She studied him carefully. "I don't remember you reading the Bible before . . ."

"That's because you were young. I kept this Bible by my bed, and I'd read through parts of it once or twice a week. Ask your mom. She'll tell you."

"Have you read anything lately that you'd like to share?"

"Do you want me to?"

After she nodded, it took him only a minute to find the passage he wanted.

"It's Galatians 5:22," he said, pressing the Bible flat in his lap. He cleared his throat before he started. "But when the Holy Spirit controls our lives, he will produce this kind of fruit in us: love, joy, peace, patience, kindness, goodness, faithfulness, gentleness, and self-control."

She watched him as he read the verse, remembering how she'd acted when she'd first arrived and how he'd responded to her anger. She remembered the times he'd refused to argue with her mom, even when she'd tried to provoke him. She'd seen that as weakness and often wished her father were different. But all at once, she knew she'd been wrong about everything.

Her dad, she saw now, had never been acting alone. The Holy Spirit had been controlling his life all along.

The package from her mom arrived the following day, and Ronnie knew her mom had done what she'd asked. She brought the large envelope to the kitchen table and tore it straight across the top, then dumped the contents on the table.

Nineteen letters, all of them sent by her dad, all of them ignored and unopened. She noted the various return addresses he'd scrawled across the top: Bloomington, Tulsa, Little Rock . . .

She couldn't believe she hadn't read them. Had she really been that angry? That bitter? That . . . mean? Looking back, she knew the answer, but it still didn't make sense to her.

Thumbing through the letters, she looked for the first one he'd written. Like most of the others, it was printed neatly in black ink, and the postmark had faded slightly. Beyond the kitchen window, her dad was standing on the beach with his back to the house: Like Pastor Harris, he'd begun to wear long sleeves despite the summer heat.

Taking a deep breath, she opened the letter, and there, in the sunlight of the kitchen, she began to read.

Dear Ronnie,

I don't even know how to start a letter like this, other than to say that I'm sorry.

That's why I asked you to meet with me at the café, and what I wanted to tell you later that night when I called. I can understand why you didn't come and why you didn't take my call. You're angry with me, you're disappointed in me, and in your heart, you believe I've run away. In your mind, I've abandoned you and abandoned the family.

I can't deny that things are going to be different, but I want you to know that if I were in your shoes, I would probably feel much the way you do. You have every right to be angry with me. You have every right to be disappointed in me. I suppose I've earned the feelings you have, and it's not my intent to try to make excuses or cast any blame or try to convince you that you might understand it in time.

In all honesty, you might not, and that would hurt me more than you could ever imagine. You and Jonah have always meant so much to me, and I want you to understand that neither you nor Jonah were to blame for anything. Sometimes, for reasons that aren't always clear, marriages just don't work out. But remember this: I will always love you, and I will always love Jonah. I will always love your mother, and she will always have my respect. She is the giver of the two greatest gifts I've ever received, and she's been a wonderful mother. In many ways, despite the sadness I feel that your mother and I will no longer be together, I still believe it was a blessing to have been married to her for as long as I was.

I know this isn't much and it's certainly not enough to make you understand, but I want you to know that I still believe in the gift of love. I want you to believe in it, too. You deserve that in your life, for nothing is more fulfilling than love itself.

I hope that in your heart, you'll find some way to forgive me for leaving. It doesn't have to be now, or even soon. But I want

you to know this: When you're finally ready, I'll be waiting with
open arms on what will be the happiest day of my life.
  I love you,
  Dad

"I feel like I should be doing more for him," Ronnie said.

She was sitting on the back porch across from Pastor Harris. Her dad was inside sleeping, and Pastor Harris had come by with a pan of vegetable lasagna that his wife had made. It was mid-September and still hot during the day, though there'd been an evening a couple of days earlier that hinted at the crispness of autumn. It lasted only a single night; in the morning the sun was hot, and Ronnie had found herself strolling the beach and wondering whether the night before had been an illusion.

"You're doing all you can," he said. "I don't know that there's anything more you could be doing."

"I'm not talking about taking care of him. Right now, he doesn't even need me that much. He still insists on cooking, and we go for walks on the beach. We even flew kites yesterday. Aside from the pain medication, which makes him really tired, he's pretty much the same as before he went to the hospital. It's just . . ."

Pastor Harris's gaze was full of understanding. "You want to do something special. Something that means a lot to him."

She nodded, glad that he was here. In the past few weeks, Pastor Harris had become not only her friend, but the only person she could really talk to.

"I have faith that God will show you the answer. But you have to understand that sometimes it takes a while to be able to recognize what God wants you to do. That's how it often is. God's voice is usually nothing more than a whisper, and you have to listen very carefully to hear it. But other times, in those rarest of moments, the answer is obvious and rings as loud as a church bell."

She smiled, thinking she'd grown fond of their conversations. "You sound like you talk from experience."

"I love your dad, too. And like you, I wanted to do something special for him."

"And God answered?"

"God always answers."

"Was it a whisper or a church bell?"

For the first time in a long while, she saw a touch of mirth in his eyes. "A church bell, of course. God knows I'm hard of hearing these days."

"What are you going to do?"

He sat up straighter in his chair. "I'm going to install the window in the church," he said. "A benefactor showed up out of the blue last week, and not only offered to cover the rest of the repairs in full, but already had all the work crews lined up. They start work again tomorrow morning."

Over the next couple of days, Ronnie listened for church bells, but all she heard were seagulls. When listening for whispers, she heard nothing at all. It didn't necessarily surprise her—the answer hadn't come to Pastor Harris right away, either—but she hoped the answer would come before it was too late.

Instead, she simply continued on as she had before. She helped her dad when he needed help, let him be when he didn't, and tried to make the most of the remaining time they had together. That weekend, because her dad was feeling stronger, they made an outing to Orton Plantation Gardens, near Southport. It wasn't far from Wilmington and Ronnie had never been before, but as they pulled onto the graveled road that led to the original mansion, built in 1735, she already knew it was going to be a memorable day. It was the kind of place that seemed lost in time. The flowers were no longer in bloom, but as they walked among the giant oaks with their low-slung branches draped in Spanish moss, Ronnie thought that she'd never been anywhere more beautiful.

Strolling under the trees, her arm looped through her father's, they talked about the summer. For the first time, Ronnie told her dad about her relationship with Will; she told him about the first time they went fishing and the times they went mudding, she described his fancy dive from the cabana roof, and she told him all about the fiasco at the wedding. She didn't, however, tell him what happened on the day before he left for Vanderbilt or the things she'd said to him. She wasn't ready for that; the wound was still too raw. And as always when she talked, her dad listened quietly, rarely interjecting, even when she trailed off. She liked that about him. No, change that, she thought. She *loved* that about him, and she found herself wondering who she would have become had she never come down for the summer.

Afterward, they drove into Southport and had dinner at one of the small restaurants overlooking the harbor. She knew her dad was getting tired, but the food was good and they split a hot-fudge brownie at the end of the meal.

It was a good day, a day she knew she'd always remember. But as she sat alone in the living room after her dad had gone to bed, she once again found herself thinking that there was something more she could do for him.

The following week, the third week of September, she began to notice that her dad was getting worse. He now slept until mid-morning and took another nap in the afternoon. Though he'd been taking naps regularly, the naps began to lengthen, and he went to bed earlier in the evenings. As she cleaned the kitchen for want of anything better to do, she realized after adding it all up that he was now sleeping more than half the day.

It only got worse after that. With every passing day, he slept a little longer. He also wasn't eating enough. Instead, he moved his food around the plate and made a show of eating; when she scraped the remains into the garbage, she realized he'd only been nibbling. He was losing weight steadily now, and every time she blinked, she had the sense that her dad was getting smaller. Sometimes she was frightened by the thought that one day there would be nothing left of him at all.

September came to an end. In the mornings, the salty smell of the ocean was kept at bay by the winds from the mountains in the eastern part of the state. It was still hot, high season for hurricanes, but as yet the coast of North Carolina had been spared.

The day before, her dad had slept for fourteen hours. She knew he couldn't help it, that his body gave him no choice, but she ached at the thought that he was sleeping through most of the little time he had left. When her dad was awake, he was quieter now, content to read the Bible or walk slowly with her in silence.

More often than she expected, she found herself thinking about Will. She still wore the macramé bracelet he had given her, and as she ran her finger over its intricate weave, she wondered what classes he was taking, whom he walked beside on the greens as he moved from one building to the next. She was curious whom he sat next to when he ate in the cafeteria and whether he ever thought of her as he got ready to go out on a Friday or Saturday night. Perhaps, she thought in her lowest moments, he'd already met someone new.

"Do you want to talk about it?" her dad asked one day as they strolled along the beach. They were making their way toward the church. Since the construction had started up again, things were moving fast. The crew was massive: framers, electricians, men who specialized in trim carpentry or drywall. There were at least forty trucks on the work site, and people flowed in and out of the building constantly.

"About what?" she asked carefully.

"About Will," he said. "The way it ended between the two of you."

She gave him an appraising stare. "How could you possibly know about that?"

He shrugged. "Because you've mentioned him only in passing over the past few weeks, and you never talk to him on the phone. It's not hard to figure out that something happened."

"It's complicated," she said reluctantly.

They walked a few steps in silence before her dad spoke again. "If it matters to you, I thought he was an exceptional young man."

She looped her arm through his. "Yes, it does matter. And I thought so, too."

By then, they'd reached the church. She could see workers carrying in loads of lumber and cans of paint, and as usual her eyes sought out the empty space beneath the steeple. The window hadn't been installed yet—most of the construction had to be completed first to prevent the fragile glass pieces from cracking—but her dad still liked to visit. He was pleased by the renewed construction, but not primarily because of the window. He spoke constantly of how important the church was to Pastor Harris and how much the pastor missed preaching in the place that he'd long considered a second home.

Pastor Harris was always on site, and usually he would walk down to the beach to visit with them when they arrived. Looking around now, she spotted him standing in the gravel parking lot. He was talking to someone as he gestured animatedly at the building. Even from a distance, she could tell he was smiling.

She was about to wave in an attempt to get his attention when she suddenly recognized the man he was talking to. The sight startled her. The last time she'd seen him, she'd been distraught; the last time they'd been together, he hadn't bothered to say good-bye. Perhaps Tom Blakelee had simply been driving by and stopped to talk to the pastor about the rebuilding of the church. Maybe he was just interested.

For the rest of the week, she watched for Tom Blakelee when they visited the site, but she never saw him there again. Part of her was relieved, she admitted, that their worlds no longer intersected.

* * *

After their walks to the church and her dad's afternoon nap, they usually read together. She finished *Anna Karenina*, four months after she'd first started reading it. She checked out *Doctor Zhivago* from the public library. Something about the Russian writers appealed to her: the epic quality of their stories, perhaps; bleak tragedy and doomed love affairs painted on a grand canvas, so far removed from her own ordinary life.

Her dad continued to study his Bible, and sometimes he'd read a passage or verse aloud at her request. Some were short and others were long, but many of them seemed to focus on the meaning of faith. She wasn't sure why, but she sometimes got the sense that the act of reading them aloud had shed light on a nuance or meaning that he had previously missed.

Dinners were becoming simple affairs. In early October, she began to do most of the cooking, and he accepted this change as easily as he'd accepted everything else over the summer. Most of the time, he would sit in the kitchen and they would talk as she boiled pasta or rice and browned some chicken or steak in the pan. It was the first time she'd cooked meat in years, and she felt strange prodding her dad to eat it after putting the plate in front of him. He wasn't hungry much anymore, and the meals were bland because spices of any kind irritated his stomach. But she knew he needed food. Though he didn't have a scale in the house, she could see the pounds melting away.

One night after dinner, she finally told him what had happened with Will. She told him everything: about the fire and his attempts to cover for Scott, about all that had transpired with Marcus. Her dad listened intently as she spoke, and when at last he pushed aside his plate, she noticed he hadn't eaten more than a few bites.

"Can I ask you a question?"

"Of course," she said. "You can ask me anything."

"When you told me that you were in love with Will, did you mean it?"

She remembered Megan asking her the same question. "Yes."

"Then I think you might have been too hard on him."

"But he was covering up a crime . . ."

"I know. But if you think about it, you're now in the same position that he was. You know the truth, just as he did. And you've said nothing to anyone either."

"But I didn't do it . . ."

"And you said that he didn't either."

"What are you trying to say? That I should tell Pastor Harris?"

He shook his head. "No," he said to her surprise. "I don't think you should."

"Why?"

"Ronnie," he said gently, "there might be more to the story than meets the eye."

"But—"

"I'm not saying I'm right. I'll be the first to admit I'm wrong about a lot of things. But if everything is just as you described it, then I want you to know this: Pastor Harris doesn't want to know the truth. Because if he does, he'll have to do something about it. And trust me, he would never want to hurt Scott or his family, especially if it was an accident. He's just not that kind of man. And one more thing. And of everything I've said, this is the most important."

"What's that?"

"You need to learn how to forgive."

She crossed her arms. "I've already forgiven Will. I've left him messages . . ."

Even before she finished, her dad was shaking his head. "I'm not talking about Will. You need to learn to forgive yourself first."

That night, at the bottom of the stack of letters her dad had written, Ronnie found another letter, one she hadn't yet opened. He must have added it to the stack recently, since it bore no stamp or postmark.

She didn't know whether he wanted her to read it now or whether it was meant to be read after he was gone. She supposed she could have asked him, but she didn't. In truth, she wasn't sure she wanted to read it; simply holding the envelope frightened her, because she knew that it was the last letter he would ever write to her.

His disease continued to progress. Though they followed their regular routines—eating, reading, and taking walks on the beach— her dad was taking more medicine for his pain. There were times when his eyes were glassy and out of focus, but she still had the sense that the dosage wasn't strong enough. Now and then, she would see him wince as he sat reading on the couch. He would close his eyes and lean back, his face a mask of pain. When that happened, he would grip her hand; but as the days wore on, she noticed that his grip was growing weaker. His strength was fading, she thought; everything about him was fading. And soon he would be gone completely.

She could tell Pastor Harris noticed the changes in her dad as well. He'd been coming by almost every day in recent weeks, usually right before dinner. For the most part, he kept the conversation light; he updated them on the construction or regaled them with amusing stories from his past, bringing a fleeting smile to her father's face. But there were also moments when both of them seemed to run out of things to say to each other. Avoiding the elephant in the room was taxing for all of them, and in those moments, a fog of sadness seemed to settle in the living room.

When she sensed that they wanted to be alone, she would go stand out on the porch and try to imagine what they might be talking about. She could guess, of course: They talked about faith or family and maybe some regrets they each had, but she knew they also prayed together. She'd heard them once when she'd gone inside to get a glass of water, and she remembered thinking that Pastor Harris's prayer sounded more like a plea. He seemed to be begging for strength as though his own life depended on it, and as she listened to him, she closed her eyes to chime in with a silent prayer of her own.

Mid-October brought three days of unseasonably chilly weather, cold enough to require a sweatshirt in the mornings. After months of relentless heat, she enjoyed the briskness in the air, but those three days were hard on her dad. Though they still walked the beach, he moved even more slowly, and they paused only briefly outside the church before turning and heading back home. By the time they reached the door, her dad was shivering. Once inside, she drew him a warm bath, hoping it would help, feeling the first twinges of panic at the new signs of sickness that signaled the disease was advancing more rapidly.

On a Friday, a week before Halloween, her father rallied enough for them to try fishing on the small dock that Will had first taken her to. Officer Pete lent them some extra rods and a tackle box. Remarkably, her dad had never been fishing before, so Ronnie had to bait the hook. The first two fish that took the bait got away, but they were finally able to hook a small red drum and land it on the dock. It was the same kind of fish she'd caught with Will, and as the fish struggled while she freed the hook, she suddenly missed Will with an intensity that felt like physical pain.

When they returned home after a peaceful afternoon at the dock, two people were waiting for them on the porch. It wasn't until she got out of the car that she recognized Blaze and her mom. Blaze looked astonishingly different. Her hair was pulled back in a neat ponytail, and she was dressed in white shorts and a long-sleeved aquamarine top. She wore no jewelry or makeup.

Seeing Blaze again reminded Ronnie of something she'd managed to avoid thinking about in all her concerns for her father: that she would be returning to court before the month was out. She wondered what they wanted and why they were here.

She took her time helping her dad out of the car, offering her arm to steady him.

"Who are they?" her dad murmured.

Ronnie explained, and he nodded. As they approached, Blaze climbed down from the porch.

"Hi, Ronnie," she said, clearing her throat. She squinted slightly in the lowering sun. "I came to talk to you."

Ronnie sat across from Blaze in the living room, watching as Blaze studied the floor. Their parents had retreated to the kitchen to give them some privacy.

"I'm really sorry about your dad," Blaze began. "How is he doing?"

"He's okay." Ronnie shrugged. "How about you?"

Blaze touched the front of her shirt. "I'll always have scars here," she said, then gestured to her arms and belly, "and here." She gave a sad smile. "But I'm lucky to be alive, really." She fidgeted in her seat before catching Ronnie's eye. "I wanted to thank you for bringing me to the hospital."

Ronnie nodded, still unsure where the conversation was going. "You're welcome."

In the silence, Blaze looked around the living room, uncertain what to say next. Ronnie, learning from her dad, simply waited.

"I should have come by sooner, but I know you've been busy."

"It's okay," Ronnie said. "I'm just glad to see you're doing okay."

Blaze looked up. "Really?"

"Yeah," Ronnie said. She smiled. "Even if you do look like an Easter egg."

Blaze pulled on her top. "Yeah, I know. Crazy, huh? My mom bought me some clothes."

"They suit you. I guess the two of you are getting along better."

Blaze gave her a rueful look. "I'm trying. I'm living back home again, but it's hard. I did a lot of stupid things. To her, to other people. To you."

Ronnie sat motionless, her expression neutral. "Why are you really here, Blaze?"

Blaze twisted her hands together, betraying her agitation. "I came to apologize. I did a terrible thing to you. And I know I can't take back the stress I caused you, but I want you to know that I talked to the DA this morning. I told her that I put the stuff in your bag because I was mad at you, and I signed an affidavit that said you had no idea what was going on. You should be getting a call today or tomorrow, but she promised me that she would drop the charges."

The words came out so fast that at first Ronnie wasn't sure she'd heard her right. But Blaze's entreating look told her everything she needed to know. After all these months, after all the countless days and nights of worry, it was suddenly over. Ronnie was in shock.

"I'm really sorry," Blaze continued in a low voice. "I never should have put those things in your bag."

Ronnie was still trying to digest the fact that this nightmarish ordeal was coming to an end. She studied Blaze, who was now picking repeatedly at a loose thread in the hem of her shirt. "What's going to happen to you? Are they going to charge you?"

"No," she said. At this she looked up, her jaw squared. "I had some information they wanted about another crime. A bigger crime."

"You mean about what happened to you on the pier?"

"No," she said, and Ronnie thought she saw something hard and defiant in her eyes. "I told them about the fire at the church and the way it really started." Blaze made sure she had Ronnie's attention before going on. "Scott didn't start the fire. His bottle rocket had nothing to do with it. Oh, it landed near the church all right. But it was already out."

Ronnie absorbed this information in growing wonderment. For a moment, they stared at each other, the charge in the air palpable.

"Then how did it start?"

Blaze leaned forward and rested her elbows on her knees, her forearms stretched out as if in supplication. "We were out partying on the beach—Marcus, Teddy, Lance, and me. A little later, Scott showed up, just down the beach from us. We pretended to ignore each other, but we could see Scott lighting up bottle rockets. Will was still down the beach and Scott sort of aimed one in his direction, but the wind caught it and it flew toward the church. Will started freaking out and came running. But Marcus thought the whole thing was hilarious, and the minute that rocket fell behind the church, he ran over to the churchyard. I didn't know what was happening at first, even after I followed him and saw him torching the scrub grass next to the church wall. The next thing I knew, the side of the building was on fire."

"You're saying Marcus did it?" Ronnie could barely get the words out.

She nodded. "He set other fires, too. At least I'm pretty sure he did—he always loved fire. I guess I always knew he was crazy, but I . . ." She stopped herself, realizing she'd been down that road too many times already. She sat up straight. "Anyway, I've agreed to testify against him."

Ronnie leaned back in her chair, feeling as though the wind had been knocked out of her. She remembered the things she'd said to Will, suddenly realizing that if Will had done what she'd demanded, Scott's life would have been ruined for nothing.

She felt almost ill as Blaze went on. "I'm really sorry for everything," she said. "And as crazy as it sounds, I did consider you my friend until I was an idiot and ruined it." For the first time, Blaze's voice cracked. "But you're a great person, Ronnie. You're honest, and you were nice to me when you had no reason to be." A tear leaked out of one eye, and she swiped at it quickly. "I'll never forget the day you offered to let me stay with you, even after all the terrible things I had done to you. I felt such . . . shame. And yet I was grateful, you know? That someone still cared."

Blaze paused, visibly struggling to pull herself together. When she had blinked back her tears, she took a deep breath and fixed Ronnie with a determined look.

"So if you ever need anything—and I mean anything—let me know. I'll drop everything, okay? I know I can't ever make up for what I did to you, but in a way, I feel like you saved me. What's happened to your dad is just so unfair . . . and I would do anything to help you."

Ronnie nodded.

"And one last thing," Blaze added. "We don't have to be friends, but if you ever see me again, will you please call me Galadriel? I can't stand the name Blaze."

Ronnie smiled. "Sure thing, Galadriel."

As Blaze had promised, her lawyer called that afternoon, informing her that the charges in her shoplifting case had been dropped.

That night, as her dad lay sleeping in his bedroom, Ronnie turned on the local news. She wasn't sure if the news would cover it, but there it was, a thirty-second segment right before the weather forecast about "the arrest of a new suspect in the ongoing arson investigation relating to a local church burning last year." When they flashed a mug shot of Marcus with a few details of his prior misdemeanor charges, she turned off the TV. Those cold, dead eyes still had the power to unnerve her.

She thought of Will and what he had done to protect Scott, for a crime that it turned out he hadn't even committed. Was it really so terrible, she wondered, that loyalty to his friend had skewed his judgment? Especially in light of the way things had turned out? Ronnie was no longer certain of anything. She had been wrong about so many things: her dad, Blaze, her mother, even Will. Life was so much more complicated than she ever imagined as a sullen teenager in New York.

She shook her head as she moved around the house, turning out the lights one by one. That life—a parade of parties and high school gossip and squabbles with her mom—felt like another world, an existence she had only dreamed. Today, there was only this: her walk on the beach with her dad, the ceaseless sound of the ocean waves, the smell of winter approaching.

And the fruit of the Holy Spirit: love, joy, peace, patience, kindness, goodness, faithfulness, gentleness, and self-control.

Halloween came and went, and her dad grew weaker with every passing day.

They gave up their walks on the beach when the effort became too great, and in the mornings, when she made his bed, she saw dozens of strands of hair on his pillow. Knowing that the disease was accelerating, she moved her mattress into his bedroom in case he needed her help, and also to remain close to him for as long as she could.

He was on the highest dosages of pain medicine that his body could handle, but it never seemed enough. At night, as she slept on the floor beside him, he uttered whimpering cries that nearly broke her heart. She kept his medication right beside his bed, and they were the first things he reached for when he woke up. She would sit beside him in the mornings, holding him, his limbs trembling, until the medicine took effect.

But the side effects took their toll as well. He was unstable on his feet, and Ronnie had to support him whenever he moved, even across the room. Despite his weight loss, when he stumbled it was all she could do to keep him from falling. Though he never gave voice to his frustration, his eyes registered his disappointment, as if he were somehow failing her.

He now slept an average of seventeen hours a day, and Ronnie would spend entire days alone at home, reading and rereading the letters he'd originally written to her. She hadn't yet read the last letter he'd written to her—the idea still seemed too frightening— but sometimes she liked to hold it between her fingers, trying to summon the strength to open it.

She called home more frequently, timing her calls for when Jonah got home from school or after they had finished dinner. Jonah seemed subdued, and when he asked about their dad she sometimes felt guilty about holding back the truth. But she couldn't burden him that way, and she noticed that whenever her dad spoke with him, he always did his best to sound as energetic as he could. Afterward, he often sat in the chair by the phone, spent from his exertions, too tired even to move. She would watch him in silence, chafing at the knowledge that there was something more she could do, if only she knew what it was.

"What's your favorite color?" she asked.

They were seated at the kitchen table, and Ronnie had a pad of paper open before her.

Steve gave her a quizzical smile. "That's what you wanted to ask me?"

"This is just the first question. I've got a lot more."

He reached for the can of Ensure she'd placed before him. He was no longer eating much solid food, and she watched as he took a sip, knowing he was doing it to please her, not because he was hungry.

"Green," he said.

She wrote down the answer and read the next question. "How old were you when you first kissed a girl?"

"Are you serious?" He made a face.

"Please, Dad," she said. "It's important."

He answered again, and she wrote it down. They got through a quarter of the questions she'd jotted down, and over the next week, he eventually answered them all. She wrote down the answers carefully, not necessarily verbatim, but she hoped with enough detail to reconstruct the answers in the future. It was an engaging and sometimes surprising exercise, but by the end, she concluded that her dad was mostly the same man she'd come to know over the summer.

Which was good and bad, of course. Good because she'd suspected he would be, and bad because it left her no closer to the answer she'd been seeking all along.

The second week of November brought the first rains of autumn, but the construction at the church continued without pause. If anything, the pace increased. Her dad no longer accompanied her; still, Ronnie walked down the beach to the church every day to see how things were progressing. It had become part of her routine during the quiet hours when her dad was napping. Though Pastor Harris always registered her arrival with a wave, he no longer joined her on the beach to chat.

In a week, the stained-glass window would be installed, and Pastor Harris would know he'd done something for her dad that no one else could do, something she knew would mean the world to him. She was happy for him, even as she prayed for guidance of her own.

On a gray November day, her dad suddenly insisted that they venture out to the pier. Ronnie was anxious about the distance and the cold, but he was adamant. He wanted to see the ocean from the pier, he said. *One last time*, were the words he didn't have to say.

They dressed in overcoats, and Ronnie even wrapped a wool scarf around her father's neck. The wind carried in it the first sharp taste of winter, making it feel colder than the thermometer suggested. She insisted on driving to the pier and parked Pastor Harris's car in the deserted boardwalk lot.

It took a long time to reach the end of the pier. They were alone beneath a cloud-swept sky, the iron gray waves visible between the concrete planks. As they shuffled forward, her father kept his arm looped through hers, clinging to her as the wind tugged at their overcoats.

When they finally made it, her dad reached out for the railing and almost lost his balance. In the silvery light, the planes of his sunken cheeks stood out in sharp relief and his eyes looked a little glassy, but she could tell he was satisfied.

The steady movement of the waves stretching out before him to the horizon seemed to bring him a feeling of serenity. There was nothing to see—no boats, no porpoises, no surfers— but his expression seemed peaceful and free of pain for the first time in weeks. Near the waterline, the clouds seemed almost alive, roiling and shifting as the wintry sun attempted to pierce their veiled masses. She found herself watching the play of clouds with the same wonder her father did, wondering where his thoughts lay.

The wind was picking up, and she saw him shiver. She could tell he wanted to stay, his gaze locked on the horizon. She tugged gently on his arm, but he only tightened his grip on the railing.

She relented then, standing next to him until he was shudder-ing with cold, finally ready to go. He released the railing and let her turn him around, starting their slow march back to the car. From the corner of her eye, she noticed he was smiling.

"It was beautiful, wasn't it?" she remarked.

Her dad took a few steps before answering.

"Yes," he said. "But mostly I enjoyed sharing that moment with you."

Two days later, she resolved to read his final letter. She would do it soon, before he was gone. Not tonight, but soon, she promised herself. It was late at night, and the day with her dad had been the hardest yet. The medicine didn't seem to be helping him at all. Tears leaked out of his eyes as spasms of pain racked his body; she begged him to let her bring him to the hospital, but still he refused.

"No," he gasped. "Not yet."

"When?" she asked desperately, close to tears herself. He didn't answer, only held his breath, waiting for the pain to pass. When it did, he seemed suddenly weaker, as if it had sheared away a sliver of the little life he had left.

"I want you to do something for me," he said. His voice was a ragged whisper.

She kissed the back of his hand. "Anything," she said.

"When I first received my diagnosis, I signed a DNR. Do you know what that is?" He searched her face. "It means I don't want any extraordinary measures that might keep me alive. If I go to the hospital, I mean."

She felt her stomach twist in fear. "What are you trying to say?"

"When the time comes, you have to let me go."

"No," she said, beginning to shake her head, "don't talk like that."

His gaze was gentle but insistent. "Please," he whispered. "It's what I want. When I go to the hospital, bring the papers. They're in my top desk drawer, in a manila envelope."

"No . . . Dad, please," she cried. "Don't make me do that. I can't do that."

He held her gaze. "Even for me?"

That night, his whimpers were broken by a labored, rapid breathing that terrified her. Though she had promised she would do what he asked, she wasn't sure she could.

How could she tell the doctors not to do anything? How could she let him die?

On Monday, Pastor Harris picked them both up and drove them to the church to watch the window being installed. Because he was too weak to stand, they brought a lawn chair with them. Pastor Harris helped her support him as they slowly made their way to the beach. A crowd had gathered in anticipation of the event, and for the next few hours, they watched as workers carefully set the window in place. It was as spectacular as she'd imagined it would be, and when the final brace was bolted into place, a cheer went up.

She turned to see her father's reaction and noticed that he'd fallen asleep, cocooned in the heavy blankets she'd draped over him.

With Pastor Harris's help, she brought him home and put him in bed. On his way out, the pastor turned to her.

"He was happy," he said, as much to convince himself as her.

"I know he was," she assured him, reaching out to squeeze his arm. "It's exactly what he wanted."

Her dad slept for the rest of the day, and as the world went black outside her window, she knew it was time to read the letter. If she didn't do it now, she might never find the courage.

The light in the kitchen was dim. After tearing open the envelope, she slowly unfolded the page. The handwriting was different from his previous letters; gone was the flowing, open style she'd expected. In its place was something like a scrawl. She didn't want to imagine what a struggle it must have been to write the words or how long it had taken him. She took a deep breath and began to read.

Hi, sweetheart,

I'm proud of you.

I haven't said those words to you as often as I should have. I say them now, not because you chose to stay with me through this incredibly difficult time, but because I wanted you to know that you're the remarkable person I've always dreamed you could be.

Thank you for staying. I know it's hard for you, surely harder than you imagined it would be, and I'm sorry for the hours that you're going to inevitably spend alone. But I'm especially sorry because I haven't always been the father you've needed me to be. I know I've made mistakes. I wish I could change so many things in my life. I suppose that's normal, considering what's happening to me, but there's something else I want you to know.

As hard as life can be and despite all my regrets, there have been moments when I felt truly blessed. I felt that way when you were born, and when I took you to the zoo as a child and watched you stare at the giraffes in amazement. Usually, those moments don't last long; they come and go like ocean breezes. But sometimes, they stretch out forever.

That's what the summer was like for me, and not only because you forgave me. The summer was a gift to me, because I came to know the young woman I always knew you would grow into. As I told your brother, it was the best summer of my life, and I often wondered during those idyllic days how someone like me could have been blessed with a daughter as wonderful as you.

Thank you, Ronnie. Thank you for coming. And thank you for the way you made me feel each and every day we had the chance to be together.

You and Jonah have always been the greatest blessings in my life. I love you, Ronnie, and I've always loved you. And never, ever forget that I am, and always have been, proud of you. No father has ever been as blessed as I.

Dad

Thanksgiving passed. Along the beach, people began to put up Christmas decorations.

Her dad had lost a third of his body weight and spent nearly all his time in bed.

Ronnie stumbled across the sheets of paper when she was cleaning the house one morning. They'd been wedged carelessly into the drawer of the coffee table, and when she pulled them out, it took her only a moment to recognize her father's hand in the musical notes scrawled on the page.

It was the song he'd been writing, the song she'd heard him playing that night in the church. She set the pages on top of the table to inspect them more closely. Her eye raced over the heavily edited series of notes, and she thought again that her dad had been on to something. As she read, she could hear the arresting strains of the opening bars in her head. But as she flipped through the score to the second and third pages, she could also see that it wasn't quite right. Although his initial instincts had been good, she thought she recognized where the composition began to lose its way. She fished a pencil from the table drawer and began to overlay her own work on his, scrawling rapid chord progressions and melodic riffs where her father had left off.

Before she knew it, three hours had gone by and she heard her dad beginning to stir. After tucking the pages back into the drawer, she headed for the bedroom, ready to face whatever the day would bring.

Later that evening, when her father had fallen into yet another fitful sleep, she retrieved the pages, this time working long past midnight. In the morning, she woke up eager and anxious to show him what she'd done. But when she entered his bedroom, he wouldn't stir at all, and she panicked when she realized that he was barely breathing.

Her stomach was in knots as she called the ambulance, and she felt unsteady as she made her way back to the bedroom. She wasn't ready, she told herself, she hadn't shown him the song. She needed another day. *It's not time yet.* But with trembling hands, she opened the top drawer of his desk and pulled out the manila envelope.

In the hospital bed, her father looked smaller than she'd ever seen him. His face had collapsed in on itself, and his skin had an unnatural grayish pallor. His breaths were as shallow and rapid as an infant's. She squeezed her eyes closed, wishing she weren't here. Wishing she were anywhere but here.

"Not yet, Daddy," she whispered. "Just a little more time, okay?"

Outside the hospital window, the sky was gray and cloudy. Most of the leaves had fallen from the trees, and the stark and empty branches somehow reminded her of bones. The air was cold and still, presaging a storm.

The envelope sat on the nightstand, and though she'd promised her dad she would give it to the doctor, she hadn't done so yet. Not until she was sure he wouldn't wake, not until she was sure she was never going to have the chance to say good-bye. Not until she was certain there was nothing more she could do for him.

She prayed fiercely for a miracle, a tiny one. And as though God Himself were listening, it happened twenty minutes later.

She'd been sitting beside him for most of the morning. She'd grown so used to the sound of his breathing and the steady beep of the heart monitor that the slightest change sounded like an alarm. Looking up, she saw his arm twitch and his eyes flutter open. He blinked under the fluorescent lights, and Ronnie instinctively reached for his hand.

"Dad?" she said. Despite herself, she felt a surge of hope; she imagined him slowly sitting up.

But he didn't. He didn't even seem to hear her. When he rolled his head with great effort to look at her, she saw a darkness in his eyes that she'd never seen before. But then he blinked and she heard him sigh.

"Hi, sweetheart," he whispered hoarsely.

The fluid in his lungs made him sound as if he were drowning. She forced herself to smile. "How are you doing?"

"Not too well." He paused, as if to gather his strength. "Where am I?"

"You're in the hospital. You were brought here this morning. I know you have a DNR, but . . ."

When he blinked again, she thought his eyes might stay closed. But eventually he opened them.

"It's okay," he whispered. The forgiveness in his voice tore at her heart. "I understand."

"Please don't be mad at me."

"I'm not."

She kissed him on the cheek and tried to wrap her arms around his shrunken figure. She felt his hand graze her back.

"Are you . . . okay?" he asked her.

"No," she admitted, feeling the tears start to come. "I'm not okay at all."

"I'm sorry," he breathed.

"No, don't say that," she said, willing herself not to break down. "I'm the one who's sorry. I never should have stopped talking to you. I've wanted so desperately to take it all back."

He gave a ghostly smile. "Did I ever tell you that I think you're beautiful?"

"Yeah," she said, sniffling. "You've told me."

"Well, this time I mean it."

She laughed helplessly through her tears. "Thanks," she said. Leaning over, she kissed his hand.

"Do you remember when you were little?" he asked, suddenly serious. "You used to watch me playing the piano for hours. One day, I found you sitting at the keyboard playing a melody you had heard me play. You were only four years old. You always had so much talent."

"I remember," she said.

"I want you to know something," her dad said, gripping her hand with surprising force. "No matter how bright your star became, I never cared about the music half as much as I cared about you as a daughter . . . I want you to know that."

She nodded. "I believe you. And I love you, too, Dad."

He took a long breath, his eyes never leaving hers. "Then will you bring me home?"

The words struck her with their full weight, unavoidable and direct. She glanced at the envelope, knowing what he was asking and what he needed her to say. And in that instant, she remembered everything about the last five months. Images raced through her mind, one after the next, stopping only when she saw him sitting in the church at the keyboard, beneath the empty space where the window would eventually be installed.

And it was then that she knew what her heart had been telling her to do all along.

"Yes," she said. "I'll bring you home. But I need you to do something for me, too."

Her dad swallowed. It seemed to take all the strength he had to say. "I'm not sure I can anymore."

She smiled and reached for the envelope. "Even for me?"

Pastor Harris had lent her his car, and she drove as fast as she could. Holding her cell phone, she made the call as she was changing lanes. She quickly explained what was happening and what she needed; Galadriel agreed immediately. She drove as though her father's life depended on it, accelerating at every yellow light.

Galadriel was waiting for her at the house when she arrived. Beside her on the porch lay two crowbars, which she hefted as Ronnie approached.

"Ready?" she asked.

Ronnie merely nodded, and together they entered the house.

With Galadriel's help, it took less than an hour to dismantle her father's work. She didn't care about the mess they left in the living room; the only thing she could think about was the time her father had left and what she still needed to do for him. When the last piece of plywood was ripped away, Galadriel turned to her, sweating and breathless.

"Go pick up your dad. I'll clean up. And I'll help you bring him in when you get back."

She drove even faster on the way back to the hospital. Before she had left the hospital, she'd met with her dad's doctor and explained what she planned to do. With the attending nurse's help, she'd raced through the release forms the hospital required; when she called the hospital from the car, she paged the same nurse and asked her to have her dad waiting downstairs in a wheelchair.

The car's tires squealed as she turned in to the hospital parking lot. She followed the lane toward the emergency room entrance and saw immediately that the nurse had been good to her word.

Ronnie and the nurse helped her dad into the car, and she was back on the road within minutes. Her dad seemed more alert than he'd been in the hospital room, but she knew that could change at any time. She needed to get him home before it was too late. As she drove the streets of a town she'd eventually come to think of as her own, she felt a rush of fear and hope. It all seemed so simple, so clear now. When she reached the house, Galadriel was waiting for her. Galadriel had moved the couch into position, and together they helped her father recline on it.

Despite his condition, it seemed to dawn on him what Ronnie had done. Ever so gradually, she saw his grimace replaced by an expression of wonder. As he stared at the piano standing exposed in the alcove, she knew she had done the right thing. Leaning over, she kissed him on the cheek.

"I finished your song," she said. "Our last song. And I want to play it for you."

36

·····♪·····

Steve

Life, he realized, was much like a song.

In the beginning there is mystery, in the end there is confirmation, but it's in the middle where all the emotion resides to make the whole thing worthwhile.

For the first time in months, he felt no pain at all; for the first time in years, he knew his questions had answers. As he listened to the song that Ronnie had finished, the song that Ronnie had perfected, he closed his eyes in the knowledge that his search for God's presence had been fulfilled.

He finally understood that God's presence was everywhere, at all times, and was experienced by everyone at one time or another. It had been with him in the workshop as he'd labored over the window with Jonah; it had been present in the weeks he'd spent with Ronnie. It was present here and now as his daughter played their song, the last song they would ever share. In retrospect, he wondered how he could have missed something so incredibly obvious.

God, he suddenly understood, was love in its purest form, and in these last months with his children, he had felt His touch as surely as he had heard the music spilling from Ronnie's hands.

37

.....♪.....

Ronnie

Her dad died less than a week later, in his sleep, with Ronnie on the floor next to him. Ronnie couldn't bring herself to speak of the details. She knew her mom was waiting for her to finish; in the three hours she'd been talking, her mom had remained silent, much the way her dad always had. But the moments in which she watched her father draw his last breaths felt intensely private to her, and she knew she would never speak of them to anyone. Being at his side as he left this world was a gift that he had given her, and only her, and she would never forget how solemn and intimate it had felt.

Instead, she stared out at the freezing December rain and spoke of her last recital, the most important recital of her life.

"I played for him as long as I could, Mom. And I tried so hard to make it beautiful for him, because I knew how much it meant to him. But he was just so weak," she whispered. "At the end, I'm not sure he could even hear me." She pinched the bridge of her nose, wondering idly if she had any tears left to shed. There had been so many tears already.

Her mom opened her arms and beckoned to her. Her own tears shone bright in her eyes.

"I know he heard you, sweetheart. And I know it was beautiful."

Ronnie gave herself over to her mother's embrace, resting her head on her chest as she used to do when she was a child.

"Never forget how happy you and Jonah made him," her mother murmured, stroking her hair.

"He made me happy, too," she mused. "I learned so much from him. I just wish I had thought to tell him. That, and a million other things." She shut her eyes. "But now it's too late."

"He knew," her mom assured her. "He always knew."

The funeral was a simple affair, held in the church that had recently been reopened. Her dad had asked to be cremated, and his wishes had been honored.

Pastor Harris gave the eulogy. It was short but brimming with authentic grief and love. He had loved her father like a son, and despite herself, Ronnie cried along with Jonah. She slipped her arm around him as he sobbed the bewildered cries of a child, and she tried not to think about how he would remember this loss, so early in life.

Only a handful of people had come to the service. She'd spotted Galadriel and Officer Pete as she'd walked in and had heard the church door open once or twice after she'd taken her seat, but other than that, the church was empty. She ached at the thought that so few people knew how special her dad had been or how much he'd meant to her.

After the service, she continued to sit in the pew with Jonah while Brian and her mom went outside to talk to Pastor Harris. The four of them were flying back to New York in just a few hours, and she knew she didn't have much time.

Even so, she didn't want to leave. The rain, pouring down all morning, had stopped, and the sky was beginning to clear. She had been praying for that, and she found herself staring at her father's stained-glass window, willing the clouds to part.

And when they did, it was just as her father had described it. The sun flooded through the glass, splitting into hundreds of jewel-like prisms of glorious, richly colored light. The piano stood in a waterfall of brilliant color, and for a moment Ronnie pictured her father sitting at its keys, his face upturned to the light. It didn't last long, but she squeezed Jonah's hand in silent awe. Despite the weight of her grief, she smiled, knowing that Jonah was thinking the same thing.

"Hi, Daddy," she whispered. "I knew you would come."

When the light had faded, she said a silent good-bye and pulled herself to her feet. But when she turned around, she saw that she and Jonah weren't alone in the church. Near the door, seated in the last pew, she saw Tom and Susan Blakelee.

She put her hand on Jonah's shoulder. "Would you go outside and tell Mom and Brian that I'll be right out? I have to talk to someone first."

"Okay," he said, rubbing his swollen eyes with a fist as he exited the church. Once he was gone, she started toward them, watching as they rose to greet her.

Surprising her, Susan was the first to speak.

"I'm sorry for your loss. Pastor Harris told us your father was a wonderful man."

"Thank you," she said. She looked from one of Will's parents to the other and smiled. "I appreciate that you came. And I also want to thank you both for what you did for the church. It was really important to my dad."

At her words, she saw Tom Blakelee glance away, and she knew she'd been right. "It was supposed to be anonymous," he murmured.

"I know. And Pastor Harris didn't tell me or my dad. But I guessed the truth when I saw you at the site. It was a beautiful thing, what you did."

He nodded almost shyly, and she saw his eyes flicker to the window. He, too, had seen the light flood the church.

In the silence, Susan waved toward the door. "There's someone here to see you."

"Are you ready?" her mom asked as soon as she exited the church. "We're already running late."

Ronnie barely heard her. Instead, she stared at Will. He was dressed in a black suit. His hair was longer, and her first thought was that it made him look older. He was talking to Galadriel, but as soon as he saw her, she watched him raise a finger, as if asking her to hold that thought.

"I need a few more minutes, okay?" she said without taking her eyes off Will.

She hadn't expected him to come, hadn't expected to see him ever again. She didn't know what it meant, that he was here, and wasn't sure whether to feel ecstatic or heartbroken or both. She took a step in his direction and stopped.

She couldn't read his expression. As he started toward her, she recalled the way he'd seemed to glide through the sand the first time she'd ever seen him; she remembered their kiss on the boat dock the night of his sister's wedding. And she heard again the words she'd said to him on the day they'd said good-bye. She was besieged by a storm of conflicting emotions—desire, regret, longing, fear, grief, love. There was so much to say, yet what could they really begin to say in this awkward setting and with so much time already passed?

"Hi." *If only I were telepathic, and you could read my mind.*

"Hey," he said. He seemed to be searching her face for something, but for what, she didn't know.

He made no move toward her, nor did she reach out to him.

"You came," she said, unable to keep the wonder out of her voice.

"I couldn't stay away. And I'm sorry about your dad. He was . . . a great person." For a moment, a shadow seemed to cross his face, and he added, "I'll miss him."

She flashed on the memory of their evenings together at her dad's house, the smell of his cooking and Jonah's shouts of laughter as they played liar's poker. She felt suddenly dizzy. It was all so surreal, to see Will here on this terrible day. Part of her wanted to throw herself into his arms and apologize for the way she had let him go. But another part, mute and paralyzed from the loss of her dad, wondered whether she was still the same person Will had once loved. So much had happened since the summer.

She shifted awkwardly from one foot to the other. "How's Vanderbilt?" she finally asked.

"It's what I expected."

"Is that good or bad?"

Instead of answering, he nodded at the rental car. "I take it you're heading home, huh?"

"I've got to catch a plane in a little while." She tucked a strand of hair behind her ear, hating how self-conscious she felt. It was as if they were strangers. "Are you finished with the semester?"

"No, I've got finals next week, so I'm flying back tonight. My classes are harder than I expected. I'm probably going to have to pull some all-nighters."

"You'll be home for break soon. A few walks on the beach and you'll be good as new." Ronnie summoned an encouraging smile.

"Actually, my parents are hauling me off to Europe as soon as I'm finished. We'll spend Christmas in France. They think it's important for me to see the world."

"That sounds like fun."

He shrugged. "What about you?"

She looked away, her mind flashing unbidden to her last days with her dad.

"I think I'm going to audition at Juilliard," she said slowly. "We'll see if they'll still have me."

For the first time, he smiled, and she caught a glimpse of the spontaneous joy he had shown so often during those warm summer months. How she had missed his joy, his warmth, during the long march of the fall and winter. "Yeah? Good for you. And I'm sure you'll do great."

She hated the way they were talking around the edges of things. It felt so . . . *wrong*, given everything they'd shared over the summer and all they'd been through together. She drew a long breath, trying to keep her emotions in check. But it was just so hard right now, and she was so tired. The next words came out almost automatically.

"I want to apologize for the things I said to you. I didn't mean them. There was just so much going on. I shouldn't have taken it all out on you . . ."

He took a step toward her and reached for her arm. "It's okay," he said. "I understand."

At his touch, she felt all the pent-up emotion of the day burst to the surface, overwhelming her fragile composure, and she squeezed her eyes closed, trying to stop the tears. "But if you'd done what I demanded, then Scott . . ."

He shook his head. "Scott's okay. Believe it or not, he even got his scholarship. And Marcus is in jail—"

"But I shouldn't have said those awful things to you!" she interrupted. "The summer shouldn't have ended like that. We shouldn't have ended like that, and I'm the one who caused it. You don't know how much it hurts to think that I drove you away . . ."

"You didn't drive me away," he said gently. "I was leaving. You knew that."

"But we haven't talked, we haven't written, and it was just so hard to watch what was happening to my dad . . . I wanted so much to talk to you, but I knew you were mad at me—"

As she began to cry, he pulled her to him and wrapped his arms around her. His embrace somehow made everything better and worse at the same time.

"Shhh," he murmured, "it's okay. I was never as mad as you thought I was."

She squeezed him harder, trying to cling to what they'd shared. "But you only called twice."

"Because I knew your dad needed you," he said, "and I wanted you to concentrate on him, not me. I remember how it was when Mikey died, and I remember wishing that I'd had more time with him. I couldn't do that to you."

She buried her face in his shoulder as he held her. All that she could think was that she needed him. She needed his arms around her, needed him to hold her and whisper that they'd find a way to be together.

She felt him lean into her and heard him murmur her name. When she pulled back, she saw him smiling down at her.

"You're wearing the bracelet," he whispered, touching her wrist.

"In my thoughts forever." She gave a shaky smile.

He tilted her chin so he could stare closely into her eyes. "I'm going to call you, okay? After I get back from Europe."

She nodded, knowing it was all they had, yet knowing it wasn't enough. Their lives were on separate tracks, now and forever. The summer was over, and they were each moving on.

She closed her eyes, hating the truth.

"Okay," she whispered.

Epilogue

·····✦·····

Ronnie

In the weeks since her dad's funeral, Ronnie continued to experience some emotional upheaval, but she supposed that was to be expected. There were days when she woke with a feeling of dread, and she would spend hours reliving those last few months with her dad, too paralyzed with grief and regret to cry. After such an intense period together, it was hard for her to accept that he was suddenly gone, unreachable to her no matter how much she needed him. She felt his absence with a knife-edged sharpness she couldn't contain, and it sometimes left her in a bitter mood.

But those mornings weren't as common as they'd been during the first week she was home, and she sensed that they'd become less frequent over time. Staying with and caring for her dad had changed her, and she knew that she would survive. That's what her dad would have wanted, and she could almost hear him reminding her that she was stronger than she realized. He wouldn't want her to mourn for months; he would want her to live her life much the way he had in the final year of his own life. More than anything, he wanted her to embrace life and flourish.

Jonah, too. She knew her dad would want her to help Jonah move on, and since she'd been home, she'd spent a lot of time with him. Less than a week after they returned, Jonah was released from school for Christmas break, and she'd used the time to make special excursions with him: She'd taken him ice-skating at Rockefeller Center and brought him to the top of the Empire State Building; they'd visited the dinosaur exhibits at the Museum of Natural History, and she'd even spent most of one afternoon at FAO Schwarz. She'd always considered such things touristy and unbearably clichéd, but Jonah had enjoyed their outings, and surprisingly, so had she.

They spent quiet time together, too. She sat with him while he watched cartoons, drew pictures with him at the kitchen table, and once, at his request, she'd even camped out in his room, sleeping on the floor beside his bed. In those private moments, they sometimes reminisced about the summer and told stories about their dad, which they both found comforting.

Still, she knew Jonah was struggling in his own ten-year-old way. It seemed as though something specific was bothering him, and it came to a head one night when they'd gone for a walk after dinner one blustery night. An icy wind was blowing, and Ronnie had her hands tucked deep into her pockets when Jonah finally turned to her, peeking up from the depths of his parka hood.

"Is Mom sick?" he asked. "Like Dad was?"

The question was so surprising that it took her a moment to respond. She stopped, squatting down so she could be at eye level. "No, of course not. Why would you think that?"

"Because the two of you don't fight anymore. Like when you stopped fighting with Dad."

She could see the fear in his eyes and even, in a childlike way, could understand the logic of his thoughts. It was true, after all— she and her mom hadn't argued once since she'd returned. "She's fine. We just got tired of fighting, so we don't do it anymore."

He searched her face. "You promise?"

She pulled him close, holding him tight. "I promise."

Her time with their dad had altered even her relationship with her hometown. It took some time to get accustomed to the city again. She wasn't used to the relentless noise or the constant presence of other people; she had forgotten how the sidewalks were endlessly shadowed by the enormous buildings around her and the way people rushed everywhere, even in the narrow grocery store aisles. Nor did she feel much like socializing; when Kayla had called to see if she wanted to go out, she'd passed on the opportunity, and Kayla hadn't called again. Though she supposed they would always share memories, it would be a different sort of friendship from this point on. But Ronnie was okay with that; between being with Jonah and practicing the piano, she had little time for anything else.

Because her dad's piano had yet to be shipped back to the apartment, she took the subway to Juilliard and practiced there. She'd called on her first day back in New York and had spoken to the director. He'd been good friends with her dad and had apologized for missing the funeral. He sounded surprised—and yes, excited, she thought—to hear from her. When she told him that she was reconsidering applying to Juilliard, he arranged for an accelerated audition schedule and even helped expedite her application.

Only three weeks after arriving back in New York, she'd opened her audition with the song she'd composed with her dad. She was a little rusty in her classical technique—three weeks wasn't much time to prepare for a high-level audition—but as she left the auditorium, she thought her dad would have been proud of her. Then again, she thought with a smile as she tucked his beloved score under her arm, he always had been.

Since the audition, she'd been playing three or four hours a day. The director had arranged to let her use the school's practice rooms, and she was beginning to tinker with some fledgling compositions. She thought of her dad often while sitting in the practice rooms, the same rooms that he had once sat in. Occasionally, when the sun was setting, the rays would slice between the buildings around her, throwing long bars of light on the floor. And always when she saw the light, she would think back to his window at the church and the cascade of light she'd seen at the funeral.

She thought constantly about Will, of course.

Mostly, she dwelled on memories of their summer rather than their brief encounter outside the church. She hadn't heard from him since the funeral, and as Christmas came and went, she began to lose hope that he would call. She remembered that he'd said something about spending the holidays overseas, but as each day elapsed without word from him, she vacillated between the certainty that he still loved her and the hopelessness of their situation. Perhaps it was best that he didn't call, she told herself, for what was there really to say?

She smiled sadly, forcing herself to push such thoughts away. She had work to do, and as she turned her attention to her latest project, a song with country-western and pop influences, she reminded herself that it was time to look ahead, not back. She might or might not be admitted to Juilliard, even if the director *had* told her that the status of her application looked "very promising." No matter what happened, she knew that her future lay in music, and one way or another, she would find her way back to that passion.

On top of the piano, her phone suddenly began to vibrate. Reaching for it, she assumed it was her mom before glancing at the screen. Freezing, she stared at it as it vibrated a second time. Taking a deep breath, she opened it up and placed it to her ear.

"Hello?"

"Hi," said a familiar voice. "It's Will."

She tried to imagine where he was calling from. There seemed to be a cavernous echo behind him, reminiscent of an airport.

"Did you just get off a plane?" she asked.

"No. I got back a few days ago. Why?"

"You just sound funny," she said, feeling her heart sink just a bit. He'd been home for days; only now was he getting around to calling. "How was Europe?"

"It was a lot of fun, actually. My mom and I got along a lot better than I expected. How's Jonah doing?"

"He's okay. He's getting better, but . . . it's still hard."

"I'm sorry," he said, and again she heard that echoing sound. Maybe he was on the back veranda of his house. "What else is going on?"

"I auditioned at Juilliard, and I think it went really well . . ."

"I know," he said.

"How do you know?"

"Why else would you be there?"

She tried to make sense of his response. "Well, no . . . they've just been letting me practice here until my dad's piano arrives—because of my dad's history at the school and everything. The director was a good friend of his."

"I hope you're not too busy practicing to take time off."

"What are you talking about?"

"I was hoping you were free to go out this weekend. If you don't have any plans, I mean."

She felt her heart leap in her chest. "You're coming to New York?"

"I'm staying with Megan. You know, checking out how the newlyweds are doing."

"When are you getting in?"

"Let's see . . ." She could almost see him squinting at his watch. "I landed a little more than an hour ago."

"You're here? Where are you?"

It took him a moment to respond, and when she heard his voice again, she realized it wasn't coming from the phone. It was coming from behind her. Turning, she saw him in the doorway, holding his phone.

"Sorry," he said. "I couldn't resist."

Even though he was here, she couldn't quite process it. She squeezed her eyes shut before opening them again.

Yep, still there. Amazing.

"Why didn't you call to let me know you were coming?"

"Because I wanted to surprise you."

You certainly did, was all she could think. Dressed in jeans and a dark blue V-neck sweater, he was as handsome as she remembered.

"Besides," he announced, "there's something important I have to tell you."

"What's that?" she answered.

"Before I tell you, I want to know if we have a date."

"What?"

"This weekend, remember? Are we on?"

She smiled. "Yeah, we're on."

He nodded. "How about the weekend after that?"

For the first time, she hesitated. "How long are you staying?"

He slowly started toward her. "Well . . . that's what I wanted to talk to you about. Do you remember when I said that Vanderbilt wasn't my first choice? That I really wanted to go to this school with an amazing environmental science program?"

"I remember."

"Well, the school doesn't normally allow midyear transfers, but my mom's on the board of trustees at Vanderbilt and she happened to know some people at this other university and was able to pull some strings. Anyway, I found out while I was in Europe that I'd been accepted, so I'm going to transfer. I start there next semester and thought you might want to know."

"Well . . . good for you," she said uncertainly. "Where are you going to go?"

"Columbia."

For an instant, she wasn't sure she'd heard him right. "You mean Columbia as in New York Columbia?"

He grinned as if he'd pulled a rabbit out of his hat. "That's the one."

"Really?" Her voice came out as a squeak.

He nodded. "I start in a couple of weeks. Can you imagine that?

A nice southern boy like me stuck in the big city? I'm probably going to need someone to help me get adjusted, and I was hoping it might be you. If you're okay with that."

By then, he was close enough to reach for the loops on her jeans. When he pulled her toward him, she felt everything around her fall away. Will was going to go to school here. In New York. With her.

And with that, she slipped her arms around him, feeling his body fit perfectly against her own, knowing that nothing could ever be better than this moment, right now. "I guess I'm okay with that. But it's not going to be easy for you. They don't have a lot of fishing or mudding around here."

His arms moved around her waist. "I figured."

"And not a lot of beach volleyball, either. Especially in January."

"I guess I'll have to make some sacrifices."

"Maybe if you're lucky, we can find you some other ways to occupy your time."

Leaning in, he kissed her gently, first on her cheek and then on her lips. When he met her eyes, she saw the young man she'd loved last summer and the young man she still loved now.

"I never stopped loving you, Ronnie. And I never stopped thinking about you. Even if summers do come to an end."

She smiled, knowing he was telling the truth.

"I love you, too, Will Blakelee," she whispered, leaning in to kiss him again.